My Second Wind

A Novel of Murder, Mystery & Love
In Modern-Day West Texas

Set on the campus of
Texas Tech University

Jeanne S. Guerra
A Loyal Red Raider

My Second Wind is a work of fiction, and the characters, events, dialogue and representations are fictional... and are in no way meant to represent any actual person, living or dead, nor events, except the few annual traditions that help make Tech a great university. In other words, I made the whole thing up, ya'll!

Prologue ~

She didn't care that the entire town of Muleshoe was in attendance despite the heavy spring rain. She didn't care that her thick black mascara ran down her cheeks and onto his suit as he held her close. All she cared about was that the pieces didn't fit. That something was dreadfully wrong.

When the funeral ended, she needed to walk. Heading away from the cars, she led him down the semi-deserted street in the small West Texas panhandle town. She walked with determination, going nowhere in particular, wanting, needing to simply get away and be alone. His umbrella couldn't keep up. They were both soaked.

After a few blocks she reached the entrance of a quiet city park. He thought they should return to the car and leave, but he'd go into the damn park with her if that was what she really wanted. He needed the rain, the day, the nightmare to be over.

She turned tearfully to her lover. "You know she wouldn't have done that. She just wouldn't!"

He turned his head away. "But she did. It's over."

"Over? It can't be over. She would never have killed herself." She took a step back, oblivious to the rain.

"I don't know," he said, rubbing his head in obvious distress. He turned to look back toward the cemetery and the car. "Maybe it was an accident."

"An accident? How could it have been an accident? There was a note!"

"Yeah, the note... Look. I don't know," he said, his usual self-control beginning to crumble. Why hadn't they simply gotten into the car and driven back to the university?

She moved around to confront him.

"What made you say it was an accident? What aren't you telling me?"

"What? Nothing!" he said, attempting to fight the growing fear that had settled inside. The fear won and he threw the umbrella down then barked, "Look, we've been over this a hundred times already. You've got to move on. She's dead. She killed herself. Forget it. Let's go."

He reached for her arm but she pulled it away.

"But I can't forget it. Something's not right."

He grabbed her roughly by the shoulders. "I'm telling you to forget it. She's gone and nothing will bring her back. Now either you drop this or... or I'm outta here."

He pushed her away, stepped back a few feet and retrieved the sodden umbrella. Turning aside again, he headed back to his car.

"How can you say that?" she shouted after him.

He stopped. His head throbbed. He rubbed it again and turned around to face her once more, then marched back to where she stood.

Shouting now, control gone, he said, "Just drop it! She's dead and buried. Don't ever mention her name again or I'm really gone. Do you understand me?"

She looked up at him, but did not recognize the stranger who stood before her. Then she closed her eyes, crossed herself, and turned quickly away. She ran up the street and disappeared around the corner.

He stood there in the rain and continued to rub his brow, intense pain creasing his head as well as his heart.

~ Part I ~ Changes To Be Made ~

Chapter 1 ~
Early February, Twenty-Three Years Later

"**Really?**" asked Carol, coming out from the stilted house on the Texas Gulf Coast, "He was that inept?" She settled into one of the well-worn Adirondack chairs on the spacious deck.

"So very inept," replied Sharon, waving her half-full wineglass for effect, "that he couldn't find his balls with a GPS."

Maggie spit out her mouthful of chardonnay as the three best friends burst into laughter at the crude, but probably accurate description of her friend's former boss. She reached for a napkin to mop up the mess on her sweater and jeans.

"Luckily, his replacement is perceptive and smart. Seems to be setting the engineering department on fire. I couldn't be happier," Sharon continued with a smug grin as she burrowed further under the afghan to keep out the afternoon's ocean breeze.

"Awesome," said Carol, and she lifted her glass in salute. "Here's to Texas Tech University and its ability to sometimes hire the right people. Like you, Sharon, and your new boss."

"Yes," Sharon said, mockingly superior, "The university is extremely lucky to have me on the faculty."

Maggie turned her attention away from the captivating ocean waves and looked at her companions. "I don't think I've ever reported to someone who was awful. President Ramsey at SMU always just lets me do my job, no questions asked."

Sharon said, "That's because he recognizes real talent when he sees it. You're one lucky woman, though. It's all too common to work for an idiot, no matter how good you are. Don't you read *Dilbert*? I'm willing to bet the majority of folks can't stand their bosses."

"Well, I like mine, and respect him. Jim's boss is decent, too," Maggie replied. "We really don't have anything to complain about... really."

"Definitely lucky, my dear. A little boring, but lucky," Sharon said as she saluted her with the wine. She looked out again at the waves.

Carol smiled, took another long drink, then added with an innocent air, "You know, sometimes I think my boss is inept, too, but I just sleep with him to get what I want. He's putty in my hands."

Her friends eyed her in mock surprise, then Sharon said, "The fact your boss is your husband wouldn't have anything to do with that, would it?"

Carol blinked her light brown eyes innocently. "No, not a thing." More laughter.

Maggie took another sip of wine as her two friends continued the discussion. She looked at them lovingly and felt the last of the tension of her boring daily life drift away.

It always happened like this at their annual weekend retreat, now in its third decade. I'm so blessed, she thought. Two of the greatest women in the world, and I get to run away with them every February to drink wine, catch up on everyone's adventures and renew friendships.

Sharon Phelps, with her red and gold streaked hair in a spiked pixie cut. It perfectly suited her short stature and her intelligent, unpredictable personality. Maggie always thought of her as a female Peter Pan. Adventure was always her goal, but it contrasted sharply with her love of engineering and her appointment as a tenured faculty member at their alma mater, Texas Tech University in Lubbock. Maybe it was the contradiction that made her so interesting, not only to her friends, but to her students who consistently voted her a department favorite.

Then there's Carol Penn, tall, lithe, blonde, sophisticated—always dressed in designer clothes, though a little on the whimsical side. Carol faithfully came to their Texas weekend retreat every year from Washington, D.C., where she and debonair husband Robert own and operate an environmental consulting business, both political and profitable.

And then there's me, thought Maggie Grant. Plain, traditional, not really sophisticated or adventurous, but thoroughly content with my life. I don't usually have any exciting stories to tell.

A ringing phone brought her back to reality and the conversation stopped as Sharon begrudgingly crossed the deck to silence whichever cell phone was disrupting their peace.

"Let it ring," Carol said. "Voicemail will get it or they'll call back if it's important."

Shrugging her shoulders, Sharon picked it up on the fifth ring. "Benjamin? Of course she's here, but you know better than to disturb your mother during this sacred retreat, and we've only been here one day—"

Her face turned ashen. "Of course, Ben." She crossed the deck quickly and handed the phone to Maggie. And the weekend ended.

Chapter 2 ~
One year later

"So this is really what you think I should do?" Maggie asked Jim. "Give up everything and start again? The girls agree, you know."

Early February rain pelted the home's French doors creating a strong symphony of weather, with the storm raging in an uneasy cacophony of power. Normally Maggie enjoyed nights like this. Dallas seemed to have more than its share of storms all through the year and she delighted in their sounds, sights and smells.

But tonight she didn't hear the rain, didn't see the lightning nor feel the power of the Almighty in the thunder. Tonight, sitting in Jim's big worn leather chair, she stared at the fireplace, where the flames somehow crackled even though the logs weren't real and the fire was powered by gas.

Maggie tucked her feet, cozy in thick socks, up under her legs, and pulled her flannel robe tightly around her for warmth. With both hands now wrapped around her customary mug of tea that was no longer hot, she was turned inward and noticed neither the storm nor the cup that had gone cold.

"They're right," he answered at last. "You've grieved long enough. It's time to think of the future instead of the past."

"But how can I leave our home, our friends, everything you and I built together?" she asked.

"Because you should," Jim said.

Something compelled her to look at her left hand. She put down her mug and slipped off the wedding ring he'd given her three decades before. She turned it and noticed the inscription, *"God and I~Always."*

She'd forgotten the engraving was there. Hadn't looked at it in years because the ring rarely left her hand.

With a wry smile she remembered Jim hadn't let her see inside the gold band until their wedding night. It was a perfect message, she thought then, and now. They had started out as friends, and as they discovered they shared so many passions, especially deep beliefs, their friendship turned to love.

They felt that God had brought them together, so the writing inside the ring was a testimony to that faith. All Maggie had engraved on his band was the date. She smiled remembering how apologetic she had been that night, because Jim's inscription to her had been so much more meaningful.

She laughed now, too, at the memories of her shyness and embarrassment on that first attempt at lovemaking. Her present-day laughter quickly turned to an angry sob.

"God and I, always. You were supposed to stay for always... not leave me alone... Why did you leave me!?"

There was a flash of light and a simultaneous clap of thunder that shook the empty house. This time she noticed, and with a deliberate look upward through tears, said in a defiant tone, "Fine, God, I know you're there, too. All right, I'll do it... but neither of you can make me like it."

The next day, Sunday, she phoned across the country to tell her older son Michael and his wife Karen her decision. She needn't call her younger son, Ben. She would tell him face-to-face. Since Jim's death, Ben and his young family came each Sunday to take her to Mass and spend the afternoon trying to distract her from her grief. Dutifully playing along, at least on that one day a week, she cooked a huge dinner and enjoyed her two precious granddaughters.

"They've made you an offer? But Mom," Benjamin pouted, "this is our home, your home. How can you simply pack up and move 300 miles away? You have a job at the university here. What will they say if you leave? Why go all the way out to Lubbock?"

"It's a good opportunity for me," Maggie said slowly, as she looked up at her tall handsome son—like his brother, the spitting image of their late father. "Oh, I don't know, Benjamin. I've been with SMU for so long, it's gotten rather boring. Sort of been there, done that. I could use a new challenge to keep me occupied."

Ben sat heavily in the chair next to her and countered, "But there are other good communications jobs here in Dallas."

"Yes," Maggie said, "And everywhere I go in Dallas I see your dad. Everything reminds me of him. I think a change of scenery would be good for me. This house is too big for just one. And I've always enjoyed West Texas."

"But Mom, Lubbock? Nobody moves to Lubbock on purpose. Really, Mother. This is just not like you at all. And you seemed to be doing so well after... after dad's accident. Have you talked to Monsignor Joseph about this?"

"No, I haven't talked to Monsignor Joseph," Maggie said, eyes flashing. "It's none of his business. I need to do this. End of discussion."

"Well, I'm going to call him right now so he can talk some sense into you." Ben abruptly stood up from the table and reached for the cell phone at his belt.

"You'll do no such thing," said Maggie and Amanda at exactly the same time, both glaring at him. They turned to each other and laughed. Maggie whispered across the table to her daughter-in-law, "I knew from the first time he brought you home you were good for him. Just another confirmation."

Amanda smiled.

Ben plopped down dejectedly knowing better than to go against the two most important women in his life. "But Mom, you know they say not to make rash decisions after a death in the family, and—"

She cut him off with "the look" and spoke slowly and deliberately. "The saying is not to make rash decisions in the first six months. Your father has been gone almost a year and this is not a rash decision.

I made a list of facts, just like he taught us. Remember? The pros and the cons. I weighed the options, and the pros outweigh the cons."

"Oh, thanks," Ben said, throwing up his hands. "Your grandchildren are outranked by what? By Lubbock! I just don't understand you. Where will we go for Thanksgiving and Christmas? To that crummy little dust bowl college town?"

"It's not a crummy little college town. There is a lot of dust though," she said with a smile. "Besides, you've never even been there."

"No, and I don't ever plan on going."

"Now, Ben," Maggie replied patiently, "It'd be nice if you came to visit once in a while. Besides, I can always come back to Dallas to visit—it's only an hour's flight—and we can be together at your house on holidays."

"Great," Amanda said brightly, then frowned as she looked at Maggie with alarm, "But you'll have to teach me how to do the turkey. My family always went out to eat. When you cook, it always looks so complicated to get everything done at the same time. And we've always just come here. I don't know." She shook her head, "I just don't know."

Maggie reached over and patted Amanda's hand with reassurance. "I was nervous the first time I tried, too, and I'll be happy to show you the magic." Then she whispered, "It's not nearly as hard as it looks, we just don't tell the menfolk." She turned to her son again, her tone more serious. "Ben, I just know this feels right for me. Besides, Sharon is there and she says the job will be perfect for me."

"That's because she never left Lubbock after you two roomed together at Tech, and she doesn't know any other place."

Maggie countered, "That's not fair. She went east for her master's and she travels to Europe almost every summer. She knows lots of other places."

"Well, she's a bad influence. You know... with Doug what's-his-name and everything."

Maggie narrowed her eyes. "She's been my one of my best friends for more than 35 years, and since when did you get so all provincial about people living together outside of marriage? As I recall, you and Amanda—"

"Okay, I know, I know," Ben said quickly raising his hands in protest, looking his daughters, ages three and four playing on the floor nearby. "But my generation does that. You guys are..." he stammered. "You are... you know... um, old... for that kind of thing."

Amanda and Maggie rolled their eyes at the same time.

"Sorry, son. End of discussion."

Chapter 3 ~

It took a month to sell the house and most of its contents. Maggie gave Ben his father's leather chair to place beside the fireplace in his own den. She shipped many of Jim's beloved books to Michael, kept a few pieces of furniture for herself, including her father's antique desk and her mother's drop-leaf kitchen table. She hired movers to transport the remaining possessions, and at the age of 53 pointed her ten-year-old Volvo west to begin again. Sharon had flown in a few days before to help pack and drive out with her, "just in case you think about changing your mind."

It took them less than an hour to get to the western edges of Fort Worth on Interstate 20, where civilization disappeared in favor of rolling hills and ranch land. It was as if the sky became clearer and they could see the country the way the pioneers had seen it—except for the fences and billboards blighting the landscape, of course. But still, as Maggie looked out across the massive fields of bluebonnets and wildflowers, she thought it had been too long since she'd driven outside city limits. Enjoying it, she wondered why.

Half an hour later as they passed through the settlement of Weatherford, they started a gradual climb to higher elevations, driving close to small towns and gentle hills, always up and almost straight west.

Just before Abilene, the halfway point, a light rain enveloped them in a cloud of dreary weather. They stopped to top off the tank and stretch their legs. Maggie was disappointed she couldn't see much of the countryside through the gloom. It had been almost twenty years since she'd driven instead of flown to Lubbock, and she'd hoped to see a few familiar landmarks. If the rain kept up, it would be a less exciting drive. At least Sharon was there to keep her company.

They made the pit stop short, eager to be on their way. Sharon took the wheel, offering to share her peanut butter cheese crackers with the stipulation her friend would share her corn nuts. They sipped their ice-cold Dr Peppers and continued their journey.

As rain clouds cleared near the small town of Sweetwater, Maggie scanned the landscape, noticing fairly flat farm and ranch land on her right, with huge fluffy clouds rolling across the sky as far as she could see.

"Look, Phelps," she said, delighted as the mid-morning sun sparkled off the puffs of white. "It looks like an upside down Georgia O'Keefe painting, *Sky Above the Clouds*."

"If you say so, Maggie," Sharon said with a frown.

Maggie could tell her friend was desperately trying to recall the painting. She was an engineering major, not an art lover like their other friend Carol, who would undoubtedly be familiar with both painting and painter.

Looking ahead and to her left to see if the clouds continued in all directions, Maggie was struck by the dark ridge of a long, low massive plateau to the south, extending west, parallel to the highway. Movement on the ridge of the mesa made her squint. "What are those things out there on the hills?"

Sharon glanced over then focused back on the road. "Wind turbines. The newest form of energy."

"There sure are a bunch of them," Maggie said as she looked west. There were dozens as a far as she could see. "When did those go up?"

"A few years ago. But wait a couple of minutes because just up the road, on the other side of Sweetwater, you'll be amazed."

Sure enough, as they crested a large hill several miles further west, Maggie was indeed amazed, and a few more miles later as they turned north onto Highway 84, she was dumbfounded. Dozens and dozens, if not hundreds of the enormous white wind turbines dotted the landscape in every direction. They were nothing more than tall tapered metal poles seemingly growing straight up out of cement ground-collars, with a motor at the top sporting three long, thin, slightly twisted blades turning in the wind. At least they looked twisted from Maggie's perspective. She squinted to look closer. Maybe they were just tapered, but they did come to a smaller curved point.

The travelers had reached the eastern edge of the plains of West Texas, and the turning giants were visible for miles all around them. Some were less than fifty yards from the highway and were irregularly spaced, often less than a tenth of a mile apart. Maggie opened the sunroof and craned her neck to see the tops of the nearby blades as they spun in the wind, seemingly directly above the car.

"Wow," Maggie exclaimed as she looked around.

Sharon said, "Yeah, they've put up thousands of these things out here in the past few years. Wind farms, they call them. We're in the middle of the Roscoe Wind Farm, the largest in the country, I think. I hate them because they're so huge and yet I love them because they're better for the world than burning coal or foreign oil or using nuclear energy."

"How big are they? They seem to block out the sky in some places," Maggie asked as she continued to stare at a scene that harkened to a science-fiction landscape.

"Yeah, blocking out the sky in West Texas is quite a feat, don't you think? I remember reading where they're anywhere from 200 to 300 feet tall. The blades, then, I would guess about 100 feet long. And the bases, let me think, I once heard that it would take almost thirty people standing shoulder to shoulder to circle the base of one — no, maybe it's thirty children or about twenty-five adults? I don't remember. Anyway, huge suckers, that's for sure."

"Guess they finally found a way to harvest the crazy wind out here," Maggie said, craning her neck to view those up close.

Sharon nodded, "Yep. They're popping up in lots of states across the country, and farmers and landowners are making good money from them. California has a good share of them, too, especially out by Palm Springs. Seems they work best where there's a big change in elevation, like up on the mesas, or here around the Caprock."

9

"I assume it's a crop that doesn't need much tending? No irrigation, no annual spring plowing and fertilizing. Maybe just a little WD-40 now and then?"

Sharon laughed, "Yeah."

"But white? Or are they light gray?" Maggie squinted again. "Look at how they seem to change from light to dark gray as the clouds pass over," she said, her artistic sensibilities kicking in. "Somehow, I doubt O'Keefe's painting would be quite as powerful if she'd put all these wind machines in it, would it?"

"If you say so, Maggie."

"White," she said shaking her head. "Why didn't they try for a nice light blue or something to match better with the sky? They really should have made them so they could change colors to blend in better, like chameleons."

Sharon laughed. "Oh, yeah. Good idea. Deep blue for nice spring days, yellow and gold for sunsets, and black for nights. And I guess sand colored for the occasional dust storm? But they do sort of disappear in the rain. Bet they're definitely invisible during snowstorms, though, not that we have more than one of those a year out here. Say, maybe the engineering department could invent some type of chameleon skin paint for these things? Might make millions! Boost the endowment fund!"

"Might," she said, smiling at the thought. "Are many of them up in Lubbock?"

"Chameleons?" Sharon asked tongue in cheek.

"No, silly, wind turbines."

"Not a lot," said Sharon. "We must be too high up on the Caprock or something. They don't blot the landscape like here. A couple at the southeast edge of town near a cotton mill, though, and I know there's one on campus out at the Tech Wind Museum. Don't know if the museum is actually pulling power from that one, but it turns when the wind blows, so probably. We'll have to go check it out once you're settled."

"Wind museum? I don't remember hearing about any wind museum. What's it like?"

"Lots and lots of windmills inside and out. Not a bad exhibit and great for school field trips, especially for the little ones. Kids love the windmills. It's out next to the Ranching Heritage Museum, northwest corner of campus, just across from University Medical Center.

"Winston, the director, Dr. Winston Whitaker, is quite a character. Very charming and extremely good at getting funding for his pet project. Used to be an engineering professor in my department but spends all his time now as the curator, director and fundraiser for the museum. No, I think he may still teach one class—on the new wind energy, in fact—but out at the museum. He's got a great collection of the history of windmills and such."

"Love to see it. I've a feeling there'll be lots of new things in town we'll have to check out. When I've visited before, or for the interviews, there never seemed to be enough time to do anything but catch up on our lives. I haven't even been to the Buddy Holly museum."

"Disgraceful, and you call yourself a Texas Tech Red Raider. Buddy's the king of Lubbock! You have to see his shrine," Sharon grinned. "It's got a huge pair of black nerd glasses out front. Just one of the many things you need to check out. I'll make a long list. It'll be fun. And you're gonna absolutely LOVE it at Tech. I guarantee it."

Maggie looked skeptical. "As much as you love it, right Phelps?"

Sharon nodded but then took her turn looking skeptical. "Well, maybe not quite as much since I Am The Ultimate Red Raider!" Maggie laughed heartily, recognizing her friend's mantra from their college days.

Flashbacks of their dorm suite, painted entirely in Texas Tech colors of red and black at Sharon's insistence, made her wince. "You even had that life-sized 'Raider Red' cardboard cutout in our room," Maggie laughed. "Whatever possessed you to ask Carol to make one for us?"

"Old Red? He was great, wasn't he? Carol was always so artsy-craftsy. How the hell did she end up pre-law? Should've had her make Red out of plywood instead of cardboard, though, so he'd still be around. I could put him in my front yard. But he was a great guy-magnet at pep rallies and outside the dorm for homecoming. That's how I met Gerald," she said with a heavy sigh.

"Ah, Gerald. Whatever happened to Gerald?" Maggie asked.

"Not a clue, but he sure could kiss. Remember when he was kidnapped by those freshmen from Carpenter Hall?"

"Gerald was kidnapped?"

"No, silly. Old Raider Red was kidnapped!"

"Oh, right! I remember now. What was the ransom demand? Dates or phone numbers or something?"

"Dates, I think. Just freshmen guys wanting to meet freshmen girls. Luckily, Carol and I stole him back before we had to pay up. Why didn't you go with us that night?"

"Sneak out after hours? My dad would have grounded me for life! I like letting you two be the adventurous ones. I'm still content to live through you guys and hear your stories every February. Speaking of which, is Carol coming anytime soon to make up for missing our retreat in February?"

"No, I think she and Robert are booked up for the rest of the year. They both work too hard. Probably accounts for why they're so damn rich. But we'll definitely plan one for next winter. This year, I'm just thrilled to have you here with me. It's like we'll have a lifelong girls' weekend."

Maggie smiled at her fun-loving, adventure-taking friend, envying as much as ever her ability to take risks and enjoy life wherever and whenever.

"Do you really still love Tech the same way we did all those years ago?" Maggie asked.

Nodding without hesitation, Sharon said in a serious tone, "Back then we knew it from a student perspective, and each day was a new adventure. Now, working in the engineering department, I can see things from an adult perspective—from a faculty perspective—and it's still a new adventure all the time. Maybe not every day, but often enough to keep it interesting."

"I'm glad to hear you say that. I thought you just liked the football games, even when the Red Raiders don't win the conference."

"Win the conference? Are you kidding? With Texas and Oklahoma? We'll never win the conference. But I love everything at Tech. Football, basketball, baseball, the theater productions, the music performances—wait 'till you hear Doug's jazz band this year—and the amazing things we're doing in engineering. I like seeing the students get turned on to the same things that turned us on back then I guess."

"You were mainly turned on by boys, if I remember right," Maggie teased.

Sharon ignored her and continued, "Wait 'til I give you the grand tour of our labs, and—"

"Ok, OK. I get that you love it. But I still have trouble seeing you in Engineering—it's such a conventional discipline and you are so unconventional, my... Look out!" Maggie shouted as she reached for the dashboard, instinctively pushing her right foot hard to the floor.

Chapter 4

Sharon nimbly braked, swerved onto the right shoulder, then smiled smugly as she eased back into the lane, having easily avoided the deer that had run into their path. But Maggie turned around in her seat, watching the large frightened doe as it ran across the grassy median straight into the path of a southbound car.

"Look out!" she shouted again, but this time not at her traveling companion. "Oh, God. STOP! STOP!" Sharon reacted this time by slamming her foot on the brake. Maggie looked in horror as the accident unfolded. The deer they had missed ran straight in front of another car and was thrown to the far side of the road. The black SUV spun completely around and disappeared!

Sharon immediately stopped the Volvo. Scanning quickly for other vehicles, and with Maggie urging her to "Go! GO!," she backed up along the shoulder as fast as she could until they were directly opposite the deer.

Maggie jumped out almost before Sharon turned the car off and raced across the deserted highway. Sharon grabbed her cell phone and looked for landmarks to describe their location to the highway patrol. She spotted a mile marker, made the emergency call and followed Maggie across.

When she reached the dead deer, Maggie looked frantically for the car, then spotted skid marks further down the road and hurried to the edge of a narrow ravine. There, about 15 feet down, the rolling car had come to a stop in the opposite direction, leaning against the far embankment, passenger side up, right wheels spinning silently in the air.

"It's down here!" she yelled to Sharon who was trying to flag down a southbound car. An older model blue Ford saw the waving figure and began to slow, but as Sharon beckoned them over, the two elderly women just rubbernecked and then sped up again. Sharon shook her head in disgust as she ran to the edge of the ravine. Maggie was making her way down to the small SUV.

Maggie's traveling attire was jeans and good walking shoes, so she had no trouble climbing—or rather slipping and sliding—down the muddy slope. The smell of gasoline was faint, and she noticed the shallow pool of water from the recent rain was slightly tainted with the slick substance. The engine was quiet, however, so she didn't think there was much chance of a fire or explosion. She hoped. The only sound was the swoosh, swoosh, swoosh of a wind turbine some 40 yards away towering above her head.

She moved quickly around to the front of the car. One person, the driver, was visible through the cracked windshield, slumped against the left window, deflated air bag resting against his chest. His eyes were closed.

"Please, God, don't let him be dead. Please God!" she prayed out loud as she moved in closer to the windshield, her mind assessing the problem. Her communications profession called for her to find the facts, then make a judgment based solely on that knowledge. Fact one: he appeared unconscious in an unknown condition. Fact two: she thought help was on the way, but how long it would take wasn't certain. Fact three: she couldn't see any way she and Sharon could move him by themselves. And if they didn't know his condition, she knew they shouldn't be moving him.

Was he alone? She climbed the opposite side of the ravine to get above the car and then peered into the passenger window. No one else. It was then she noticed the deflated air bag moving slightly, being pushed by his chest. He was still alive, thank God, but for how long?

The window was halfway down, so she knew he'd be able to hear her. "Hello? Are you awake?" she called out. "We've called for help. Hello?" She thought he moved a little and was rewarded with a guttural sound. The young man's eyes fluttered but closed again after another moan.

"Phelps!" she yelled up the embankment. Sharon's head appeared. "There's just the one I can see and he's alive but hurt. Get that wool blanket from the back of the car... it's wrapped around the big mirror. How soon before they get here?"

"They said 10 minutes. They're sending a rescue squad and ambulance. I'll bring the car over!" She disappeared and Maggie was once again alone with the unconscious young man. She guessed he was in his early 20's, probably a Tech student, judging by his red "Wreck 'Em Tech" T-shirt and the jumble of books in the back seat. Heading home for spring break?

He was thin and wiry, dark brown skin and closely cropped tight curly black hair. Probably tall, judging by the length of the one arm and the one leg she could see. She saw no rips in his clothes, thank goodness, and no blood was visible. Sending up another prayer for him, she moved back down the ravine to squeeze between the embankment and the car hood. She knelt at the front of the windshield, directly in front of him.

She tapped on it and called to him again through the cracked glass, telling him help was on the way. His eyes fluttered, and he moaned again. Quickly she said loudly, "Don't try to move. You've been in an accident but help's coming."

He opened one eye, then the other, slowly taking in his surroundings, and Maggie repeated her command not to move. He saw her and smiled weakly, and Maggie sighed in relief.

"Hey, son. You've been in an accident and help is on the way. It's really best if you don't try to move. Do you hurt anywhere?"

Moving only his eyes, he said weakly, "My head, my left arm. I think that's all."

"You're alone, right? No other passengers?" Maggie asked to be sure she hadn't missed someone.

"Alone? Yes. What happened?"

"A deer. We missed it on the other side of the road and it ran right into you—or you into it—and you ended up down here. You're in a ditch, but we'll get you out. Don't worry. Just be really still."

Sharon appeared overhead again and called down, "Maggie? I moved the car to this side. Here's the blanket. Should I come down?"

"No. We're fine. There's only one guy and he's awake. You need to flag down the troopers. Throw the blanket to me." She caught it and moved part of the way back up the ravine to the side—now the top of the car—and made her way to the passenger's door. She pulled on the door handle as she squatted on the embankment. To her amazement, it opened easily. She pulled the door up and out of the way, being careful not to kick dirt inside on the young man.

"Don't move now, remember? Not even your head. I'm going to put this over you to keep you from getting chilled. You're not allergic to wool, are you?"

"No, just to deer," he said in a rich deep voice.

Maggie smiled and stretched herself out on her stomach across the passenger side second door. She reached in and laid the open wool blanket across him, covering as much as she could, letting it drape over his chest. In doing so, she could see his left arm seemed to be at an odd angle, probably broken. She wished the ambulance would hurry. She could just reach his right shoulder, and knowing nurses who swore a human touch could often heal better than any medicine, she placed her hand there and gave him a gentle squeeze, eliciting a smile.

She climbed back down to again wedge herself next to the windshield. His eyes were closed again. "Are you still with me? What's your name?"

"Still with you, Ma'am. Thanks for the blanket. Josh. I'm Josh," he said refocusing on Maggie's face.

"Good, Josh. How ya' doing?"

"Okay, I guess. How's the deer?"

"Dead, I'm afraid."

"Too bad I don't like venison," he said, his dark brown eyes smiling in spite of his precarious circumstances and obvious pain.

Maggie smiled, too and then cocked her head. A distant siren? Thank you, God, she thought. Thank you for keeping him alive.

Thinking it best to distract him and keep him awake, Maggie asked questions. He was a Tech student, a junior, majoring in pre-med, heading home to Sweetwater for Spring Break. "Do you want me to call your parents?" Maggie asked. If it were one her sons in the bottom of a ditch, she'd certainly want to know.

"Sure, but my dad's gonna be pissed. Just finished paying off my car. But sure."

By now, Sharon had succeeded in flagging someone down—a man in his thirties was climbing down the side of the steep ditch to see how he could help. Maggie borrowed his cell phone and asked him to look for the easiest way for paramedics to access the scene. She reached Josh's dad who was thankful to hear his son was awake and joking—he would come quickly. He wasn't far away. He'd call his wife once he got there, as she was "prone to worry."

Another good Samaritan arrived and agreed with Maggie the best course of action was for Josh to remain still and awake. Despite the cramping in her legs, Maggie continued kneeling by the windshield and talked to the young man about Tech and life and his family. The sirens grew louder, signaling arrival of the rescue team and ambulance up above.

One by one, rescuers came down the ravine, the scene quickly swarming with professionals. Maggie finally pulled herself up and moved away so they could work. Her parting words to Josh were that he'd be fine, now.

After hearing paramedics confirm her prediction, she was helped back up to the side of the road. Sharon had given her statement to the Texas Highway patrolman, who tipped his hat and said, "Thanks, Ma'am. We might never have seen him down yonder if ya'll hadn't a been here. We appreciate your help. Sorry about the mud," he said looking at Maggie's filthy jeans and shoes. "You can go on along now, if ya'll want."

He glanced past them at a late-model car speeding their way. Moving across the median as Sharon had done, it stopped behind the ambulance, and an older version of Josh jumped out and walked quickly toward the patrolman.

Seeing no reason to stay since Josh's dad had arrived and the young man was in good hands, Sharon and Maggie turned away and got back into their car. Sharon made a u-turn at the nearest crossover, and they resumed their journey northwest to Lubbock. They had lost less than an hour because of the errant, and now dead deer.

Chapter 5 ~

A few miles down the road Sharon noticed Maggie was twirling her salt and pepper shoulder-length hair in and out through her fingers. She knew her friend only did that when she was upset. Sharon looked back at the road and said, "You okay?"

"Me? Sure, I'm fine. Just thinking, that's all."

"About Jim? His accident?" she asked gently.

"Hard not to. Just wish someone had been there for him at the end."

"They said he died instantly, Maggie," Sharon said tentatively.

"I know, but still. Anyway, I'm glad we were there today. And I'm thankful Josh had his seatbelt on. That and the air bag probably saved him."

Sharon said, "He's one blessed kid. Did you get his full name?"

"No, just Josh. Guess it was lucky we were there to see it happen. Also lucky thing for us you missed the deer. Hmm, although not so lucky for Josh, was it? But nice driving there, Phelps."

"Thanks, but if you drive outside city limits often enough in West Texas, you get used to watching for critters. Deer and armadillos, skunks and coyotes. Even those wild feral pigs cross this road sometimes. I once saw a whole herd of those huge hogs next to the shoulder. Dodging them is definitely a learned art. And thankfully there's normally not much traffic on this road. Just critters and tumbleweeds. But I've had to swerve around them now and then, just like today. Now, what were we saying before all the excitement?"

"Well, let me think. I said I have trouble seeing you teaching engineering and being so unconventional, that's all." Maggie said.

16

"Oh, yeah. That's right. But as I tell my students over and over, engineering is a creative science."

"Right. You know about Jansen... Theo Jansen?"

"I don't think so," Sharon said.

"Sure you do. He's the kinetic art guy. The one who said, 'The walls between art and engineering exist only in our minds.'"

"Oh, yeah. Like that quote. Is he the one who does those huge pieces that move along the beaches?"

"One in the same."

"Yeah, I like his work. And I agree, then, with what you said he said. We engineers find solutions to the world's problems, and you have to be creative to do that."

"I guess you're both unconventional *and* creative, then," Maggie said. "The most accepted vision of an engineer is a middle-aged white male with thick glasses, white short-sleeved shirt and pocket protector. Like George McFly in *Back to the Future*." She reached over and patted Sharon's spiked and streaked hair do. "You certainly don't fit that image!"

"Well, I would hope not. And where my hair is concerned, I have always been creative. And so were you, once upon a time... well, not about your hair, but other things for sure. One thing I told Doug we're gonna do is get you back to your creative, idiosyncratic... is that a word? ...back to your eclectic old self. I know you and Jim were happy, but a lawyer's wife? Formal dinner parties for clients? I can't imagine it."

"Well, imagine it," Maggie said, laughing as she wiped some of the mud off her hands. "We even had the Bishop over for dinner regularly."

"The Bishop? Woo, woo, Maggie. We've got a lot of serious loosening up to do. We'd better start by making our first stop at you-know-where for re-indoctrination."

"You-know-where? Where?" Maggie said with a puzzled expression.

"Wow. It's definitely been way too long since you've been out here for fun. You'll see. And now you're here to stay! Yippee!" she cried at the top of her lungs with both hands off the wheel and up in the air. Maggie covered one ear and quickly reached to steer the car from the passenger side, but smiled just as enthusiastically.

Later, still heading northwest, Maggie noted the dwindling number of wind turbines, except for what seemed to be one noble last stand, high up on a large plateau northwest of the small town of Snyder. She counted close to 50 of the giants up there, away from the highway's surrounding craggy terrain.

As they worked their way up the Caprock that would take them to the High Plains at the southern end of the Texas panhandle, both took more care to scan the sides of the highway for sudden movements, but nothing further crossed their path except the occasional tumbleweed. They'd been steadily climbing as they moved across the state, but here the change in elevation was more dramatic as they traversed the rugged country to Llano Estacado, the "staked plains." Mesas and buttes rose on either side of the road, with dry gulches, ravines, scrub brush, the occasional cactus, and craggy boulders dotting the red earth.

As they drove through the tiny town of Post, named for the breakfast cereal king C.W. Post, the town's founder, Maggie knew they were close to the end of their journey, but couldn't resist pulling over at the state historical marker.

"Why are we stopping?" Sharon asked.

"Just wanted to read about the famous Mr. Post, that's all," Maggie replied. She read it aloud to her skeptical passenger. *C.W. Post established the town in 1907 as a utopian colonizing venture with his purchase of 200,000 acres to establish the Double U ranch, building and selling houses, a hotel, textile plant and cotton gin, planting trees along every street, and prohibiting alcohol and brothels.*

"No booze or brothels?" Sharon deadpanned. "No wonder the utopia failed."

Chapter 6 ~

On the northern outskirts of Post, they drove up the last major geographical transition of the Caprock, a dramatically steep hill, often impassible in icy weather. At the top, on the Llano Estacado at last, Maggie looked east out over the vista stretching at least twenty miles, most of it a thousand feet below them. Gullies, ravines and arroyos made a beautiful rugged display of red earth before leveling out to the eastern plains known to some as "redbed country," the transition land between East and West Texas—most of it used for ranching.

To her left, the flat level plain above the Caprock began its seemingly endless journey west to New Mexico. She remembered reading about this vast region lying at the southern end of the country's High Plains, part of what was once called the Great American Desert. About two hours north of Lubbock was the panhandle city of Amarillo. And just north of Amarillo was the Canadian River, the largest tributary of the Arkansas River. It sets Llano Estacado, or the South High Plains, apart from the rest of the High Plains. The Caprock Escarpment on the east defines the boundary with sharp, often precipitous cliffs, 300 to 1,000 feet tall. The Mescalera Escarpment on the edge of the Pecos River forms the western boundary. Part of the Caprock is Palo Duro Canyon, just south of Amarillo. Wasn't there a famous outdoor stage production there during the summers?

"There still is," Sharon said. "I've been a couple of times. Definitely worth the drive."

Maggie had camped there in college with her friends, but never seen the show. Maybe she and Sharon could put it on their "To Do" list.

To the south, near Big Springs, the Llano blended into the Edwards Plateau with a subtle beauty of rolling stark terrain. In total, almost 38,000 square miles of West Texas and Eastern New Mexico claim the title of Llano Estacado. By comparison, it is slightly smaller than the whole of South Carolina. Twenty-four Rhode Islands would fit comfortably in the area.

"What does Llano Estacado mean, Phelps? I know it translates as 'staked plains,' but what's that?"

"Hmm?" she replied, turning from the eastern view that always intrigued her. "Oh, I don't know. Doug would know. I think he has a book on it. Something to do with 'staking out a trail' or something. Seems there's more than one theory as to what it means, though. He'll know."

As Maggie and Sharon drove the last 40 miles to Lubbock, Maggie's pulse quickened at the first sight of the South Plains cotton fields, many of them freshly tilled and waiting for planting, with the promise of quick sprouting seedlings in acre upon acre of rich red land. Other fields still held stubble from last season's crops, thin ragged brown sticks poking up from the earth at odd angles with the occasional green weed stubbornly growing nearby. The stalks and weeds helped keep the topsoil from blowing away in the windy environment.

Here and there a discarded piece of plastic was caught on the broken stalks, blowing furiously in the wind, trying to free itself for further adventure. It's said that all things finally end up in America's rivers, but since this was a semi-arid climate, there were no nearby rivers—no steady surface streams heading for the ocean. Perhaps this plastic was destined to be buried in a sandstorm. Better than polluting the waterways, Maggie thought.

There had been a few cotton fields back down around Roscoe—some in fact where both wind turbines and oil pump jacks sat in the middle—but the soil was a little different down there. Maybe more brown? Less sandy, Maggie wondered? But up here on the South Plains, the fields extended for miles, and no metal giants with turning blades marred their beauty. There was an occasional pump jack, but they were lower to the ground and she didn't think they broke the terrain's visual rhythm as obnoxiously as those huge wind turbines.

As the cotton grew, it would alter the point at which land meets sky, and out here there was a lot of sky. Seasonal growth and harvesting created a natural undulation of horizontal change making the South Plains now a "sea of growth" rather than the "sea of grass" as described by Spanish explorer Francisco Coronado, the first known European to cross this area in 1541.

As always, South Plains farmers prayed this year for abundant rain with alternating warm sunshine. Cotton was king in this part of West Texas, and more than one harvest over the years had been slight because of drought, or ruined by fierce hail storms. Each year was a gamble, and one could never be sure of a good harvest. But the percentages favored good crops, because the farmers kept planting year after year.

Wasn't that just like all of life, Maggie thought. You plan and work hard and know where you want to go, but then nature throws you a curve, changing everything. She thought of the plaque she'd hung over her desk in her old SMU office, "We plan, God laughs." So true, she thought, and then turned her attention back to the beckoning cotton fields.

About ten miles south of Lubbock, the fencing on the west of the highway became uniform, and rather than posts of old Mesquite trees and barbed wire, it was black steel stakes with evenly spaced wire fencing. Miles of it. Running inside the length of the fence was a wide dirt road, broad enough to accommodate the turning of a tractor or a cotton picker during harvest.

Here, next to the highway, the rows were straight, but further in, the ground had been plowed into giant circles to use the latest irrigation systems set up on towering thin wheels. Maggie couldn't imagine how a tractor pulled the huge sprinklers. They were so tall and gangly looking. Maybe they were self-propelled by motors or hydraulics on the wheels instead? She'd have to ask someone at Tech. Maybe in the Ag department. Surely they would know.

Even though the huge circles couldn't be easily detected from ground-level, Maggie envisioned the area from the air, as she saw it on recent trips to and from Dallas. Hundreds of gigantic circular fields dotted the landscape, edges almost touching each other. Different throughout seasonal growing cycles, the circles were of dark green, yellow, brown or red. She also envisioned the small lakes shimmering in the sunlight after a rain. Playas, they were called. Man-made or God-made? Another question to put on her list.

The fields behind the black fencing seemed a little more well kept than those previously passed, and the huge irrigation wheels lightly dotted the land for as far as the eye could see.

Farmers planted some fields and then irrigated to help Mother Nature along, but they also planted dry fields, allowing Mother Nature to tend those by herself. Less than half of the fields in this area were left to grow naturally, and because West Texas conditions are often perfect for the cotton, the dry-land farming normally produced reasonable-yield crops, with really good crops coming on average once every three years. About one in seven years, however, dry-farming crop yields are poor–but not bad enough to justify the high costs of irrigation. Maggie related all this to her traveling companion.

"How do you know all these facts?" Sharon asked.

"Bought a Texas Almanac and looked them up. I thought I should reacquaint myself with the area, that's all," she shrugged. "I like to know the facts about where I'm living."

"Well, I've lived here for more than thirty years, and I didn't know all that. You sound like a walking encyclopedia. And how the farmers have the faith to gamble their livelihood each year is amazing to me. I guess it's either feast or famine. I think it's a definite sign of strength. I doubt I'd have the fortitude to work all year for only one payday. I like the security of a regular paycheck that doesn't rely on the weather. Especially since the stupid weather changes so much out here."

Maggie smiled. "Well, now you'll know almost as much as I do." She resumed her soliloquy, noticing Sharon was listening with interest despite her protest. Far in the distance, Maggie could see more oil pump jacks jutting up here and there, bringing up the black gold from deep underground. However, the wells were still more prevalent below the Caprock and down into the Permian Basin, nearer Midland and Odessa where a pipeline infrastructure made pumping more profitable. Here, she'd read, the oil was stored until transport trucks came to move it to either a refinery or a pipeline station. The dark metal pumps jacks always reminded Maggie of giant praying mantises, heads slowly bobbing up and down, up and down.

After several miles of the black fencing, they passed a gate with a three-foot tall iron cotton boll interlaced with the capital letter A brand welded on top of a high metal arch. Sharon said it was one of the relatively new entrances to the Cotton A ranch, one of the largest in the area, extending west into Hockley County, with cattle and cotton and oil.

"Don't know how many acres, but the family is pretty influential on the South Plains. Been here for several generations, from what I know. I also hear they're big Tech supporters. Probably have a suite at the stadium. All the rage among the wealthy."

As far as the eye could see, the dark red earth had been turned over and peaked in long, unending rows. Maggie felt this unexplained desire to walk through them, to see the plowed rows up close, to smell the fragrant freshly turned soil. She'd loved spring in her small garden at home, but never seemed to have enough time to devote to it, hiring out much of the work.

She thought about pulling over—she was at the wheel since their quick stop in Snyder—but now wasn't the time, especially since she was freshly clean, having changed out of her muddy clothes. She vowed to return soon.

Chapter 7 ~

Texas Tech University is the heart of the city of Lubbock, population 218,000. Spread over 1,840 acres of flat land, the school was established in 1923 as Texas Technological College and opened two years later to serve West Texas' growing population. It was known back then mainly for animal husbandry, agriculture and home economics. In time, other schools were added, and Maggie knew today the university boasted more than 30,000 students studying in hundreds of different disciplines within 13 colleges. Students attended Tech from all over Texas, as well as from across the country and around the world.

Texas Tech was home to Maggie, Sharon and Carol when they were students. It had been Maggie's choice of colleges more than 30 years earlier because it was the one state college far enough from Dallas—five to six hours, depending on who was driving—far enough to "get away," yet close enough so she could go home for holidays. But she was pleasantly surprised when she first saw the city and the campus back in 1969. Hundreds of thousands of lush trees had been planted and were thriving, making parts of Lubbock resemble the green acres of her Dallas neighborhood, minus the hills, of course. And the Tech campus, huge in comparison to others she'd visited, was as stately as Dallas' SMU with decades old trees in abundance.

During her four-year stay, the Texas Legislature, at the request of Tech administration and alumni, changed the name from Texas Technological College to the more appropriate Texas Tech University, given the size and disciplines taught. There was controversy over the new name, and students and faculty were divided between the names Texas State University (now used for a school located in San Marcos) and Texas Tech University. The "Tech" in the name referred to its long history, but it was opposed by many as "tech - no - logical." Maggie remembered that message being displayed in huge letters on a campus construction fence, obviously painted by protesting students late one night. The "Tech" name prevailed however, and Texas Tech University, as it has been called for three decades now, was able to keep the beloved Double T symbol.

Maggie was still at the wheel as they entered Lubbock. She took a straight shot down Avenue Q, past where the old traffic circle had been converted into a regular intersection with stoplights.

"Progress, schmogress," complained Sharon. "The old circle was fun, especially if it was late at night and we'd downed a few. But boy we were stupid, thinking we were invincible."

Maggie agreed, recalling a few adventurous trips of her own around the infamous circle.

They continued north on Avenue Q to 19th Street, past Orlando's original Italian restaurant. Agreeing it was still among the best places in the city to dine, they vowed to visit it soon. She turned west on 19th and drove past the historic Lubbock High School and then just another half mile to the southeast corner of the Tech campus. On an open lawn dotted with huge trees, the old president's home was set far back from the street and, Maggie noticed, its west side was currently under construction. For several years now, the large house had served as the Alumni Association headquarters and was also used for fancy receptions and gatherings. As enrollment grew, the president had moved off campus, and the University now owned a larger house across 19th Street, which bordered the campus on the south, affording a little more privacy for the president and his family.

A contented sigh escaped Maggie's lips as it always did when first sighting her alma mater. There were just so many good memories here. Here where she'd met her life-long friends and earned her independence. She loved the almost century-old university.

Sharon directed her to turn north up University Avenue, past their old dorm, Drane Hall, no longer used for student housing. Drane is where the girls first met back in the days when rules were stricter and only girls lived there. Having a 9 o'clock curfew on weeknights gave the young women needed time for bonding and allowed them to focus on studies because quiet hours began after 10 p.m.

Now, she understood, both boys and girls lived in most of the residence halls, sometimes alternating floors, but she thought in this case the old ways were better for all concerned. There definitely could be too much exposure to the opposite sex. How did they concentrate on studies? Did they even have quiet hours? Was there time to make lifelong friends?

At Broadway Street, Maggie turned left between the stately entrance porticos marking the main access to the university. Just beyond the entrance, she passed the familiar fountain with the towering Texas Tech University seal. They'd been students when it was first built and a favorite prank was to either fill the fountain with soap suds or red dye. She remembered one year the fountain's waters mysteriously turned orange the week the University of Texas Longhorns came to town. The entire campus was in an uproar.

At Sharon's insistence, she drove up the long tree-lined east-west esplanade, past the famous Will Rogers statue, reportedly positioned so the horse's rear pointed toward Texas A&M University in Central Texas. Memorial Circle with its cascading fountains and flags was just beyond, with the north-south esplanade off to the right. Imposing three-story Spanish-Renaissance-style buildings lined the esplanades and the circle, defining the university. As she drove the circle, Maggie slowed for a few pedestrians scurrying around campus.

"I thought it was Spring Break," Maggie said.

"It is, but not all the kids leave. A lot of studying going on. Only about six weeks until finals," Sharon said.

Directed to park in front of the majestic administration building on the south side of the main circle, Maggie immediately realized exactly where the "you-know-where" was Sharon had mentioned earlier. An imposing three-stories of ornately carved stone and brick, the Administration Building was the first edifice constructed for the university. Its red clay mission-tiled roof continued the Spanish style and added needed color. Maggie remembered seeing old black and white photos of it, alone on the flat prairie land, seemingly not a tree or house or building around for miles. There had been a lot of progress in the past 75 years. Majestic trees and dramatic arched buildings were everywhere, patterned after that first template.

Rising high above the Administration Building, elaborate two-story, brick-and-stone domed towers marked the two corners of the building as it turned away from the circle into a U-shape, its opening toward the south. Both stunningly ornate towers housed bells that rang out songs for special occasions or celebrated victory at the end of home athletic games.

Numerous domed windows on the main building, designed for air flow before the advent of air conditioning, were encased in detailed carved borders of the off-white stone. The stone continued throughout the facade with embellished bas reliefs depicting angels, plant life, columns, and words spelling out not only the disciplines of the university in 1925 - agriculture, manufacturing, homemaking, literature, science and art—but also home, state, church, school and industry, the five great institutions of democracy in the early 20th century. The products of those institutions—virtue, patriotism, religion, enlightenment, wealth, and good citizenship—also were engraved and rounded out the philosophical theme.

Ornate seals were incorporated in the early 20th century design for historical reference. Maggie thought of the popular amusement park in the Dallas area, Six Flags Over Texas. It, too, highlighted the six landowners of Texas—Spain, France, Mexico, Texas, the Confederacy, and the United States. The Texas Tech University seal was incised as well, a shield containing symbols for church, home, state and education, quartered by crossing bands of cotton bolls, with an eagle perched on top, wings spread in a majestic pose.

A large archway cut the bottom floor of the Administration Building into two even sections and allowed easy passage to the inner sanctum of the courtyard to the south. It was through this archway Maggie and Sharon headed with wide grins. They stopped in their tracks on the opposite side under an elaborate domed arcade.

The you-know-where lay directly ahead—a 23-foot long concrete bench, in the shape of a Double T, the school's most recognizable symbol. Sacred to students and alumni alike, tradition dictated only upperclassmen and graduates should rest on the gift from the class of 1931.

The women stood just inside the courtyard sheltered by the east and west wings of the three-story stately building, looking at the bench for a long moment, smiling with their individual memories. Then as they kept their gaze on the monument, they slowly circled in parallel directions, around the intrusive Gov. Preston Smith statue—an unpopular addition since their graduation—and turned back toward the open archway to reverently settle themselves in the upper inside corners of the main T. They laid their arms over the back and clasped hands.

"I'm so happy to have you here with me at last," Sharon said.

Maggie leaned her head back and sighed, soaking up her share of the afternoon's warm spring sunshine. "I'm so happy to be here."

After a few minutes of reverent silence, Sharon asked, "Which window is yours?"

Maggie quickly came back to reality and gulped, her feeling of well being diminished slightly as she gazed up at the imposing old building.

"Um, it's there, up in that corner, but it actually faces the flagpoles and Memorial Circle," she said, pointing west to the third floor where the red and brown bricks made a 45-degree turn. "A little office tucked up in the northwest corner, next to the student ombudsman office and an ancient elevator."

"Really?" said Sharon in surprise. "The president's office is on the first floor in the east wing, way over there," she said, unclasping their hands and pointing in the opposite direction. "I thought the director of communications and marketing would be right next to him."

"I did too, but Mr. Boyle said all those offices were taken, so I, or rather the entire department, was relegated to the other side."

"Bennett Boyle, the Chief of Staff," Sharon said with disdain.

"You know him? What's he like?"

"I thought you met him? Wasn't he in on the interviews?"

"He was, but he seemed preoccupied so we never really got a chance to talk. The first interview he just observed. It was kind of creepy. Remember? I told you about it. Never even asked any of the questions. Jonathan Long did the talking."

"Jonathan Long is his second. Him I don't know much about, but what I do know is favorable. Hmm. I vaguely remember your telling me about Boyle. Tell you the truth, Mags, I was too damned excited thinking about your moving here. I guess I didn't listen well. Sorry."

"That's all right. In the final interview, Boyle at least said a semi-polite welcome, but he barely glanced at me. He had Long show me the office space and introduced my assistant."

"Don't take it personally. Boyle treats everyone like that. Did you get a load of his hair? Stiff as, um, what's the old Cowboys' coach's name?

"Jimmy Johnson?"

"Right, Jimmy Johnson's hair. Boyle's rug is so stiff even a West Texas tornado wouldn't disturb it."

"He wears a rug?" Maggie asked in surprise.

"No, I don't think so, but it's stiff enough to be one. And I know he didn't purchase those fancy threads here in Lubbock—much too uptown, even for an Aggie."

"An Aggie?"

"Yep. Graduate of Texas A&M. I'd stay out of his way if I were you."

"Sharon, he's my boss! How can I stay out of his way?"

"Well, at least be careful. How much staff did you say you have?"

Maggie sighed, a trickle of doubt beginning to form about her decision. But she couldn't quit before she had even started. She'd just take it one day at a time.

"Staff? I think there are five of them—two writers, a photographer, the graphic artist and the assistant. Met the assistant briefly and she seemed really nice, professional, but a little apprehensive about another new boss in just under two years. Was my predecessor really that bad?"

"Well, everyone referred to her as 'that bitch in communications.'"

"Oh great, Phelps. Something you conveniently neglected to mention?"

"Did I?" Sharon said innocently. "Well, truthfully, I was afraid you wouldn't come," she cringed. "Sorry, again. In the president's eyes, though, she could do no wrong. Everyone thinks they were sleeping together, but personally, I think she had better taste than that. Anyway, that's probably one reason why she's gone. That and the fact she didn't have a clue about how to run a communications office. And her office was right next to his. Too close for comfort for President Stone's wife, I'd say."

"What else have you conveniently forgotten to tell me? You'd better tell me everything. Forewarned is forearmed, you know."

"All I know is the gossip, which normally is 80 percent true, but when President Stone came three years ago, the communications director—he'd been here forever—you know, old man Leonard—retired within the year and Stone hired this own wife's best friend from California. California for God's sake. Why in the world would someone move to Lubbock from California?"

"I'm moving from Dallas!" Maggie cried.

"I know, but Dallas is not as hip as California."

"Hip? You still use that word, Phelps?"

"Well, certainly not anywhere except here in Lubbock. Lubbock's still behind the times in many things, but that's one of the reasons it's so great. Anyway, Danielle, from California, was about 36 and a real beauty."

Maggie frowned. "Oh great, and I'm coming in more than 15 years older and 20 pounds overweight with gray hair. Just great."

"Don't be silly. You at least know what you're doing, and you don't look that old. Besides, climbing up to your new office every day will quickly take away those extra pounds. But I *have* been meaning to get my hands on that gray hair of yours." As she playfully reached for her friend's head, Maggie held her hands up to protect herself and moved out of reach.

"What? No way, Sharon. My hair stays natural, just the way I've always worn it and just the way I'll always wear it. If God gives me gray hair, who am I to change that?"

Sharon gazed down at the capri pants Maggie had changed into. "God gave you hair on your legs, but I see you shave that off regularly."

Maggie frowned at her with narrowed eyes.

Knowing she'd scored points, Sharon smiled. "Okay, we'll leave that battle for another day. Anyway, Danielle came in with no communications experience that I know of. Rumor has it she was a lingerie model."

"What!"

Sharon nodded. "That's what they say. Pretty enough. Really pissed people off, though, especially when she was made a vice president by Stone. I'll bet I can guess just what she was communicating with him. Anyway, they say when Mrs. Stone heard about their rumored affair, Danielle hustled her cute little butt back to California. And now rumor is President Stone won't be here much longer. Tsk... And her best friend, too." Sharon mockingly eyed Maggie with suspicion and added, "You know Doug and I are really happy."

"I know." Maggie's eyes widened as she understood the implications. "Don't be ridiculous," she laughed. "Besides, you know I'm through with men. There'll never be another Jim."

"Yeah, he was a real keeper," Sharon said seriously with regret. "Even if he was a lawyer."

Maggie shrugged to hide her pain at remembering Jim and then said teasingly, "And I have gray hair."

"Oh, yeah, not Doug's favorite thing," Sharon flounced her red and gold streaked hair as she brightened. "But seriously, Maggie, you can't help but impress them with your genuine communications background. They're lucky to have you, and your staff will be thrilled you know what you're talking about."

"Well, we'll see. Does seem odd, though, my office so far away from the president's. How do they get things done expeditiously?"

Sharon blanched mockingly. "Expeditiously? You're in Lubbock, remember? All things are a little slower out here. Except the wind, of course."

"Oh, right. And just think of all the added exercise I'll get running— rather walking—up and down from my office to the president's and back."

"Yup. Come on, Maggie. Let's get you expeditiously moved into our guest house at the Nest."

Chapter 8 ~

Maggie smoothed her pulled-back chignon-styled hair, straightened her pin-striped black suit and entered the Administration Building. Instead of the stairs, she headed for Bennett Boyle's first-floor office next to the president's suite.

She was about 30 minutes early, thinking she would get a jump on her first day at work. Boyle's outer office was open and empty, but the door to his inner sanctum was closed. Through the semi-frosted glass insert she could tell he was at his desk.

Hesitant to disturb him, she went instead to the massive ornate marble stairs in the middle of the building and walked up to the third floor in the opposite wing only to find her new office locked. She leaned against the wall in the hallway and took several deep breaths to recover from the steep climb and to calm her nerves.

"Don't be silly, Margaret Riley Grant," she sternly told herself. "You're quite capable of handling this job. Just use your instinct, intellect and skills." She looked up, "But I could use a little help, God."

"Did you say something?" came a female voice from behind her. Startled, she turned to see Elaine, her assistant, hurrying toward her. *Elaine, Elaine ... what's her last name?*

"Oh, no," Maggie said recovering. "Well, actually, just a little pep talk to myself. First day nerves and all that, I guess."

Elaine smiled.

"How are you, Elaine?"

"I'm good, Mrs. Grant, now that you're here. The stairs get easier, trust me. Here, let me get the door. I've got keys for you inside and all the things you'll need to get settled in."

Elaine unlocked and opened the door, turned on the lights and headed for the small inner office. Maggie followed the cocoa-skinned woman into the second room. *Easton,* she thought, remembering Elaine's last name. She wondered how old she was. She guessed about mid-forties, although her tight, smartly fashionable short skirt showed off well-toned bare legs that didn't look a day over thirty. Two-inch heels accentuated her slim figure. Noticing that Elaine wasn't at all out of breath from the stairs, Maggie silently chided herself about getting back into shape.

"There's barely room in here for your desk, but I think we got it situated all right for you, Mrs. Grant," Elaine said as she cranked open the only window.

"Maggie. Please call me Maggie." She looked around at the cramped room. "It's fine. Thank you. I don't really need more than a desk, computer and phone, and the window is a nice bonus." She moved over to the view of the familiar flagpole circle and noticed she could hear the water cascading in the fountains. Soothing, she thought. Elaine squeezed around the other side of the desk and disappeared into the outer office, which was about twice the size of Maggie's.

Over her shoulder Elaine called back to her, "It's just a shame to put you, and us, way up here. Mr. Leonard had an office area about six times this size, and we were all housed around him on the first floor, east wing. But Boyle confiscated all the space when Ms. Danielle left just after Christmas, even though it was our office space forever."

"Mr. Boyle took the Communications offices?"

"Yep," she said. Then Maggie heard her mutter under her breath, "The bastard."

"You worked for Mr. Leonard?" she asked as Elaine returned to Maggie's office.

"Oh, yes, we all did," she said as she brought in keys and some paperwork. "He was, is, the nicest man and definitely knew what he was doing. I started with him about sixteen years ago, along with Charlie. Susan and Steven worked for him a while, and just before he retired, Ricky was hired. You'll like the guys. Ricky's an incredible graphic designer and knows everything about computers. He's the reason we have these fairly up-to-date models and all the software we could ever want. So you should be okay with at least a modern computer, even if the office and furniture are from the middle of the last century."

She continued talking as she efficiently moved around the room checking for dust, straightening the few files and books fit snugly in the office. "Charlie is a great photographer—been here forever and knows all there is to know about Tech. Worked for National Geographic right out of college before he came back and settled down. Whole family went to Tech.

Susan and Steven keep up the website news and news releases and anything written. Both have been here 'bout five, six years, somethin' like that. Their offices, if you can call them that—more like closets similar to yours—are just across the hall. When I need to tell 'em something, I just pop from room to room to room.

"They should all be in soon. We like to get in early in case Mr. Boyle stops in first thing, which he does, or did, often. Even though he's our boss now, he hasn't come by as much this semester—either because Ms. Danielle isn't here to gawk at—the man's a damn sexist—or maybe because of the stairs. Darn elevator only works one or two days a month. Anyway, about Boyle. Here's hoping the elevator *stays* broken so he stays *away*."

Maggie smiled and shook her head slightly in amazement at her new assistant's unapologetic opinions.

Elaine smiled back, "Let's get you settled, OK?"

Maggie and Elaine fell into an easy, almost one-sided dialogue, with

Elaine trying to relate everything to her new boss at once, and Maggie imitating a sponge, attempting to soak it up as quickly as it was spilled. Even when the other staff came in, were introduced and quickly left for their own offices, Elaine kept up her rapid-fire soliloquy on the department's procedures, accomplishments, quirks and shortcomings.

Finally, when she began to describe the postal process at the university in detail, Maggie stopped her with, "Let's save some of this for later, shall we? How about..." but stopped herself when Elaine's eyes widened like a cartoon character as she looked over Maggie's shoulder to the outer office. Maggie turned around to see an enormous plant spanning the doorway to the hall.

"Oh, my," she said softly as Elaine stepped around her and headed for the door squealing, "That's huge! Where'd it come from? Is it for me? Where did you get it?"

An out-of-breath voice from somewhere behind the immense foliage replied, "Um, a...pant, pant...a...delivery...pant, pant...for Mrs....Grant?... pant...Margaret Grant?"

"Yes, yes, come in," Elaine said excitedly. "Put it down right here," indicating the middle of the floor in front of her desk. "I'll sign for it," she said, stepping around the greenery to the deliveryman, who deftly slid the heavy plant off a dolly. She sent the winded man on his way back down the stairs and handed the card to an open-mouthed Maggie.

"It's for you. It's gigantic! What a gorgeous philodendron bipinnatifidum! It's as tall as me! Who's it from?"

Maggie read the card silently and smiled, shaking her head.

> *Mom- A new plant for a new adventure.*
> *Know you'll kick ass!*
> *Love, Michael & Ben, et al.*

"From my sons. I'd forgotten. We have a tradition of sending a small plant to each other's office when we start new jobs... this is my first new one in about 15 years. I'm... it's huge!" she said with a laugh. "What did you say it was?"

"Oh, it's a philodendron bip-in-nat-if-id-um. They grow really well under florescent lights. Don't they have the prettiest leaves? Bipinnated. If I take good care of it, which I will, it might reach the ceiling!"

It took both of them to drag the plant into one corner of the outer office. There was no way it would fit in Maggie's small space. Elaine promised to water and feed it faithfully, proudly relating her green-thumb prowess with all things growing.

Maggie liked her new assistant and worked with her to set up regular weekly staff meetings, filling out the necessary first-day-at-work paperwork for Human Resources, and then headed downstairs to a scheduled mid-morning meeting of the university's administrative staff, still smiling about the plant. She'd have to call her sons tonight to thank them.

Bennett Boyle, hair sprayed firmly in place, stood at the door of the president's conference room and looked startled when Maggie greeted him. He frowned even deeper than his usual scowl, massaged the side of his head and said, "What are you doing here?"

"Reporting for my first administrative staff meeting," she said brightly. "I noticed it online. Did I get the time wrong?"

"Yes, I mean, no. It's the right time, but you don't need to be here. I'm your direct supervisor and I attend this meeting. I'll relay to you anything I think you need to know."

Maggie looked at him for a moment before answering. "All right, Mr. Boyle. I'm just accustomed to being on the administrative team."

"Well, you're not," he replied tartly.

"May I meet with the president then, later this afternoon?"

"You may not. There's no need. You don't report to him. You report to me. You can talk with me if you need anything. Call my secretary for an appointment later in the week. I'm busy now."

"An appointment?"

"Yes, an appointment," Boyle said coldly, dismissing her by turning his back and entering the conference room.

"Okay, then. An appointment it is," she said looking up to the ceiling and heading back upstairs. "Not going to make this easy, are you God?

Chapter 9 ~

A week later, Maggie was still trying to get in to see Bennett Boyle. His secretary, Katherine, was kind and apologetic about it, but could not convince Boyle to see her. Not one to twiddle her thumbs at her desk while waiting for assignments that didn't seem to be forthcoming, Maggie had spent the first days getting to know her competent and likable staff, asking lots of questions, looking at the department's meager budget and reviewing files from her predecessor. It didn't take her long to determine that, indeed, the woman might have been a lingerie model for all she seemed to know about running a university communications office.

On day two she'd called her first staff meeting in an empty conference room, as none of their offices could hold more than two people, except Elaine's, but certainly not all in chairs, especially now with the new plant.

Charles White, photographer, was of medium build, light brown thinning hair, in his early fifties, Tech T-shirt under an ancient sports coat, well-worn Levi's, complete with the latest fashioned Nike running shoes. His weathered skin and stained fingers revealed him as a longtime smoker, but Elaine had told her a cancer scare last summer had him quitting cold turkey. He chewed gum constantly. His wife of twenty-four years was head of the Admissions Office at University Medical Center. They had no children.

Ricky Sanchez, artist, was in his early thirties, slightly overweight, dark eyes showing intelligence and wariness at the same time. His design work was as good as Elaine had said, and Maggie liked his quiet manner and his penchant for loud Hawaiian print shirts. Single, Elaine confided earlier he still lived with his parents a few blocks from campus, but Elaine was working on "findin' him a girl."

Susan Davis, the younger of the two writers, mid-twenties, was taller than any of the staff, most of her vertical measurement in her legs. Her Mary Travers-style straight blonde hair added to the illusion of height. Maggie wondered if she could sing. She fairly floated into the room, a confident smile on her face. She was a graduate of the Columbia School of Journalism, and had followed her husband, Peter, to Lubbock when he was accepted into the graduate biomedical sciences program. They had one son, whose name was not Paul, but Trey. Maggie told herself she must remember not to call her Mary... or to ask what she would do if she had a hammer.

Steven Jackson, the veteran writer, was, like Maggie, roughly thirty years older than Susan and only tall enough to reach his colleague's shoulders when standing but equal in height when seated next to Mary... er, Susan. His ebony bald head was normally covered by a stylish tweed cap. He wore a starched, designer button-down-collared shirt, expensive slacks and Italian tasseled loafers. His dark eyes sparkled. An Alabama graduate, he'd been recruited from *The Dallas Morning News* by Leonard and liked the collegiate atmosphere and stability much more than the low pay and newsroom chaos of reporters. He was married to a nurse and they had four grown children, all in either Alabama or Dallas.

After introductions, Maggie asked her staff, "So what's your... I mean our... internal communications vehicle? Newsletter, hard copy, electronic? I'm not finding anything in the files."

Steven shrugged, "We don't have one."

"No internal communications? Nothing at all?"

"Nope," Susan said, mimicking Steven's shrug. "Not in the last two years."

"Does gossip count?" said Elaine brightly.

Maggie smiled, "Uh, no... Wow. What about when Mr. Leonard was here? Surely he knew the value of communicating with staff?"

It was Elaine's turn to shrug. "We had a weekly hard copy newsletter, *Insight*, but Boyle cut it out of the budget as soon as Mr. Leonard retired. And Ms. Danielle didn't think it was important. I can have the old copies brought up from archives if you want to see them. They go all the way back to the 1940s."

"Um, no, thank you. But I'd like to talk with Mr. Leonard. He's still in Lubbock, isn't he?

"Oh, yeah. I see him at the baseball games," said Charlie. "Big fan, great guy."

"Good. Elaine, see if you can set up a lunch with him this week—oh, and at his favorite restaurant, whatever it may be."

"Sure thing. Hope you like barbeque," she said as she wrote herself a note.

Maggie continued, "We probably need to start our own newsletter, but let me do a little research first. Now, what about news releases? Do you have a good relationship with the local media? I noticed recent releases on the website from different departments across campus. I assume you all take care of those?"

Steven answered. "We do, and our relationship used to be great with local media, but recently we've just been handling the normal, everyday news."

Maggie looked puzzled. "How do you mean?"

Susan said, "He means we just do the boring stuff. Bennett Boyle's office handles the media, or I should say, Boyle tries to handle it."

"Really? How's that working?" she asked skeptically.

"Not well," said Ricky. "We are a 'día late y a peso short' as mi mamá used to say. We know nada about what goes on in this building until we read it in the local paper, so most of the time the media doesn't bother with us for important stuff."

"Hmmpf," was Maggie's reply, not ready yet to openly declare she thought that was clearly the wrong way to handle communications. She prodded them further with, "How do you contact all the faculty and staff in an emergency?"

"We don't," Ricky said. "There's software that can help us do that, but nobody in this ivory tower seems to think the unwashed public employees need to know what's going on, especially in an emergency."

"Really?"

"With all the shootings on campuses across the country, and even with our West Texas tornados, we have no way of getting word out to everyone," Steven offered. "I told them I think it's criminal, but they don't listen."

"Okay, good to know. Let me think on it awhile. Might have to fix that first. Now what about social media? Whose in charge of twittering, texting, blogging and all that?"

Susan answered. "Once again, we did all that, but our former boss didn't think it was necessary, so it has fallen by the wayside. Tell you the truth, I don't think she had any idea what we were talking about."

"What about approaching Boyle about it?"

"Good luck with that," said Charlie. "We *know* he knows nothing about social media. I'm certain Bennett will tell you to take a flying leap."

Maggie laughed, imagining Bennett Boyle saying those exact words. Looking at her crew, she said, "Well, sometimes you just have to ask forgiveness instead of permission. How about you all have social media proposals to me by the end of the week?"

"I knew I was going to like you," said Elaine, smiling broadly as the others nodded.

They finished the meeting with discussions of the outside marketing firm the university hired for statewide billboards, magazine ads and national story pitches. Maggie thought she could bring some of it in-house. She had seen the previous work of her staff and knew they were competent enough to handle more. Besides, it would help with her paltry budget.

Chapter 10 ~

Just before noon two weeks later, Sharon walked into Maggie's office. "Hi, I was downstairs for a meeting. Can you get away for lunch? Next class isn't until three." Sharon worked and taught in the Civil Engineering Building, on the east side of the north-south esplanade. It was a short five-minute walk, and the friends were able to meet easily, if not often, for lunch.

"Sure... give me a minute and we can go over to the Student Union." She finished an e-mail then spoke to Elaine on the way out, "I'm heading out to lunch for a few minutes. Got a call into Jake Humphrey. If he calls here, send him to my cell, will you, please?"

"Sure thing, boss."

"Jake Humphrey? Who's that?" Sharon asked as they started down the stairs.

"*Lubbock Avalanche Journal* reporter. Nice guy. Tech graduate, lifelong Lubbockite—or is it Lubbokean?

"Definitely Lubbockite," Sharon said, raising her eyebrow.

"Okay. Anyway, he does a pretty decent job with his stories," Maggie explained. "I'm trying to get on his good side."

"I didn't know reporters had good sides."

"Most of them do. They're just people who have a job to do, like you

34

and me."

"Not like me. I don't make it a habit of going for the jugular. It's gotten where I don't believe anything I read in the papers or hear on the nightly news any more."

"It's true there's a lot of 'gotcha' journalism out there, but I think the majority of reporters try to be honest and objective. At least that's what I expect until they prove me wrong."

"That's optimistic of you, Maggie."

"Not really. I've had good experiences with them. But I do remember we had a reporter from the *Fort Worth Star Telegram* who was unbelievable. He'd ask leading questions he could twist to get the predetermined answers he wanted for the lies he printed and then complain when we complained. We called it the 'Startlegram' when he worked there. His lies finally caught up with him and the ethical editors booted him out the door. But, personally, I think he did a lot of damage to that once-credible rag."

"Startlegram? That's clever." Sharon smiled. "Amazing the difference one little letter can make."

They reached the outside and headed through the courtyard across to the Student Union Building, or SUB. Sharon said, "Haven't seen you for a while. Late nights at the office?"

"Yep. Just trying to get a handle on things. Guess we have been like ships passing in the night."

"Things getting any better? You've been at work, what, two weeks now? Is Boyle letting you handle the media yet?"

"Nope. The staff's right. We seem to be the last to know about anything, so I'm doing a lot of clean up with the reporters. But Bennett Boyle pretty much ignores anything I send over. You would think the Chief of Staff has too many other things to do besides my job, but I'm trying to get things done right."

"Still no appointment?" asked Sharon as they entered the cafeteria.

"No, but I have sent him work summaries."

"Summaries? How?"

"By e-mail, of course. Why?"

Sharon smiled and said, "Because the man ignores e-mails. Well-known fact."

"Really? No wonder I haven't heard from him. Hmmm. That might work to my advantage."

They selected their salads and sat down at a corner table in the main dining area. Maggie asked, "Do you know our photographer, Charles White, very well?"

"Charlie? Sure. Everybody knows Charlie. Great guy. Awesome photographer. Been here forever and is all over campus getting photos. What about him?" She frowned. "Don't you like him?"

"Oh, no. I like him fine. And he *is* a great photographer. It's just he seems... well yesterday, we needed a photo shoot done at the Biology Building. I assigned it to him, and he turned red and said that he couldn't. Steven cut in quickly and said he'd take care of it, not to worry. I sensed everyone in the staff meeting seemed a little uneasy, so I let it go. As they left, I heard Charlie thank Steven, and he said 'no problem.' That he was 'always there for him.' I just wondered what that was all about?'

"His sister."

"His sister? Whose sister?"

"Charlie's sister."

"Charlie has a sister?"

"Charlie did have a sister. She was about 10 years younger than Charlie and was attending Tech when she died."

"Oh, what a shame. How?" Maggie asked.

"Took a dive off the top of the Biology Building."

"Suicide? Good grief! No wonder he didn't want to go there. Poor guy."

"From what I understand, he hasn't been in the building since it happened. Remember the murder of the cleaning lady a year or so before we came to Tech?"

"Of course. My parents were questioning my choice of schools. Luckily, the guy was caught pretty quickly, wasn't he?"

"Yep. But it was in the same building. And then about two years ago, there was a brutal rape on campus."

"Don't tell me. Biology Building?"

"Yep. Not the luckiest place at Tech. I'd give it a wide berth, if I were you."

"Definitely."

"Now, what about President Stone?" Sharon asked.

"Well, Elaine and Charlie both say rumor has it Stone is leaving at the end of the semester, but I've no idea. Have you heard anything in engineering?"

"The same. People think he's leaving. Probably will announce it at the next Board of Regents meeting. If he does, there won't be too many tears shed in my department."

"Yeah, I haven't found many faculty who are loyal to him, and nobody seems to like Boyle either. I've made headway in making friends with all the media in town, but it doesn't do me much good if I don't get the news first so I can get it to them. I had lunch yesterday with Jake at the *Avalanche Journal*—"

"*A-J*," Sharon corrected. "Everyone in Lubbock calls it the *A-J*."

"Okay, the *A-J*, then, and I think we hit it off. The problem is he often knows about things before I do. And he still feels like he has to go to Boyle before he comes to me just to keep from getting shut out. I don't blame him, but it makes me wonder why I'm really here other than for the mundane stuff. I tell you, my previous communications jobs were a lot more exciting than this."

"Sorry about that, Maggie. Didn't you say you were going to talk with old man Leonard, the previous communications guy? Did you get a chance?"

Maggie smiled remembering, "I did. He's quite a character. I took him to lunch at his favorite place—Tom and Bingo's Hickory Pit Bar-B-Q."

"Tom and Bingo's? We used to go as students, didn't we? I'd forgotten about it. Where is it again?"

"Thirty-fourth and Boston. No, Elgin. Thirty-fourth and Elgin. Remember? It's a little hole-in-the-wall with benches along the inside as the only place to sit. Can't be more than twelve-feet wide, but service is quick and the food is really good. I love their sign—'*We start serving every day at 11 TIL WE RUN OUT*.' That pretty much sums up West Texas' style, don't you think?"

Sharon nodded with a mouthful of lettuce.

"Anyway," Maggie continued, "I met him there my first week and we had a good chat about the department. He's the one who came up with the current tagline for Tech, *From Here It's Possible*."

"I've always liked that. What'd you call it? Tagline?"

"Yeah... some call it a branding slogan or marketing one-liner. One of the better ones across the country, in my opinion," Maggie said. "And Leonard confirmed the staff does quality work, but for the last couple of years their hands have been tied. He was extremely unhappy with his replacement and said he went to Stone about it, but obviously it did no good."

"Obviously," Sharon said with chagrin.

"But he gave me insight into some things. It was a good meeting... and worth the time, and definitely worth it for the barbecue! I'll bring some home one night soon and give Doug the night off."

"Tom and Bingo's Bar-B-Q. He'll love it. You know, Maggie, maybe if and when Stone leaves, it will get better. Heard anything about who the new president might be?"

Maggie shrugged. "I would be the last to know, remember? They're really keeping a lid on this one, but I have heard Bennett Boyle might be in the running, or at least he'll apply."

"They wouldn't dare, would they? Nobody likes Boyle, the prick." Sharon made a face to further display her displeasure at the idea.

"It'd be a total disaster for my department, that's for sure. Stranger things have been decided by regents, though."

"Amen to that."

They finished lunch and headed back outside. "You ready to go house hunting again this weekend?" Maggie asked, looking sideways at Sharon.

"No. We like having you at our house, even though we don't see enough of you. But yes, of course I'll help you look. Let's hit it really early Saturday morning, OK? Doug's got a faculty concert Saturday evening you can't miss. He's playing his sax in the jazz band. You'll love it. Really turns me on when he has that sax in his hands."

"The way you two carry on, I don't think you need any help from a musical instrument," Maggie teased. "How long have you two been together now?"

"Twelve glorious, wonderful, sexy, romantic years."

"You're a lucky woman. He's a real keeper. I don't remember you ever being as happy as you've been with him. An engineer and a musician. Who would've thought that'd work?"

"I keep telling you—engineering is a CREATIVE science!"

Chapter 11 ~

Sharon and Doug's elegant two-story home, the Nest as they laughingly called it, was two miles west of campus on 19th Street, and Maggie had easily settled into the large guest cottage at the back of the two-acre estate. With her quarters already completely furnished, the majority of her belongings were put in a nearby storage facility, ready for whenever she found her own home, which she hoped would be soon.

Not that the arrangement wasn't both comfortable and comforting. She was alone but within throwing distance of one of her two best friends in the world. And Sharon's significant other, Tech music professor Douglas Pucci, agreed with Sharon on the need for Maggie to have as much privacy as she desired and as much company as she needed. It reminded Maggie of her first experience in Lubbock—she was alone, but help from her parents back in Dallas was just a phone call away. Now she was alone but her friends were just a few steps away.

At first, Maggie shared dinners with them in the main kitchen, previously only faintly aware of, and now delighted by Doug's gourmet culinary skills. Italian food seemed to be his specialty, probably due in part to the annual summer trips the two made to Tuscany visiting his family "in the old country." Maggie was worried her extra pounds would be harder to lose as she gained an appreciation for his cooking, especially his lasagna.

Once she began her work in earnest though and realized she would have little or no direction from her supervisor, she spent long hours at the office, passing through the kitchen only late at night either looking for leftovers to take for reheating in her own kitchenette, or to see if anyone was still up to discuss the day.

Sharon and Doug had individually mentioned, casually but not too subtly, that they expected her to be with them at least six months, if not a full year. Maggie, though, knew the arrangement was only short-term, and looking for a house of her own needed to be a priority if she was to get a complete start on her new life. She'd promised to stay at least through the end of July to watch the big house while they made their annual trip to Italy. And besides, finding a house of her own was harder than she'd imagined.

Just south of campus, in the area of older homes she'd loved as a student, houses of brick and stucco from the 1930s and '40s were in various conditions. Many were still the original size and shape, owned by older occupants, some who rented out a bedroom or garage apartment to students. Others had been restored and enlarged, with beautifully manicured lawns and decades-old oak or elm trees gracing their lawns. A few of the lovely old houses had been torn down completely and replaced by McMansions—gigantic two- or three-story brick cookie-cutter monstrosities taking up almost all of the green space, forever changing the appearance of a street. There should be an ordinance against those teardowns, she thought ruefully as she toured one Sunday after church.

Maggie favored the older homes with character, if not closet space, imagining herself in the middle of the landscape, happily tending an iris bed or two. She'd actually brought some of the irises from her gardens in Dallas, not being able to bear parting with them since they had been her mother's. They were currently planted temporarily next to Sharon's guest cottage.

With only a few homes for sale meeting her criteria, quick calls to the real estate agent's listing found she was always too late. "Just sold this morning" was a common refrain. Maggie was resigned to wait patiently for the right house and enjoy Sharon and Doug's hospitality a little longer.

Chapter 12 ~

Every other day or so, Maggie dutifully attended either early morning or Sunday Mass. The constancy of the universal Catholic liturgy gave her a comfortable link to her old life and made her radical upheaval seem not quite so radical. There were several Catholic churches in the area and she thought she needed to try them on to see which one fit best.

As a student at Tech, she attended Protestant services because she'd grown up Lutheran. Only after she and Jim were married did she become Catholic. She had wanted to be a participating member before their first child was conceived. Because she'd conceded to Jim their children could be raised Catholic, Maggie had attended a class for potential converts.

Jim jokingly told their friends the first time it "didn't take." Truth was the priest who ran the classes couldn't, or wouldn't, answer her many questions. A year later she'd tried again with a different, younger priest, Father Joseph Turner. Extremely patient and interested in her intellectual points, he not only satisfied her curiosity but was also convincing enough about the validity of the teachings that she joined the church whole-heartedly, much to Jim's surprise and her mother-in-law's relief.

She was obliged to admit there really wasn't that much difference in the two religions. While Martin Luther had made some valid points a few centuries back, they were not legitimate enough to make a huge difference for her in this century. Being strong in her faith since childhood, she felt comfortable enough with what she'd learned in class to make the change, or she wouldn't have done it. It certainly would be easier if they worshiped as a family.

It was praying to the saints and the Virgin Mary that baffled her at first. "Why in the world," she had argued, "do you need to pray to statues when you can go directly to God?"

Father Joseph's simple explanation was Catholics don't actually pray to statues, as most Protestants mistakenly believe. Rather the likenesses are there to keep the saint in mind while conversing with them, much as you look at someone's picture when reminiscing.

He asked her, "In times of trouble, don't you ask your friends to pray for you?" She had, in fact, often asked others to intercede for her, as she felt the more prayers the better. She continued to ask her parents to watch over her family, even though both had died in a plane crash shortly after her graduation from college. There was a certain comfort in asking and then in believing they were on duty along with her guardian angel.

"So," continued Father Joseph, "we are merely asking the saints for the same. Intercession and prayers."

It made sense to Maggie, and so it was added to the list of things she took on faith. Confession was another hurdle, however. Telling your sins to a priest instead of to God? Again, why not talk directly to Him, she asked. "Surely He's not too busy to hear me?"

Once again, Father Joseph, now Monsignor Joseph, listened to her concerns and then explained enough to allow her to try it. After her first confession and absolution, Maggie had been astonished by the feelings of genuine relief. It was true, then, confession *was* good for the soul. She became a believer in the sacrament, and Father Joseph became a friend to the young couple as well as their spiritual guide throughout their marriage.

Chapter 13 ~

Two miles southwest of the loop in Lubbock, a huge gold-domed sanctuary had recently been built on several acres of treeless grasslands, surrounded by freshly constructed starter homes and across from wide open fields, also treeless. Most of the worshipers were young families. It was an incredibly beautiful building, but the majority of the congregation was too young for her.

Saint Barnabas, the 1960s-built church inside the loop, was architect-turally interesting and the greeters were friendly and welcoming, but the middle-aged pastor's voice was such a monotone that she, along with several others, had a hard time stifling their yawns and staying awake.

This particular Sunday, she headed for St. Elizabeth's University Parish, the huge Spanish mission-styled "campus" church, a few blocks east of Texas Tech on Broadway, and across the street from the Christian church Sharon and Doug attended. The services and Masses scheduled at the two sanctuaries were conveniently staggered, either by accident or design, so traffic wasn't too bad at either church. Maggie would get out that morning about 20 minutes before Sharon and Doug and had promised to rush to Café J to secure a table for brunch. Her mouth was already watering in anticipation of their famous seafood crepes.

From the rear parking lot, Maggie studied the church. The tan brick building could have easily been a part of the Tech campus architecture with its red clay-tiled roof, carved stone columns set into the walls, and deep-cut ornate stone window frames. At the entrance, Maggie went through a massive double oak door, then made her way across the three-story, 30-foot wide vestibule. Additional massive oak doors led into the sanctuary. Above those doors, a wall of clear glass allowed light to stream between the entry foyer and the sanctuary.

A back pew was the perfect place to observe other churchgoers as well as the entire service. She took a moment to study the architecture. The open, light-filled sanctuary had an immense vaulted oak ceiling sharply contrasting with the thick, whitewashed adobe walls. The simple oak altar and ambo, or pulpit, stood up on a raised carpeted platform. Directly behind and above the altar was a large wooden crucifix, nearly 12 feet tall but dwarfed by the massive walls. Further above, a Spanish-style stained glass window was set back from the wall into the outer brick, as in a niche, showing the walls to be three to four feet thick. A white dove soared in the middle of the window's brilliant blues and reds of colored glass.

To the left of the altar was an open iron gate leading to a much smaller chapel, no bigger than 12 feet by 12 feet, lined with stained glass windows from floor to ceiling. Dazzling colors drew the eye to the center of a smaller altar where the sacred host was kept in an ornate gold tabernacle.

Along the two side walls of the main sanctuary, flanking the pews, 20-foot-tall stained glass stories of Christ's life were set up high and deep. Maggie was surprised to notice the brightness of the church was not from the daylight, but achieved through the stark white walls and strategically placed lighting, both hanging and recessed. A well-designed sanctuary to reflect the light of the Lord.

She knelt to give thanks for her new adventure, her boys and their families, her friends and her health, and then asked for guidance—not for anything in particular this time, but just for general guidance in all decisions. She crossed herself and stood as the music signaled the beginning of Mass.

Subconsciously noting the St. Elizabeth congregation was made up of all ages, ethnicities and levels of wealth and poverty, including the expected large number of college-aged students, she felt comfortable here. A young Hispanic family sat next to her, obviously close to the back door to make a quick exit if either of their offspring, the preschooler or the newborn, began to participate too loudly.

Directly in front of her was another family, a couple in their late thirties with four, no, five children. She judged them to range in age from fifteen down to about three, all tow-headed and ruddy freckle-faced like their father, with the exception of the middle girl who had dark silken hair like the mother. Next to them, an elderly woman who looked to be about 95 hobbled into the pew with the help of an older well-dressed gentleman, probably her son. She was elegantly dressed in a yellow spring suit, an understated fashionable hat framing her small weather-worn face.

A bell clanged and the congregation rose at the signal. Because Maggie was so far back and to the left, her line of sight to the procession was blocked by others until the priest, deacon and acolytes stepped onto the higher level of the altar. She was pleased to see one of the two young altar servers was a girl—not all churches complied with the Vatican dictate that servers could be of either gender, just as not all churches interpreted the rules the same way. The young girl's presence meant that at least the pastor here was a little forward thinking.

Squinting and standing on tiptoe, Maggie studied the priest more closely. He was tall, dark headed and looked to be around her age, comfortably somewhere in his 50s. He moved with an athletic grace much like Jim's. When he spoke, his deep rich voice was pleasant, but it seemed to Maggie it was his enthusiasm for his faith that flavored his speech to the point of making him charismatic—even from a distance.

Just a week after Easter, the gospel reading was one familiar to her—the story of the disciple Thomas, who said, "Unless I see the mark of the nails in His hands and put my hand into His side, I will not believe." Scriptures say Jesus replied, "Blessed are they who have not seen and believe."

Maggie's throat constricted and she closed her eyes to force back threatening tears. She could see Jim give her a skeptical look and recite his frequent line, "I'll believe it when I see it." Lovingly calling him "Doubting Thomas" since the beginning of their marriage, she often reminded him many things in life just had to be taken on faith.

Now it was Maggie who was the "Doubting Thomas," wondering about her unlikely move to West Texas. Had she really heard both Jim and God tell her to come? Or was it an illusion she created to get away from the relentless grief of being in a house that was no longer a home without the man she'd loved for thirty years?

She was renewing her prayer for guidance as the priest's soft, yet commanding voice interrupted and then captivated her. His message wasn't the mundane patronizing normal sermon, but an intellectual query on how this particular scripture was relevant today. Her mind had to work to keep up with his ideas and hypotheses.

She tried to convince herself it was his words that moved her—uninfluenced by her curiosity of whether he looked as appealing up close as he did high up on the altar. Oooh, get thee behind me, Satan, she thought as she closed her eyes to listen without the visual distraction. She was mesmerized.

When he stopped, she thought it was too soon. She wanted more, and she looked at her watch, the time showing he had talked for a little more than the normal sermon. Maggie stood with the congregation for the Profession of Faith, then realized this is what she wanted... what she needed. Intellectual religion, much like Monsignor Joseph provided back in Dallas. Of course it wouldn't hurt if the celebrant wasn't hard to look at, either.

During communion, she walked up the left aisle to the front, but again she was too far away to really see him. She received the sacred host from a much older priest who seemingly appeared out of nowhere, but in reality had stepped out from the small chapel. She smiled as she bowed, thinking he was probably at least as old as the hat lady at the back; then she took the host as he said in a high-pitched thick Irish brogue, "Aye, da body o' Christ." She looked him directly in the eyes and he held her stare, then nodded as if to say, "OK, me darlin', time to move on." Maggie shook her head as she moved to the lay Eucharistic minister who held out the communion cup to her.

All thoughts of the dark-haired priest vanished as she contemplated those ancient, intelligent, all-knowing and obviously Irish eyes. She returned to her seat, wondering just how old he really was. Quickly admonishing herself for her lack of piety and her intense curiosity of things, she followed the remainder of the Mass more reverently.

At the end of the last hymn, though, Maggie strained again to catch a closer glimpse of the "younger" priest in the recessional. But once again her view was blocked.

Thinking she might see him outside on the porch as he greeted worshipers, she made her way through the vestibule and out the main doors only to find herself at the end of the line leading directly to the older priest. She noticed the taller cleric nearby, but his back was to her and he was surrounded by a crowd of obviously admiring and adoring parishioners, mostly women. She sighed and focused her attention on where she was.

"Margaret Grant," she said smiling when it was her turn to shake the old priest's hand. "Newly arrived from Dallas."

"Well, then, an' I'm Monsignor Fitzpatrick. From Dallas, is it now? Ya wouldn't be knowing me good friend Father Joseph Turner, now would ya?" he asked with a wink.

"Monsignor Joseph?" Maggie replied with surprise. "From Saint Mary's parish? Why yes. He's a dear friend."

"Well, now, an, didn't 'e call me up just da other week ta be on da lookout fer ya. And here ya be. Welcome ta Saint Elizabeth's. I hope ya will be comfortable 'ere."

"Why, yes," she said slightly flustered at this unexpected connection to her past life. "I, um, I enjoyed the homily very much," she stammered, remembering too late he wasn't the one who should receive the compliment.

"Oh, aye. Father Murphy talks a great lesson on da scriptures, 'e does. Couldn't do without 'em here a' tall. Not a' tall. Been 'ere giving good sermons an' serving da parish goin' on 'bout fifteen years now. Good priest, hard worker. Lucky ta have him as me assistant."

"Your assistant?" Maggie stammered. Most priests were long retired by the age of 70, and Monsignor Fitzpatrick had to be 90 if he was a day.

"Oh, yes, meself's the pastor of Saint Elizabeth's. Been here since yon cornerstone was laid at da old chapel some 60 odd years back. This is me home, but da parish, don't ye know, has gotten so grand, thanks be to God, dat I had to take on a little help. And de Bishop asked me to be kind to young Father Murphy, there." He inclined his head toward the other priest. "So I humor 'em by letting 'em do much of da legwork—and da homilies. He doesn' like ta be idle, as day say. So, I pretty much let 'em run da place, but 'tis meself who's really da boss." He winked conspiratorially at Maggie as he gave her a direct look. "E'er seen da movie *Going My Way*?"

She smiled, delighted, and looked again at Father Murphy's back. The crowd around him had dispersed somewhat and he was making his way back into the church.

"There now," said Monsignor Fitzpatrick. She quickly turned her attention back to him. "I hope ta be seein' ya again soon, Mrs. Margaret Grant?"

"Thank you, Father. You will, you will." She glanced once more at the church, looked at her watch and hurried to her car, thinking she might not be the first to arrive for brunch.

Father Murphy wasn't the celebrant at either of the two early morning Masses Maggie attended that week, and again absent at the next Sunday Mass, but the deacon did a pretty fair job of the homily, while the Monsignor presided at the altar. She liked the atmosphere at Saint Elizabeth's and thought perhaps she had found a new church home.

A few days later, Elaine sent a call into her office from "a priest." Startled, Maggie picked up the phone, puzzled until she heard the distinctive Irish brogue on the other end of the line. It took Father Fitzpatrick forty-five seconds flat to coax her into volunteering for the summer's Vacation Bible School.

"Don't ye know," he said, "Our dear Mrs. Bodecker, bless her soul, has been doing the same popsicle stick crosses nigh on ta twenty years, and me friend Father Joseph happened ta mention dat ye were right good at some rather progressive craft projects for da children when you were at Saint Mary's back in Dallas."

He added quickly, "Now don't ye know dat wit' yer important job at da university an' all, meself is sure dat ye canna be 'ere everyday for da morning classes come summer, but if ye could just give our teachers some new ideas an' da like, it would be much appreciated, it would. Father Joseph himself assures me dat 'twill be an easy task fer someone as talented as yerself. Can you help me, do ye think, Mrs. Margaret Grant?"

Maggie laughed. Every priest she'd ever known had an amazing ability to recruit volunteers, but Father Fitzpatrick might just be the best she'd encountered.

And so, working with the church secretary to find out this year's theme, gathering information on ages and numbers of expected children, a teacher workshop was set up for the Saturday before the early June Vacation Bible School. Now all she had to do was figure out five projects for the week for each of the five different age groups. Twenty-five projects in all—and with an extremely limited budget, because, "We're a wee poor parish, we 'ere," Monsignor had said pitifully enough.

Piece of cake, she thought rolling her eyes at her own gullibility, knowing she'd be opening her wallet. She'd also be calling Carol, the real craft lady, for advice, and visiting the storage facility to dig out her supply boxes. She spent the next several evenings and weekends getting prepared to teach. In the meantime, her day job kept her busy during the week.

Chapter 14 ~

The Texas Tech University Board of Regent's meeting, held monthly in the east wing second-floor boardroom of the Administration Building, normally drew minimal crowds and the obligatory one or two reporters.

Today, the room was crowded, due, Maggie knew, to persistent rumors President Stone was going to announce his resignation. Just outside the boardroom, she ran into Bennett Boyle.

"Mr. Boyle, what a nice coincidence," she said as he frowned at her. "I have been trying to set up an appointment with you. Maybe we could talk today?"

"I've, um, I've been busy. You've only been here a week."

"Three," she said looking at him sweetly.

"What?" he said.

"Three," she repeated. "I've been here three weeks and have been trying to get an appointment with you for three weeks."

He ignored her statement and took another tack, "Why are you here? You don't need to be here. I'm covering the Board meeting."

"Yes, I understand that, and I am sure afterward you'll relay anything you think I need to know, but seeing as how it's a public meeting, I'm here to be part of that public," she said looking directly at him. "I can take the morning off to make it legal if you prefer?" She silently dared him to object.

"It's not necessary for you to be here," he said as he regained his composure.

"Perhaps not, but nevertheless, I'm here and intend to stay unless you absolutely forbid it. I'm meeting the *Lubbock Avalanche Journal* reporter, but I can certainly tell him you won't allow me to be here."

He looked at her hard, turned on his heel and entered the board room.

Maggie gulped, said a small prayer and followed him in. She found a seat next to Jake, the *A-J* reporter she had treated to lunch the previous week. She was glad he was there—they hadn't actually discussed it.

To no one's surprise, President Stone did announce his resignation, effective at the end of the semester. Maggie went up to get the word out.

Early the following morning Maggie received a call from Boyle's office asking to meet with Boyle that afternoon.

"Will wonders never cease," she said to Sharon over lunch. "He actually wants to talk with me."

"More likely talk *at* you," opined her friend.

Maggie arrived right on time, armed with a list of suggestions for revamping the department. Boyle's secretary, Miss Katherine, apologized, saying someone had just popped in, but it shouldn't be but a minute or two. Maggie sat down in a comfortable leather chair to wait.

Twenty minutes later, the door to Boyle's inner sanctum opened and a neatly dressed man quickly exited. He moved directly to Katherine and gave her some papers. Only then did he realize someone else was in the outer office. He turned to Maggie with a nervous smile and introduced himself.

"Jonathan Long, assistant to the Chief of Staff, at your service. And you are?"

"Margaret Grant, director of Communications and Marketing. You interviewed me, Mr. Long, about two months ago."

"Oh, yes, of course! Sorry I haven't been up to officially welcome you. Please call me Jonathan," he said as he looked her up and down as men are wont to do. She smiled, for some reason not in the least offended by his frank appraisal, and then returned it, confirming her earlier assessment that he was about thirty-five, married, unassuming and competent.

Politely excusing himself, he retrieved a different set of papers from Katherine and left in a hurry, calling over his shoulder to Maggie, "We'll talk. I'll call." His brisk footsteps, wide smile and fast-paced mannerisms reminded Maggie of a ferret, who spends its entire waking day in rapid motion. She liked him.

"I didn't realize it had been three weeks," Boyle said. He didn't bother to look up as she entered his office. She quickly surveyed the large neatly arranged paneled room and noted the lack of personal touches with the exception of his two professionally framed diplomas from Texas A&M University. No family photos, no sports memorabilia. All business.

"As Chief of Staff, I'm rather a busy man, as I'm sure you can understand."

"Of course, especially with President Stone's announced resignation," Maggie said.

"Yes, yes. But be that as it may, let's talk about your job response-bilities."

"OK, good," she said. Without an invitation she sat down directly across the desk from Boyle. He still didn't look at her, but continued rifling though some papers.

Maggie waited, and cleared her throat. Boyle seemed to be surprised someone was there. He said, "Oh, yes, well, I am your direct supervisor, so you report directly to me with everything you do, understand?"

"Yes, of course," said Maggie.

She waited for his next statement, but he only continued to look through the papers on his desk. Finally, she broke the silence. "I *have* been sending you weekly work summaries. Have you had a chance to read them?"

He looked up at her sharply. "You have? No." He dug back into the mountains as if looking for the summaries. "When?"

"Every Thursday, but they're probably not on your desk. I sent them through e-mail."

"E-mail? I don't have time for e-mail. I've got stacks of paperwork to do each day. I'm too busy to look at useless e-mails."

"Oh, well, that would explain why I haven't heard back from you about the new software."

"What new software?"

"I noticed the lack of emergency notification software, and knew it must be an oversight, so I worked with the IT department and we've purchased a new system. We were able to find the funding in both our budgets. It was installed just this week, in fact."

"An emergency notification system?" Boyle's brow was furrowed.

"Yes. All universities have them in light of recent national campus events, and it makes sense. I was certain you would approve and President Stone seemed pleased. We announced it in the employee newsletter."

"What do you mean, you were certain I would app– What employee newsletter?"

"You haven't seen our new version of *Insight*?" she asked innocently.

"*Insight*? I cut it out of your budget. You don't have money for that nonsense."

"We don't exactly need money. It's electronic. Through all-campus e-mail."

"What! You sent out an e-mail to everyone on campus? Who author-ized you to do that?" He reached over for his computer keyboard and tried to boot the blank screen, then shouted to the outer office, "Miss Katherine. Come fix this infernal thing for me."

Miss Katherine, the polished dark-suited matronly secretary, quickly and efficiently obliged, saying to Maggie as she worked, "Oh, thanks for the *Insight* update yesterday afternoon. It was nice to be among the first to know, and I'm looking forward to next week's issue. Here, Mr. Boyle, I'm printing a hard copy for you."

Boyle emitted what appeared to be a painful growl. "That will be all Miss Katherine," he said sternly.

"Yes, sir, Mr. Boyle," she said sweetly. She left as efficiently as she had entered.

Boyle pulled the copy from the printer as Maggie hid a smile. It read:

President Announces Resignation at April Board Meeting

Texas Tech University Board of Regents accepted the sudden resignation of its president at their monthly meeting this morning. President Stone said, "I have enjoyed my tenure at Texas Tech, but family issues are compelling me to move on. I will finish up projects this semester so the new president can be hired before the fall term."

The resignation was accepted by the Board of Regents chairman who expressed gratitude to Stone for his service. A committee was appointed to immediately begin looking for a replacement.

The article went on to list Stone's accomplishments and tenure at Tech.

Boyle looked up after reading the first paragraph. "Who the hell authorized you to do this?"

"Well, sir, it's news from a public meeting the employees needed to know. In my last weekly work summary, I reported to you we were planning on publishing *Insight*, and would begin this week if in fact there was a resignation announcement, which there was.

"And I e-mailed President Stone after the Board meeting to make certain I had the quote correct. He thanked me for getting the word out to employees. I copied you on the e-mails, sir. I just assumed if you didn't want me to do so, you would've let me know."

Boyle stood up and walked to his window, his back to her.

May as well give the screw another turn, Maggie thought. "You know, sir, I attended the faculty senate meeting the first week I was here, and they—"

"You did what?" he said, as he turned toward her with a hard look.

"Went to the faculty senate meeting and asked what I could do to facilitate open communications. The senate told me they wanted to know university news before they read it in the local newspaper. They were 100 percent in favor of reviving an employee newsletter, so we pulled it together. I put all this in my weekly summary to you... sir."

She stoically sat there while he stared at her. After what seemed an eternity, he turned back toward the window.

Another uncomfortable silence followed. Finally Maggie said, "I'm a firm believer our most important audience is our internal audience, so I directed our first communication efforts toward them. I've also reached out to the university student newspaper, and to local media and have met most of the relevant reporters, and even a few irrelevant ones."

Boyle rubbed his head as if trying to regain his composure. He returned to his desk, looked at Maggie and calmly said, "No more quotes from anyone unless they go through me. And you clear all contact with reporters through this office. Do you understand?"

"Yes sir, I understand," said Maggie mildly.

"Dismissed." He sat down looking once again at his desk clutter.

Maggie retreated to the outer office where she gave a nod and wink to Miss Katherine who mouthed silently, "Well done!"

Maggie fairly floated up the stairs to her office, with a silent prayer of thanks, thinking, "Round two to Margaret Grant."

Chapter 15 ~

The next few weeks were busy for Maggie, and not just because of her extracurricular project for the church. At work, she was building contacts through faculty and staff and deciding what news to include in *Insight*, looking for the right mix of hard news, basic information and a little fun. Hers was an astute, educated audience, and the newsletter they sent out needed to respect that audience as well as inform and entertain.

Her philosophy on what mattered was based on the possibility of a member of the community bumping into a faculty or staff person in the grocery store—which happened often—and what they might ask about the university. Communications' job was to supply enough information in a timely manner so Tech employees couldn't and wouldn't say "no idea because they never tell us anything." The 2,600 people on the Tech payroll were her first and best ambassadors to the local public and she intended to keep them knowledgeable and informed.

Judging from the feedback to the weekly Tech trivia contests, the positive response was growing steadily, proving the faculty senate members to be as smart as she thought they were in requesting a revival of *Insight*.

And then trouble.

It was a Thursday morning, and as usual, she headed into the office long before the others. Her unread morning newspaper was tucked under her arm. She made a cup of green tea to sip as she settled down to shake the cobwebs and see if there was anything in print about Tech, perhaps gleaned from the news releases Steven had sent out earlier in the week.

She knew Jake was good at using almost everything they sent him, trusting her office to only send out releases readers would care about. Jake, the reporter turned friend, was out this week, though, taking a short vacation for his brother's wedding somewhere back East, but a cub reporter might have picked something up and run with it.

On the third page, a headline caught her attention, her right hand stopping with her cup in midair. "Oh, God," she said aloud, and then looked up apologetically. She put down her teacup hard enough to spill it.

"How in the world did that happen?!"

She dialed Jonathan's number and reread the short article while his phone rang. The headline said:

Local Philanthropist Donates $30 million to Tech Wind Museum

Jonathan answered on the fifth ring and without Maggie uttering a word, he said quickly, "Just read it, too. No idea. Let me see what I can find out. I'll call," and hung up. Thirty million dollars, she thought. That's huge!

Her phone rang before she could take her hand away. As she scanned the brief article for the third time, she answered "Communications and Marketing. Margaret Grant speaking."

The voice on the line was loud and angry. "Third page. What in the hell do ya'll think you're doing over there? I get the largest donation in the history of the university and it only makes page three of the god-damned local newspaper?! You should be fired, you know what I mean?"

"And you are?" Maggie asked defensively.

"Dr. Winston P. Whitaker the third, director of the Wind Museum. Who the hell are you?"

"Margaret Grant, director of Communications. Listen, I'm sorry, Dr. Whitaker, but this office knew nothing about the gift."

As if he didn't hear her, he continued, "And no god-damned state or national coverage anywhere!"

"Well, Dr. Whitaker, I can assure you if we *had* known, we would have put together a marketing plan for the announcement to garner better results. Who did you talk to about it?" she asked, desperately hoping one of her staff hadn't dropped the ball, although she couldn't imagine they had.

"Bennett. Bennett James Boyle—chief of god-damned staff. And he assured me your office would handle this professionally."

"And we would have, Dr. Whitaker, but unfortunately, it seems Mr. Boyle forgot to tell us about it."

"Well, obviously, Miss. This is a disaster! This is all your fault!"

"I hardly see how it can be my fault, Dr. Whitaker, if we knew nothing about it. But perhaps it's not a total disaster, sir. It's Thursday, so we can get information out to major outlets this afternoon for Sunday's papers. Why don't I come over to see you right now and get some facts. I'll have my staff start working on a state and national package immediately. Will that work for you?"

Maggie's heart was racing as fast as her brain. She began thinking of the myriad details needed for such a quick campaign. Finally, he answered, "I'm in my office at the museum. Come now." And he hung up.

After a quick call to her troops to get the ball rolling on background of the philanthropist, the director, the history of the museum, needed photography and another quick consultation with Jonathan, Maggie raced to her car to drive to the Wind Museum in the northwest corner of campus.

On the way, Steven called her back telling her his wife was friends with the donor's daughter-in-law, and he might be able to use the connection to get in to see him this morning. She sent him down that path, being thankful for small towns where everyone is somehow connected to everyone else. She knew Steven would do a good job with the interview.

Although Lubbock early morning traffic is virtually nonexistent in comparison to Dallas, it still took her a good 15 minutes to get to the museum what with dodging students on bikes and foot. The low speed limit didn't help either.

She found Dr. Winston P. Whitaker III pacing in his office. His Texas Tech University Ph.D., master's and bachelor's diplomas hung prominently on his wall.

About her height, he was half-again as round as he was tall, white-headed with an equally-white bushy mustache, nattily dressed in tweed, complete with weskit, bow tie and pocket watch on a long shiny gold chain. She guessed from the spring in his animated walk that he was younger than she was but dressed as though he was in his seventies. He looked almost comical, like a character straight out of a play.

As he ushered her in, his eyes were shooting sparks in accompaniment to the smoke coming out of his ears.

It took about ten minutes to get him calmed down, with Maggie assuring him her staff had the talent to do the job right. This was her forte, gathering facts and information to be regurgitated to the media in the appropriate way. Probing Dr. Whitaker's knowledge, feeling his excitement for the work he did, examining his dreams for the museum—under her careful questioning and delicate nudging, he gradually revealed his passion for wind power and technology and what he believed the future held.

He gave her a quick tour of the exhibits. She was surprised at how much slower he walked and talked once he had calmed down. She listened intently while taking notes and calculating where the best photos could be set up later that morning.

"Dr. Whitaker, tell me about the donation specifically. What will you do with the money?"

"Oh, my dear," he said almost breathlessly. "We have such plans. We will, of course, expand our facility as well as our outreach to the community, to Texas and even to the nation. We will become THE place to go for information on windmills and wind energy. After all, the high plains are where it all began, you know what I mean?"

"Yes, sir, I do. Now what's your first step?"

"Well, my dear, first we'll expand the exhibit hall. We'll blow out the back wall and the roof," he said pointing up animatedly, "and go out and up. We're going to have a room big enough to house the actual newfangled turbine blades, so their 'grandglorius' size can be seen, so the little children can come in and touch them and say 'wow' with their eyes popping."

Twinkles had finally replaced the sparks in his own popping eyes and Maggie couldn't help but get caught up in his excitement.

"Projections on construction timeline?" she asked.

"Oh, yes. This first phase should be complete just after the first of the year. I'm planning on throwing a big party!"

Another twenty minutes of questions gave Maggie a fairly complete picture of the five-year plan, and she had to admit she was impressed. At the end of the interview she said, "Thank you, Dr. Whitaker."

"Windy, please call me Windy. Everybody does."

"Seriously?" Maggie asked skeptically.

"Oh, yes, my dear. Since I was knee-high to a cotton patch. Mama couldn't keep me from climbing the windmill out back of the barn. I think I was three the first time I climbed to the top. Just sat there on that old wooden platform under the turning big wooden blades, blowin' in the wind, you know what I mean? She was sure I was going to fall and kill myself, but heights never bothered me. And, oh, that windmill just called to me. As did every other windmill in the county. I don't think there is even one left in West Texas I haven't climbed at some time or another, unless it was put up last week. That big one out front?" he said pointing out the window. "That's the one from my family farm—the Axtel Standard—the first one I climbed. Built around 1915."

Maggie looked out at the almost 70-foot wooden windmill with the 20-foot turning blades and thought it was no wonder his mother was scared.

"So, everyone calls me Windy. Seems rather apropos now that I have all this, you know what I mean?"

"Um, yes, it rather does. Um, thank you, Windy."

With notes in hand and a promise to send him a copy of the marketing package, she left Dr. Whitaker—Windy—an almost satisfied man. "It will be fine," she assured him once more as he escorted her to the front door.

"Well, my dear, the proof is in the 'pudmometer,' you know what I mean?"

Maggie smiled at him and left, saying to herself, "I think I know, but what an odd expression." She dismissed it, making a mental list of which impossible tasks had to be done next.

Two minutes before the end of the day, Elaine pressed the fax button to send the final media release while Ricky simultaneously pressed send on the electronic version of the same.

A collective sigh went up from the staff as they sank into the nearest chairs.

"Whoa," Susan said as she propped her long legs up on Charlie's lap and let her arms fall. "I'm totally whipped."

"Drink," moaned Steven. "I need a drink."

Elaine handed him a cold bottled water saying, "Sorry, whiskey's not allowed on campus."

He looked at the bottle and her in mocking disgust, but took a long gulp anyway.

"Great job, folks," beamed an exhausted Maggie, leaning against her office doorframe. "It's a great package. Good stories to pull from, great photos linked on the web, a variety of ways the various media can approach the story, and just an overall quality marketing approach. Thanks so much for all your work."

"I haven't worked this hard and this fast for years," said Charlie. He pushed Susan's legs down and stood to stretch dramatically. "I loved it!"

"Me either," said Ricky.

"You're too young to have *ever* worked this hard," Charlie teased, playfully punching him in the arm, which started a brief shadow-boxing match.

"So true," said Elaine, "but your fingers were flying on that keyboard, Ricky. Good job. Can we go home, now, Boss?"

"Of course. But remember, tomorrow we'll have to do all the work we were supposed to get done today plus all of tomorrow's normal load. And hopefully talk to lots of reporters and handle TV news crews at the museum. So, another busy day, troops."

Steven smiled and shrugged as he got up to leave, "Just makes the weekend come faster." He then stood straight and saluted them saying dramatically, "Good night, my comrades in arms. Today we won the battle, but tomorrow we carry on the war!"

Laughing, they headed out the door, congratulating each other, giddy with the satisfaction of a job well done. Maggie retreated into her office to get her briefcase, thinking today they had really become a team—a team of professionals who put out quality work. She too, smiled with satisfaction.

This was one evening she wouldn't stay late, hoping Doug was cooking something wonderful, and had lots of wine for her to consume while she related the day's efforts to her friends.

Chapter 16 ~

The something wonderful was chicken alfredo accompanied by a delicate white wine and fresh spinach salad with strawberries and feta cheese. Maggie devoured a healthy portion as she related the news of the donation.

"Russell Arbuckle is the donor. Some big philanthropist from around here. Wealthy beyond measure, is what I was told," Maggie said between delectable bites.

"Must be beyond measure if he can give $30 million for windmills," Doug said. "Arbuckle? Isn't he the owner of the Cotton A Ranch south of town?"

"He is," Maggie said. "Steven did a great story on his family. He and his wife—Dorthea, I think—have been here in West Texas for several generations. But it's a ranch and a farm. Money was made through cotton, cattle and not a little bit of oil. Think he has lots of property near Odessa, too. That's where most of the oil wealth comes from."

Sharon asked, "Isn't he on the Tech Board of Regents?"

"Yep. And a graduate of Tech's Ag program. I saw him briefly at the April Board meeting when Stone announced his resignation. Arbuckle is just an average-looking, unassuming guy. He's got a crew cut just like my dad used to wear. Asked some intelligent questions, too."

Sharon said, "Dr. Whitaker must be ecstatic."

"He is, or was, after he got over his mad. I swear, it's as if Boyle wants us to fail... or he's just too dense to know he needs to let us do our jobs."

"I vote for dense," Sharon said. "I hate conspiracy theories."

On Friday, several local and state newspaper and television reporters called to do stories. The team fielded numerous calls from print reporters across the state and one exploratory call from "Good Morning America."

Dr. Whitaker was interviewed for the local evening news. To Maggie's horror, as she stood to the side watching him being filmed at the museum, he used several words that weren't really words. Oh, the meaning came across, all right, but it made him appear as though he was making Archie Bunker mistakes. Thankfully, his piece was edited heavily. His rambling sentences didn't make for good sound bites, and the non-words weren't aired. Maggie would have to work with him or else keep him away from cameras.

At 7 a.m. on Sunday, Steven called a sleepy Maggie to relay the news that the story had been repeated on the front page of the *Lubbock Avalanche Journal* with a new angle, and picked up by major newspapers across the state. There was even a short blurb in the *New York Times*. After she hung up the phone, she nestled back under the covers contentedly and said aloud, "Yep, there's proof in the 'pudmometer.' "

On Monday, Jonathan discovered that the previous week Boyle had called the news desk of the *A-J* and told them about the donation. Seems he thought the *A-J* cub reporter would then pass the news on to other media outlets, so he didn't contact anyone else. He told Jonathan his plan had worked, ignorant of the fact Communications and Marketing had rescued the situation. Maggie had asked Jonathan and Dr. Whitaker not to mention their last-minute operation, at least not on Thursday so Boyle couldn't object before it was done. Evidently they did as she asked because Boyle seemed to take credit for the wide coverage.

And that was fine with Maggie. Dr. Whitaker was happy. The donor was happy. And Bennett Boyle was as happy as Bennett Boyle could be. All was right with the world.

At least for a little while.

Chapter 17 ~

When Maggie arrived at work on Monday the following week, she could hear the commotion from two doors down the hall. She stopped just short of the doorway and peeked in. Elaine was pacing, picking things up and then putting them down heavily, muttering rather loudly to herself.

"Stupid, egotistical man... typical male chauvinist... tell him a thing or two... good swift kick in the ass... all the way back to Aggieland... stupid! Stupid! STUPID!" Elaine screamed. She then took off her right shoe and threw it against the far wall, barely missing Maggie's plant.

Maggie stepped in quickly, saying, "Elaine! What in the world?"

Elaine whirled around as if to strike her, but seeing it was Maggie, thankfully held herself in check. She comically limped back to her desk and sat down with a thud. Her head went down on her desk, and she began theatrically beating her fist against a stack of papers.

"Elaine! What is wrong?!"

Elaine raised her head and looked hard at Maggie, saying with clenched teeth and balled fists, "Your boss just got rid of Katherine. Just got rid of her! After 23 years in the Chief of Staff's office, he just got rid of her!" She was standing again now, lopsided on one shoe, face flushed.

"Miss Katherine?" Maggie said, incredulous. "Boyle fired Miss Katherine? Whatever for?"

"For a better looking piece of ass, that's what for!"

"Okay, Elaine, take it down a notch or two and give me more information. You're a communications major, remember? And I'm not getting all the facts... so sit and talk. Now!"

Elaine sat, crossed her arms and took several deep breaths as Maggie retrieved the errant shoe. Finally she said, "I just heard from Nancy in the President's office. Boyle got rid of Miss Katherine."

"Fired her?" Maggie asked, surprised.

"No, moved her to the open receptionist position in the President's office. How humiliating for her!"

56

"And why did Boyle do this? Do you know?"

"Because he can!" she said, her voice rising again. "He thinks because Stone left last week and he's interim president he can do as he pleases. He moved that Allison slut from HR..."

"Slut? That's sort of harsh, isn't it, Elaine?" said Maggie. "Do you know for certain she sleeps around?"

"Everybody says she does... but no, I don't know for certain. Okay," she said, a bit sheepishly, lowering her voice. "I won't say that, but she wears these really tight, short skirts—"

"Ah, Elaine, my friend, *you* wear really tight, short skirts."

Elaine was indignant, "Yeah, but I wasn't hired because of that!"

Maggie looked at her skeptically, so Elaine explained, "Mr. Leonard was a friend of Uncle William, so he hired me sight unseen. But it didn't take him long to find out how good I am." Then she laughed, "And I look damn good in tight, short skirts!"

"Yes, you do!" Charlie said as he stuck his head in the door. "Say, did you guys hear about Miss Katherine? Asshole Boyle replaced her with that slut from HR."

As the facts came in, it turned out to be true Bennett Boyle had moved Miss Katherine. And done it in an extremely abrupt and tactless manner.

Seems she'd found a note on her desk early that morning telling her to take her personal items to the empty receptionist desk in the office next door because he no longer needed her services as his secretary. She'd been so distraught she'd immediately taken a sick day, carrying home her family pictures, framed business school diploma, 15-year-old African violet, one Kleenex box and a half-eaten package of chocolate covered raisins that didn't last the morning.

By 8:30 a.m., Allison the slut from HR had happily moved her personal items into Boyle's outer office. They included a mirror, a jumbo pack of Juicy Fruit, six bottles of nail polish, a framed photo of herself—obviously taken at a cheap shopping mall glamour studio—and an eight-inch-tall stuffed purple elephant named Baby, now proudly displayed on the front of the desk where Miss Katherine's African violet had sat since infancy.

The entire building was in an uproar. Miss Katherine was much loved and justifiably respected throughout the campus. More than one person whispered their threat to quit on the spot if by some horrid mistake the Board of Regents made Bennett Boyle the new president. Everyone knew he'd submitted his application, and insiders said his ego wouldn't allow him to doubt that the office would be his soon. Maggie was nauseated at the thought.

She was also nauseated when she remembered she'd scheduled an appointment with Boyle for later in the day, needing to go over next year's budget one more time before turning it in to Finance. Boyle had so far refused to discuss even a modest increase. Armed with facts and numbers, she headed downstairs at the appointed hour.

Interesting, she thought, that Boyle was still in the old Communications offices rather than moving into the now-empty presidential suite next door. Maybe he thought it might be a tad too presumptuous—or maybe too humiliating to move out if he didn't get the job. Or maybe he just didn't want Communications moving back in down there? In the meantime, he was obviously taking full advantage of his newfound power to make some less-than intelligent changes, at least according to gossip.

Well, she thought as she entered his outer office, time to meet the infamous Allison.

Jonathan Long was standing at Katherine's old desk, arms out in exasperation, talking to the person seated behind the desk, and blocking Maggie's view. "You don't understand. I'm Mr. Boyle's second-in-command, and I'm allowed to see him whenever I need to see him... and I need to see him now."

A sugar-sweet, high-pitched voice replied in an almost comically slow Texas drawl, "Well, Mr. Long. It's you who don't seem to understand. Since this mornin', ah am in charge of Mr. Boyle's appointments, and you don't happen to have an appointment according to this here little appointment book, so you cain't see him right now."

Maggie stepped up next to Jonathan, put on a big smile and said sweetly, "Well, I have an appointment, and I can give up my time slot to Mr. Long if he needs it."

"Thank you, Maggie," Jonathan said in his usual quick manner. "I really just need five minutes."

Allison narrowed her eyes at Maggie and frowned. "And just who the hell are you, darlin'?"

Maggie raised her eyebrows at the new secretary, quickly assessing her mannerisms, speech, attire and attitude, and didn't like any of the above. The thirty-something woman had massive bleached blonde hair curling out of control, even under a wide headband of neon green. Her matching tightly stretched top was cut so low over her obviously implanted breasts Maggie thought she could have easily hidden her cell phone inside the visible cleavage.

"Margaret Grant, director of Communications and Marketing, and I *do* have an appointment with Mr. Boyle. You can check in that there little appointment book," she said sweetly. "Go ahead, Jonathan, I'll just sit out here until you're finished."

Before Allison could think to protest, Jonathan knocked once on Boyle's door and entered, closing the door behind him.

Allison still had her mouth open in surprise when Maggie turned her back and sat down in one of four leather chairs lining the wall. Maggie opened the folder she'd brought, and without looking up and with a considerable amount of sugar dripping from her mouth, said, "You might want to close your mouth, Allison. Your gum's about to fall out."

Mouth now snapped shut, Allison stood up revealing her way-too-tight, way-too short, brown pleather skirt and neon green stilettos. She sashayed past Maggie and drawled, "Ah'm goin' to the ladies' room."

Four minutes later, Jonathan came out and looked at the empty secretary's desk. Allison hadn't returned. He whispered to Maggie as he hurried to the hallway, "Whatever is he thinking!?"

Maggie smiled again, straightened her suit and marched into the inner sanctum—after all, she did have an appointment.

She stood in front of Boyle's desk and waited. And waited. He loves to play this game, doesn't he, she thought. Making people stand as if at attention until he acknowledges them. She didn't want to play today, and said curtly, "What happened to Miss Katherine?"

Without looking up, he said, "She moved next door. What do you want?"

"Why was she moved?"

At that, he looked up sharply. "I don't report to you—you report to me. It's none of your damn business why she was moved. What do you want?"

"We have an appointment to go over my department's finances. I brought some facts and figures I'd like to discuss—"

He interrupted, "Put them on the secretary's desk."

"But I need to discuss them with you."

"But *I* don't need to discuss them with *you*," he said with a caustic snarl, "so put them on the desk outside and leave. Dismissed." He returned to his work, looking down.

Maggie clenched her fist, and before she could stop herself, clicked her heels together, stood at attention, saluted, and marched out.

Bennett Boyle pretended not to notice.

Chapter 18 ~

"What is *wrong* with that jackass?" Sharon said the next day at lunch. She was trying to once again reconstruct her *Texas Tech Special* sandwich that fell apart each time she attempted a bite.

"No clue. I'm so frustrated with the man. How does he expect me to do my job if he won't give me the tools I need? I know the university has enough to increase my budget, but he won't even talk about it. And every time I do talk to him, I get all tied up in knots because he's so unreasonable! No matter which way I turn, he puts roadblocks in my way. He micromanages with fear and intimidation. How in the world did he get to be Tech's chief of staff?"

"Extremely good question, and if you find out the answer, I'll make you the queen." More black olives fell out from between the rye bread.

"And how can the Board put up with his moving Miss Katherine? I just don't understand that level of incompetence," Maggie said, taking a bite of her tuna salad on croissant. "Yum, this is good."

They'd left campus to try out a new sandwich shop downtown next to Maggie's favorite thrift store, both establishments run by the Disabled American Veterans. If they ate really fast, they'd have time to look over the new donations for sale. She'd found a couple of pieces of furniture on previous visits to the shop she thought were real bargains, including a 1940s lime green vinyl chair with yellow painted wooden legs. Sharon had looked at it with a jaundiced eye, but Maggie loved it at first sight and happily forked over the reasonable asking price. It was currently in her storage shed, awaiting successful house hunting.

"Well," Sharon said, struggling again to keep the onions, avocado, turkey and bean sprouts from falling out, "I don't know what to tell you to do... Damn sandwich. It tastes great, but won't hold together long enough to get in my mouth, even as big as my mouth is!"

Maggie laughed. "Why don't you just use a fork?"

"Guess I'll have to," she said in exasperation, putting it down and picking up her utensil. "Doug always says 'when it doesn't work the way it's supposed to work, work it another way.'" She stabbed up a piece of the sandwich with the fork and triumphantly stuffed it in her mouth, chewing happily. She raised her fork in the air in a victory salute.

"That's it!" Maggie said excitedly. "If it doesn't work the way it's supposed to work, work it another way. Now, we know it doesn't work, so... so how can I work it another way?"

Sharon swallowed and said, "Work what?"

"Work."

"What?!?!?

As Maggie drove them back to campus, Sharon said, "Now explain this again? You're going to change the way you work?"

"Yep. Obviously, the way I work with Bennett Boyle is not producing the results I need to get my job done successfully. So, I'll change the way I work with him and hopefully get better results."

"Change how?"

"Well, for one thing, instead of fighting it and wishing it weren't true,

I'll accept the fact he's a micromanaging tyrant. He seems to get worse when I lose my temper, so I won't lose my temper. He hasn't a clue on how to communicate effectively, so I'll teach him, and make him think it's his ideas we use. And he likes to play those little power games, like having people wait for him, so I'll just refuse to play them but within parameters he can't object to without losing face. And then, well, then I'll outflank the bastard."

Chapter 19 ~

First thing the next day, Maggie got a chance to activate her new plan, although it wasn't exactly the way she'd envisioned. First to arrive at the office again, as she came in from the hallway something immediately bothered her, but she couldn't put her finger on it. Dismissing it, she continued to her desk and began processing e-mails.

A few minutes later when Elaine arrived, Maggie called out a good morning greeting. Elaine didn't answer, but a moment later stuck her head in Maggie's office. "Why'd you take it home? And how?" she asked.

"Why'd I take what home?"

"Phil."

"Phil?"

"Your plant. The plant your boys sent you. I named it Phil. Why'd you take it home? I was taking good care of him," she said with obvious hurt.

"My plant? I didn't take it home." Her eyes went wide. "It's gone?!" she asked, rushing out to Elaine's office. "It's gone." They both stared at the huge empty space where Phil once proudly stood. "I thought I noticed something different when I came through earlier."

"If you didn't take him home, where is he?"

"I've no idea, but as big as it is, it couldn't be far, could it? Okay, Elaine, go see what you can find out. Surely someone saw it... saw Phil leave. Report back and we'll figure out what to do."

Elaine headed out the door.

Twenty minutes later she was back, and fuming. In a restrained voice, she said, "I found him."

"Great!" Maggie said. "Where? What happened?"

"In Boyle's office."

"What? Bennett Boyle stole my plant?" Maggie asked, incredulous.

"No, Allison stole your plant. When I went looking for him... for it, no one knew anything until I got down to the first floor. Then Ted in Finance said he'd stayed late last night and saw two maintenance guys hauling a huge plant toward the president's office. So I headed in that direction, but I glanced in Boyle's office as I walked past, and there he was... big as life... Phil, sitting in the outer office. He looks so sad..." She shook her head.

"I calmly went in, because I thought that's how you'd want me to handle it... but the little twerp was all over me, telling me Phil was hers now... something about outranking me... that anything the Interim President wanted he could take... and she was standing right in my face, chomping her gum at me like a heifer... then... then..." Elaine's face was flushed, and her eyes started to water as she looked away.

"Elaine, what happened? Tell me. You need to tell me."

Maggie couldn't imagine what that crass woman could say to unnerve Elaine.

"She called me a nigger."

"What!?"

"I tell you, Maggie, I almost flattened the bitch." Elaine was now past tears and into rage.

Maggie was stunned. She knew there were people who were still ignorant enough to be racist but not stupid enough to show it at a public university. That was not only stupid, it was against the law. She quietly said to Elaine, "But you didn't? Flatten her, I mean. Right?"

"No. I decided I'd come get you so you could flatten her." Elaine smiled weakly, tears and anger forestalled.

Maggie thought she'd figure out a way to do more than that. But first she had to get all the facts. "Tell me everything you said and she said, word for word."

Elaine complied.

Then Maggie asked, "How'd she even know about the plant? Has she been up here?"

"Yesterday when you were at lunch. She brought up the graduation report I gave you from Boyle. Sort of threw it at me, but I let it go. Must have seen Phil then," Elaine said shaking her head again at the empty corner.

"Yeah, it's... he's kinda hard to miss. Okay, give me a few minutes to think about this because I can't just march down there and take him back. But I can guarantee Phil will be back where he belongs soon. And Allison will get her due." As she retreated to her office, she echoed Jonathan's words, "Unbelievable! Whatever was Boyle thinking?"

Two hours later, armed with determination and a sure-fire offensive plan, Maggie strode into Bennett Boyle's outer office—and found it empty, except of course for Phil. She put down the small box she was carrying and walked over to the plant. Leaning toward it, she whispered, "Don't worry, darlin'. I'm here on a rescue mission." She reached up and patted Phil's top leaves.

Voices floated out of Boyle's office. She turned, and noticed his door was slightly ajar. She sat down to wait for Allison's return. At least Boyle was here and she needed him, too, if her plan was going to work.

The voices grew louder, but she could only catch snatches of the conversation of Boyle and another man. "...not smart..." "...as I please..." "...too much attention..." "...taking her..." "...don't care..." "...Katherine..." "...mark my word..."

She was startled when Allison suddenly appeared in front of her, drawling, "You'd better not be here about that there plant."

Maggie reached into her pocket and then said calmly, "Well, I am here about the plant. Elaine—"

"I've already told that nigger girl of yours—"

"Elaine," Maggie said forcefully, immediately standing up. She was bristling.

But Allison continued, undeterred. "I told her to take her black ass outta my office. I outrank her and she has no business telling me what to do, so you keep her outta here, ya' hear? I don't like working with niggers. You understand?"

Maggie had her hands in her pockets, her own rage balling them into fists. It was all she could do to keep her anger in check. Maybe I *should* flatten her, she thought. Taking a deep breath, she folded her arms in front of her chest, looking squarely into Allison's eyes and said with a quiet force, "Her name is Elaine Easton. She's my assistant. Watch your mouth and show some respect for where you are and who you work with, or you'll be out on *your* ass faster than you can find someone to kiss it. Am I understood?"

Allison took a step back, her mouth gaped, gum threatening to fall again. For a moment, she looked a little frightened but quickly regained her bravado. As she was about to protest, they were interrupted.

"Mrs. Grant, my dear!" Maggie wheeled around to find Winston Whitaker stepping out of Boyle's office, followed by the ogre himself.

"How delightful to run into you! I was going to call you. We need to do lunch, you know what I mean? And I promised to give you a more thorough tour of my museum! How about Thursday? Can we do it on Thursday? We'll dine first, and then spend the afternoon windmilling!"

Maggie recovered quickly but noted Boyle seemed astonished she and Dr. Whitaker knew each other. "Thursday would be great, Dr. Whitaker. Just name the time and place and I'll be there," she said pleasantly.

"Wonderful, wonderful," he said, delighted. "I've just been telling our Interim President Boyle here how the museum project is coming along nicely, and he has kindly given me permission to steal Miss Katherine away from the president's office. She's going to be my new assistant. Isn't that grandelicious?"

So that's what they were arguing about. Good for Miss Katherine.

"That's great news," Maggie said. I know she'll be an asset to the museum."

Winston smiled and then looked smugly at Boyle, who gave him an unreadable look. Then Boyle turned to Maggie and said flatly, "Did you need something?"

Allison interrupted quickly, "She's tryin' to take mah plant."

The men looked at her, then at Maggie, who smiled sweetly. "I'm sorry, Mr. Boyle. There's been a little mistake."

"Mistake?" he said, genuinely puzzled.

"Yes, sir. While it's true that as Interim President you have the authority to use anything in the building you need, according to the university's guidelines, Chapter Three, Section Six, page 56, personal property of employees is excluded from that right. And that beautiful plant over there," she said, pointing to Phil, "is my personal property."

"Did you buy it?" Allison asked sarcastically, hand on hip.

Maggie continued, calmly and professionally. She picked up her folder. "No, I didn't buy it. It was a gift from my sons. I have a copy of the florist's delivery receipt right here, along with the name and phone number of the deliveryman who will testify that this particular plant is the one he delivered on that date. I also have a copy of a work order from Maintenance to attest to their removal of it from my office last night after hours and placement here at the direction of your office. And I have a copy of the university guidelines, if you would like to see them, Mr. Boyle?"

Boyle was dumbfounded, obviously unaware his new secretary had taken anything from anywhere, and simply replied, "No."

Winston was highly amused and had stepped back, watching the scene with fascination.

Maggie continued, "Thank you. Now I've arranged for some men to return it to my office, again if that's alright with you, Mr. Boyle?" Looking at her watch, she said, "They should be here any minute now."

"No," whined Allison. "This office needs some sprucin' up and it looks better here."

Boyle looked at Allison, then at Maggie, then the plant. When he turned back to his new secretary he said forcefully, "No." To Maggie, he said flatly, "You may take your plant. I'm... it won't happen again."

Allison whimpered, "But..." and stopped with a pout when Boyle gave her a stern look.

"Thank you, Mr. Boyle. If you don't mind, I'll just wait here until the men arrive to take it back upstairs... just to ensure it's safe return. Wouldn't want it to get suddenly broken or anything. Oh, and I brought this," Maggie said, picking up the small box, "to take it's place." She triumphantly pulled off the cover to reveal another philodendron bipinnatifidum, a miniature version of Phil. She handed it to Allison who glowered at her.

Chapter 20 ~

A few minutes early for her Thursday lunch date with Dr. Whitaker, Maggie waited in the foyer of Café J, the quaint-yet-sophisticated restaurant just south of campus on 19th Street near University Avenue. She'd been delighted to discover its interesting and elegant cuisine in a city more well-known for barbeque and chicken-fried steak. Café J's website declared, "Blending French techniques with Southwestern influences, an extensive wine selection, and original paintings—haute cuisine meets impeccable hospitality and service."

Maggie had eaten here at least half a dozen times since her arrival in March and agreed whole-heartedly with the description. The original artwork was an interesting and ever-changing part of the ambience.

That was another surprise for Maggie. The art scene in Lubbock seemed to be vibrant. Learning of monthly art walks and several active galleries, she was pleased to find a much more broad-based variety of art than the expected genre of western landscapes and Cowboy campfire scenes.

She was certain it was due almost entirely to the art professors at Tech. Their department had grown significantly since she was a student, with a few of her old professors still teaching classes today. Shortly after her arrival in March, she was looking for Tech T-shirts for her granddaughters in the campus bookstore and had been pleased to recognize Terry Morrow, her printmaking professor from more than 30 years ago, and one of her favorite teachers. Confessing he didn't remember all his students from years gone by—at least not by their faces or names—he thought perhaps if she could show him some of her college artwork? That, he was certain, he would remember. She only had one piece he might recognize, a woodblock print from his class, but it was currently buried somewhere in her storage unit. Maybe another time she might show it to him.

Funny, he hadn't looked too much older than she did that day. Must have been just out of school himself when she was a student, but her memory of him was of a much older professor. Appearances could be deceiving, couldn't they?

Maggie and Winston settled into their corner table at Café J and scanned the mouth-watering menu. Winston opted for salmon salad with champagne vinaigrette, served on a bed of mixed greens with cherry tomato, red onion, cashews, asiago cheese and poached pears. As usual, Maggie ordered the seafood crepes, salmon and shrimp, topped with Swiss cheese and a white wine lemon dill sauce, served with vegetable medley. But being considerate of her waistline, she opted for one crepe instead of her normal two or three.

The two exchanged pleasantries until the food arrived. After his first bite, which he enjoyed with a wide grin and closed eyes, Whitaker looked at her admiringly. "My dear Mrs. Grant, I can't tell you how much I appreciated your work with our donation publicity. Our patron was pleased as punchade. We shall need to work together more often."

"I'd like that," Maggie said sincerely.

"And I do apologize for exploding at you over the phone earlier that morning," Whitaker said. "I was just so upset about the lack of coverage. I can't believe Bennett didn't tell you, or ask for your assistance."

"You haven't told Mr. Boyle about what we did, have you?"

"Oh, no, my dear. Haven't breathed a word. Better to let him have the illusion of glory. No sense rocking the boat, you know what I mean?"

"Yes, I do. Have you known him long, Dr. Whitaker?"

"Windy. You must call me Windy, please. And yes, I've known Bennett Boyle a long time. I must say, I was quite amused the other day... the plant drama, you know what I mean? Brilliant way to handle the situation, Mrs. Grant, just brilliant. Perfect way to work with Bennett."

"Thank you, Windy, but now you've got to call me Maggie, please. And I wonder if you could tell me a little more about him, if you wouldn't mind. I'm, well... if I knew more about him, maybe I could..."

"Giving you a hard time, is he? Interfering in your work?"

Maggie smiled but kept silent.

Winston patted her hand, saying, "That's just his style. Never been an especially happy person. In fact, now that I think about it, I don't remember seeing him smile in years! What a shame. Life should be lived to its fullest, don't you think?"

At that Maggie nodded, but wanted more. "Is he married? Children?"

"B.J.? Oh, heavens no!" laughed Winston.

"He's not... ?" Maggie left the question unsaid.

"Gay? Oh, definitely not. He doesn't join me in that particular persuasion."

"I didn't mean to..." Maggie said quickly.

"No, no. No offense taken. I'm quite comfortable with my choices and preferences in that area, you know what I mean? And these days it's perfectly acceptable to come out. Even in West Texas. But Bennett is definitely straight. Just look at his new secretary. He certainly didn't hire her for her brains. What's her name again?"

"Allison," Maggie replied, unable to disguise the disgust in her voice.

"Yes, yes. Allison. Oh, don't worry, my dear. I'm sure our little Miss

So Native Americans, and then Spaniards, would drive tall stakes into the ground as guides across the terrain. They 'staked out' a trail.

"Others say yucca flower stalks served as stakes to tether horses on the open plains. But the most recent theory, which I think is extremely interesting, was proposed by a Spanish-speaking Tech student. Llano Estacado could be a bastardization of *llano estancado*, meaning 'plain of many ponds.'"

"Referring to the playas?" Sharon asked.

"Definitely. There are thousands of the shallow depressions here on the South Plains. They fill up with water during rains and then don't drain well because of the hard caliche soil they're made from, so they support the wildlife around here. Without the playas, we wouldn't see the migration of those Canada geese you like, or several other species. Anyway, I think it's quite possible estancado is the right theory."

"Hard to know which one is correct without all the facts," Maggie said, a twinkle forming in her eye. "Maybe we could pile them all together? Let's see, 'Francisco Vásques de Coronado came upon the Caprock that looked like a stockade, scaled the palisades to conquer the land, finding full playas and stakes made of yucca plants dotting the landscape, so he watered and then tethered his horses.'"

Sharon groaned, "That was as pathetic as Doug's joke. Good thing you don't write history for a living, Maggie."

Not long afterward, Maggie was sitting in her office doing just that, only she was writing recent history about the graduation ceremonies she'd attended that morning. Her first at Texas Tech since her own long ago, Maggie had been impressed with the pomp and circumstance and the excitement of the graduates and their parents, but was disappointed that Interim President Bennett Boyle represented the university that day. Although donned in regalia as all the other assembled faculty and administrators, he was the only one without a mortar board, tam or cap on his head. Maggie thought he probably didn't want to muss his helmet hair.

Not only did he look out of place without a hat of some type, but he also gave a lackluster speech and showed no enthusiasm for the proceedings, as if he couldn't wait to get out of the arena. Not a good way to impress the Regents, Maggie thought, although that might be a good thing for all concerned.

Luckily, a keynote speaker had been engaged months ago by the former president. Rousing the crowd to laughter and tears, she did an outstanding job and received a standing ovation. The contrast between the two, as Winston might say, was "mindbludgeoning."

The day after graduation, Maggie came back from a quick lunch to find

Elaine fuming once again. Seems she had passed Allison in the hallway. Boyle's new assistant made another racial remark, under her breath, but loud enough for Elaine to hear. Although again tempted to deck the stupid woman, Elaine instead reported it to Maggie as she had been instructed. Maggie calmed her down, then gave her a gift.

A few days later, another gift arrived. Elaine brought in a package delivered through campus mail. Maggie was delighted to find an expensively framed surprise from Winston. She showed it to Elaine, then together they looked for a place to hang it. Elaine read it out loud:

JABBERWOCKY by Lewis Carroll
(From *Through the Looking-Glass and What Alice Found There*, 1872)

'Twas brilling and the slithy toves,
Did gyre and gimble in the wabe;
All mimsy were the borogoves.
And the mome raths outgrabe.

Beware the Jabberwork, my son!
The jaws that bite, the claws that catch!
Beware the Jubjub bird, and shun.
The frumious Bandersnatch!

He took his vorpal sword in hand:
Long time the manxome foe he sought—
So rested he by the Tumtum tree,
Ad stood awhile in thought.

And as in uffish thought he stood,
The Jabberwork, with eyes of flame.
Came whiffling through the tulgey wood.
And burbled as it came!

One, two! One, two! and through and through,
The vorpal blade went snicker-snack!
He left it dead, and with its head,
He went galumphing back.

And hast thou slain the Jabberwock?
Come to my arms, my beamish boy!
O frafjous day! Callooh! Callay!
He chortled in his joy.

'Twas brilling, and the slithy toves
Did gyre and gimble in the wabe;
All mimsy were the borogoves,
And the mome raths outgrabe.

That same day, yet another present arrived, this one enjoyed by the entire building, with the exception of Bennett Boyle. Allison turned in her resignation, effective immediately saying her brother desperately needed her to help out at his construction business. She packed up her nail polish, juicy fruit, glamour photo, elephant and left. She didn't take the plant.

Only Maggie, Elaine and the university's general counsel knew what had really happened. After the hallway insult, Maggie had presented Elaine with the tape from the small recorder she'd had in her pocket the morning she'd rescued Phil. It contained Allison's racial slurs, loud and clear. Elaine took the tape to University Counsel Bobby Jones and filed a formal complaint against Allison for racial discrimination and harassment.

Bobby Jones had then called Allison into his office to discuss her options. She opted to resign.

The job opening was posted. Miss Katherine did not apply. Ten days later the little plant in Bennett Boyle's outer office died from lack of care.

Chapter 22 ~

Scheduled for the last Saturday in May, the craft session for Vacation Bible School instructors was planned with the precision of a military invasion. General Maggie had arrived at 7 a.m. to set up the workstations in the musty old church fellowship hall. Starting with the preschool teachers at 8 a.m., each of the five groups of volunteer instructors would come for an hour-and-a-half session, learning how to make the different craft projects for each day of the week, five in all. If all went well, and with a half-hour in between each of the sessions reserved for cleanup and the next set up, Maggie would be crafting nonstop until dinnertime.

As the first group was coming in and finding seats at the tables, two elderly women approached Maggie, one tentatively, the other one confidently, sort of pulling the other along. The confident lady was dressed simply in jeans and cotton checked blouse, had short gray hair, a weathered face and intelligent eyes. She looked to be in her mid- to late-70s, and smiled as she introduced herself.

"I'm Fern," she said offering a hand. Maggie took it and was surprised at the strength in the handshake. "And this is Jenny Bodecker, Mrs. Grant."

Uh-oh, Maggie thought, the popsicle-stick queen. She too, was mid-to-late 70s, but with rinsed hair in sort of a soft blue hue, shirtwaist dress, and bright pink lipstick. She was perhaps twice as thick as her pencil-thin friend. Maggie hoped her surprise hadn't shown on her face, and she turned to offer Mrs. Bodecker her hand. But Jenny Bodecker stood stoically, arms crossed over her ample bosom. She nodded slightly, but wouldn't look at anything but the wall behind Maggie.

Fern put an arm around her and said firmly, "Now, Jenny. We'll have none of that. You shake hands with Mrs. Grant here and give her a proper Christian welcome or I'll tell Father Fitzpatrick on you."

Jenny Bodecker's eyes widened. Scowling at her companion, she reluctantly took Maggie's still offered hand for a speedy shake. She quickly returned to her seat and crossed her arms again, still frowning.

"Sorry about that," Fern said in a soft West Texas accent. "She'll come 'round, I reckon. Just take some time. I'm glad you're here, though, and you can count on me to help in any way. Oh, look at the time. You'd better get a move on, Sweetie. I'll bet you've got a full schedule today!"

Maggie greeted her class warmly and decided the direct approach might be the best. Immediately after she introduced herself, she said cheerfully, "I've heard such wonderful things about the crafts of years past." Mrs. Bodecker unfolded her arms and sat up a little straighter, surprised but still frowning as all eyes turned toward her. "And I understand we owe it all to Mrs. Bodecker, who is here with us this morning." Maggie looked at her and smiled broadly. "Monsignor Fitzpatrick tells me she has been a tireless and unselfish volunteer, so much so that when another pre-school instructor was needed this year, she was willing to move into the role as soon as he asked. Thank you so much, Mrs. Bodecker. Shall we give her a round of applause to thank her for her work?"

And with the popsicle-stick-queen flattered and happy, Maggie dived into the teaching.

After the third group ended early, thrilled with the new project ideas and supplies, Maggie's stomach growled for the second time, reminding her she'd skipped lunch as well as breakfast. Other volunteers were working in the building preparing the classrooms for VBS on Monday, and rumor had it pizza might have been brought in. Sniffing the air, trying to detect telltale aromas, Maggie only caught the stale odor typical of older buildings. Since she had about 20 minutes until group number four arrived, she went in search of quick sustenance.

Asking the first person she saw in the hallway, a college-age Hispanic volunteer moving furniture, he replied, "Yes, ma'am. I think there's some left in the kitchen, down around the corner to the right. Father Murphy was looking for some, too." As he moved down the hall, he called back over his shoulder, "There wasn't much left, though."

Dodging three more volunteers with heavy burdens, Maggie made her way down the long classroom hallway and peeked around the corner. She spotted the kitchen door, and crossed quickly to avoid the constant movement of people on a mission. Just as she stepped inside, she was flattened against the doorframe. Startled, her attacker dropped the pizza slice in his hand and turned to grab her by the arms, holding her up as she gasped for air. He looked down regretfully at his victim, still tight against the door.

"So sorry, I wasn't looking! Are you alright?" he said in a familiar voice.

Maggie starred up into the most amazing green eyes and her knees buckled. He gently held her as she involuntarily slid down on the floor. He knelt down beside her with a worried face. "Really, are you hurt?" he said quickly. "I wasn't paying attention. I'm so sorry. Seriously, are you OK?"

Dark mid-length hair framed a handsome, athletic face. His tattered Notre Dame Football T-shirt was probably authentic—he was certainly big enough to have played, although it had to have been thirty years ago, at least. His strong large hands continued to grip her arms, and she had considerable trouble catching her breath and replying. She'd been right. Father Murphy was just as good-looking up close.

Once she finally assessed nothing was broken, she sputtered, "Yes, I'm alright... I think. Just let me get up." He helped her up. She continued to lean against the door and he continued to hold her. The top of her head came to the top of his chest, so she had to crane her neck to meet him eye-to-eye. She was mesmerized by the depths of those eyes. "I... I was looking for some pizza..." she said weakly.

"Uh, oh," he said as he looked around on the floor, quickly spotting and picking up the slice he'd dropped. "Afraid I took the last piece. Want a bite?" He held it close to her mouth.

"Uh, no thanks," she said, nose wrinkling as she put up her hand in protest. Unconsciously her other hand had gone up into her hair and was twisting it through her fingers. "I really have to get back anyway."

"Yeah, me too. Duty calls," he said as he took a bite for himself, "Really sorry to have run into you. You sure you're OK?"

"Fine, just fine."

He continued to eat, staring at her, leaning closer in with his arm over her head. Too close, Maggie thought, as she was caught up again in his emerald eyes. Her knees threatened to fold once more, but she forced herself to lock them in place to keep her balance. He took another bite, barely an inch from her mouth, seeming to enjoy the effect he had on her.

"Thank you, Father," she said quickly as she ducked under his arm and hurried out the door.

"Colin!" he called out after her.

"Father Colin," she whispered. Her stomach pains had vanished but another hunger had taken its place.

Chapter 23 ~

"I am telling you, Sharon, I am going to Hell," Maggie said decidedly to her friend after she took another long sip of wine. The craft day finished, Maggie had declared it a success in that she'd given away all the supplies and ideas and was confident the volunteers would do a decent job. She'd handed out her business cards, though, just in case the volunteer teachers needed some help during the week. She also planned on checking on them in person each day during her lunch hour just to be sure.

After feasting on Doug's leftover ratatouille while he attended a summer student recital that evening, Maggie and Sharon were comfortably seated on the back patio next to the shimmering swimming pool, half-empty glasses in hand. That was another amazing perk to living in Lubbock. Even in the summer, the evenings cooled off so pleasantly it was hard to believe you were in Texas. Most nights, even in late August, air conditioning was turned off and windows were opened to let in the fresh breezes.

"Don't be ridiculous," Sharon said. "Just because the priest is gorgeous and turns you on? That happens all the time. Don't you remember that handsome blond priest Carol used to talk about in college? What'd the girls call him? Father What's-his-name...?"

"Father What-a-waste," Maggie said with a grin.

"Yeah! Father What-a-waste! That was it. Seems a shame the Catholic church insists on celibacy. But quit worrying. So he turned you on? At least it's good to know you're still alive on that front."

Maggie gave her a hard look and then turned away, surprised at her flush of emotion.

Sharon put down her glass and moved over to hug her friend. "Oh, Maggie, I'm sorry. I didn't mean to... But it has been more than a year... oh, I'm so sorry."

"It's OK, really. I'm just tired from today, I guess, and more than a little surprised to have been, as you say, 'turned on' by a priest, of all men! But you're right. I guess it's nice to know I can still at least get bothered by the opposite sex. I'm just not sure I ever wanted to get bothered again."

"You're still young, Maggie—well, relatively speaking. And sex is healthy! How about finding someone from work to casually sleep with?"

"You're joking, right?"

"Yeah, for you, nothing is casual about sex, I guess." She got up to get more wine for them both.

Maggie said thoughtfully, "It's not that I wouldn't want it, but I don't believe sex outside marriage is right for me. My faith... well, you know. And since I don't ever plan on marrying again..."

"I know, and I understand that's the way you feel, but I just don't happen to agree, obviously. In fact, I'd like for you to show me where it says in the Bible sex is only for marriage."

Maggie looked at her with surprise. "I, well, I don't know offhand, but I'm sure it is. You know, wedding vows and all, 'Keeping thee only unto thyself' —no, wait, that's not right."

Sharon giggled. "No, that sounds like you should only pleasure your-self. Say, why don't you ask Father Murphy?" Sharon teased, and then deftly dodged the cracker Maggie threw her way. "Then how about Bennett Boyle for sex? I hear he's available since Allison left."

Maggie shivered as she grimaced and laughed simultaneously. "Celibacy for eternity has to be better than Boyle!"

"At least you're laughing again. Let's go in and watch an old movie, say, *Thornbirds*?"

Maggie threw a second cracker, scoring a direct hit on Sharon's nose. Then she put her arm lovingly around her diminutive friend's neck as they walked inside.

"No! But I'll take *Going My Way* and a lot more wine."

Chapter 24 ~

On Monday, Maggie didn't see or run into Father Murphy when visiting St. Elizabeth's at noon. She did see Jenny Bodecker, however, who gushed about the successful craft project completed that morning. Fern reported teachers had placed each child in front of the poster Maggie had made and taken a photo of them as per Maggie's instructions. The poster said, "Jesus Loves Me! This I Know!" positioned so the child's head was surrounded by the letters. All the digital photos would be printed by the end of the week, and the Friday craft project was to decorate a foam frame for their pictures to take home to mom and dad.

Several of the teachers complimented Maggie on how well their own sessions had gone that day and thanked her again for the project ideas and supplies. She caught Monsignor Fitzpatrick's eye as she left, and he nodded appreciatively to her and winked as he talked with a parishioner.

"Wonder how long it will be before his next call for help?" she said to herself as she left. But it was fine. She'd enjoyed the experience and had met several volunteers she was sure would become friends, especially Fern. A successful adventure all around.

Maggie was still high on happiness when she returned to her office. Sharon had been right, the stairs had done her good, and she could make it all the way up without panting. Her next goal was to take the stairs two at a time... but all in good time, she thought.

Elaine was still at lunch, but had left a note on Maggie's door. *Call Bennett Boyle ASAP!!!!*

"Great," she groaned. "A good day ruined."

Five minutes later she was standing in Boyle's office, listening with astonishment. He actually wanted her to contact the media about a just-released short list of possible new presidents. "Give them some background on all of us."

Damn, Maggie thought glancing at the list... his name was on it.

"I don't have the resumes, but you can dig them up. Get it out this afternoon. The Board wants it out today and I don't have time."

"We'll be happy to," Maggie said as she took the list he offered.

"That will be all," Boyle said sharply when she made no move to leave.

"Do you want to see the release before we send it out?"

"What do *you* think? Go. Wait... put them in alphabetical order. Now go."

She went, amazed he'd actually given her an assignment. Was her new way to work paying off? Well, we'll just show him how good we are, she thought. And they did. Boyle approved the first draft of the release, especially since the alpha order put his name first. Again he dismissed her quickly. Wow, a good day had gotten even better—except for Boyle's inclusion in the list of possible new presidents.

On Tuesday, Maggie once again headed to St. Elizabeth's to check on her students, but this time she did run into Father Murphy... literally. As she stepped inside the door to the fellowship hall, he was stepping out, looking at some papers in his hand instead of where he was going, and he ran right into her, once again knocking her back against the wall, his papers flying everywhere.

"Ouch," she said, rubbing her banged elbow as he reached for her and then let go abruptly.

"I am so sorry!" Father Murphy said with another pained expression, as he picked up his papers.

"This is getting to be a habit, Father," Maggie said as she straightened

78

her suit.

"What? Oh, yes. You're the craft lady, aren't you? Your second crushing! We need to be a little more careful," he said with a smile as he stepped back, straightening his long black cassock before continuing to pick up his papers.

She looked into his green eyes and smiled and was surprised that she didn't feel the same deep tugging. Must be the cassock, she thought as she stood up straight. Catholic guilt was still alive and well, even at her age.

"Yes, we do need to be more careful. We haven't been formally introduced, though. I'm Margaret Grant," she said, extending her hand. "Moved here from Dallas a few months ago."

"Yes, I know. Father Fitz knows you. You work on the university campus, in Communications, I believe? You've done a great job with the kids' crafts. Thanks so much."

"My pleasure, Father. Now, if you'll excuse me, I need to go check on today's projects."

"Not at all. Nice running into you!" he said pointedly and headed out the door.

Maggie sighed as she continued down the hall. At least she wouldn't have to worry anymore about facing the fires of hell over him, clumsy man.

Chapter 25 ~

By Thursday, Maggie didn't really have to check on the projects, but she enjoyed talking with her new friends as they told amusing stories about their morning classes. She hadn't seen either of the priests, but Jenny Bodecker had become a loyal fan and Fern was a constant pleasure.

Elaine had asked for the afternoon off, so Maggie hurried to get back to cover the phones in their small offices. The niece of the first African-American professor at Tech, Elaine was a Red Raider through and through, much like Sharon, although Elaine was the only one of seven siblings and cousins who hadn't finished her degree at Tech.

"I fell in love with Reginald, and we couldn't wait to get married and have kids," she'd explained as she rolled her eyes heavenward. "Now they're all grown and gone and I'm finishing up where I left off. Should graduate in another year."

Taking night classes and an occasional Saturday class, Elaine was, not surprisingly, majoring in Communications. Maggie thought she already knew enough to be considered a professional communicator, but all universities insisted on a degree for the official "professional" status and accompanying larger paycheck. Maggie hoped she could keep her once she was official—she was a valuable member of the team. She'd have to check with Finance into how much of a salary increase she could offer once her degree was completed.

Elaine's request for the afternoon off was a family matter rather than a school one, though. Her aunt Frances, widow of the professor, was "getting on in years," and at her own insistence, the family was moving her to a nearby assisted-living facility. Elaine had mentioned Maggie might want to look at her aunt's house. It was going on the market. The family hadn't chosen an agent, but Maggie could come to look it over after work. It was an older home on a large corner lot near Tech Terrace Park, just the area Maggie hoped to settle into.

Right after work, Maggie pulled her Volvo in front of the address Elaine had provided—the northwest corner of Gary St. and 22nd. Elaine came out of the bright red front door and motioned her to come inside.

Maggie's heart gave a slight leap as she gazed at the 1930s-style one-story dark stone house. Two identical archways dominated the front of the structure, the first tall-peaked arch presiding over a fair-sized covered porch and the main entrance. It was supported by wide stone columns and surrounded by a thick stone wall about three feet high. To the right, the other archway crowned a portico serving as a wide carport, but could make a great screened-in porch. A large south-facing picture window on the left was flanked by a huge red oak tree, towering over the yard with welcoming shade.

On the east side, also in the irregularly shaped stones, Maggie could see the detached garage which had been converted into an apartment. Elaine had told her she and Reginald had lived there when they were first married. It had probably housed either relatives and/or Tech students for several decades. Maggie quickly scanned the surrounding neighborhood. Not a McMansion in sight!

As she stepped inside, Elaine greeted her in a small foyer. It opened into a large front room flooded with light from the picture window and two smaller windows on the west side. A front stone fireplace graced the corner, original to the home. Hardwood floors throughout, the house was crowded with vintage furniture, obviously lovingly cared for by Aunt Frances. The attached dining room was behind the main room and led to the kitchen and adjoining laundry off to the left, both of which could use an update, although Maggie rather liked the ancient red, yellow and green-splashed linoleum floor. Two fair-sized bedrooms on the east side and one full bath, complete with pink and maroon deco tile, finished out the early 1930's house.

"I know it needs a lot of work," Elaine said, "but I think it has a lot of possibilities."

Oh, definitely, Maggie thought, as she fell in love with the quaint place. She'd already imagined moving a wall here and there, expanding out back to add a master bedroom with much needed walk-in closets, enlarging the kitchen, putting in a pantry, opening up the ceiling in the main room and perhaps even the dining room. Her mind reeled with the possibilities.

Further exploration showed the back yard was big enough for a large deck, and a huge pecan tree shaded half of it. The kitchen area could be bumped out to the west, and the area near the garage was certainly big enough for a good-sized addition with master bath. The other half of the yard could be reworked into a wonder of a garden. It looked as though Aunt Frances had once delighted in tending it herself, but both the front and back areas were in need of restoration landscaping.

Perhaps the garage apartment out back might make a good studio? She didn't need the extra income from a rental space. Could the south side be turned into a wall of windows to let in the light? How fun it would be to paint again and to have an area for messy projects!

Within a week, Maggie had bought herself a house, with Sharon and Doug reluctantly approving the impending move. They were impressed, however, with the location—three short blocks south of campus, eight minutes from the Nest by car—and with the soundness of the structure. Older houses were built to last.

The price was certainly reasonable because Elaine's family didn't want to work through an agent. And they were asking fair-market value, which Maggie was willing to pay.

Their only stipulation was Aunt Frances had to approve of the new owner. Maggie was a bit nervous as she accompanied Elaine to afternoon tea at the assisted living residence on Sunday. A tiny lady with fire in her eyes, Aunt Frances was direct, polite and asked her frankly what would be done to "her house" if she allowed Maggie to move in.

Briefly outlining her thoughts about vaulted ceilings, window walls and granite countertops, Maggie was delighted when Aunt Francis approved with enthusiasm, asking to visit at least once when it was completed.

Doug knew several contractors who would bid on the remodeling, one in particular who had done some work on the Nest, and Maggie filled her off-work hours with planning the first home she had ever bought by herself.

It was a job she knew would consume her, so it was with great reluctance she answered another call from Monsignor Fitzpatrick a few days later. He needed her help on a committee he was forming, or rather one Father Murphy was forming. The Newman Club for Catholic college students would be celebrating its 75th anniversary next year, and St. Elizabeth's, being the original site for the area's club, wanted to throw a year-long party to would draw in new members.

"Surely," he had pleaded, "with yer great experience at da university," they couldn't do it without her. Why, she would be the "most valuable member o' da committee." They would meet only occasionally, and she could just give ideas, not have to serve regularly.

She didn't have the heart, or courage, to say no to the loveable old priest, so she agreed to meet with them for the initial planning meeting the following week.

Chapter 26 ~

That Saturday evening, after spending a long day looking at cabinet styles for the kitchen and going over the third revision of design plans from her architect, Maggie consented to meet Sharon and Doug at La Diosa, a fashionable wine bistro downtown. Set in an old warehouse with high ceilings and picturesque brick walls, the eclectic restaurant was a favorite haunt of Tech faculty, especially for happy hour. Numerous vintage couches and chairs were settled around tables of all shapes and sizes. Artwork lined the walls as if in a gallery and she noted several were for sale. She liked Walter Patterson's landscapes, thinking one might look good in her new house, but getting closer, she winced at the prices.

She spotted Doug on a purple couch across the room and joined him as he finished ordering a bottle of wine and hors d'oeuvres.

"Hi, Handsome," she said, kissing his cheek as he rose to greet her. "Where's Sharon?"

"Running late. She's at the hairdresser's and there was some problem with the coloring or something. She'll be here directly as soon as she's properly 'spiked.' How's the house coming? Not well, I hope, so you'll be with us longer," he teased.

"No, not well. And yes, I may just give up and live with you guys forever!"

"Great! But seriously, what's wrong now?"

"Oh, just the normal renovation stress and problems. I've done this before, but not on such a major scale and not by myself. There are so many decisions. And right now, the architect and I aren't communicating as well as I'd hoped. I tell him I want the ceiling torn out in the living and dining rooms and he tells me fine... then brings me plans without that included. Seems he 'just can't see it working with the integrity of the house.' Thinks I should just re-plaster them with vintage swirls!"

She reached over for an olive on the just arrived plate.

"So, fire his ass," Doug said.

"If only."

"If only what?" Doug asked as he poured wine for them both. "If only what?" he repeated and looked at Maggie when she didn't answer.

She was staring, mouth open, olive in mid-air, at the couple just entering the bistro across the room. Doug followed her gaze as the pair headed in their direction. "Who's that?"

The tall man and scantily dressed woman draped on his arm crossed the room and stopped in front of Maggie and Doug. "Mrs. Grant," the man said easily as he nodded to Maggie and then to Doug.

Maggie replied coldly, "Shouldn't you be in church or something?"

"What?" he asked.

Tugging on his arm impatiently, his lady friend said, "Come on, Colin," then dragged him away to a dark corner table.

"Who was that, Maggie?" Doug asked as he watched the 'lady' sashay away.

"That," she said with disdain as she chomped on the olive, "was Father Murphy."

"Are you sure it's him?" said Sharon when she arrived ten minutes later, craning her neck to catch a glimpse of the man in the dark recess.

"Of course I'm sure. The man knocked me over twice and was inches from my face. It's him all right. She called him Colin." Maggie was still fuming.

"Well, maybe she's his little sister, or something," Doug offered in defense of his gender.

"Not a chance, the way she was hanging all over him. And you don't put on perfume like that for a big brother," Maggie stated flatly. Damn, she thought. How could he be so blatant about seeing a woman of that type right here in the community? And damn those eyes of his—she'd felt the familiar unsettling tug inside as he'd looked at her tonight—no black cassock to trigger her guilt, or his, obviously. Double damn.

Maggie skipped Sunday Mass, instead joining Sharon and Doug at their service across the street. She prayed for tolerance. On Wednesday, she arrived early for Father Murphy's committee meeting, deliberately sitting at the far end of the table between two other volunteers. When the cassock-clad Father Murphy arrived and greeted everyone, she gave him the coldest stare she could manage... her boys called it "the look."

Normally "the look" could melt any male within 20 feet into submission, but it seemed to have no effect on Father Murphy, who brightly ran through the meeting agenda with equal skill and cheerfulness. Maggie squirmed the entire hour, unhappily remembering the "lady" on his arm a few nights before, and left abruptly as the meeting ended. She couldn't even stand to be in the same room with him. Before she made it out to her car, she decided she would resign from the committee and find another church. But how was she going to tell Monsignor Fitzpatrick?

Early the following Saturday, Maggie headed to Saint Elizabeth's to follow through on her decision. Best to just get it over with, she thought. The Monsignor wasn't in the parish office, but was "supervising the repainting of the old parish hall," his secretary had said. Maggie headed in that direction, wondering if it was a huge sin to lie to a priest, especially one as nice as Monsignor. She'd decided she would skirt the truth about Father Murphy. God could punish him in his own way, she thought. It wasn't *her* place to put him in *his* place. Besides, surely someone else from the parish had seen them? Yep, she would skirt the truth, say something about more convenient location of churches, or something, and then make sure she went to confession, but not here at Saint Elizabeth's.

Concentrating on her speech, she stepped in the parish hall door and was immediately bowled over and knocked to the floor by a madman with a wet paintbrush, which left a wide swath of ivory paint across the front of her dark green cotton blouse. Deciding this was God's sign that she definitely had picked the wrong church, and wondering why she'd ignored His first two signs, Maggie was surprised to find her attacker was not Father Murphy but a rather familiar-looking young Hispanic man with soft brown terror-filled eyes, fumbling to put down the brush and help her up at the same time. He only succeeded in getting more paint on both of them.

Where had she seen him before?

She heard footsteps and voices coming in her direction, as she tried to stand while assuring the young man she wasn't hurt. She definitely couldn't say the same for her blouse. Several strong hands helped her to her feet, including, damn it, those of Father Murphy, once again in his torn Notre Dame T-shirt and tight-fitting jeans. And he was grinning at her like a Cheshire cat. Maybe she *would* tell Monsignor Fitzpatrick what she saw after all, the fiend.

She was standing on her own now, and the others were slowly returning to their work. Father Murphy reached down and picked up her purse to hand it to her. She snatched it away as she once again assured those around her that no, she wasn't hurt, and yes, she should've been more careful. The young man with the paintbrush was offering myriad apologies, almost to the point of panic. Father Murphy put his hand gently on his shoulder and said, "It's all right, Jamie. Mrs. Grant is used to getting knocked down, and she's not hurt. But you probably should buy her a new blouse, don't you think?"

Jamie looked at her stained garment and said, "Of course, I'm so sorry. I'll take care of it, Ma'am, I promise! But, I..." He looked at Father Murphy for help. "Mi madre... I've gotta go, really."

"Yes, of course, Jamie. Go, but call me when you get there and know more. Do you need some cash?" He quickly took several $20 bills from his wallet and stuffed them in Jamie's shirt pocket.

"I'll take care of this," he said, pointing to Maggie, "and this," he said as he took the wet brush from Jamie's hand. Jamie hesitated only a moment and then hurried out the open door.

Maggie turned to watch him sprint across the parking lot.

"Just got a call that his mother is ill. He's heading home. We'll keep him in our prayers."

"Of course," said Maggie as she turned back inside, "and he doesn't need to replace the blouse, Father Murphy. It was as much my fault."

"Colin," he said.

"Yes, Father Colin," she said avoiding his gaze and looking instead for the more friendly Monsignor.

"Father Colin?" he said, eyebrows raised. "Don't you mean Father Sean?"

She looked at him and wished he had on his cassock so her heart wouldn't do flip-flops.

"No," she said flatly, "I mean Father Colin Murphy."

"OK," he said slowly, "Stay right here a minute. Promise you won't move?"

"No, I won't promise you anything. I'm looking for Monsignor..." But he'd already turned and walked briskly around the corner of the short entry hallway. She stomped her foot at his arrogance, straightened her clothes, pulled her purse over the shoulder not covered in paint, and stepped into the main room where men and women of all shapes and sizes were busily turning the walls the same color as the wet swath on her blouse.

The smell of fresh paint was overpowering but not overwhelming, signaling a renewal in the musty old room. Orderly chaos seemed to prevail, and she marveled again at the old priest's powers of persuasion. At the rate this army of volunteers was working, the huge hall would be finished long before lunchtime. Too bad she wouldn't be around to enjoy it. Now where was the old priest?

Before she could spot the Monsignor, Father Murphy had stepped back in front of her. "Mrs. Grant! Again you have met with catastrophe at St. Elizabeth's. I think this is a parish record. Are you all right?"

She looked at him hard and stammered, "What?" Then she involuntarily stepped backwards against the wall when a second Father Murphy came into view and said, "Surprise!"

Her purse slid off her shoulder, but she grabbed it before it fell and clutched it to her stomach as she looked from one face to the other. No, she wasn't seeing double... but she was! They were identical, both dark haired, green-eyed, tanned, tall and all male. The only difference was their ND T-shirts didn't match and one had a little more gray hair.

"Twins!" she said much too loudly and then clapped a hand over her mouth.

"Yep," said one grinning Father Murphy.

"Since birth," said the smiling other one.

Laughter started to bubble up from inside Maggie, and even with her hand covering her mouth, it spilled out in loud unfeminine guffaws that had both men grinning even more broadly and had Maggie soon doubled over, leaning against the thankfully unpainted wall. Sliding helplessly to the floor, she gasped for air, looked at them and started laughing all over again.

The Fathers knelt down beside her as she held her stomach while trying to suppress the giggles spewing from her mouth. She laughed so hard it hurt, and tears started streaming down her face. One of the Father Murphys retreated to find tissues, and she said to the other between gasps and giggles, "I... need... to... sit... down."

"You are sitting down," he said flatly.

She looked surprised, then narrowed her eyes first at his face, then the floor, and wheezed, "Oh, so I am. I need to... to stand up, then." He reached for her, pulling her up, a little too closely for her comfort, his arm snugly around her waist, her hands flat against his chest. Her laughter stopped and she sighed, looking deep into his green eyes and said, "Where's a black cassock when I need one?"

"What?" he said with obvious confusion.

Triggered, her laughter spewed forth again, and this time she spit and blubbered all over his face as she couldn't contain it. Maggie pulled away, leaned once more against the wall, then turned away, holding her stomach and laughing hard again.

The second Father returned with tissues, giving one to his brother for his spit-strewn face and several to Maggie. Then they just stood shoulder to shoulder, arms folded, watching her, and waited.

Finally, wiping her eyes, she regained most of her composure and faced them to apologize. "Oh, my. I'm so sorry... really, so sorry... So, which one of you ran into me?"

"That would be me, the first time," one said, raising his hand.

The other one, the one with a touch more gray said, "And me, the second time. I'm Father Sean Patrick Murphy, priest."

The first one said, "And I'm Cailean—Colin—Patrick Murphy, professor."

Looking at Colin, Maggie said, "And you were the one I saw last week at La Diosa with a date?"

"Yep, that was me all right... Wait, and you thought I was him?" He laughed out loud, and slapped his brother on the back. "No wonder you weren't very civil."

"I'm so sorry," Maggie said sheepishly.

Sean looked at his brother, frowning. "Who was it this time? Kate?"

"No, Dixie."

"Ah, yes, Dixie. Definitely not my type," Father Sean deadpanned.

Maggie looked at him quickly, then got the joke and started laughing again.

"Oh, no you don't," Colin said, grabbing her elbow and steering her farther into the room. "Come here and let me get you some water or something. If you don't stop laughing, you're going to hurt yourself."

Maggie clutched her purse to her stomach and allowed herself to be pulled further into the large room. Father Sean followed. Colin sat her down next to a refreshment table, put a bottle of water in her hand, and commanded, "Drink."

"Yes, sir," she said, complying. As she drank and the giggles subsided, she couldn't stop looking up from one face to the other.

"You guys are really identical!"

"Yes," Father Sean replied dryly, "All our lives. Listen, I've got to get back to work, Mrs. Grant. Duty calls."

"Oh, of course, but when you ran into me the other day, how did you know who I was? We hadn't been introduced."

"Colin told me. After *he* ran you down, he sent Jamie to find out from Monsignor Fitz who you were and then told me about the crash, describing you to a T."

Colin rolled his eyes and shrugged as Maggie looked at him.

Then she said, "Jamie? I thought he looked familiar. I hope his mother's all right."

"Me, too," Father Sean said. "We're remembering her in the Masses tomorrow. I really need to go, if you'll excuse me now. Duty is still calling. I'll see you at church in the morning?"

"Of course, Father, wouldn't miss it," Maggie replied happily.

Father Sean smiled, turning to rejoin the volunteers. Colin sat down in the chair next to her as she sipped more water, shook her head and smiled.

"What?" he said, when she grinned broader.

"Nothing, nothing at all," but she was so relieved—relieved she wouldn't have to leave Saint Elizabeth's, and relieved her physical attraction hadn't really been to a priest.

Colin cleared his throat. "Listen, Mrs. Margaret Grant. Are you free for dinner tonight?"

Maggie turned to look at him with surprise, smile gone. "You're asking me out? I have a wedding ring on or doesn't that matter to you?" She said it with a little more acerbic vigor than she intended. Leftover anger from when she thought he was a priest who dated, she supposed. Although Jim had been gone almost a year and a half, she couldn't bear to take off the simple gold band, and besides, it kept unwanted men at a distance.

Obviously, though, not this one.

"It does matter, Mrs. Grant, but I happen to know you are widowed, since February a year ago, and weren't you out with someone when I saw you at La Dioso?" Without waiting for an answer, he quickly said, "So I thought you might like a little dinner and conversation. That's all. Unless you have another date? Besides, I ate your lunch a few weeks back and figure I owe you some pizza, at least.

"Oh," was all she could say.

Colin continued. "Like Sean said, I had Jamie check you out and Monsignor told all. You work at Tech in the Administration—but I'll forgive you for that—and you moved here in March from Dallas. You have two grown married sons, one in Dallas and one out somewhere in the Northwest. And two young granddaughters, though you don't look like any grandmother I've ever seen. So, thought you might like dinner and a little conversation, that's all."

Maggie's mouth hung open. She shook her head, closed her mouth at last and said, "So if you know everything about me already, what'll we talk about tonight?"

Colin smiled. "Well, you obviously know nothing about me, seeing as how up until about ten minutes ago you thought I was a wicked wayward priest, so I can make it a one-sided conversation. Seven o'clock?"

Maggie looked at her watch and jumped up. "Yikes! I'm late! I've got to go! Make it 7:30 at Orlando's. The old one on Avenue Q."

He stood quickly as she fished for her keys, "7:30 at Orlando's. That's good. What's your rush?"

She headed out the door and called back, "Sorry! I've got to go fire an architect!"

Colin stood there, thumbs in jeans pockets, looking after her for a long time.

Chapter 27 ~

"Seriously? Tonight?" Sean asked. "She doesn't look your type."

"My type? I have a type? Since when?" Colin asked his twin as they washed the last of the paintbrushes.

"Since forever, big brother."

"Oh? And what type is that?" Colin asked, irritated.

"Well, you know, the kind you wouldn't take home to Mom." Colin scowled at him, but Sean continued. "The kind you can have a good time with, but you don't have to get serious with. That kind."

"Oh, and you, of course, know all about women, Father Sean," Colin said, emphasizing the Father.

"I'm still a man, Colin, so, yes, I know a little about women. But more importantly, I know a lot about you."

"Just because I've never brought a woman home to Mom, doesn't mean..." Colin protested, then stopped, not exactly sure what he meant.

"Doesn't mean what? While you were with the Bureau, you couldn't settle down, moving all over who knows where. Now that you're here, you can, if you wanted to... but the women you choose to date, at least the ones I've heard about or seen, aren't the settling-down kind. Mrs. Margaret Grant just might be."

Colin finished the last brush and reached for the towel to dry his hands, turning to face his brother.

"Well, *I'm* not the settling down kind. There's just something about her, though. She's not a bombshell, in fact, rather plain looking, and a little plump in places..."

"A little what?" Sean said in surprise.

"Could stand to lose few pounds, I guess, but when she smiled today, I don't know how to describe it. There was just a spark—of course not when she was drooling and spitting in my face," he said, remembering her doubling over in uncontrolled spasms of glee. "But, there's just something there I liked. I'd like to get to know her a little better, that's all."

"O.K." Sean said. "But remember Monsignor Fitz is rather fond of her, so be gentle, please."

"Gentle? I'm only going to have dinner and conversation. Nothing more, I swear."

"Fine," Sean said skeptically. "But be gentle just the same."

Sharon sat on Maggie's bed as she watched her pull clothes from the closet and try them on. "So you're having dinner with the priest?" she asked.

"Yes, I mean no... I'm having dinner with the one I thought was the priest, but he's not. He's a professor of some kind," she replied as she pulled on a red linen blazer. "The other one's the priest. How's this? Casual enough?"

"Everything you've tried on in the last 15 minutes has been casual enough. Just pick one. You look great in anything."

"I should have been taking the stairs two at a time by now. Still got a few pounds to lose. Damn."

"Damn, what? You look great! And lucky you are about to have dinner with a man who makes you quiver and he's NOT at priest, thank God. What are you upset about?"

"It's just that it has been forever. Am I ready for this?"

"Ready for what? It's just dinner. You don't do sex, remember."

"Yeah, I remember," she said wistfully.

Colin arrived early at the decidedly Italian restaurant, typically decorated in red checked tablecloths, plastic grapes and wine bottles, but there was an ambiance to the decades-old Orlando's restaurant that made it a little more sophisticated than the usual pizza place. And he knew the food was amazing.

After asking for a corner booth away from the door and ordering a bottle of wine, he fidgeted with the breadsticks, wondering why in the world his stomach seemed to be in knots. It's just dinner, he thought. I've had dinner with hundreds of women. He took a gulp of wine, willing himself to be calm and then took another.

He stood as she arrived right on time, and promptly spilled his wine. He hurriedly wiped it up and motioned for her to sit. She smiled, then quickly slid onto the seat, wincing a little as she bent down.

"You all right?" Colin said, noticing the grimace and sliding in across from her.

"Fine, just a little sore from all that laughter this morning. My ribcage may never be the same." She smiled shyly, a little nervous herself, he thought. He liked that smile but could tell he wasn't alone in wondering what he was doing here. She reached up and twisted her hair, then stopped herself when she noticed he had noticed.

"Hello, Professor Cailean Patrick Murphy," she said a little anxiously, putting out her hand.

"Hi, Mrs. Margaret Grant," he replied, amused, taking her hand for a business-like shake, his nervousness melting with her touch.

She pulled hers away quickly and cleared her throat. "Please call me Maggie. Is that all right?"

"Perfect, Maggie. Mine's Colin to my good friends and family. Wine?"

"Yes, thanks, Cailean." At his raised eyebrow, she shrugged and said, "I don't know you well enough to call you Colin."

He smiled, thinking he might have to remedy that pretty quickly and then poured a glass for her, refilled his own. They ordered from the over-sized menus.

Maggie took another sip of wine and then said, "Okay, talk."

"What?"

"You said you'd tell me all about yourself since you already know all about me. So talk."

"I don't know everything about you, but okay. Hmm, let's see. Where to begin?" he said with a mischievous smile.

"Well, start with what kind of professor you are, where you work, how long you've been in Lubbock, where you were born, are there more Murphy's besides your twin, the priest? Have you always been a Notre

Dame fan and what does Cailean mean?"

"Whoa! What are you, a reporter?"

"Sort of. Just start talking, and I'll ask questions along the way." She'd always been comfortable in interview situations, and weren't first dates just that? Interviews? With people she was writing a story about, the exchanges were a game to see if she could pull out information the person didn't necessarily want to reveal, or didn't know was important. And when she was the one being asked the questions by a reporter, it was an even more interesting contest to make sure she only revealed enough to satisfy, but never revealed too much. She seldom lost a match.

And so he started talking, and she asked questions and he answered, and then he asked questions and she answered. They talked through the appetizers, through spaghetti and veal Parmesan, and through Italian cream cake topped with spumoni ice cream. And through a full bottle of wine.

Colin—from the Gaelic Cailean, which means "young creature"—was the older of the twins by a few minutes and the second of eight children, seven boys and one girl, the youngest. They were born and raised in Chicago, and most of the family was still there, including mom and dad, who now had seven grandchildren to spoil, none of which were offspring of Colin or Sean, he assured her with a wry smile.

"And one great-grandchild on the way," he added.

"You and your twin have the same middle name, Patrick?"

"Yep. Mom gave it to all of us as a middle name. In fact, our older brother is Patrick Patrick Murphy."

"You're kidding, right?"

"Nope. It's his actual given name. Until he got big enough to beat us up, we called him 'PP.' "

"I'll bet that went over well," Maggie said.

"Not so much, really. But mom's maiden name was Patrick, Molly Kathleen Patrick, so she wanted to keep it in the family. Even my baby sister is Margaret Patrick Murphy."

"Margaret?" Maggie said.

"Yep, but we call her Peggy... and she's now a Jones... married a good Catholic, but not Irish."

"Okay, Cailean Patrick Murphy, tell me more."

He'd graduated from Harvard, but Sean and several other siblings attended Notre Dame, hence the T-shirts. And besides, it was every Irish Catholic's duty to love the Fightin' Irish. He had spent 20 years "doing stuff" before being asked by Sean to come to Lubbock after retirement.

"Doin' stuff?" she asked. "What kind of stuff?"

"Just stuff," he said. "And now I'm a professor here at Tech. Industrial design."

"Industrial design? You're a designer? Wait, don't change the subject. What stuff? What exactly did you do for those twenty years?"

"Well, promise you won't laugh? Just some stuff with the government."

She laughed. "The government? Which government?"

"Our government, of course. The United States government."

"Which branch?"

"Goodness, are you sure you're not an interrogator? All right, I was with the FBI."

She laughed again. "Right. You spent twenty years doin' stuff with the FBI and then you retired and moved to Lubbock?"

"Yeah, sure," she chuckled. "Nobody moves to Lubbock on purpose."

He crossed his arms, leaned back and just looked at her, smile gone.

Maggie raised her eyebrows. "Seriously, Professor? You were with the FBI? A G-man?!"

"G-man? They don't call us that anymore. But, yes, seriously, I was with the FBI, retired, and moved to Lubbock. Sean's a great brother, and Lubbock is an interesting place to live, don't you think so? You moved here."

"Yes, but I graduated from Tech and love it. Seriously, FBI?"

"Something wrong with the FBI?"

"No, no, I just... I just find it easier to think of you as a priest than as a G-man, that's all." This time they both laughed. Try as she might, though, no more details about his "stuff" with the government were forthcoming, so she moved on to other topics.

Over coffee, which they both needed after consuming the entire bottle of wine, she learned how when he first came to town, he took a few university classes out of curiosity and found he had talent in design. He'd always liked drawing things and then building them—gadgets, furniture, almost anything made of wood—but it had only been a hobby, and one he hadn't had much time for with the agency. At retirement, he had the time, and one thing led to another. He'd thought he'd move on right after the next class, then the next semester, then the next year, but he got hooked. Within a few years, he was teaching a class or two. Then he was asked to apply for the full-time position that opened up.

"So, I meant to come visit Sean for a month or two while I decided what to do next, and I've been here almost ten years now. It's... It's comfortable."

"And I meant to stay happily married in Dallas where I was comfortable. But things happen," she said with a touch of sorrow, looking out across the restaurant.

He looked at her thoughtfully, then leaned a little forward to softly say,

"Yes, they do happen. I'm sorry for your loss."

After a moment, she refocused and said, "Oh, sorry. Thanks. Seriously. Sorry. Didn't mean to get like that... too much wine." She sighed, recomposed, and took another sip of coffee. "Speaking of things that happen, though, did you hear from the young man? What was his name? The one whose mother was ill?"

"Jamie Chavez. He's a senior at Tech. And no, but he said he'd call me. He's got a long drive ahead of him. She's in Idaho."

"Idaho? Wow, that *is* a long drive."

"Yeah. He has grandparents just up the road in Canyon but grew up with his mother in Idaho. Good kid. Worked a couple of years out of high school to afford college, so he's a little older than most seniors but still a kid to me. Should graduate next spring."

"I promised your brother I would remember him in my prayers, and speaking of which," she said, looking at her watch, "it's getting a little late, so I'd better say good night."

"Right," Colin said, just now noticing they were the last patrons in the restaurant. He looked up and called the relieved waiter over to settle the bill. "Let me walk you to your car."

Outside, there were only two vehicles left in the dimly lit front parking lot, Maggie's ten-year-old Volvo and an even older pickup truck Maggie thought looked like it hadn't seen the inside of a car wash for at least a year. Colin walked her to her car, and she turned to offer her hand again, saying solemnly, "Thanks for dinner, Professor Murphy."

Surprised, he reached for her hand, shook it firmly, but didn't allow her to pull away this time. Holding it now in both hands, and looking deep into her hazel eyes he smiled slowly and waited for her reaction. She returned the smile, amused. Satisfied that the beauty was still there, he said, "The pleasure was all mine, Mrs. Grant." He let go, turned abruptly on his heel and strode away toward the filthy old pickup.

Maggie's knees had threatened to buckle again when he took her hand, but willing herself steady she got through it without embarrassing herself. Once in her car, she turned the key and drove away without another glance at him. "Damn those eyes," she muttered. She needed a long cool swim in Sharon's pool, and not just because of the summer temperature.

The next morning, after going to early Mass and seeing Father Murphy but not Professor Murphy, Maggie drove Sharon and Doug to the airport for their annual pilgrimage to all things Italian, assuring Doug she would take good care of their house for the next four weeks, and assuring Sharon she would call her if anything developed with "the non-priest," as Phelps kept calling Colin the professor.

On the drive home, Maggie was struck by the fact that she was truly alone for the first time since coming to Lubbock. Sharon and Doug had been a lifeline, so to speak, and had been there for her when loneliness or sadness had shown the slightest signs of emerging, just as Ben and his family had been in Dallas the previous year. She would just have to keep busy, that was all. Luckily, the house renovation details should take up most of her off-work time. And then there was always her office. Oh, boy, she thought ruefully, her office.

Chapter 28 ~

Communications staffers partnered with Information Technology for the care and feeding of the university's voracious website, a huge beast of information with more than a million pages linked. Yes, a million. Many pages and sites were controlled by different departments, but it was a daunting task to keep the information updated and correct. The main Tech website was frequented more than 700,000 times a month—current and prospective students, their parents, community members interested in any of the thousands of campus activities, by staff, faculty, other colleges looking at the competition, and those looking for news of Texas Tech, especially loyal alumni.

Steven and Susan did the majority of the writing. When a department had changes for their pages, a request form was available online. Because everything was under strict graphic guidelines along with writing and design standards, Ricky and Tech's IT department were tasked to make those changes after they were approved by the Communications office. Several older students were hired each year to assist with keeping the website current, and Steven, Susan and Ricky did a great job of supervising them.

It kept them all hopping, as faculty came and went and organizations changed leaders. Working with the website was a constant endeavor—especially on this day as Maggie questioned her new way to work with her micromanaging boss.

"I want the front page changed," Boyle told Maggie when she reported to him as requested early Monday. "The president's office needs more exposure and I want the page to reflect the responsibilities of this office. Here's a list of what I want. Make the changes."

Maggie looked with incredulity at the list of his demands, including a photo of himself as the interim president and his personal message of welcome, poorly written, she thought, along with design changes. These were major changes to the content, format and design.

"The front page? You mean the home page? It's not really that simple,

Mr. Boyle. We have a committee of students, staff and faculty, along with IT personnel that meets once a month to discuss and approve major changes, so I'd have to take your request before them."

"No. Just do it," Boyle said flatly.

"I'm afraid I can't just do it, Mr. Boyle. A change of this magnitude, the home page that's linked to everything... it just can't be changed on a whim... I—"

He looked up at her sharply, "A whim?" He said sternly. "I assure you, I do not make decisions on a whim."

Maggie immediately pictured his former secretary, Allison, but thought better of contradicting him. Think, Maggie, what's an effective way to deal with him this time that won't get you fired?

She straightened up and said, "Normally, once the committee makes recommendations for major changes, sir, the Board is informed. Would you like me to let the Board know of your request for changes?"

"No. Just do it. I tire of reminding you that I am your direct supervisor and you must do as I ask. Dismissed."

Once she was back upstairs, Maggie called Ricky in to help her think this through. Would her tried and true analytical approach help solve this problem?

"He wants to do what?" Ricky said. "He can't. We can't. There are guidelines in place... and who wants to know about the president on the home page anyway? We can't."

"I know we can't, but we've been directed to, so let's look at it logically. Fact one—"

"Fact one," Ricky interrupted, "is that Boyle has a frickin' ego the size of Texas and he just wants the publicity a photo on the home page would give him, hoping it will influence the Board of Regents to give him the job permanently."

"I know, Ricky, but let's figure out a way to not comply with his directive and still keep our jobs, shall we?"

"Sure, Boss, but how?"

"Fact one is that major changes must, by university guidelines, go to the committee for approval. Fact two: Boyle wants us to bypass the committee. Fact three: we like our jobs," she said with a sardonic smile. "So, what are our options?"

"Well, we could sabotage his computer so he can't see we haven't made his changes?" Ricky suggested brightly.

"Punishable by firing squad, I'm sure."

"Right. Let me think. He's not computer savvy, is he." It was a statement rather than a question. Everyone in the building knew Boyle didn't use e-mail and barely understood the on/off switch, another reason to wonder how he even knew the home page was influential. "So, he probably doesn't understand how long it would realistically take to make a change like this."

"You're right. I think he expects the changes this week," Maggie said.

"We could stall him, couldn't we?"

"Yes, we could. Hmmm. How long *would* it take to make the changes?" Maggie asked.

"I can't do it all here. I'd need to work with IT, and they'll be furious. It took us more than a year to get approval for the current homepage layout and then design all the other pages following that template. I'd say, without having to get any of the approvals, it would still take us several months. And that's only if we do nothing else."

"That's great. Let me talk with Pat in IT and let her know what we're trying to do. See if she'll go along with the stall tactic. Within a month, the Board should have named the new president, and odds are it won't be Boyle—then problem solved.

"In the meantime, Ricky, my graphic genius, work up three or four new design drafts for the homepage with what Boyle wants so we can show them to him. But make each and every one so awful that he'll keep sending us back to the drawing board. You could deliberately leave out one or two of his demands in each design, but different ones each time. And use the worst picture you can find of Mr. Bennett Boyle. If we can stall him on the design long enough, we might not even have to get IT started on any changes. And remember, Ricky, what is *said* in this office *stays* in this office."

"Not a problem, Boss. I can have some ideas by mid-week... and although I'm not used to doing ugly work," he said with a gleam in his eye, "this might actually be fun!"

On Monday evening, Maggie met with her new architect for the second time. She'd hired him shortly after she settled with the last one. This one assured her that tearing out the ceilings and installing paneled, cream-painted crossbeams in both living and dining rooms would be doable and still be in keeping with the design integrity of the house. She was pleased she would be able to see the revised drawings later in the week.

On Tuesday afternoon, Elaine put through a call from "a Professor Murphy" and took note of the expression of surprise and delight on her boss's face as she asked Elaine to close her office door.

"Didn't know if you were headed to Dallas for the long weekend," Colin said after they'd exchanged pleasantries.

"No, no. I'm here. The long weekend?" she asked, puzzled.

"Monday's the Fourth... of July," he added when she made no reply.

"Oh, yes, of course! No, I'm here... in the middle of constructing an addition to a house and sort of housesitting for friends. So, no, I'm here. Just forgot it was a holiday, that's all."

"A house addition, huh? That's hard work. Yours?"

"Of course it's mine," she said laughing, "and I love renovating houses, don't you?"

"Can't say if I do and can't say if I don't since I've never done it, to tell the truth. Never needed to."

"I've done it before in Dallas. Jim and I..." She kicked herself for mentioning her late husband again—stupid, stupid—but continued on, "We added two extra rooms—for a larger den with a pool table for the boys and a study. The construction was a mess, but I enjoyed the process."

While waiting for Colin to reply she silently chided herself again for bringing up her late husband.

At last he said, "So, if you're not too busy house-additioning and housesitting, wonder if you'd care to join me at the street fair Monday afternoon?"

"Street fair? Where?"

"Where? You have been busy. In front of St. Elizabeth's on Broadway. Lubbock does the Fourth up right with a huge *Fourth On Broadway* street fair and then fireworks at McKenzie Park. Anyway, Sean has asked me to help again at the church's booths... they set up games for the kids and sell tacos. I'm on duty until 1:30. I could come pick you up after that?"

"Oh, well, no, it's close to the office, so I'll just walk over to the church, I mean if that's okay with you? Don't know if I can stay through fireworks, though. I'm really behind on things with the addition, but I'll come to the fair for a while. Will that work?"

Disappointed that she didn't sound too enthusiastic, he decided he would take what he could get and see where it went. They agreed to meet at the church booth.

Chapter 29 ~
July 4

After putting in a few hours at the office, Maggie was comfortable in Skechers, capris and a sleeveless cotton blouse rather than her usual summer linen suit. She was, after all, the only one in the building. She locked up to walk the few blocks to St. Elizabeth's. As warm as it was, she was thankful for the lighter clothes. Besides, it was supposed to be a holiday. Just as she reached the top of the esplanade key, she stopped at the sound of the carillon bells behind her. She looked at her watch—one o'clock—and wondered why they were ringing. Recognizing *The Star Spangled*

Banner, she held her hand over her heart and watched the American flag on Memorial Circle flutter slightly in the light breeze. When it was over, she resumed her journey to the street fair.

From her office window, she'd seen the crowds gathering on Broadway just after noon, and even before she stepped off campus she could smell the delicious aromas of street-fair food floating on the hot afternoon breezes. Her stomach rumbled, but she resisted the barbeque, corn on the cob and hotdogs offered in the booths she passed, remembering Professor Murphy had mentioned St. Elizabeth's was selling tacos. She'd hold out for three more blocks for the sake of loyalty to the church. She could always come back to sample the others later.

Colorful patriotic bunting and banners, balloons, kites and throngs of happy people decked in all manner of red, white and blue swarmed like bees on a hive. Music seemed to pour from everywhere, from rock 'n roll to reggae to mariachi. Maggie caught the infectious excitement even before she spotted Colin in khaki shorts, sandals and a fairly new Notre Dame shirt and cap. He was helping preschoolers with the beanbag toss. Thankfully, Father Sean, next door at the ring toss booth, had on his cassock, so it was easy to tell them apart even from a distance.

Monsignor Fitzpatrick was there, too, donned in his own regal cassock and seated up on the sidewalk under the shade of a canopy. Seems he was the official prize-giver-outer, so any child who won a prize—and they all won something—had to come up to him. He talked quietly with each one, telling a joke, or somehow coaxing a smile or giggle from even the shyest of youngsters. It was hard to tell who was more delighted, the children, their parents or the Monsignor.

Maggie bought a taco and bottled water, quickly downing both as she stood among the crowd watching Colin interact with little children. A few minutes later he spotted her and recruited her as his assistant. She helped move kids in line to the appropriate throwing point, and retrieved errant beanbags, wishing her granddaughters had been here. They would've loved it all.

When Colin's replacement finally arrived, they said their goodbyes to the priests and headed east up the street. He glanced at her sunburned nose and declared she needed a hat because the sun was blazing. He found several being peddled at a nearby booth.

"No, really," she protested as he placed a cowboy hat on her head. "I don't look good in hats."

He looked at her critically, taking the hat off and trying on another, this time a broad brimmed red straw hat. Once more he looked at her, and this time she comically crossed her eyes at him.

As he reached up to take that one off, too, he said, "You're right. You don't look good in hats. Here, just plop on this cap and maybe no one will notice." He handed her his Fightin' Irish cap. He bought one of the straw cowboy hats for himself, which looked quite fetching, Maggie thought. She smiled, adjusted the size of the cap and said laughingly as she pulled it low over her sunglasses, "Thanks... I think."

Next they stopped for "meat on a stick" and fresh lemonade, then walked companionably for the next hour, weaving their way through the heavy crowds, trying their luck at some games of chance, stopping to admire crafts, or listening to one of the dozens of entertainers up on small stages dotting the sidewalks. It was hard not to bump into each other often, and Maggie felt each touch, inadvertent or not, enjoying the moments, pushing all thoughts of "what's next" out of her mind.

Colin sometimes reached up to gently steer her elbow or put a hand on the small of her back to guide her, and he, too, felt each connection as if it made his hand tingle. He knew exactly what he wanted to happen "next," but was taking it slow and gentle, as Sean had requested. She laughed easily at his wit, and he was enjoying her company, deciding he definitely liked making her smile, hat or no hat.

Professor Colin Murphy seemed to be well known, as he exchanged greetings with dozens of people, most of them either college-aged men or middle-aged women. She was introduced to everyone he met as Margaret Grant. Interesting, she thought. Not my friend or my date, but just Margaret Grant. Not even Maggie.

It was especially interesting when they ran into Dixie, his lady friend from La Diosa. She popped out of the crowd squealing his name and jumped up to plant a messy kiss before he could even speak. Gushing about how happy she was to see him and why hadn't he called her, she was oblivious to Maggie, who'd stepped back, watching the normally in-control professor blush as he tried to hold an exuberant Dixie at bay.

After clearing his throat, he introduced them and Dixie's smile vanished. "Nice to meet you," she lied with daggers in her eyes, looking Maggie over from head to toe, sizing up the competition. She sniffed, obviously deciding this new woman posed no threat to her, then turned quickly back to Colin.

"Well, darlin', call me anytime. I'm available." Turning on her heel, she spotted another acquaintance in the crowd and called out loudly to him, making her way to his open arms. Colin steered Maggie in the opposite direction with decided haste.

The only person Maggie seemed to know in the mass of fairgoers was Jenny Bodecker, who was busy in a craft booth, selling birdhouses, planters filled with daisies, and, of course, her famous crosses—all items made from popsicle sticks. Mrs. Bodecker already knew Colin, so Maggie didn't need to make an introduction. Jenny blushed and giggled as Colin bought one of her biggest planter boxes telling her, "You can never have too many of these beauties."

"Murphy!" Maggie heard from behind them, and Colin stopped once again, turning to shake the hand of a handsome young wiry African American, almost as tall as himself. "Josh. Good to see you, man."

Josh smiled, then looked at Maggie who had recognized him the minute she'd turned. His eyes widened when she took off her sunglasses and cap. "My angel!" he cried, picking her up in a tight hug and twirling her around —a difficult thing to do in the dense crowd.

"Oof!" Maggie said as he crushed her to him.

"Oh, sorry," he grinned as he put her down. It was Colin's turn to stand to the side and watch.

Maggie smiled up at the young man. "You look great, Josh. Are you all healed?"

"I am! Just a broken arm and some cuts and bruises. You saved my life! Murphy, this is the angel I told you about. I thought I'd dreamed her, that she wasn't real, but she called Dad and gave me a blanket... and kept me awake... Oh, I still have your blanket... or Mom has it. She wanted me to find you so she can return it personally. I'm so glad I found you!" He finally took a breath and just stood there, grinning.

Colin watched them for a moment, then said, "You're the angel who saved him?"

"No, I didn't really save him. We, Sharon and I, were there when he went off the road, that's all, and we called for help. The rescue squad saved him." Turning again to Josh, she said, "I'm happy to know you're doing so well. Sharon will be, too."

"Sharon. That's the only name we had," Josh said. "The trooper only had that one name written down, so we didn't know who you were or how to find you. I'm telling you, Mom will be so happy."

Colin looked from Maggie to Josh, the two of them standing there, grinning like fools at each other. It truly was a small world. He turned to Josh, "I thought you were going home for the summer."

"I was, but it was easier to find a job here. Too many high school kids taking the summer work back home. I'm still waiting tables at McAllister's on 19th. Stop in some time, Murphy, and leave a big tip?" he said hopefully.

Colin told him he'd be by in a few days.

"Say, did you hear from Jamie?" Josh asked, serious now.

"Yeah. He called Sunday night."

Uh-oh, Maggie thought, she'd forgotten to ask about him although she'd continued to keep him in her prayers.

Colin frowned. "Things don't look too good with his mom. It's cancer. Stage four. He's decided to spend the summer at home. Don't know if he'll be back in the fall. Keep him in your prayers, will ya? Oh, and his room is available until then, if you're interested. Aren't you moving in this fall when Joe graduates?"

"That's tough for Jamie. Thanks, man. Yeah, I'm next on the list, and I might be interested in moving in early. I'll give you a call tomorrow. I've got to go to work in a few minutes, but listen, Ma'am," Josh said, turning to Maggie, "will you give Murphy here your full name and phone number so I can give it to my parents? They really wanted me to find you."

"Um, happy to get that for you, Josh," Colin said with a slight smirk. "I'll talk to you tomorrow or the next day about the room."

"And thanks again, Ma'am. You'll always be my angel." He leaned down and kissed her cheek, then turned and blended into the crowd.

"His angel, huh?" Colin asked.

"Hmmm," Maggie replied. "Nice young man."

"The best. I'll add my thanks to you for saving his life."

"Right place, right time, that's all. And speaking of nice young men, I'm sorry I forgot to ask about Jamie. Cancer? That's too bad."

"Yep, it is. It's just Jamie and his mom. Don't think he ever knew his dad. Died when he was a baby, if I remember right."

"His room?" Maggie said questioningly.

"His room? Oh, yeah, he lives with me and his room is going to be vacant, so I thought Josh might like to bunk there for the summer," he said nonchalantly and started walking through the crowds again.

"He lives with you? You live with a student?!" Maggie exclaimed as she followed hurriedly in his wake.

"Four of them, actually," he said casually over his shoulder, walking as though looking for someone or something.

She grabbed his arm to make him stop and looked up at him squarely. "Professor Cailean Patrick Murphy. You live with four students! Whatever for?" She couldn't comprehend a fifty-something professor actually living with twenty-something college guys.

"I'm hungry again. Are you?" he said and headed for the corny dog stand he'd spotted. He bought two, with drinks for them both, then walked to a vacant shaded bench nearby to add the necessary mustard. Maggie stomped her foot and then followed, undeterred.

She accepted the fare and then persisted, giving him "the look."

"Talk, Professor Murphy," she commanded.

Between bites and gulps, he told her about his unusual living arrangement. At first, thinking his move to Lubbock to be only temporary, he'd rented a room for himself. Then, after deciding to stay, he found a small one-bedroom furnished apartment. He'd never owned a home so had few possessions and didn't see the need to buy things even when he found a little larger, and quieter, garage apartment—again furnished.

About six years ago, one of his promising students was having a hard time financially, and Colin tried to help him out by letting him sleep on his couch. This student was a Tramp, and about the same time that group asked Colin to be one of their faculty sponsors.

"A tramp?" Maggie asked. "A Saddle Tramp?"

"Yeah, Saddle Tramp, the men's service organization at Tech."

"I know about Saddle Tramps. Dated one in college. Hmpf..." she said as she looked off with a wistful smile. "Loved those red corduroy shirts." Then she turned back to Colin, "You were a sponsor?"

"Still am," he replied with a surprised smile at the red shirt comment. Interesting woman, he thought.

"You volunteer to sponsor the Saddle Tramps?" Maggie asked.

"You don't exactly volunteer. You have to be asked by the Tramps, and I've been asked for about six years now. Anyway, getting to know the Tramps a little better, seems there were others who were financially strapped, too, so I tried to figure out a way to help them. I found a larger furnished apartment and then two years ago bought one of the five-bedroom condos in the new development just over there, The Cottages of Lubbock." He pointed northeast across Broadway.

"It's student housing, actually, but the owner and I are poker buddies, so Tom cut me a good deal on the one in the far southwest corner. I rent out four of the rooms to junior and senior Tramps each year at reduced rates—they pay what they can—it's a good investment property and everyone's happy."

"You live with four college guys... four Saddle Tramps."

"Yes, I do. Look, most of the time I'm on campus teaching or working in the studio until late at night or just out. Sean volunteers me a lot, too. Just not there much at all, really, and I have pretty strict rules about parties, cleanliness, etc. It's seriously not bad at all. I'm sort of like a dorm mother, I guess, but not actually," he shrugged. "Gives us all a place to lay our heads at night and allows them to concentrate their energies on studying and serving the organization instead of worrying so much about money. It's comfortable."

Maggie sat back, staring at him. "Amazing," was all she could manage to say. Who is this man, she thought. Spends twenty years "doin' stuff" for the government he won't or can't talk about, retires to Lubbock—definitely not a destination location—and helps preschoolers at a street fair and college kids at life.

"You gonna eat the rest of that?" he said, looking at her half-eaten corny dog. She handed it to him and drank her water while he finished off the dog along with his beer.

"Do the Saddle Tramps ring the bells in the tower?" she asked after the last drop. "I heard them ringing earlier today."

"They do, but they don't, but you did. It was the carillon bells in the west tower today. Played by keyboard, I think, but not by us. Music department takes care of it if I'm not mistaken. At one o'clock every Fourth of July. Supposed to coincide with the ceremonial Liberty Bell ringing in Philadelphia, or something like that. Tramps ring the victory bells after games—in the east tower." He grabbed her hand saying, "Come on. It's almost time for the bluegrass fiddlers, and I'd like to get a good seat."

She allowed her hand to stay in his as he led her back up the street, passing St. Elizabeth's, where he presented Mrs. Bodecker's craft to his wary brother. He took her hand again as they wove their way up another three blocks and found two empty chairs to watch the show, but she put her hands in her lap once they sat down. Then, absorbed in the music, they clapped, whistled and stomped along with the enthusiastic crowd.

In the end, Maggie begged off from late night fireworks—she had an early morning meeting with her latest architect—so Colin walked her back to her car on campus. Purposefully putting her hands in her pockets, they walked companionably along, talking about her renovation. She also explained about her housesitting duties, saying it was Doug, as in Sharon and Doug, who she had been with at the bistro. She thanked him for the afternoon, laughing when he stuck out his hand for yet another handshake. Instead, she reached up and gave him a quick kiss on the cheek, as young Josh had given her. "Thank you, Cailean."

He lingered as she drove off, tucked his thumbs in his pockets, and whistled on his long walk home.

Only when she got home did Maggie realize she hadn't returned his cap.

Chapter 30 ~

Ten days later, there was still no call from Professor Cailean Patrick Murphy. She hadn't seen him at Mass on Sundays or the few early morning weekday services she'd attended. And Father Sean was always surrounded by admiring parishioners—besides, what would she say to him, "Why hasn't your brother called me?" That was totally out of the question.

So she concentrated on work at the office and her new house, stopping every day to check on the progress, consulting with the architect and the contractor who oversaw the subcontractors, and making crucial decisions. She'd have to start shopping for more furniture soon, she thought, but it could wait until Sharon got back. Wish she were here now to talk to, she thought almost every day. Since there really wasn't any "news" about the "non-priest," she hadn't made any overseas calls and realized just how much she missed her friends.

She also missed Doug's cooking and found herself doing takeout for dinner most nights, once even stopping at McAllister's. Maybe she'd see Josh and could casually ask if he'd moved in to Colin's house, or something? But Josh wasn't working that night, and Maggie chided herself all the way back to the house. "Silly, foolish woman. That's what you are Margaret Riley Grant. Acting like a lovesick teenager. I just won't think about him anymore." And she didn't, at least not until she crawled into bed at night.

Damn him was what she thought whenever she did allow Professor Murphy to come to mind. He's just not interested in plain, middle-aged me, she decided.

Remembering the La Diosa encounter, she reasoned that if he'd been even a little interested, he would've glanced in Maggie's direction that night and surely seen Sharon instead of assuming Doug was *her* date.

Damn him. What a fool she'd been to think a handsome, charismatic guy would be the least bit interested in her. He'd asked her out to dinner because he felt guilty about running her over and eating the last piece of pizza. And Monsignor Fitzpatrick had probably asked him to show some pity for the new widowed parish member, that's all.

Then why ask her to join him on the Fourth? And why hold her hand? She could still feel the heat of his touch. Damn him. He was probably holding more than Dixie's hand right now. She wrapped her arms around herself for comfort but found little.

Chapter 31 ~

Just before noon in mid-July, a shadow darkened Maggie's office door and she looked up, startled to see Professor Murphy standing there, hands shoulder-high on the doorframe, leaning in, looking at her.

"Hi," he said, a tentative look on his face.

"Hi," she replied. What was he doing here? An errand from Monsignor Fitz?

"Free for lunch?" he asked. She started to say no, but heard instead Elaine's unusually loud voice quickly saying, "Yes, she's free!"

Colin turned toward Elaine and smiled as she moved to the door, calendar in hand. Sticking her head inside in front of him, a little quieter now, Elaine said, "Well, you are free, Boss. Not a thing on your calendar for at least two hours or so."

Maggie gave her "the look," and Elaine retreated to her own desk. "Guess I'm free, Professor Murphy," she said, resigned. She picked up her purse and as she walked past him, he was still smiling. "I have my cell if you need me, Elaine."

"Oh, we won't need you, Boss. You just go and have a nice long lunch. Don't worry about a thing. Have fun now, you two!" And with that, Elaine ushered them out into the hallway, grinning widely as she watched them walk toward the stairs.

"My truck's out front, or we could walk? Thought we'd go to Gardski's. I'm pretty hungry," Colin said tentatively.

"Gardski's is fine. Haven't been there in a while," she replied in a cool tone.

They opted for a quicker trip in the truck as it was sunny, 94 degrees with a little bit of hot dust kicking up in the dry wind, and Gardski's was at least a half-mile up Broadway. Maggie was a tad apprehensive about her freshly dry-cleaned linen suit as they approached the old brown pickup truck—at least she thought it was brown—it was hard to tell with the amount of dirt and grime covering the exterior. But climbing into his filthy vehicle, she marveled at the pristine condition of the interior, especially as opposed to the mud-caked outside. It even had modern air conditioning and seatbelts, obviously not factory installed judging by the age of the truck.

"Nice ride," she said sincerely.

"Thanks. Had it for a while."

A while, indeed. Must be from the early 60s, with its brown leather bench seat, chrome dash instruments and old radio. A vintage Chevy pickup. If he cleaned the exterior, she thought it could have been used in the latest Chevrolet commercials touting durability.

As they drove the few blocks down Broadway to the restaurant, they talked minimally of the weather and not much more. When they parked, Colin jumped out and started to walk around to her side, but Maggie was already out and had closed her door before he could help her. They walked silently to the restaurant's front door.

Gardski's was a two-story European-style building with high-pitched gables and dark beams crisscrossing the light olive green exterior stucco walls. Sometime in the 1940s, it had been built as a fashionable residence on Lubbock's main brick street. A wide stone porch now served for outdoor seating, and the living areas downstairs, as well as the upstairs bedrooms, had been converted into small, intimate dining rooms, complete with white tablecloths and decent china. A small bar was also upstairs.

Maggie was once again taken back thirty years, as this had been a favorite fancy-date destination, but then the restaurant was called the Brookshire Inn. Not much had changed except the name—the food was still unusual and delicious and the hospitality unmatched in the city. Oh, well, there was no bar in the place back then. Lubbock was dry and you had to head south to the Strip to get something to drink. Traffic to the Strip was usually quite heavy late afternoons right before the weekends.

They settled into a small corner table in the front room and ordered. Colin evidently *was* hungry, as he asked for their biggest steak with all the trimmings. Maggie loved their spinach artichoke chicken, but opted for the lighter club sandwich on such a hot day.

When the waiter left, Colin unexpectedly reached across and took Maggie's hand in his. She looked up in surprise, started to pull away, but the pain in his face made her change her mind.

"I'm sorry I haven't called. I had to go out of town. Jamie Chavez's mother died and I went to help him take care of things."

"Oh, Colin, I'm so sorry. I didn't know." She put her other hand out to him, and he took that one, too.

"I wanted to call, but... but I didn't," he said squeezing her hands and then letting go and sitting back, looking away. "Hard thing to lose your mother."

She hadn't wanted him to let go. In fact, wanted to move around the table to comfort him. Instead, she looked at him with compassion and said simply, "Tell me."

He smiled a little and told her. Jamie had called him around four-thirty the morning after the Fourth, saying it looked pretty bad. His mother had gotten the terminal diagnosis just after Christmas but kept it to herself. When she was hospitalized in mid-June, she allowed the hospice worker to call him. They thought she had only a month or so left. When Jamie came, they moved her home, Jamie and hospice volunteers tending to her around the clock.

She worsened sooner than the doctors anticipated, and Jamie called Colin to help him figure out how to get his elderly grandparents to Idaho as quickly as possible. They lived in Canyon, a mid-sized community ninety miles north of Lubbock and were unable to get to their daughter's side by themselves—both were in their late 70s and spoke only rudimentary English. Living on a small Social Security pension, they didn't have the means to fly, nor the necessary skill sets, especially in this time of uncertainty and sorrow for them.

Colin would bring them—he didn't have classes just now. Jamie had protested, but Colin had said, "Do you need me, son?"

When the answer was a simple "yes," he'd made some quick arrangements and headed to Canyon, picking them up in a rented full-sized sedan—his truck obviously not suitable for this trip. Knowing a parishioner who owned several of Lubbock's largest car rental facilities and who would, of course, do anything for Father Sean's brother, allowed Colin to lease the car long before normal business hours. He arrived in Canyon early that morning.

They drove straight through, stopping only for food, fuel and restrooms, the grateful grandparents—abuelos—taking turns napping comfortably in the large back seat, or praying fervently for their only daughter, worn rosaries constantly moving in their hands. The speedometer showed a steady pace of about 15 miles over the legal limit, but if the grandparents noticed, they understood the urgency of their journey and didn't protest. Although Colin's Spanish was much better than their English, conversation was limited since each was preoccupied with their own thoughts.

Heading north through Amarillo, then across a sliver of the Oklahoma panhandle, they easily reached southeastern Colorado. Colin couldn't remember if the Caprock made as dramatic a showing this far up on the plains as it did in West Texas. Maybe someday he would drive up here and find out.

Their journey took them north, northwest up to Interstate 70. Making a left turn, they headed for Denver, and in early evening turned north again to Cheyenne. He knew the route through southern Wyoming was a little less up-and-down than traveling straight west from Denver to Salt Lake City. They stopped for a late dinner at the Crossroads Cafe in Cheyenne, a clean, mid-sized truck stop Colin was familiar with. When they entered, heads turned toward the unlikely trio of travelers.

Jamie's grandmother was a tiny woman with the smallest hands Colin had ever seen on an adult. She was slim, plainly attired in an inexpensive print dress, shawl draped over her thin shoulders. Her gray hair was pulled back and piled in a bun, slightly askew from the trip. Standing, she was only as tall as Colin's elbow. At six feet, three inches he felt like a giant with a china doll, tiny and frail. When she sat in the booth, her feet didn't reach the floor.

Her husband's feet touched, but only with the help of the thick heels on his snakeskin boots. He wasn't much taller than his esposa. He wore his best jeans and a Wrangler-style shirt with pearlized snaps. His weathered face under the straw cowboy hat revealed decades of hard outdoor labor.

When they settled in to order, other diners lost interest and returned to their own meals. Along with their hearty dinner entrées, Colin suggested the fried pickles, assuring them there were none better in the entire country.

When the cheeky, heavily made-up waitress brought out the order of half a dozen warm sliced pickles with crisp brown crusts, Jamie's grandfather gathered the courage to try one, declaring it as "No es mala... no es mala," but his wife wrinkled her nose, stubbornly refusing to even taste the "evil-looking unnatural things" while crossing herself several times.

The waitress turned indignantly on her heel and marched back to the kitchen in a huff, obviously insulted. They could hear her loudly relating the "unbelievable behavior of those stupid Texans" to the cook, who peered out at them menacingly through the small order-up window. Although restrained, the men had their first laugh since the beginning of their journey. Jamie's grandmother was calmly devouring her chicken-fried steak, feet swinging, seemingly oblivious to it all.

As it grew dark, they followed Interstate 80, part of which was the old Oregon Trail. Colin had been here before and was sorry his passengers couldn't see the amazing landscape as they crisscrossed rivers and drove through fascinating rock formations. There was one stretch, he remembered, where huge 50-foot boulders looked as though God had been playing on a beach, dripping gigantic globs of wet red sand into softly molded piles resembling make-believe castles.

As the trio drove along in the dark, Jamie's grandparents slept, and Colin thought about Yellowstone National Park and the Grand Tetons, which, according to signs, were directly to their north now. He'd been through that area twice, the first time as a young FBI agent. The assignment had gone terribly wrong and one of his fellow agents had been killed before they "got their man." Colin had never experienced the death of someone close to him before, and although he knew he was not to blame, he was surprised at the intensity of his feelings. He had requested, and received, an extended leave of absence.

After gathering his hiking gear, he'd spent the next few weeks exploring Yellowstone and the mountains high up around Jackson Hole. Living off the land and army meals for most of the hike, he had serious discussions with "the big man" about the nature of life and living, right and wrong, good and evil. Sean had joined him for one weeklong leg of the journey, and they'd grown even closer, the young priest and the young government agent exploring their spirituality in the face of the world's reality.

Colin had come back to the agency with a new determination, and a newfound inner strength that had served him well during many subsequent assignments and missions, and deaths.

Much of the reminiscing, the geography and spiritual journey he left out of his accounting to Maggie. When the waiter appeared with their food, Colin seemed surprised and stopped his narration. They ate in silence—automatically and without tasting.

"You speak Spanish?" Maggie asked matter-of-factly after several bites.

Without looking up from his plate, he replied in the same manner, "Comes in handy working in Southern California and Arizona."

Maggie was curious, but now wasn't the time.

After a few more bites to quiet his hunger, he continued the story. By dawn's light, he and Jamie's grandparents were skirting the northeastern corner of Utah and driving into Idaho, north of the great salt lakes. They'd ended their journey in Blackfoot, Idaho, population just over 11,000—billed as the Potato Capital of the World. Situated between the western edge of the Salt River Mountain Range and the eastern edge of the Snake River Plain, Colin immediately saw a resemblance to Llano Estacado... endless flat fields of potatoes could easily be mistaken for endless flat fields of cotton. Not only was Blackfoot the agricultural center of east Idaho's potato industry, it was home to the Idaho Potato Museum. Colin didn't think he would visit it this trip.

After taking the grandparents to Jamie's home, Colin had checked into the nearby Super 8 Motel of Blackfoot, complete with a modest price and complementary Super Starter Breakfast. After some much-needed sleep, he remained on the periphery of the small family to give whatever assistance he could.

Jamie's mother had lingered for a full three days after their arrival, accepting Last Rites from her parish priest and spending a little time alone with each of her family members and close friends before she died peacefully in her son's arms.

"Jamie was devastated," Colin said. "He immediately bolted the house and ran down the street. I followed and found him a few blocks away at the high school football field. He was so angry. Angry with God, with the world, with himself for not realizing she was ill."

Maggie said gently, "Everybody grieves in their own way. And sometimes, especially if it's the first time they lose someone close, they act out because they don't know how to act. My boys... they grieved so differently from each other for their father. I tried to help, but I was grieving, too. It's a hard thing to go through, but necessary. I'm glad you were there for him."

"I am, too, but maybe Sean should have been there instead of me."

"But he didn't call Sean... Father Sean... did he? He called you. He needed you."

"Maybe. Anyway, I planned to stay only through the memorial service but then there were so many details to take care of, it seemed appropriate for me to be there for the boy. He was still so lost. His mother had been his whole world. Maybe it did help that I was there."

"I'm sure it did, Colin. It was an amazing thing to do."

He quickly shrugged off the compliment, not even aware she had twice now called him Colin instead of Cailean, thinking instead of his brother and of their large family, which always had and always would be there for each other. How fortunate he and Sean were.

Jamie's mother had asked to be cremated and have her ashes rest in the cemetery at the small church in Canyon where she grew up.

Wanting to get away from the memories and return to Texas, Jamie had said, "There's nothing left for me here now." Maggie knew exactly what that felt like, twice over.

So the young man gathered what he wanted of his mother's possessions and arranged with friends to sell the small house and the rest of the furnishings.

More than a week later, Colin, Jamie and Jamie's grieving grandparents caravanned back through the Rockies—a little slower this time—to the modest home in Canyon. Jamie was still up there with them, waiting to return to Lubbock in another month for the fall semester, his senior year.

To his amazement, the first thing Colin had wanted to do when he returned was talk to Maggie. He'd learned long ago to trust his instincts, and sitting there with her he knew he'd been right. The burden had been lightened in the telling.

"When he gets back," Maggie said tentatively, "I'm willing to talk with him... I, um, I lost both my parents when I was about his age."

"Maggie, I'm so sorry. I had no idea."

"It's not something you would know. But I can tell you it's hard, just starting out in life to be independent, to be on your own, and then all of a sudden you *have* to be on your own. There's no one at home to run to if things don't go right, or if you get scared."

Now it was Colin's turn to take her hand and share the pain.

"I don't know how I would have gotten through it without Sharon and Carol. They were everything to me. And Sharon's parents, too." She looked away, remembering. After a few moments, she shook her head and took back her hand, saying, "So, I do know what he's going through, and if he'd like some reassurance that it will get easier, I'm your man... or woman." She smiled bravely at him, and he gained a new respect for this interesting woman who was, as his brother had said, not his type.

When he dropped her off back at the office, he asked to see her the next weekend. "I'll phone you later in the week," he said, and she smiled, already looking forward to the call. Guess he does like me a little, she thought quietly as she walked up the stairs. Good... because she liked him more every time she saw him.

Chapter 32 ~

"Soon," the contractor said. "Soon, Mrs. Grant."

"Soon is a relative term, Mr. Campos. Can you give me a firm date?" Maggie asked as they stepped over, around and through construction, looking at the week's progress, which actually was considerable. Workmen were present on this Saturday, currently setting tile in the master bath, finishing cabinet installation in the expanded kitchen and pantry, and installing pot lights high up in the newly vaulted ceilings in the living and dining areas. Last week they had finished laying tile in the kitchen. Maggie had seriously wanted to keep the old linoleum, but Campos had shown her several patches beyond repair and warned of the dangers of asbestos. She'd relented and picked out a durable tile to match the cabinets he was installing.

"I think I'll have it all finished by August 15th, including the final walk-through. It's gone really well. The weather has held. Now if we can just get those granite countertops from Fort Worth, we'll be in good shape."

"If?"

"Don't worry. I'll have you in by the fifteenth. I promise. Contract calls for penalties if I don't, and I'm not real fond of penalties," he said with a smile. "By the way, is that yellow tabby cat hanging around yours?"

"What? No, it's not. What yellow tabby cat?"

"I think she's lying on the back deck right now. Been here almost every day... makes herself at home. Real friendly gato."

"Well, not my gato. I'm sure she belongs to one of the neighbors. August 15th you say?"

She liked this man and thought he was doing a great job with her additions. He'd even made some suggestions for improvements beyond the architect's plans, and Maggie had taken some and left some, choosing to spend her money wisely on quality upgrades with no frills.

"Definitely."

"That'll work. Thanks," Maggie said, relieved somewhat. An original estimate by the architect of six weeks' work had been stretched to eight by the contractor, and Maggie was eager to get settled in her new house. She was excited this afternoon because Colin was coming to see it for the first time. She hoped he approved. Then she asked herself what would happen if he didn't. "Nothing," was her answer. She loved it, and that was all that mattered. Nevertheless, it would be interesting to see what he thought.

Late afternoon Colin knocked on the open front door, peering in, curious about what type of house Maggie would live in, and what type of additions she'd approved. He didn't much like changing the feel of a house, and he hoped she hadn't modernized the charming cottage too much. But who was he to judge? It was her house, after all. Still, it would be interesting to see what she'd done.

Hearing the knock, Maggie stepped out of the kitchen area and invited him in. He began looking around and then heard a deep voice bellowing, "Murphy!"

Turning, he smiled broadly at Maggie's contractor. "Campos! Don't tell me you're here robbing this little lady blind? How are you, my friend?" They shook hands and slapped each other's shoulders enthusiastically as Maggie frowned... Uh oh, she thought. Robbing me blind?

"Bueno, Murphy, but tell her the truth. I'm the best damn contractor in Lubbock County, with the most reasonable and fair prices, and you know it. 'Fess up, amigo!"

Still smiling broadly, Colin turned to Maggie, "He's right. He really does quality work and is honest to the core. How'd you find him? Yellow pages luck?"

"Uh, no. Doug recommended him."

"Doug? The guy you were with at La Diosa?"

"Yes, Sharon's guy. Remember?" Why did it bother her he thought she was with another man?

"Oh, Sharon's Doug. Yeah, I remember." Turning back to Campos, he said, "So show me around, mi amigo. What damage have you done to this beautiful old house?"

"Damage?" he said in mock horror. "I've brought out her full potential, my friend. Wait 'til you get a load of this master suite... it's a beauty... and then there's the studio outside, but we're not near done with anything yet... there's still..." and they disappeared into the back of the house, leaving Maggie standing by the front door, arms crossed in wonder.

"Maggie?" she heard Colin yell a minute later. "You comin'?"

I'm coming, she said to herself. After all, it is *my* house.

By the time they'd finished the contractor's grand tour, all the workmen had gone for the day, and Campos left the two alone, promising to be back to work early Monday and to call Colin soon for a night of poker.

Colin was still looking around at all the details. Maggie followed, amused at his "mms" and "oohs," wondering if he really liked it.

Going through the entire house once more, opening drawers, cabinets and closets, looking at the workmanship, the style, running his large hands over the corners and carvings, he returned to the living area and stood next to the huge stone fireplace, then turned to Maggie. "This is well done, Margaret Grant. Well done."

"Thank you, Professor Murphy. Your admiration is appreciated."

"Actually, it's better than well done. I'd say you upgraded the charm and functionality of the house without sacrificing its character. I can't imagine how it could be better. If you paid a fair price for this—and I'm sure you did—you're turning it into a good investment property. And I'd kill for a studio like that —the wall of windows was brilliant. Did you know you can see the park from there?"

"Yes," Maggie said laughing, "I did know. But I'm turning it into a home, not an investment property."

"Right, a home. But still, the return on your dollar would be quite impressive."

"I'm planning on staying quite a while in my home," she said, again emphasizing the word "home."

"Okay, I got it. I'm impressed. You seem to be a woman of many talents." He moved toward her, giving her a direct gaze before putting his arms loosely around her waist.

Surprised, she put her hands on his upper arms, leaned back and looked up at him skeptically. He bent down and kissed her forehead lightly, releasing her suddenly and saying, "I'm starved! What's for dinner?"

Startled, and a little breathless, she said after a moment, "Ah, Murphy, as you saw when you walked through three times, I don't have —"

A solid knock on the front door cut her off. Colin went to the door, opened it wide and grinned. Josh stood there, a huge McAllister's restaurant bag in one hand, two giant drinks in the other.

"Josh!" Maggie said, pleasantly surprised.

"Mrs. Grant! How nice to see you. Mom said she'll be in town in a few weeks and wants to personally deliver your dry-cleaned blanket. Said she'd be in touch, so she'll call you soon."

Colin took the food, handed it to Maggie, and gave Josh several bills that included a large tip, judging by the young man's grin as he left, calling out, "Good night! And thanks, Murphy!"

"Dinner's here, m'lady. I remember you eat club sandwiches, and I ordered one sweet tea and one regular. You choose." He made a makeshift table with discarded wood and two saw horses. Then found boxes for chairs, brushing away sawdust.

"Well, bring it here, Mrs. Grant, don't just stand there. I'm hungry, remember?"

She moved toward him, handing him the fare. Just then, a flash of yellow caught her eye, and she turned to see an enormous tabby cat nonchalantly walking down the hallway to the master bedroom, tail high in the air.

"Your cat?" Murphy asked.

"No! Can you help me get her or him out of here?"

"Why? There's lots of windows open. She'll probably leave in a few minutes... just curious about the renovations, I'm sure. You sure she's not yours?"

"Of course I'm... Let's eat, Murphy."

He grinned as he opened the bag to set food on the table, "I'd told Josh I'd be by McAllister's the week after the Fourth with a big tip but didn't get the chance, so I thought I'd kill two birds with one stone. My promise to Josh and seeing this house you're renovating. I got you an oatmeal raisin cookie. Figured you for the oatmeal raisin cookie-type. Is that right? Sit, sit."

Maggie laughed as she sat, saying, "Oatmeal raisin's one of my favorites." This man was full of surprises, wasn't he? She opted for the regular tea to balance out the cookie.

They spent the evening eating their take-out and then walking the block, commenting on the quaint old houses, planning her garden tasks, and getting to know each other better. With relief, she noticed the visiting cat cross the neighbor's yard. She needed to make certain all the windows were shut tight.

Maggie showed Colin the studio space again, talking about her desire to start drawing and painting, although it'd been years since she'd touched either sketchpad or canvas.

"It was hard for me to get started designing when I first came here, too... to Lubbock, that is. The classes helped, and one thing just led to another. I think the first step is always the most difficult in the creative process. At least it is for me. But then once I get going, I sort of lose myself in it and love transforming wood into something useful as well as good-looking. Functionality and form, as I tell my students."

"What type of things do you build or design?"

"Design and then build. Mainly furniture. Cabinets, desks, benches, things like that. I like detailed work but in a finished product that looks simple, like the wood was always meant to be that way. Like Campos did on those kitchen cabinets of yours. That's real quality there, you know. You're lucky to have him on the job. It'll really pay off for you in the long run... great investment."

"Home, Murphy. Home. And I like quality. Do you hire out? Do commissions, I mean?"

"Only for special people," he said smiling at her. "What'd you have in mind?"

"Oh, nothing, yet. I haven't enough furniture to fill this place, just some mattresses and box springs in storage, so I don't know what I need or want. But maybe we can talk about it after I've moved in... hopefully in mid-August."

"Is that when Campos said he'd be finished?

"Yes. August 15th."

"His word's good as gold, so August 15th it is. I know some Saddle Tramps who'd love to earn a little cash by helping you move in. You have some furniture in storage you said?"

"Yes, but not much. Probably need only two guys. Who would you recommend? Josh? Jamie? Will he be back by then do you think?

"Josh for sure, and if Jamie's not back, I volunteer my services, but mine won't cost you. I'll check with them if you'd like, and we'll plan the move for the first Saturday after the 15th. How does that sound?"

"That's great, thanks. I'll count on it," she said, pleased he would commit to helping several weeks away. That meant he was either an extremely considerate man, or he enjoyed her company enough to imagine seeing her through the next month, at least.

"That way, I can see what furniture you do have and how large of a commission I can talk you into," he said with a mouthful of leftover cookie and a twinkle in one impossibly green eye.

Mercenary, she thought.

When darkness fell, they sat on the stone wall of the front porch and looked out over the serene park, watching stars begin to twinkle in the sky.

"As a student," Maggie said, reminiscing, "I played in that park. Flew kites, kissed a boy or two, and made snow angels on the slopes of the playa over there. But we called it Flint Park back then because Flint Street runs right next to it."

"Makes sense. What's it called now?"

"Tech Terrace Park."

"Doesn't exactly roll off the tongue. Isn't that the name of the neighborhood?"

"It is, but it's still Flint Park, to me."

"Kissed a boy or two, huh?" Colin asked playfully.

"Or three," Maggie said smiling, remembering again the Saddle Tramp with the red corduroy shirt.

Around 10 o'clock, Colin bid her good night with a light peck on the cheek, saying he needed to be up for early Mass. He wanted to see her again. Could he call next week?

"Yes, especially if you bring cookies," Maggie told him playfully. She closed all the windows because of the nosy cat and locked the doors because of the construction equipment inside. Then climbed into her Volvo and headed for the Nest, grinning like a schoolgirl who'd just been asked to the prom. Of course he could see her next week... with or without cookies... and the next and the next.

Chapter 33 ~

In late July, the Board of Regents announced the sole finalist for the position of president of Texas Tech University, one Phillip Parker, Ph.D., graduate of Dartmouth and the University of Texas, an economics guru. Of the finalists announced earlier, Maggie thought he had the best credentials. His last position was as Chief Financial Officer at the University of Illinois.

When the decision was announced, a collective sigh of relief went up from the administration building, no doubt echoed in departments across the university. Boyle was more sullen than usual, and Maggie tried to stay out of his way. Thankfully, they wouldn't be changing the website's home page as directed, and Boyle didn't ask about it again.

Maggie had hoped the new president might be Catholic and fall under Monsignor Fitz's influence so she might have some access, but no luck there, he was Methodist. He was also the first African-American president at Tech—definitely an anomaly in this part of the country.

Although Maggie's group handled the news releases about his selection and arrival, she had yet to meet him. And even though her staff had sent Boyle a detailed outline of suggestions for introductions to the staff, students and community, they heard nothing in return. The plan had included an interview with the *Daily Toreador* student newspaper during Dr. Parker's first week and then guest editorials in the *Lubbock Avalanche Journal*, as well as appearances at as many campus activities as he could fit into his schedule. The Faculty Senate, the Alumni Association and the department chairs should be visited as soon as possible.

They'd suggested the president's office contact various local civic clubs, the mayor's office, the University Medical Center administrators and the student body president, as well as the presidents of all active student organizations. The Lubbock public radio station would welcome him as a guest for a lengthy interview program. Communications had offered to work with him to write a series of articles for their *Insight* employee newsletter on his mission and goals. Different student organizations could place ads in the school paper to welcome him. And it certainly wouldn't hurt to frequent local restaurants and introduce himself.

Unfortunately, he didn't seem to be using any of those ideas. She wondered if he'd even seen the plan because he wasn't marketing himself at all. Maggie thought he wouldn't last long without a good exposure plan.

She knew better than to bring it up to Bennett Boyle, though. There wasn't much more she could do except wait and hope for the best. Luckily, it wasn't all she had to think about.

Chapter 34 ~

"**Are** you free Saturday morning? I found some vintage curtains I think will look good in here, but I wanted to get your opinion." She had brought Sharon over to the new house after she'd picked them up at the airport and deposited Doug and the luggage at the Nest.

"I haven't been home a full day yet and already you're dragging me out shopping!" Sharon exclaimed. "Okay, but only if you'll tell me when I get to meet this beau of yours."

"He's not my beau," Maggie said defensively. "He's a friend. But he's promised to help me move in, so you can meet him then if you promise to behave yourself."

"When you move in? That's another two weeks away. We could double date before then, couldn't we?"

"No. We're not dating... we're just friends. And besides, I'm too busy to go out."

"Well, then I guess I'll just have to be content to wait. But speaking of this house you're renovating, Maggie," Sharon said, moving from room to room, admiring the work, "it's really the most charming stylish house I've seen in the entire town. You've done so much while we were gone! It really suits you so well. I never did think you were a traditionalist like your home in Dallas. This house is definitely much more like the old Maggie. You feeding the cat yet?"

"What? No, I'm not feeding the cat! But she still won't go away. Though I am getting a worried about her. I think she looks a little thin."

"Where is she?"

"I haven't seen her this evening. She could be anywhere."

"Well, she's probably already devoured the entire neighborhood's mouse population. If she comes around as much as you say, Maggie, I think she's looking for a new home. You should feed her."

"Not until I find out where she came from. Surely she lives around here somewhere. I checked with Miss Frances, and she'd never seen her before. I'll ask around and maybe put up a flier or something near the park. Will that satisfy you?"

"Yes, but I can hardly wait to meet them both."

"Both?"

"Yes. Your new cat and your new beau."

"Friend," Maggie said quickly. "He's my friend."

"Yeah, and I'm a puffed-up peacock. Ooh, shoot. A bird reference. Sorry."

Campos had been true to his word and work was finished by the 15th. And Colin had been true to his word and helped move her in the following Saturday, with both Josh and Jamie assisting. She generously paid the students even though both had objected loudly. Finally, Colin told them to take it, that Mrs. Grant's feelings would be hurt if they didn't.

Sharon and Doug had come early to help, and while the four men picked up furniture and hauled the big stuff, the two women thoroughly discussed every possible location for every piece of furniture from the storage unit, making a list of pieces they'd need to start shopping for.

At one point Maggie found an opportunity to talk with Jamie alone, and she expressed sincere condolences to him about his mother. His usual smiling face had been more sober than normal, but when she mentioned it, Maggie noticed the raw edges of still-fresh grief cloud his vision.

"I don't know if Professor Murphy mentioned it," Maggie said gently, "but I lost both my parents at about the same age you are. If there's anything I can do other than pray, please don't hesitate to call me. I know you might have questions about your feelings... it's just that I have been there and can try to help navigate you through it." She didn't know if she had said too much, so she was silent for a moment.

He met her eyes for the first time and said softly, "He told me. Thanks. Mrs. Grant... does it go away? The pain, I mean?"

She reached out and touched his arm. "No, it doesn't. But it gentles with time. My parents have been gone more than 30 years and I still get ambushed once in a while with the grief. It's something you learn to live with. Mom and Dad would have wanted me to get on with my life and to be happy. I'm sure your mother wants the same for you."

He looked at her as if saying he could never imagine being happy again. He turned away.

"I promise it will be easier with time, Jamie. Call me if you need me."

He nodded and went outside to bring in another load from the truck. Maggie's heart ached for him knowing how hard it was going to be for a very long time.

The hardworking crew was rewarded with pizza for arranging and rearranging furniture, unloading books and carting numerous boxes. Doug had left earlier when the heavy lifting was done. Josh had to head to work right after the pizza, and Colin left shortly thereafter with Jamie to work on some business for the Saddle Tramp organization—last spring Jamie had been elected this year's president and because he was absent most of the summer, had a lot to catch up on. Colin promised to call Maggie later in the week.

"Ooohhh," Sharon said as Colin drove away. "What a hunk! No wonder you've got the hots for him!"

"Phelps, I don't have the 'hots' for him. He's just an interesting man who's generous with his time. A friend in the making."

"A friend with a face and body that are unbelievably handsome. You might need to rethink the sex thing, you know."

"No, I don't want to rethink it. And speaking of which, I looked up what the Bible says about it outside of marriage. Do you want to know?" Maggie asked as she walked to a bedroom with another box.

"Not really, but tell me anyway so I can refute it," Sharon said as she followed.

"Seems there's no real prohibition in the Bible against it between an unmarried man and an unmarried woman..."

"See? That's great! I'm happy for you!"

"But," Maggie continued, "sexual immorality is denounced in more than two dozen passages in the New Testament. In Corinthians, Paul says it isn't good for a man to have sexual relations with a woman, and then he goes on to talk about how each man should have his own wife and each woman should have her own husband." Maggie stopped, looking at her friend's reaction before continuing. "Seems Paul states marriage is a cure for sexual immorality."

Sharon sniffed and said, "Paul also hated women and said in Corinthians they should keep silent in assemblies and if women want to learn anything, they should go home and ask their husbands. Says it's a disgrace when women speak in an assembly. Also, according to Paul, in Timothy, I think, he says he doesn't allow women to teach or to wear their hair in fancy styles or to even adorn themselves with pearls."

Maggie's eyes widened, thinking of her mother's pearl necklace, which she wore for special occasions and often to church.

Sharon continued, "But that's Paul... not necessarily God. So, if we don't believe that garbage any more about speaking, teaching and wearing pearls, why should we believe what he said about sex outside of marriage? One of the Ten Commandments said not to commit adultery, not that we couldn't enjoy one of His gifts without marriage—that is if neither partner is married. I'm confident God won't send me to hell because I'm sleeping with a man I love dearly."

"I don't believe He will either. However, I'm not ready to say it's right for me. So, as usual, we respect each other's opinions on the subject, right?"

Sharon laughed. "Right, girlfriend. But you might at least give it some thought when that gorgeous man takes you in his arms next time."

"Maybe I will, but I doubt it. And it's *if* there's a next time."

Close to midnight, Sharon finally said good night, and Maggie was alone in her new home. She poured a glass of wine and then walked slowly through the entire house, looking critically at every room once more before making up the mattress in her master suite. She raised her glass up high and said a prayer of thanks, draining the last dregs before turning in. Great house, she thought to herself as she drifted off to an exhausted sleep... and so little furniture. Must shop...

Chapter 35 ~

At Mass the next morning Maggie ran into Fern in the vestibule, accompanied by a tall man with a crew cut. He looked familiar, but Maggie couldn't immediately place him. Must be Fern's husband, she thought, the way he's holding her hand. How sweet.

"Maggie, my friend," Fern said. "Let me introduce you to my better half. Russell, this is Margaret Grant, the creative lady I told you about who did such wonderful crafts for the children this year. Maggie, this is Russell, my husband of too many years to count."

Maggie smiled at the tall man in the western suit with bolo tie, desperately trying to place him. He was so familiar! Where??? Shaking his hand, she said, "Pleased to meet you, Mr..." What was Fern's last name? Did she ever know?

"Russell Arbuckle, Mrs. Grant. And I've seen you often at Tech regents meetings."

"Of course, Mr. Arbuckle!" Maggie said with sudden recognition. "You're a regent. I hadn't realized... Oh, oh, and you're the generous donors for the Wind Museum." Looking at a smugly smiling Fern, she said, "You keep things close to the vest, don't you!" Looking back at Mr. Arbuckle and hoping she'd recovered her manners quickly enough, she said, "But how nice to finally meet you."

Fern was so unpretentious, and yet they were probably the wealthiest family on the South Plains, if not in most of Texas. Amazing.

Russell smiled and said, "I've heard good things from my Fernie about you, and from Monsignor Fitz. And Winston Whitaker thinks you're quite a smart woman. We 'preciate your sending Steven out to interview me about the museum gift. He did a some nice stories."

"It was our pleasure, Mr. Arbuckle," Maggie said, smiling. Then searching their faces, she tentatively asked, "I, um, I thought the article said your wife's name was Dorthea? Did we get it wrong?"

Fern smiled, but it was Russ who answered. "No, it is. Dorthea Fern Cavenaugh Arbuckle. But we're not that formal around these here parts. Fern is what everyone calls her and Russ is what everyone calls me, so please, no Mr. Arbuckle, if you don't mind. Just makes me feel old!" he said with a wink.

Maggie remembered Steven's article said he was 83, his wife 77.

"Thank you, Russ. And I'm Maggie."

"And we'll be late if we don't go in pretty soon," Fern said. "Monsignor likes to start on time, or is it Father Murphy today? Isn't he the best homilist? Just love his interpretations of scriptures. Oh, Maggie, we're starting another round of Bible study at the house this fall, after Labor Day and you're welcome to join us. I'll let you know the details, but we really must go in now, Russ, darlin'. See you later, Maggie."

"Yes, see you later, Fern. Nice to meet you Russ."

It *was* Father Murphy who celebrated that particular Mass, and once again Maggie lost herself in his thought-provoking sermon. Lately, she'd given fleeting thought to trying to attend the earlier Mass so she might see Colin—he was an early morning person, he'd said, and liked attending as the sun came up—but she thought it might be too forward of her, since the

10 a.m. service was her normal routine. Besides, after the physical work of the previous day, she was surprised she'd made it up in time for even this mid-morning service. She'd planned to spend the rest of the day unpacking a few more boxes, especially in the kitchen so she could start cooking, but her sore muscles and the hot weather made her think instead of a relaxing afternoon in the pool at the Nest. She opted for an hour in the pool and then went back to her own house to dig through more containers.

Chapter 36 ~

Her new house. It was the first one she had owned by herself, and she felt a mixture of pride and panic each time she crossed the threshold. Owning a house was a huge responsibility, but she felt up for the challenge. After all, she'd run their Dallas home alone for more than a year after Jim died. She could do this, especially since she loved the quaint house so much.

She was particularly pleased with the original stone fireplace—a real fireplace where she could burn real wood. Jim had hated the smell and mess of ashes, so they'd enjoyed the highest-priced artificial gas logs they could find—for both their living area and den. Gas logs were warm, but just not nearly as satisfying to Maggie as the real thing. She looked forward to the cold West Texas winter to try it out.

Getting rid of most of the furniture from her Dallas house had been a way to heal, and to not remember Jim quite as much, not that her heart still didn't hurt when she thought of him every day. But once she found the quaint house and completed the additions and renovations, she decided to furnish it completely opposite from what she'd lived with for the last 30 years. Out went the Martha Stewart everything-matched-and-everything-perfect style. In came odds and ends and interesting, comfortable things, like the lime green chair she'd found earlier in the summer.

Not that her Dallas house hadn't been comfortable. When the boys were young and Jim had made partner in the firm—youngest partner ever—they'd moved up from the old East Dallas neighborhood to the "right neighborhood."

Once they'd added the huge den and the clichéd paneled study for Jim, their two-story traditional home, complete with white-columned-front porch was better suited for entertaining Jim's clients and important members of the church. You just couldn't invite the Bishop over for dinner with mismatched chairs at the dining room table. Well, you could, but Jim wouldn't have liked it. So, they lived well, surrounded by designer furnishings, and they entertained fashionably.

But that was when Jim was alive and loving her and when her whole world revolved around him and the boys. Now he was gone, the boys were grown and she was on her own.

Over the next few weeks, Maggie and Sharon scoured the thrift stores, garage sales and flea markets for older pieces to be refinished, for comfortable chairs to be recovered, and for lots of little eclectic treasures like the wire shelf and the old game board now hanging in the hallway. Sharon refused to let her buy a second-hand couch for the living room, saying couches were like mattresses... you just didn't sleep on someone's discard. So Maggie found a lovely and expensive non-traditional sofa at one of Lubbock's finest furniture stores and was convinced to purchase the matching chair because it was on sale. Almost everything else, though, was second- or third-hand including a vintage Scotch cooler, red and black plaid, that she placed next to the new chair as an interesting side table. Her father had owned one decades ago.

The Disabled American Veterans Thrift Store provided most of her finds, but she'd bought a few pieces of quality furniture at Aunt Frances' estate sale. Some of them fit perfectly where they were, and nothing else seemed to work in those special places. Like the old telephone table sitting under the alcove at the end of the hallway. Maggie had stripped its well-worn painted finish and re-stained it.

And when she couldn't find just the right treasure to fill a wall space, she painted... something she hadn't done since before her older son Michael was born. Buying boards and canvas, she delighted in the stretching and priming, the wonder of a blank canvas filling her with both joy and terror.

Maggie had majored in art at Tech. Her undergraduate degree was in studio art with drawing as a minor. She actually was pretty good at it but slowly gave it up because "messy projects" in the house didn't work with two growing boys and so many obligations, and because the boys left her happily exhausted at the end of each day. There simply wasn't time in her life for painting or drawing.

The garage apartment of her new house was her first real studio. Ready to enjoy her wall of windows on the south side, she'd eagerly set up an easel, canvas and paints in the bright new room.

Curled up lazily next to the warm window, Maggie's new cat eyed her activity with interest. Maggie had posted signs in the neighborhood and the *A-J* for a week and received no word from a possible owner, so she had allowed the cat to move in. Because the tabby kept walking into the house with prissy little steps as though she already belonged, tail high in the air, Maggie called her Miss Priss.

The cat normally roamed the neighborhood by day. At night she nestled in a corner of the living room on a soft basket bed. Maggie was glad for the company and had Campos install a pet door in the back for Miss Priss' convenience. The cat had stepped through it the first time as if saying, "what took you so long?" Her steady diet, courtesy of her new owner, was showing in a fuller figure and shinier coat.

But Maggie had yet to pet her or pick her up. She'd tried a couple of times, wanting to take her to the vet for a checkup, but Miss Priss was having none of it, hissing at her and backing away. So, they had an unusual relationship—Maggie fed her and Miss Priss tolerated Maggie. It seemed to work for them both.

As Maggie picked up a paintbrush for the first time in more than three decades, she asked the cat what she thought. "Should I really do this?" Miss Priss turned her head away and closed her eyes, soaking up the sunshine. "Thanks for your help," Maggie said, staring at the blank canvas, wondering where to start.

She stopped again, suddenly remembering Sharon and Carol coming to Dallas about 18 years before. Marathon shopping and a late lunch at the Zodiac Room at the downtown Neiman Marcus was topped off by a visit to the Dallas Museum of Art. There was a special exhibit of works by members of the Wyeth family, favorites of theirs from college days.

Halfway through the exhibit Maggie fell apart. Overcome with emotion, she literally wept at the beauty of a John Kennedy portrait, so masterful was the younger Wyeth's genius of capturing the strength and vitality in the famous face. As she stood there, quietly sobbing, arms folded around herself, her friends were at a loss.

"Mags," Sharon said protectively putting her arm around her waist. "What is it? Are you ill? Do we need to leave?" Carol handed her tissues hastily retrieved from a purse. Maggie was unable to answer and continued crying quietly, staring at the portrait.

Truth was, she was ashamedly overcome with jealousy. Jealousy of these Wyeth men, that they had this enormous God-given talent and were allowed the freedom to show it to the world in all its glory.

She'd once had talent, or so her professors told her. She could get lost in a painting so quickly— shut out the world and revel in the magical realm of creating. But now it was buried inside her by life... by family... by obligations. Buried so deep she hadn't realized it was even there any more, still wanting to be used, to be allowed to emerge. For some mysterious reason, seeing this particular painting forced to the surface acknowledgement of her own talent. The recognition overflowed and took control of her emotions and actions. "I can do that," her head silently screamed at her. "Why can't I be allowed to do that?"

Desperately ashamed of her selfish and egotistical thoughts and her loss of control, she let her friends think she was simply overtired from volunteer work and taking care of her growing family. Sharon and Carol were worried because their normally unflappable friend was, well, "flapped," but no other logical explanation came to mind, and Maggie didn't enlighten them. She let them escort her protectively to the outside sculpture garden to compose herself, swearing them to secrecy about her breakdown. They had kept their pledge. She'd been grateful, and none of them mentioned it again. Until today.

Paintbrush still in hand, she called Carol and asked if she had time for a girl talk. Of course she did, was Carol's quick answer, and Maggie relayed the remembrance.

"Does it ring a bell?" Maggie asked tentatively.

"Absolutely it does," Carol said. "I didn't think you were really exhausted. I think you were wishing you had time to draw, to paint. You wanted to be able to show the world you had talent, too. Right?"

"How... how did you know?"

"Because I sort of felt the same way, that's why. Seems to me if God gives us talents and we discover what they are, we shouldn't waste them. You majored in art in college, I took some classes, and we were pretty damn good, weren't we?"

"We were. I especially remember the photo you showed me of your Lincoln portrait."

Carol continued, "But neither of us uses those drawing talents in our profession. And something else..."

"What's that?"

"We artistic types are an egotistical and competitive bunch and when someone gets recognition for something we think we might have been able to do, it rubs us the wrong way, no matter how nice we might be. So, I paint... and I do a lot of crafts, and enter all these women's group contests and local competitions... and rejoice a little each time someone admires what I do."

"Exactly! I, goodness, Carol, I should've known you'd understand. I didn't paint or draw after that but found a pretty good creative outlet. I went home that day feeling such a need to do something..."

In the days immediately following the museum visit, Maggie had taken action to remedy those needs. Late one evening after the boys were tucked in bed, she told Jim of her desire to go to work, of her need for an outlet for her creativity, even if it wasn't as an artist.

"The boys are in school," she had argued. "And I need to get out. I don't want to waste my education just being a social director for the Grant family." Jim was reluctant, as he enjoyed having her home to tend to all the activities of their lives. Everything was so orderly now.

"Let me find something I might like to do and try it for year," she pleaded, "and if it isn't working for everyone, I'll quit."

Although harboring serious reservations, he relented. A year later he had to admit things were just as orderly at home, even though she was busier. He was proud of her work in the Communications office at SMU, the boys were thriving, and she seemed to be handling it all quite well. And there was a glow about her he hadn't noticed since earlier in their marriage.

Little by little, Maggie incorporated her creativity into her work, taking over design of the university newsletters, organizing and decorating banquets and creating marketing plans. She'd even taken up writing and seemed to have a knack for it, remembering she'd actually enjoyed research paper assignments other students dreaded. Working with the media was a game to her, one she almost always won. She had made a quality career from the need to be creative.

"So, Carol, my dear friend, I'm about ready to start again, painting, that is. I'm just scared to death I'm not as good as I think I am... or was."

"Truly good artists never think they're as good as they are... not even the greats. Michelangelo doubted his Piéta, remember?"

"Yeah, but his work I'm not jealous of. Just in awe!"

"Me, too, Maggie. But go for it. Can't wait to see what you do. Take pics and e-mail 'em. And have fun!"

So, now, back in her light-filled studio, she tentatively took brush in hand and began outlining a giant flower on a six-foot square canvas. Standing back to analyze it after a few carefully laid strokes, she decided it wasn't half bad... not half bad at all. She painted with more boldness, spending the rest of the afternoon immersed in paint and hope. She hung the still-wet canvas in her living area and sighed with contentment. "Great therapy," she said out loud. "Must buy more canvasses."

The joyful struggle of creating, though, was in direct opposition to the painful struggles of her work at the university.

Chapter 37 ~

With her new house only two blocks south of campus, she could comfortably walk to work, and often did, including this already hot late August morning. Reaching the office, thankful for air conditioning, she found Jonathan Long, Boyle's second in command, outside her door, pacing the hallway.

"Jonathan," she said as he noticed her. "What a nice surprise." Looking at his frown, she quickly said, "What's wrong?"

"Wrong?" he said hurriedly as she unlocked the doors and he followed her into her office almost stepping on her heels as he went. "Nothing. Everything. Just the usual chaos from Boyle. He called me late last night, woke the baby for God's sake, and demanded I have this report ready for him to look at by 9 this morning. I'm telling you, Maggie, the man's a tyrant! And he's gotten worse now that Parker got the presidency he wanted. He's driving me to distraction, not that he wasn't doing that already, mind you."

"So how can I help, Jonathan?" Maggie interrupted, amazed any human could talk as fast as this one did.

"Oh, yes. The report is done, but I need you to look at it for coherence. I'm not sure it makes sense, and you're good at being objective. Will you look at it for me? I brought it on a flash drive." He handed the blue flash drive to Maggie who plugged it into her computer. He continued, "Stayed up most of the night getting it done. I swear, since Stone left and Boyle threw Miss Katherine away, it's been harder and harder to know what the man wants. Sometimes I think even he doesn't know what he wants. And then that mess with that girl he brought from HR. Now he doesn't even have a secretary and uses mine or Nancy from the president's office. Guess word got around how difficult he is and nobody who is even remotely qualified wants the job... can't say as I blame them... wonder myself why I stay, but the wife..."

"Jonathan," Maggie interrupted again. "Sit down and give me time to go over this report if it's due by nine."

"Oh, yes, of course. Sorry. I've a tendency to ramble."

She smiled and thought 'yes, you do.' They spent the next 45 minutes working to rearrange sentences and paragraphs, adding and deleting enough information to make a quality report, one she knew Boyle couldn't dispute.

Jonathan called later to thank her, saying Boyle had approved it immediately. Maggie thought it a good thing Jonathan hadn't told the idiot she'd helped. Work was getting to be more than a pain... it was getting harder to get the work done at all with Boyle's constant ignorant interference. As settled in as she was, she hoped this wasn't as good as it was going to get, because she knew it could be so much better... and so much easier for all at the university.

While she pondered her growing frustration, Jonathan interrupted, almost in a whisper, "Um, Maggie, I think I need to see you about something else. Do you have time?"

"Of course, Jonathan. Come on up or do you want me to come down?"

"I think I'd better come to your office. Be there as soon as I can slip away." He hung up and Maggie wondered what that was all about. He sounded more nervous than usual.

Five minutes later he was standing in front of her desk. He had closed her office door behind him. She looked at him questioningly.

"Now don't go getting all mad or anything, Maggie, because you're not supposed to see this... but I thought you should." He handed her a piece of paper he took out of his leather folder.

"What is it?" Maggie said, taking the page. She scanned it quickly, then looked up at him in astonishment. "Who wrote this?" she said quietly, trying to contain her fury.

"Boyle said President Parker wrote it and I was to send it out to media without telling you," Jonathan said with obvious guilt.

"Without telling me? Why? I don't understand? Our department writes news releases and sends them out and this... this is drivel. No newspaper worth its salt would publish something this mundane. Certainly not the *AJ*. What in the world is he thinking?"

Maggie reread the short paragraph, an extremely unprofessional excuse for a news release stating that President Parker had met two weeks ago with the local chapter of the Tech alumni association, which wasn't even named correctly. Attached was a badly centered photo of the president shaking hands with a person whose back was to the camera. There was no caption for the rather blurry snapshot.

"I don't know," Jonathan said apologetically. "All I do know is when I turned in the report this morning to Boyle, I was directed to obtain a media list from your office so I could send this out... and I was not to show it to you. And Boyle said Parker would be writing all his own news releases from now on and wanted this to appear all over the state."

"Well, that's not going to happen. Fact one: No reporter is going to write about a routine meeting that happened two weeks ago. Fact two: It is definitely not news. There's nothing in it readers will care about. Where's the hook? The interesting action? Space is money, and newspapers won't waste their space for something as routine as this. Fact three: The photo is terrible and without proper id. Fact four: Why the heck didn't he tell us about the meeting beforehand so we could find some angle to pitch it with if he wanted publicity? Was there an alum there Parker went to high school with? Did they present him with a donation for one of Tech's good causes? Did he make any statements about his vision for the university? Tell them anything new and exciting?" Maggie's voice was getting louder now and Jonathan closed his eyes. "This release tells me nothing!"

"I'm sorry, Maggie," he said sheepishly. "But can I have the media list?"

"No, Jonathan, you can't. I'll go talk to Boyle right now," she said determinedly, getting up and moving to the door.

"Maggie, wait," Jonathan pleaded. "He'll kill me!"

Maggie stopped, took a deep breath and handed the paper back to him.

"Sorry. You're right. I'll let you go back to your office. Then I will calmly go see our esteemed Mr. Boyle and ask why you need the media list. I'll feign ignorance of the news release and take it from there. I promise you won't be blamed, Jonathan. And thank you for showing it to me."

Thirty minutes later, a much calmer Maggie stepped unannounced into Boyle's office. He glanced up, surprised, the usual scowl on his face. "What do you want?" he said, looking back down at the papers on his desk and rubbing his forehead.

"Excuse me, Mr. Boyle," Maggie said in her best professional manner, "But we were asked to provide our media list to Jonathan Long's office and I wondered why? If you have something you need to send out, my office is more than happy to do that for you."

He looked up at her suspiciously, but could detect no malice. "We just need the list, that's all," he said, hoping that might pacify her, but knowing it wouldn't.

"What for? Perhaps we can assist with whatever you need it for and make it easier to accomplish. We are..."

He put down his pen as if exasperated and looked at her. "If you must know, President Parker has decided to send out his own news releases and wants to bypass Communications. That's why I need the list." He shifted self-satisfactorily, as if he knew it would wound her.

"I see. May I ask why he wants to bypass the university's department of professional communicators?" Maggie asked, trying to control her temper.

"Because he doesn't like you, that's why."

That was the last thing Maggie expected to hear. She was dumbfounded. "Doesn't like me? How can he not like me? He hasn't even met me!"

"He just doesn't. Doesn't think you're doing a good job, so he's writing all his own releases. Send the media list to Long's office as directed," he said briskly.

Maggie involuntarily reached up and twisted her hair, coming to a decision. She stood straight, almost at attention and said firmly but calmly, "No, I won't, sir. If the president wants news releases sent out, my office is the best place to handle them. We have contacts all over the state and can make calls... and... Do you have a press release he wants sent out? May I see it?"

Boyle looked at her a long moment. Then he opened a file and gave her a copy of what Jonathan had shown her earlier. She read it again and sighed. "Mr. Boyle." He didn't look up, but continued his work. She sat down directly in front of him and repeated a little louder, "Mr. Boyle. This is not in standard release form, there's a mistake in it, there is no university logo, there is no contact information, no photo caption or I.D., and nothing that any newspaper would print. It's not really news, and it's two weeks old. No one will print it."

He put his pen down again and looked at her hard. "He wants it in newspapers all over the state. He wants it sent out today. He doesn't want you to make any changes in it. Send it out as it is."

"But if we send it out, it reduces our credibility with the media. They will not only ignore this, but they will ignore future releases we send out that *do* contain something worth printing. We'll be wasting their time and they won't appreciate it. Let me talk with President Parker so I can convince him how wrong this is."

"Do you want to keep your job, Mrs. Grant?" Boyle said sternly and loudly, staring at her hard. Maggie was silent. "Then send it out! And bring me a list of who it went to. Do NOT contact or bother the president! Out!"

Maggie returned dejectedly to her office where she instructed her crew to send out the news release, but to call all the media outlets first and apologize.

That night, over a large glass of sorrow-drowning wine, Maggie and Sharon discussed the serious implications of the afternoon's encounter with Boyle.

"But you can't trust Boyle," Sharon said. "Maybe he's setting you up."

"Setting me up? How?"

"I don't know how, but no matter what you do, you're damned-if-you-do and damned-if-you-don't. Send out the crappy releases and lose credibility with the media and never again get anything good published. Don't send out the crappy releases, and lose your job."

Maggie sighed, "Definitely not good in either case."

"Parker can't be that stupid, can he?" Sharon asked.

"How would I know? I've never even met the man. Maybe I should just give up and move back to Dallas."

"What? No way, Maggie Grant. We're not the giving-up type of women. And you're not... repeat NOT... moving back to Dallas. Besides, as much as I hate conspiracy theories, I think I smell a big conspiracy here. I think Boyle is flat out lying."

"You may be right. Maybe I should do a little investigating before I put the house up for sale," Maggie said only half-kiddingly.

Over the course of the next week, Boyle called every day to see where the article appeared. The only place the information ran was in the local alumni association newsletter and they misspelled the president's name. Most likely because their organization's name was misspelled in the release.

Maggie put in a discreet call to her counterpart at the University of Illinois, President Parker's last place of employment. What she learned made her decide to stay in Lubbock and duke it out with Boyle.

~ Part II ~ Hearts To Be Broken ~

Chapter 38 ~

"It's another damn news release from the president," Steven said as he stomped into his boss's office. Working carefully, Maggie had managed to avoid further explosive encounters with her boss for a few weeks. He'd sent up two other nonsensical news releases purportedly from President Parker, each badly written and poorly constructed.

"Send it out, but apologize again first."

Maggie's staff dutifully sent out the bad releases, but with discreet apologies, and newspapers across the state dutifully ignored them. Maggie documented every directive from Boyle and every action by her staff—except the apologies. And she waited patiently for her chance to turn things around. She was too committed to quality communications to let an idiot like Boyle do harm to the university she loved. With a good staff, with supportive friends, and an increasingly interesting personal life, she could afford to bide her time.

If their busy schedules permitted, Maggie and Colin were seeing each other at least once a week, for dinner or a movie or a trip to the Cactus Theatre downtown to take in a live show. One night she'd invited him for a light supper and a movie she'd rented. He'd laughed heartily when she put on James Cagney in *G-Men*, a 1936 black and white film. Often they met just to talk about their days, enjoying each others company, as two old friends might. It was all casual and comfortable.

A favorite place of theirs was the J&B Coffeehouse, 26th Street and Boston. With the typical mishmash of furniture in small intimate seating groups, free Wi-Fi, and great coffee, it was a comfortable hangout for students as well as professors. This particular weeknight, she sipped her honey-almond tea as she waited for him. Normally punctual, tonight he was running about 20 minutes late. Had she gotten the time or place wrong?

Her cell phone rang and it was Colin apologizing, saying he'd gotten caught up in his work at the shop. Would she like to meet him there? He still wasn't finished for the evening, and she could see his latest project. She took her tea to go as well as his usual coffee with cream and drove to the west side of campus.

She wasn't sure exactly what she'd expected, but this well-lit workshop was huge, the smell of fresh-cut wood mixed pleasantly with aromas of coffee, glue and sweat. Three students were in their respective workstations, concentrating on drawings or fitting pieces together on their latest projects. Colin, his back to her, was in the far corner that held a large drawing board, tacked-up blueprints, and a half-completed dresser, which he was sanding by hand. He was covered in sweat and sawdust, even though the air conditioning seemed to be working fine.

Maggie stood there and watched him work a few minutes, not wanting to disturb his intense concentration. Finally, he stopped and ran a hand over the corner he'd been working on, moving around to the other side of the piece, seemingly satisfied those three square inches were smooth enough.

He saw her and smiled, "Hi," he said, walking toward her and placing a light kiss on her cheek, raising eyebrows from his students. If he noticed their interest, it didn't show.

"Sorry about this, but I couldn't get myself to a stopping point and lost track of the time. Oh. You brought coffee. Thanks," he said as he took it from her, tasting.

"Not a problem, Murphy. This is beautiful work," she said admiring the craftsmanship of the five-foot high oak dresser with multiple drawer openings. "You're making yourself furniture?"

"No. It's... it's not for me." When she raised her eyes questioningly, he shrugged, "My mom asked me to make it for dad, for his birthday in December, so I'm taking the opportunity to do it here while using it for demonstration purposes for my students. I buy all the wood, and most of the tools are my personal ones, so it's kosher to use the space.

"Anyway, I need to get it finished and sent to Chicago, but it'll take me until Thanksgiving at least to get it done. I'm way behind. Haven't even started on the drawers yet. Was planning on doing most of it those two weeks in July, but... well, you know."

"It's beautiful. I'm sure he'll love it." She walked around it admiring the workmanship and then noticed the drawings on the wall next to the drafting table. "These the plans for it?"

"They are," he said, taking another sip of coffee. "I make the kids create complete blueprints for their projects, so thought I needed to do that myself."

"They're quite accomplished drawings, Murphy. The perspective, the detail. It's remarkable for someone without a degree in art or design. Maybe you should've gone into that in college instead of law?" she asked in all seriousness. How could he have ignored this talent when he was younger, she thought, and then realized she'd done the same thing... ignored her art to raise a family.

"And miss all the fun of hunting down the bad guys?" he laughed but then turned serious. "No, I'm content to do this now—at this stage in my life. I needed those years of adventure and movement. I don't think I would've been happy teaching and staying in one place when I was younger. There's so much of the country and the world to see. I needed to see it, and I did."

Maggie smiled at this new insight. He was indeed an interesting man, and she was enjoying the new friendship. It was a friendship, wasn't it? It certainly wasn't a romantic relationship, she mused. He's never offered more than a quick soft kiss goodnight—and for now that suited her just fine. She wasn't sure what she would do if it headed to something less platonic. Yet, the desire was certainly there. It was just pushed to the side while she got to know more about him... and about herself. It was comfortable, and she liked comfortable almost as much as Colin Murphy.

Chapter 39 ~
Early Fall

Doug led Sharon and Maggie through the excited crowd, which got louder the closer they got to Jones Stadium at the northeast corner of campus. One of the first orders of business when she'd arrived last spring was to purchase a football season ticket next to Sharon and Doug's usual seats. Deciding to walk the mile from Maggie's house to the stadium, knowing it would be quicker than fighting traffic in and around campus on the day of the first home game, they were caught up in the enthusiasm as soon as they stepped on campus. The Goin' Band from Raider Land marched smartly across campus with throngs of cheering, hopeful red-and-black-clad fans following in their wake, Maggie, Sharon and Doug included.

This was the first game Maggie had attended since her college days and she wondered if the magic would still be there. The ever-changing West Texas weather had cooperated, and the forecast was for sunshine and clear skies into the evening hours. The game was scheduled to start in early afternoon, but it should still be light when it was over and warm enough to leave jackets at home.

As they were crossing Memorial Circle, Maggie looked once again at the Will Rogers statue. Late Thursday evening, Saddle Tramps had wrapped the legendary man and horse in flowing red crepe paper, covering them head to hoof without so much as an inch of bronze showing. It was a tradition begun after her graduation, and yesterday she had stood by her office window to admire the transformed statue and watch Saddle Tramps, posted at each campus entrance, hand out red and black streamers for entering cars. They were fulfilling their roles as spirit leaders.

Steven had walked in at that point and she remarked on the Will Rogers' wrapping.

"Yeah, it makes for great pictures. We just hope it doesn't rain between Thursday nights and game times," he said with a smile. "When wet, crepe paper can get pretty ugly pretty fast."

"Do they always use red?" Maggie asked.

"For games, yes. But they wrap it in black for special mourning events, like the campus shooting at Virginia Tech. It really symbolizes the mood."

"And no one ever messes with it? I vaguely remember Will being splashed one year with maroon paint when the Aggies came to town, but that was a long time ago."

"Nope. Saddle Tramps guard it 24/7 along with the Masked Rider statue closer to Jones Stadium, and of course the real Raider horse. No pranks in at least a decade, although I'm sure it's not for lack of trying by some rival teams."

Once in their seats near the south 35-yard line, Maggie scanned the crowds behind them for Colin and Sean. Monsignor Fitzpatrick was probably at the game also, more than likely in a luxury suite high above the masses with one of the wealthier parishioners. Being a part of the crowd in the open air was more appealing to the Murphy brothers, who also had season tickets. Maggie had agreed with them wholeheartedly and settled into the crowd, happy to be part of the enthusiastic unwashed public.

Still not seeing the brothers, she left her seat to find the nearest corny dog stand. She hadn't had one since July the Fourth, and she hoped the stadium corn dogs were as good as she remembered from years ago, or at least as good as the ones from the street fair.

Concession stand lines were long, but moving quickly. At the counter, Maggie was pleasantly surprised to see Fern Arbuckle on the other side, sprightly stepping to fill orders. For a small lady in her late 70s, Fern was surprisingly quick, much like Jonathan Long, Boyle's assistant, but in a calmer manner.

Maggie gave Fern her order and asked about Russ. "He's up in our suite with Tom, Julie and the boys," Fern said. Then to Maggie's questioning look she added, smiling conspiratorially, "I don't really care for football, but I love the excitement and the kids, so I volunteer at the concession counter while he talks football with the guys. It's great fun. That'll be seven bucks, please!"

Maggie returned to her seat to find Colin standing talking to Doug. Turning, he smiled at her, then noticed her partially-eaten corny dog. "You really like those things, don't you?" He pulled a napkin from her hand, reaching up to gently wipe away a spot of mustard from the corner of her mouth.

Sharon noted the gesture seemed natural for both of them, as if they had been together for years. Interesting, she thought, tucking that piece of information away for later exploration.

Maggie had eaten half of the corny dog already and swallowed her mouthful before answering in the affirmative. "Love 'em. Where're your seats?" she asked.

"Three rows up and in the next section over. Why not come up for a bit?" he asked hopefully. "Sean's not here yet. Should be along mid-quarter, though."

Pleased with the invitation, Maggie looked questioningly at Sharon, who said, "Go ahead. We'll see you when the priest kicks you out."

It was closer to the middle of the second quarter when Father Sean finally showed up, and Maggie had spent nearly an hour comfortably next to Colin, enjoying the game, joining in the singing of the school alma mater, cheering the Red Raider black stallion racing across the field, and whooping with the crowd for the two Tech touchdowns. She also groaned at the two touchdowns and a field goal scored by the opponent. But there was plenty of time, and Tech had one heck of an offensive passing game. But mainly she was enjoying being with Colin, and marveled at how relaxed she felt.

One of the long-standing traditions at Tech football games was the Saddle Tramp participation before and during the games. She craned her neck to spot the two Tramps she knew, Jamie and Josh, and found them easily among the red-shirted men on the field. They rang their cowbells as the team entered the field through the traditional Bell Circle. Standing at attention, they then led the students and fans in the Tech Alma Mater, guns up, a tradition that began just after Maggie, Carol and Sharon graduated. The Raider Red mascot carried a six-shooter, so the Guns Up sign—thumb and forefinger extended in a pistol shape—was Tech's answer to the rival University of Texas' Hook 'em Horns sign.

As the band was leaving the field, Saddle Tramps fanned out to the sidelines to toss miniature red Tech footballs into the crowd, a tradition newly revisited from decades before.

Maggie stood, ready to catch one, but they weren't coming anywhere near their section. "Will you reach for one if it's close, Murphy?" she asked.

He laughed. "I would, but the guys know where my seats are and make it a game to not throw any this way. They think it's hilarious that I've never caught one in all these years."

"Poor thing," she said feigning pity. "I caught one more than three decades ago. Want me to dig it out of storage for you?"

"Thanks, but I can live without one... Threw them way back in the dark ages, did they? Ooff!" he cried as Maggie elbowed his side in reply.

"Colin, do you know why they're called Saddle Tramps?"

"I do," he answered. She looked at him expectantly, but he was silent, ignoring her.

Stomping her foot, she cried, "Murphy! Tell me why they're called Saddle Tramps!"

"Oh, you wanted to know why? I thought you just wanted to know if I knew," he teased.

She readied her elbow again, but he quickly said, "Mercy, woman! I'll tell you."

"Today would be good, Professor," she said as she sat down with the crowd to await the impending kickoff.

"Saddle Tramps were started in 1936 by student Arch Lamb. He was a cheerleader and along with two others conceived the organization to channel students' sometimes overly exuberant and unruly nature into more positive and productive activities. They thought the school needed a men's organization to boost school spirit. It has grown in to a school spirit and service organization."

"And the name, Murphy?"

"Oh, yes. Early Texas ranchers would hire a nomad saddle tramp for his ability and willingness to tackle any task assigned. Then the tramp would move on after a while, having done all he could to contribute to the improvement of the ranch. That's why Lamb named the group as he did. Saddle Tramps would be hard workers when in school at Tech, moving on after their college years were done."

"That fits," Maggie said. "Sounds like you recited it, though. Did you?"

"Most of it directly from the Tramp's website." He shrugged, "I have this extremely non-useful talent of being able to memorize text after only one or two readings and recall it at will."

"Non-useful? You're kidding, right? Didn't it help in school?" Maggie asked, immediately jealous of his peculiar talent.

"Oh, yeah, absolutely, and at other times later, but not much need for it now. Anyway, that's the history. Let's see, the website also says," he put his hand over his heart, sitting up straight, "'Saddle Tramps attend all men's home football, basketball and baseball games. Our primary focus remains to further the spirit and uphold the traditions of Texas Tech University. Some of the traditions that we uphold are: Raider Red–the mascot–Wrapping of Will Rogers and Midnight Raiders, Homecoming Bonfire and Parade, Bell Circles, Victory Bells, Shotguns, UT/A&M Watch, Carol of Lights, Bangin' Bertha–the traveling bell–and many more. Along with attending sports games, Saddle Tramps are also very involved in the Lubbock community by helping out with several local charities and... and'... oh, yes, 'philanthropy events annually.' Probably should be philanthropic."

"Fascinating," Maggie said, laughing.

"Yeah, they're a great bunch of guys. I enjoy working with 'em."

"No, I mean that you can memorize like that..." she said, shaking her head.

Colin shrugged as he stood with the crowd for the kickoff.

Chapter 40 ~

By the time Father Sean arrived and she returned to her own seat, Maggie was stuffed with half of a second corny dog. Midway through devouring it, Colin, who had consumed his own dog in record time, eyed hers saying, "You gonna eat the rest of that?" She laughed and gave it up happily, knowing the calories would be distributed better on his large frame than on hers.

At the end of the game, a narrow victory for Tech, Sharon and Doug asked the twin brothers to join them for a late casual dinner at the Nest, but Sean begged off, saying his sermon wasn't quite ready for the next morning. Colin accepted, though, and walked with them as far as the Administration Building before heading in the other direction to his truck. They passed the tower where the victory bells were ringing, and would continue for thirty minutes, two Saddle Tramps fulfilling the duty call.

Once at home, Maggie waited for Colin to get through traffic while her friends went to the Nest to light up the grill. She also fed Miss Priss.

This time, Colin's truck was fairly clean on the outside and still pristine on the inside. Maggie climbed in, directing him to the home on 19th Street, on the way answering his query as to why her friends called it the Nest.

"Sharon's mom is an avid birdwatcher," she explained. "Spends every spare moment with the Houston Audubon Society, looking through binoculars to find and confirm new sightings, traveling to exotic places around the world hoping to discover new species. Mrs. Phelps' home is filled with everything birds, from photos to cutely decorated birdhouses, with expensive porcelain bird figurines on every possible flat surface." Old nests and jeweled birds with bright colors were the decorations for the family Christmas trees, and their back yard was the feeding station for hundreds of migrating species that enjoyed the pounds of birdseed put out each week, even though the Audubon Society frowned on the practice.

Sharon had grown up in the world of Audubon, and although she loved birds, too, she refused to decorate their Lubbock house with them, Maggie explained. There was only one small bird feeder on the premises sporadically refilled by Doug.

At Christmas, birthdays and on her infrequent visits, Sharon's mother inevitably presented bird-themed gifts, but they were all put away somewhere in the attic, gathering dust. To pacify his pseudo-mother-in-law, Doug started calling their home the Nest—a cozy, comfortable place to come home to after a busy day flying around campus, he'd told her.

"That makes no sense," Colin said. "I mean, how does that pacify the mother?"

"You're right, it doesn't make sense. But some things about Sharon and Doug you just have to accept without questioning. Maybe Mrs. Phelps gets some satisfaction thinking of birds whenever they mention their Nest? I've no idea... you'd have to ask Sharon, or Doug, or Mrs. Phelps, though she rarely visits since her husband died about five years ago," she said, shaking her head. "Oh, and never bring Doug or Sharon anything to do with birds. I made that mistake once—found a great Audubon print... just a small one for Christmas one year. Sharon was speechless, but apparently not from joy. Never hung it up, at least not in any place where I've ever seen it. Probably in the attic, also gathering dust."

"So... references to our fine feathered friends are out?'

"Absolutely."

"No, 'birds of a feather flock together.'"

Maggie grinned, "No, definitely not."

"A bird in the hand is worth two in the bush?"

"No!"

"How about 'The early bird catches the worm'? 'As the crow flies?'" he continued.

"No!" Maggie said, giggling. "That's enough."

"'One swallow does not a summer make?'"

"Stop!" Maggie said, stomping her foot and laughing.

"Wise as an owl. Naked as a jaybird. Sitting duck?"

"Stop, Colin!" she sputtered.

"Out on a lark? A feather in your cap? Eagle eye?"

She was clutching her stomach and laughing hard. "Colin, please!" she begged between gasping breaths. "It hurts!"

"Okay, I forgot your penchant for splitting your sides. I'll stop," he said with a straight face.

Maggie took deep breaths and composed herself, or at least tried to until he added, "Guess my goose would be cooked if I tweeted more, huh, Grant?" She was too far away to elbow him, but vowed revenge.

Casual dinner for Doug meant thick grilled steaks and baked potatoes, with juicy grilled corn on the cob. Luckily, it wasn't ready until late in the evening, so the corny dogs were no longer an issue, and they all ate as if famished. Settling comfortably around the pool after dinner, they talked of Tech and their different departments—Music, Engineering, Communications and Design. Comparing challenges, Maggie won the prize for having the most difficult boss, an honor she was not pleased to accept, but nevertheless did.

Lately, though, her new way to work was sort of working, except that she still had no access to the new president.

Chapter 41 ~

Last night's weather forecast predicted rain in late afternoon, and Maggie was glad she'd listened and brought her umbrella to work today. Dark clouds rolling in from the southwest were starting to spit as she headed home through the Administration Building parking lot. She sneezed, her nose stuffed and irritated from a slight cold she was trying to shake. The wind kicked up and the rain came harder. Even if she hurried, she'd be soaked by the time she walked all the way home, and that wouldn't help her cold. Should she turn around and go back to her office?

She decided to wait out the storm at the SUB or the library, both closer now than the Admin Building. She opted for the library. Earlier that afternoon, she and Ricky had worked on the design of a brochure and neither thought the typestyles available to them were exactly what they were looking for. Maggie envisioned a classic typeface she couldn't recall the name of, and told Ricky she'd look it up. Here was her chance to do that research while waiting for the storm to pass.

She hurried up the library steps and closed her dripping umbrella as she entered the terrazzo-tiled foyer. Designed in the late 1950s, the university library was an anomaly among ornate campus buildings—the architecture was not much more than a huge rectangular box set up on a smaller box of windows serving as the ground floor. The façade was a series of tall white stone arches reaching from the ground to the top floor across all four sides. Each six-story, narrow arch framed sunscreens made from thousands of 8-by-8-inch red clay octagonal cylinders stacked horizontally, set back close to the windows and walls on all four sides of the building.

Presumably, supervising architect Nolan Barrick was "modernizing" the distinct Spanish-Renaissance style of the main campus buildings, but Maggie had read a history of campus buildings where Barrick said the stark geometric form was simply a result of "a spectacular increase in enrollment coupled with severe limitations on funding for required expansion of facilities. Building costs became the major controlling factor, and continuity of character in newer structures through the use of similar materials rather than traditional forms was necessitated."

Maggie thought it was his way of apologizing for the building that looked so out of place. She wished they had found the money to stay true to the classical architecture of the Memorial Circle area. One thing was certain, area birds loved the horizontal cylinders as they made for perfect houses. Sharon's mother would no doubt be in favor of that.

The library's interior hadn't changed much since her days as a student, either, at least not the large east entrance with its sunken fountain and study areas, still crowded with comfortable black leather reading chairs.

Maggie was pleased to see plastic umbrella bags available for patrons, and took advantage of one as she entered. When wet, the marble floors were definitely slippery.

Still on the ground floor, Maggie headed for a computer rather than the old manual card catalog, which was nowhere to be found. She missed the sturdy, beautifully made catalog cabinets with their multitude of small, narrow drawers and brass hooked pulls. These days, card catalog cabinets were mainly found in antique stores, the price tags normally too high for her consideration. Maybe the thrift store might get one in. She could always ask to be called if one was donated. They might not ask as much as an antique shop, and a cabinet like that would be great for her studio. Maybe she could commission Colin to make something similar for her when he finished his father's gift?

Her brief computer search revealed several books about typefaces and settings on Stack Level 5, under Z. Maggie wondered if that meant the subject was not as important as those listed earlier in the alphabet. Not really understanding the logic of the Dewey Decimal System, she didn't have an answer. But she was glad someone at least considered typography interesting enough to write a few books on it, no matter where they were shelved.

The west elevators, still located in the east part of the building but facing west, took her to the sixth floor, or seventh, depending on whether you counted the administrative mezzanine as a floor—the first floor was labeled G for Ground floor. However it was labeled, Stack Level 5 was still the top floor, and offered a spectacular, if limited view of the campus. The thousands of shallow cylinders on the façade broke the landscape into small segments with rounded edges, like looking through hundreds of ineffective telescopes. Maggie had seen some interesting student photos utilizing this unusual architectural feature.

Many of the stacks, or shelves in Stack Level 5 were moveable, another innovation in the last decade or so. All books were there as promised, but not visible at the same time, because shelves could be moved, separating or collapsing aisles, allowing for more stacks when needed in the limited space of a still growing library. Stacks, or bookcase shelves, were made of metal and sat about two inches up off the original floor, raised on metal tracks, with hinges on top of each shelf to help open or close the stacks. Presumably more hinges were attached at the bottom, but they were hidden by the raised platform floor where metal tracks were evenly spaced to move the rolling shelves. Walking from the rows at the ends of the stacks required a half step up to the raised aisles.

Z — let's see, turn north, U, V, farther back... ah, there, Z. In the farthest northwest corner, after 37 stacks, Maggie found the right area, but the stacks she needed were compressed. Control panels stated whether it was safe to move the huge bookcases, obviously triggered by some sensor to keep the shelves from shifting if obstructions were in the aisles—such as students. Good thing, she mused, as crushed students would make for unwanted headlines. Following the arrows on the controls, she easily manipulated a stack to the left to open an aisle. The movement, preceded by a single ping, was barely audible, suitably quiet for its environment, and made Maggie marvel at the wonders of technology.

Typography—at the northern-most end of the stack. She chose a few books, noticing the numerous signs posted imploring patrons "Do not reshelve books." She took her bounty to a nearby table next to the north windows and settled in for a leisurely journey into all things Gutenberg while she waited out the storm. Wonder what the inventor of moveable type would think of moveable book shelves?

It was then she noticed just how quiet it was up on Stack Level 5. Was she the only one up here? With stacks pushed against each other, her line of sight was limited to the ends of the shelves, the few tables around her and an exit door behind her she assumed opened to stairs. She hadn't seen anyone during the book search, nor did she remember hearing anyone. The elevator was quite a distance away, yet in this silence she certainly could have heard it open if, in fact, it did. "Eerie," she said out loud. "Bet it's not quiet like this during finals week."

Returning to her books, she searched for the next twenty minutes and found several examples of what she wanted to show Ricky. Marking pages with scraps of paper, she took them to the copier at the other end of the floor, next to the elevators, and decreased her Red Raider account card by several dollars. After checking on the weather, she returned to her table. It was still pouring, so she decided to look more closely at "The Typographic Book 1450-1935," published in 1965. The largest book she had pulled from the shelves at almost tabloid size, it contained fold-out copies of type used by Gutenberg himself, looking like well-scripted calligraphy.

Fifteenth-century illuminations gracing the pages were captivating, and Maggie recalled a study of illuminations she'd made for one of her master's classes. It had been, as Jim quipped after reading it, "Quite an illuminating paper." She smiled as she thought of him and then suddenly turned her attention to her right as she heard a noise. She thought the exit door in the southwest corner closed, or was it a stack being moved? She heard nothing else. No footsteps, no shuffling of papers.

Probably some student who'd fallen asleep and just left quietly. Tables were placed on the south wall, too, close to the other stairs. A great place to nap. Although the sudden noise had startled her, hearing nothing else she quickly dismissed it and returned to her treasure.

She read, *"Letter forms may well begin with geometry, but only the sovereignty of eye and hand can transmute a diagram into a work of art."* That's what Colin does with his blueprints for furniture, she thought. Even if he didn't build the pieces, the blueprints would be works of art in and of themselves. I wonder if he realizes he's an artist in that respect? She sat back, thinking of him, picturing him tall and all masculine, sweating in his workshop over a chair or bench he had designed, sans shirt, of course, blueprints on the wall next to where he worked. With a decided smirk, she thought maybe he just might let me watch him work. Or even let me sketch him working.

Goodness, I'm getting sidetracked. As my son would say, I'm too old for that sort of thing, but gracious, the man is definitely all man. Maggie sighed, trying to ignore the sudden sensations deep inside and forced her attention back to the book. She resumed exploring each page with the thrill of discovery.

Several minutes later, she was startled from the silence again as the elevator dinged. She heard the doors open and then close as a squeaking sound headed her way, stopping, then starting again, and stopping, starting, again and again. Within two minutes, a pimple-faced young student came into view, pushing an ancient squeaky-wheeled library cart filled with books. Obviously, WD-40 was in short supply.

He looked startled to see her, but smiled shyly, then shrugged at the nearest "Do not reshelve books" sign, and disappeared down an aisle, apparently attending to the proper placement in the Dewey Decimal System, noisy wheels notwithstanding.

Hunger made her stomach growl, so she decided it was time to head home before it got dark. Maggie glanced out the window again. "Yep, still raining buckets," she said to the walls. "At least I have an umbrella." She'd probably be soaked by the time she got home, but she *had* accomplished her research. And she was hungry.

After putting the copies for Ricky in her briefcase, she picked up her books and moved toward the stack, then remembering the signs, turned back around to leave them on the table. I guess it's job security for the students, or else they just don't think patrons are smart enough to put books back where they got them. Now that I think about it, most libraries ask the same. But with a reminder every two feet on the walls, it seems a little like overkill. Oh, well. Saves me the trouble.

Just as she placed her books back on the table, she heard a crash. Turning to face the stacks, she heard, "No, no... um, help? HELP!"

"I'm coming!" Maggie yelled as she hurriedly zig-zagged through the aisles, turning up one row, down the next aisle and up another row. "Where are you?"

At the opposite side of the floor she found the young student librarian standing stock still against the south wall, dropped books at his feet, one hand over his mouth, the other clutching the book cart, looking wide-eyed at the ceiling.

"What?" she said as she, too, looked up. Dark gray smoke was rolling along the ceiling, appearing to come from the center of several stacks that had been moved together. "Fire!" she yelled at the boy, as she became acutely aware of the distinctive smell despite her stuffy nose.

"Where's the fire extinguisher?" He didn't move or speak. "Go get help! Use the stairs and go get help!" she said, pushing him toward the southwest stairs. She quickly moved down the row next to the wall. Where is it? Is there no sprinkler system? Of course, not... it's a library... it would ruin everything... there has to be an extinguisher... there it is!

Opening the small bright red door, Maggie grabbed the canister of fire suppressant and headed back to the stacks, smoke now threatening to come down the side walls. The pungent smell was becoming overpowering.

She pushed aside her panic as she hit the control of the outside stack, knowing she would have to move them in succession to get to the middle where she thought the fire was—at least that's where the smoke seemed to be thickest. Nothing. It didn't move. Was it stuck? She set the extinguisher down and pushed, but the shelf didn't budge. I can't get to the fire, she thought, panic rising.

Maybe the other end? She raced there with the canister. That stack wouldn't move either, not with the controls nor with brute force. She fell back against the wall, trying to determine her next move when the sudden loud shrill and blinking lights of a pulled fire alarm had her dropping the canister on her foot. "Yeowch!" she cried, reaching for her foot. She heard coughing, and realized the student librarian hadn't left after all. He must have found the alarm and pulled it.

She made her way to him, limping slightly, eyes watering, lungs beginning to sting. He was huddled on the floor near the stairwell door, covering his head with his arms and sobbing between coughs. Maggie got down on her knees in front of him, pulling his arms down, cradling his head in her hands to make him look at her.

Calmly, but firmly she said over the screeching alarm, "We're going down the stairs together. You and me, right now. It will be all right. Get up and come with me. Now!"

Not taking his terror-filled eyes off her, he allowed her to help him up. She steered him quickly to the door, opened it and heard the thunder of footsteps on the stairs below as hundreds of students evacuated the building. Apparently other floors weren't as deserted as Stack Level 5.

Maggie pulled the metal door tight behind them and guided her charge downward, taking gasps of fresher air. When they reached the next landing, the student librarian halted to cough violently. Twisting around, he vomited up his burrito dinner, scoring a direct hit on Maggie's slacks and shoes, even though she'd tried to jump back out of the way. "Oh, yuck!" she cried, then thought, well, nothing to do about it now. She turned him back around and they continued down the stairs.

The closer they got to the first floor, the slower the going was because the number of those leaving increased with each floor. But she was impressed with the orderly manner of the evacuation. She glanced back up the stairs, and saw no signs of smoke.

The students in the stairwell proceeded rapidly down the steps without pushing or running over one another. Most had taken their backpacks with them; and most were on their cells, phoning or texting a friend about the excitement. Good thing they can't see or smell the smoke, she thought, or it might be a different story.

Once outside in the downpour, she looked around for someone to take the young librarian. As she scanned the crowd through the rain, she noticed the back of a tall student, Saddle Tramp patch on his backpack, and realized with surprise it was Jamie Chavez. He was helping guide the others safely away from the building and didn't seem panicked.

"Jamie!" she shouted. He turned in her direction, spotted her and pushed his way to her.

"Mrs. Grant! Were you in there? I was in the basement when the alarm went off. What is it? Did you see anything? Ugh, what's that smell?" Looking down, he pulled back from her in disgust.

"Don't worry, the rain should wash it off. Listen, Jamie, I need your help." Explaining that the young librarian needed to see the paramedics, she confidently left him in Jamie's care. She glanced up to the top floor as she started to make her way through the throngs of people to the main entrance on the east side of the building. Was that an orange glow through the tile cylinders, or just the alarm light? She calmly thought it would make an interesting picture. Amazed that something like that would pop into her head in the middle of a disaster, she chided herself and focused on the facts. When she heard sirens in the distance, she pushed harder through the throngs of wet students.

Campus police were arriving at the east entrance as she climbed the front steps. "It's on the top floor," she said quickly to the first officer she reached. He looked at her questioningly. "I work in Communications here at Tech. I saw the fire. The stacks are pushed together and wouldn't move so I couldn't get to it. I can show you where the firemen need to go in." He grabbed her arm and took her with him into the lobby.

It didn't take long for the Lubbock Fire Department to put the fire out completely. As per established procedures, and because thanks to Maggie they knew exactly where the fire was, Campus Police had already sent eight officers up elevators to the floor beneath the fire and then over to the back stairwells with crowbars, fire extinguishers and oxygen masks—standard equipment carried for just such emergencies. Because of their training, they'd not only been able to search the entire floor for any victims—even though Maggie thought she and the student librarian had been alone—they'd succeeded in moving the stacks apart and were containing the fire when the city firefighters arrived.

Although the library didn't have a sprinkler system, it did have several fire-hose wall units on each floor connected to the water main with stout hoses long enough to reach all areas. Campus police knew their locations and how to use them, and their quick actions kept the damage, although considerable, contained to the southwest quarter of the floor. City firefighters did the rest.

Maggie was asked to stay in the lobby to speak with the authorities when things settled down. Her phone still upstairs in her briefcase, she couldn't call her staff and wished she'd asked Elaine to order a belt holster for her smartphone. First thing tomorrow, she thought.

Through the glass wall, she could see the barricades police had set up outside below the library steps. Photographers and reporters were gathering despite the continuing rain, and shouted questions to the officers. Great, she thought, I'll look like a drowned rat on camera. But at least I can give them a first-hand account.

"Ma'am," an officer said, and she turned her attention to him. "The chief would like to talk to you upstairs, if you don't mind. The elevators are useable and most of the smoke is cleared. Will you come with me, please?"

She looked wistfully at the wet scene outside, wanting instead to do her job out there, but it would have to wait. She accompanied the officer to Stack Level 5.

A long half-hour later, after extensive questioning, Maggie was allowed to gather her briefcase and umbrella. She'd told her story twice, to the Lubbock Fire Chief, and to the arson investigator, and then was asked to repeat it for the head of Campus Police, Chief Callahan.

The tall, gray-headed mustached man with ostrich boots and crisp, immaculate uniform under his rain slicker, eyed Maggie slowly, then drawled, "Tell me what you saw, Sweetheart."

Maggie was leaning on the edge of a library table. She looked up at his cragged, pockmarked face and decided he didn't fit the stereotype of a West Texas lawman. In fact, with his menacing stare he looked more like the proverbial bad guy. But even though his presence and demeanor commanded respect, Maggie wasn't in the mood to give it.

She replied wearily, "I've told it twice already, and don't call me Sweetheart. I'm wet, tired and hungry and not in the mood for male chauvinism. I also need to go downstairs and talk to the reporters."

"Do you know who I am?" Chief Callahan asked her, moving closer to her face. "Not playing nice with the police chief can make for lots of parking tickets, Miss... Miss..."

She drew herself up and looked at him squarely. "Margaret Grant, Tech's Director of Communications and Marketing. And, Chief, not being respectful to the person who writes about the university's various departments can make for lots of bad publicity for the Campus Police."

He studied her with surprise, pleased to find an administrator with some backbone. He took a step backwards and held up his hands in surrender. "Okay, let's start again, shall we Margaret Grant? I'd appreciate it if you could briefly tell me what you saw and did, and we'll call it a draw. Then you can go talk to your reporters. Is that acceptable?"

She gave him a wry smile, and quickly recounted the scene one more time. She also told him she'd call him early tomorrow with questions about his investigation. He said he'd be pleased to help her.

When she finally stepped outside, there were no reporters to be found. So she checked on the student librarian—he was fine and had been sent to his dorm to rest. Returning to the lobby, she glanced at her cell phone. One call, from Sharon, of course. Quickly calling her back and filling her in, she refused an offer to come right over for a large glass of wine. Instead, she would opt for a hot bath and something to eat when she got home. She headed out once again.

The rain had stopped, and only a few people were still outside. Then she spotted Jake, the *A-J* reporter, finishing an interview with a student, and headed his way.

"Jake," she said as he stood alone now, scribbling in his notebook. "My favorite reporter. Where are the others?"

"Hey, Maggie. They're all gone. They got their interviews and left, I guess to make the ten o'clock news, although it's not much of a story."

"Not much of a story? What do you mean?"

"Your Chief of Staff briefed us all about 15 minutes ago. Took us next door to the Student Union and set up a news conference of sorts. I wondered where you were."

"I, uh, I was in the library."

"No kiddin'? Well, Boyle said... let me look at my notes... yeah, he said, 'a small electrical fire triggered the alarm. No injuries and minor damage on the top floor.' That's it."

That bastard, Maggie thought, then made a quick decision. "Um, Jake, you probably don't want to print that."

"Why not?"

"Because not one word of it is true. Join me for a cup of hot tea and a sandwich and I'll give you an exclusive."

Chapter 42 ~

At 10 p.m., every news station had the same story with Bennett Boyle on camera, lying to reporters and to the world. Then each reporter had interviewed students, whose reactions swung the gamut from panic to amusement to annoyance that they'd had to leave in the rain. She called her staff, briefing them and asking them to come in early the next morning. She set her alarm accordingly then took that long hot bath.

Sure enough, early the next morning while staff answered the angry calls from television reporters who had been lied to, she was summoned to Boyle's office. "What is the meaning of this?" he shouted angrily, throwing a copy of the *A-J* newspaper on his desk as she entered his office.

"Just doing my job, Mr. Boyle. I don't believe in lying to the media. It wasn't an electrical fire, it didn't trigger the alarm and it wasn't minor damage."

"How the hell do you know?"

"I was there, on Stack Level 5, and tried to put it out. I actually think it was arson, although I didn't tell the reporter that."

"What? You'd better be damn glad you didn't tell the reporter that!"

Now she was angry, too, and quickly dismissed the tactic of remaining calm. Her new way to deal with him definitely wouldn't work in this situation. Looking at him defiantly, she said, voice rising, "I know how to do my job, Mr. Boyle. I know what to say and how to say it, and *I* know you should never lie to the media. Whatever where *you* thinking?!"

Boyle blanched. No one talked to him like that. No one ever questioned him like that. Yet he felt an inexplicable need to explain and did so with extreme displeasure. "That if there was no story, they'd go away. You're inviting them to write about a possible arson, for God's sake. How can you be so reckless?"

Maggie took a deep breath and with her voice now calmer, but still defiant and strong, said, "I am not reckless, and the media always finds out the truth, so better to tell them up front than to have them make us out to be liars. So, I told the truth, that the fire is under investigation and we would provide more information as soon as the investigation is complete. I've talked with Chief Callahan and as soon as he knows anything, we'll put out a statement. Much better for the reputation of the university. And," she said pointedly, "why did you go on camera when you didn't have any facts or couldn't say anything positive? You could have talked about the heroics of the Campus Police, about the calm way the students evacuated with no injuries, about Saddle Tramps and library personnel directing students away from danger. Any number of good things instead of lies we'll now have to refute."

He stood there, staring at her in disbelief.

She continued, undeterred, "My staff is now upstairs fielding calls from irate TV stations who last night reported misinformation. My staff is cleaning up your mess, again. And I should be up there helping instead of trying to explain my job to you... again. Good day, Mr. Boyle."

Maggie turned sharply on her heel and marched out, leaving a bewildered and decidedly annoyed Chief of Staff looking after her.

"Again?!" he fumed.

Chapter 43 ~

"**Glad** you weren't hurt," Colin said later that week when he called her. "Stood up to Boyle, huh? Bet that went over well."

"Not exactly, no."

"Well, he hasn't fired you yet, has he? That's a good sign he's realized you were right and he was wrong."

"Here's hoping. I'd hate to be fired right after buying a new house." Maggie said ruefully.

"Good investment opportunity," Colin said quickly, smiling, which she swore she could "see" over the phone. "Listen," he continued, "can you clear Saturday afternoon and evening?"

She could, wondering at his instructions to wear heavy jeans, boots and a long-sleeved flannel or corduroy shirt... and to bring a hat, which of course she didn't have. The Tech cap she wore to football games would have to do.

"Where are we going and what in the world are we doing?" she asked Saturday as he picked her up dressed in roughly the same type of attire. His truck's exterior was filthy again.

"Cotton pickin'," he said with a smug grin.

"Cotton picking? As in going out and harvesting the cotton? In a big tractor?" she asked.

"Nope. By hand."

"By hand? By our own hands? Picking cotton with our bare hands? Whatever for?"

"It's a tradition. The Cotton A has a decades-long unwritten law of bringing in the first acre of cotton by hand. Once that's done, they harvest the rest with 'big tractors,' as you call them."

"The Cotton A? You know the Arbuckles?"

"I do. Church, remember?"

"Oh, yeah. Wait, we're going to pick an entire acre of cotton?" Maggie said with alarm. "Us and what army?"

150

"You'll see."

And she did. As they got close to Russ and Fern Arbuckle's large old farmhouse on the Cotton A ranch/farm, the cars and trucks lining the long drive told the story of the army. Farm hands, neighbors, friends from the parish, and all their families, even children as young as toddlers were there to join in the tradition.

Hovering around the east side of the huge two-story yellow clapboard house next to an enormous deck, the large crowd waited in good humor to begin their labor. Maggie greeted several parishioners, including Mrs. Bodecker and her husband, Ned. They, too, were in pants and heavy shirts and boots.

Father Sean and Father Fitzpatrick were present, and about ten minutes after Maggie and Colin arrived, the two priests were up on the deck along with Russ and Fern. A hush fell over the crowd as Russ welcomed them to the beginning of harvest season. He thought it had been a reasonably good growing season, and he thanked his workers for their diligent labor since last spring's planting.

"As you all know, each spring here on the Cotton A, we ask Monsignor Fitzpatrick to bless the planting, to ask God to watch over our crops and our workers, to keep each safe in their growing or their hoeing, and once again, God has answered our prayers. He gave us an earlier than usual killing freeze about a week ago, and these lovely bolls just started popping open when the sun hit them the next morning. So, with a crop now ready to harvest, we need to get this event under way.

"Since I was knee-high to a cotton boll, this ranch has picked the first acre together by hand to celebrate the ritual of our fathers and grandfathers and to keep us close to the good earth. We thank you for joining us today to keep tradition alive.

"And now, we ask Monsignor Fitzpatrick and Father Murphy to bless our harvest. Fathers?"

With the help of Father Sean, Monsignor Fitz ambled up to the small platform on the deck, slowly gazed over his audience, trying to look into the eyes of each person, young and old. He did the same before each Mass, and Maggie thought Father Fitz a showman at his best, looking for all the drama to be found. Once assured all eyes were on him alone, he began by crossing himself, "In da name o' da Fadder an' o' da Son an' o' da Holy Spirit. Amen."

Father Sean then said, "Our help is in the name of the Lord who has made heaven and earth. The Lord be with you. And with your spirit." Most of the audience answered in unison, "And also with you."

Father Fitz continued, "Almighty Lord God, Ya keep on giving abundance ta men in da dew o' heaven, an' food an' sustenance out o' da richness o' da soil. We give tanks ta Yer most gracious majesty for da fruits o' da field which we are 'bout ta gather. We beg o' Ya, in Yer mercy, ta bless this harvest, which 'as been received from Yer generosity. Preserve it, an' those who reap it, an' keep 'em from aul harm. Grant, too, dat aul dose whose desires Ya have filled wit dese good tings may be happy in Yer protection. May dey praise Yer mercies forever, an' make use o' da good tings dat do not last in such a way dat dey may not lose dose goods dat are everlasting through Christ 'er Lord. Amen."

Father Sean finished with, "In the name of the Father and of the Son and of the Holy Spirit. Amen."

Russ thanked the priests as they left the platform, and said, "Okay, now remember, we've got some prizes at the end of the day, but the main job is to have fun, and of course to get it all picked 'fore the food gets cold. If you don't have an assignment, see Tom up here to get one. Then head for your row and wait for the gun... let's get pickin'! There's a feast awaitin' for us when we're done!

Fern spotted Maggie and Colin and made her way through the crowd to them, throwing her thin but strong arms around Maggie for a hug. "I'm so glad you were able to join us, Maggie!"

"I'm so happy to be here," Maggie said. "I've never picked before."

"No? I can't imagine anyone not pulling it at least once in their lives, but Colin was a novice at one time too, weren't you, dear?"

"I was, but I learned quickly. Tom and Russ sort of threw me out there and said pick, so I did. I'm such a city-slicker and did such a poor job on the first few plants they had to come behind me to do it right. There's definitely an art to it."

"Almost a lost art, I'm afraid," Fern said wistfully. "All this technology. It's just not the same as when I was a girl. Now we spray it all and turn it crispy brown, then the pickin' machines clean eight rows at a time. They've already started to defoliate the outer acres. Can't stand the sight of those withered up branches, but I know it's the best way to harvest nowadays. Doesn't mean I have to like it."

"Have they harvested any of the fields yet?" Maggie asked.

"No, that'll start on Monday. We always have the hand-harvest first if we can. If you get tired of pickin', Maggie, you can help in the kitchen, although there are plenty of folks working in there, so feel free to stay outside until it's all picked—especially since it's your first harvest."

Colin said, "Cotton A feeds us well for our work, but each person here will pull at least one boll, even down to the smallest child. I've seen some mothers carry out their children who aren't even walking yet. I think if they can grab something, they let them pull a boll."

"That's right," Russ said, walking up to put his arm around his diminutive wife of more than 55 years. "It symbolizes how it takes all of us, working together, to have a crop. A healthy crop to provide for all the workers and their families throughout the year. And again this year, we've been blessed."

He kissed Fern tenderly on the top of her head. "But they're pickin,' Colin, not pullin'."

"What's the difference?" Maggie asked.

Fern answered. "Pickin' is reaching inside the boll to pull the locks of lint and seeds out of the burr. Pullin' cotton is pluckin' the entire boll off the plant, burr, lint, seeds and all."

"So what does your equipment do? Pick or pull?" Maggie asked.

Russ answered, "Our harvesters pull and strip the cotton, then spit the burrs back out into the field as they go along. Our machines are actually stripping the plants, but nowadays it's not exactly politically correct to say we're stripping, because it's looked upon as inferior crop. But with the advanced technology and quality seeds, our cotton is as premium as they grow in Arizona or California. So we call 'em harvesters. Just rhetoric, but no matter what we call it, it gets the cotton to market."

"Hadn't you two better get pickin'?" Fern said. "There won't be any left in a short while!"

"On our way!" Colin laughed. He grabbed Maggie's hand and led her to the field.

Colin had been assigned a row and given two burlap sacks before they headed out. She noticed Father Sean helping Monsignor Fitzpatrick toward the end of a nearby row, sack in hand. She didn't think they'd pick much but knew Father Fitz wasn't one to sit on the sidelines and be content to watch.

Colin handed her a pair of leather gloves. "You'll need these," he said. "But pick the first couple of bolls without them to get the feel for it. But not yet," he warned as she reached down. "Wait for the gun." And with that, a shot rang out and the pickin' commenced with shouts and whoops of spirited competition.

Maggie looked at the knee-high withered cotton plant before her with its fluffy white fibers exploding out of sharp brown burrs and said a little prayer for assistance.

"I'll show you," Colin said, expertly pulling the fibers from between the sharp pricks without incident. Maggie tried it, gingerly putting her hand into the plant. It's so soft, she thought, pulling when her fingertips reached the underside, gathering her first wad of cotton. She moved her thumb around feeling the weighty seeds deeply impeded in the fiber and wondered about the patience needed to pull them out by hand.

She grinned with her success, and Colin smiled with her, delighted in her pleasure as she popped it into her sack. They attacked the plants with determination.

As they worked their way down the row, Colin told her more about cotton. She learned the average yield per acre is normally one and one-third bales, but with the newest developed seeds that allow herbicide to be sprayed on top without damaging the cotton plants, farmers expected two to three bales per acre. Colin said a bale weighs approximately 500 pounds without seeds. Maggie's eyes got wide when she learned more than 600 pounds of seeds would be taken from this one acre, but they'd let the cotton gin remove them from the fiber. As Maggie had thought, it was much too time consuming to do by hand. That's why the invention of the cotton gin by Eli Whitney more than 200 years ago revolutionized cotton farming.

"In the 1700s, even under good conditions, a worker could clean no more than one pound of the crop a day. The cotton gin made it possible to clean fifty pounds per day back then, the simple invention streamlining the work and making profits soar."

When Maggie looked at him questioningly, he said, "Yes, it's one of those things I read way back when and it just sticks in my brain. I've got tons of useless stuff in here," he smiled, tapping himself on the head with one leather-gloved hand. Maggie laughed, but asked what else he knew.

He talked about how raw cotton from the field is fed through a cylinder in the gin with wire teeth spinning around. The wire teeth pass through small slits in a wall, pulling the fibers of the cotton all the way through but leaving the seeds behind.

Cotton is still a relatively easy crop to grow, requiring not much more than God's good earth, rain, sun and air. Today, five million acres of cotton are grown annually in the country. And West Texas, with its abundance of wide open spaces and good air, was a perfect environment for the crop. Colin said proudly, "Today the South Plains is the largest contiguous cotton growing region in the world.'

"In the world?" Maggie asked, surprised.

"Yep. Too much civilization everywhere else," Colin answered. "Irrigation and chemicals have enhanced the yield per plant, too, but many of the fields are without irrigation. Farmers plant dry fields at much lower costs, praying for weather conditions to be favorable."

Maggie asked about the large center pivot irrigation pipes she had seen. She learned they are not pulled by tractors as she originally thought, but instead are mechanized to move on command, each section constantly adjusting to keep in alignment with its neighbors. They can even be monitored by satellite systems through a farmer's cell phone.

The acre they were picking today, however, was a dry field, he told her, and this year's dry crop was good.

Maggie thought of the successful marketing campaign of the National Cotton Growers Association, "Cotton - the fabric of your life," with their images of happy people floating and romping in billowing pristine white cotton fabrics. Brilliant branding tagline. Roughly half the fibers worn in the entire world come from cotton because of the comfort and its ability to easily absorb skin moisture.

Tenacious seeds, necessary for regeneration, were once the plague of the crop because of the difficulty of removal, but now are harvested and pressed into cottonseed oil used in snack foods, salad oils, candles, cosmetics, detergents, paints and soaps... and of course, more cotton plants. The remnants of seeds are used in some cattle feed because they're high in protein.

When Colin's knowledge of the crop was exhausted, he called Russ and Fern's son Tom over to give the next lesson. Seems Tom Arbuckle was the current president of the Cotton A Co-Op, a cooperative where not only the Arbuckles, but many other nearby farmers pooled their resources to run a gin and get their product to market with a higher profit.

"We also work together to learn the newest technology, look at the latest products in seeds and equipment, and sort of use our combined experience to bring about the highest, best quality yields," Tom said. "In our area, we take advantage of every local resource we can, including the Plains Cotton Growers, Inc. It's an active organization promoting and protecting the interests of all the area's cotton farmers."

"How do they do that?" Maggie asked.

"How?" Tom mused. "I guess I'd say they foster improvement of conditions for the Plains cotton to be produced and sold. And they encourage standardization and improvement in the quality of cotton and cottonseed, among other objectives. Then we pray a lot."

Maggie smiled. "Pray for the right amount of rain?"

"Yes, for that and for no hail, and no dust storms. I think most of the farmers would say they spend a proportionate amount of time working during the day and praying at night. Each year it's a risk, but one that once it gets under your skin, keeps you coming back year after year. It's a good life."

Maggie asked a few more questions as they moved down the rows together, the men picking quickly and waiting for her to catch up.

She learned today's cotton farmers don't just plant seeds and water the ground or hope for Mother Nature to cooperate. Today's cotton farmers use technology and science to enhance their productivity and yield, as well as charts and graphs and precise calculations of all types to their advantage. There is nothing simple about successful farming in West Texas.

Today, however, technology wasn't helping Maggie one bit. She picked the cotton as fast as she could, but in no time fell far behind Tom and Colin. They were leaving one or two full bolls on each plant for her to pick after them. They filled their ten-pound sacks and turned them in, hurriedly bringing back empty ones to start where they left off. She thought Colin and Tom were competing against one another. Had Colin asked Tom to answer her questions to slow him down? She wouldn't put it past Professor Murphy.

It didn't take long for the enthusiastic newness of the manual labor to wear off and a healthy tiredness to set in. Maggie thought about past workers, those who picked cotton prior to harvesting machines and wondered how they did it, day in and day out, hour after hour. A matter of necessity, she supposed. And the slave labor of the south, before the Civil War? This was definitely back-breaking monotonous work. Although the cotton gin had been a great invention, it was one of the reasons slavery had grown and flourished in the American South. The gin made cotton a more profitable crop to market, which meant more farmers could plant more acres, which in turn meant the need for more slaves. It was a cycle that transformed a country, and not for the better, in Maggie's opinion. Now the harvester, or cotton stripper, did the work of slaves, but she knew there were still small farms across the country where tenants worked almost the same as the slaves, scratching out a living from the dirt without the benefits of technology. She had a new respect for their labors.

By the end of the first hour, Maggie noticed most of the women had left the fields, all the young children with them. Although about a quarter mile from the house, every once in a while she caught the aroma of mouthwatering barbeque, roasting on the huge mesquite-lined pit she'd seen earlier. It made her stomach growl, and she wondered about the wisdom of being stubborn and picking until the end. Her back ached, her fingers were scratched and sore despite the gloves, her shirt torn, her feet muddy, and her face was sunburned, even under her cap.

The priests had abandoned their row long ago, Monsignor Fitz to the cool shade of the deck, iced tea glass in hand, and Father Sean back to town to officiate at the late afternoon Anticipatory Mass. He would be back shortly afterward, however, to enjoy the feast and to collect his elderly housemate who needed to retire early so he would be alert for the Sunday services.

When the final boll was picked clean, another shot rang out, and weary pickers headed back to the house. Maggie, hand holding her aching back, turned away from the house and looked out over the seemingly endless acres of cotton, stretching as far as the eye could see. It was so peaceful out here—well, except for the hungry crowd behind her thundering back to the house. Maybe Russ and Fern would let her come out sometimes to walk the fields and meditate. Maybe they'd think she was being silly, but there's just something about it that called to her.

"Maggie? Coming?" Colin called, halfway back.

"Coming!"

156

They were met with cool sweet tea, cold beer and table upon table of down-home food, including more barbeque beef than Maggie had seen in her entire life. It made her think of what Steven had told her about when Texas Tech was first built. Ever the history buff, Steven said at the 1926 dedication ceremony of the Administration Building a cotton bale was symbolically used for a speaker's podium, and that 35,000 pounds of barbeque had been prepared for the multitude of visitors and dignitaries. She thought the number had more than likely been exaggerated over the years, but she was certain the excited town folk had made a feast to be remembered.

Maggie knew they didn't have quite that amount of beef today, but it still was an impressive pile, most probably Cotton A cattle, and she was hungry enough to eat her fair share.

After taking their turn to wash up at the old tank under the turning windmill, she and Colin joined the line for food—aromatic barbeque, potato salad, pinto beans, corn on the cob and fresh baked pies and cakes. Sitting on hay bales placed around the yard, they unashamedly stuffed themselves as the ever-faithful cool evening breezes began to blow. Much to the delight of the youngest generation, games for the kids had begun shortly thereafter, including burlap sack races, hay bale rolling and the more-fun-to-watch-than-participate-in three-legged race. Tech was playing an away game, and several men had wandered in the house to watch, returning regularly to announce the score to the crowd.

An hour or so later, Russ stood on the deck again and awarded prizes for this year's best pickers, in categories divided by age. Mr. Bodecker won the over-60 category and was awarded a case of local wine. Younger winners took home various prizes such as six-packs of cold beer, or movie theatre tickets. But everyone won the satisfaction of knowing they'd helped get the harvest off to a good start.

Someone picked up a guitar and started strumming and humming, and before Maggie knew it, they were in the middle of her first ever full-blown hoedown, fiddlers' bow strings flying. Large sheets of plywood had been made into a temporary dance floor, and it wasn't long before it was crowded with boot-scooters.

Colin proved he could boot-scoot with the best of them, and Maggie laughed as he twirled her around to the *Cotton-Eyed Joe.*

Near dark, when most of the guests had gone home, Maggie and Colin stayed to help clean up, then were ready to head out themselves. After she thanked Fern again for the wonderful afternoon and evening, and the new experience, Maggie felt bold enough to ask about her desire to come walk the cotton fields.

"Why of course, Maggie," Fern answered. "Feel free any time... but tell me what kind of car you drive so I can pass the word along... hate to have you shot for trespassing!" She winked, but just to be safe, Maggie immediately wrote down her car's make, model, color and license plate number.

Chapter 44 ~

After she climbed in the truck to leave, Maggie was surprised when Colin opened the passenger door, case of wine in hand and said, "Tom's finally paying off an old bet. Slide over to the middle, will you? I don't want to put this in the back. Gets bumped around too much."

She undid her belt and moved over to the middle, fastening the middle seatbelt and resting her hand on top of the case even though Colin had cinched it up with its own belt. Precious stuff, she thought.

When he got in the driver's seat, she was immediately conscious of his closeness, although he seemed unfazed. As they drove away, she noticed every bump and every touch, and tried to ignore it. He was a friend, and they were comfortable the way things were. Just friends, dammit, she said to herself.

It was rare for Colin to drive her home. Normally, they each drove their own vehicles to their "dates" so a goodnight kiss at the door or an invitation in for a nightcap wasn't an option. It was always a light peck on the cheek or a soft brush of the lips as they parted, nothing more as each went their own way. Maggie had wondered why he'd always asked to meet her. She supposed it was because he just liked her as a friend. This way it didn't get complicated.

But tonight? It was late, they were tired and she was sitting close to him, their bodies touching. What would he do if she just casually laid her head on his shoulder?

Don't be ridiculous, she chided herself. You're not in high school, Maggie. He's a friend... get over it. He'd probably be horrified and then you'd be embarrassed. Rubbing her arms and stretching her sore fingers, Maggie tried to take her mind off the way his jeans fit tightly, the way his cowboy hat tilted just so, the way he'd held her as they'd two-stepped.

She said, "I hurt in places I didn't know I could hurt!"

"But it's a good hurt, isn't it?" Colin asked.

"Good hurt?" Maggie laughed. "Yes, I guess it is. Do you do this every fall?"

"Ever since I've been here. I met Tom through Sean, and we started playing poker. That's how I met your contractor, Campos, through Tom and cards. We don't play as much as we used to, although Tom's wife Julie doesn't mind if we gather at their house. We all seem to be so busy. Anyway, Tom invited me out the first year."

"I know Tom and Julie live at the other house, but this one is big enough for them all isn't it? I thought ranch and farm families were often inter-generational?"

"They are sometimes, but I think where Tom and Julie are it's a different, larger school district for their kids. And I know Julie likes the one-story, adobe-style house."

Maggie had been out there once. Tom and Julie's house was beautiful with a huge courtyard and swimming pool. It was about ten miles west, and in Hockley County, not Lubbock County, but still on Cotton A property.

Colin said, "From his office out there, Tom mainly oversees the oil and cattle production side of the ranch which is away from the cotton. Someday his kids will live in the big house here, and then his grandkids will probably inherit his, if they take to ranching and farming. Unfortunately, it's a dying profession. But they've been a family of farmers and ranchers since the early 1900s. Tom told me once his granddad first farmed this land with a mule and plow."

"Wow," Maggie said. "What a difference. And in just three generations? From mule and plow to a tractor that plants... how many rows at a time?

"I think they use both eight- and sixteen-row planters now. And it *is* amazing. Good land, good people."

"And Father Fitz blesses each harvest?"

"And each spring planting. That one's much easier and mainly ceremonial. We meet at sunup at the end of the rows to sow the seeds in that same acre and then consume a breakfast along with the blessing."

"When in the spring? The fields hadn't been planted when I drove through last March."

"March is way too early. Normally they wait until about the 10th of May to plant. Timing's kind of tricky, depending on West Texas weather. You've got to get all those acres planted between the heavy rains, and then once the plants emerge five or six days later, you pray the hail storms don't come."

"And if they do?" Maggie asked.

"If they get hailed out? Then they plow the damaged fields under and replant with milo—sorghum—if it's too far into the season to replant with cotton. Or some plant sunflowers. Tom calls it their 'catch crop.' Happened a couple years back. Storm came up after the seedlings were about eight inches high and wiped out more than half the plants. It was a bad one. They plowed it under and started again. Wasn't a great crop that year but good enough to keep them afloat."

"I thought they were wealthy from the oil?"

"They are. Incredibly wealthy. And from property investments, too. They just refer to the cotton, cattle and oil as separate businesses, and they still want a success in each."

"Property investments? Is this Tom the 'Tom' you bought the student housing from?" Maggie asked, remembering a conversation from last July.

"One and the same. His oldest son Heath has a business degree from Tech and thought it would be a good idea to invest in property east of the university. Tom thought it would be good experience for Heath to learn the hard way, so he allowed his son to make some deals. Turns out Heath sorta has the Midas touch—those deals worked exceedingly well, and the student housing project came into being and made the family even wealthier. That's one of the reasons they can afford to give so much of it away. They dare to take risks, knowing they still have other ventures to fall back on. They work hard and have been blessed with more success than most."

"You certainly wouldn't know it, though. They're so genuine, so nice. I like them both, or all... how many Arbuckles did I meet today?"

"I think there's about a dozen of them all together. Russ, Fern and Tom, Julie and their kids. Then spouses and more kids. Russ' dad, Ted Arbuckle, died about four years ago at the age of 98, a couple years after his wife Hazel. He and Monsignor Fitz were good buddies. Tough old guy, but I liked him. Had two sons, but Russ' older brother was killed at the end of World War II—a long time ago. So it fell to Russ to continue the farm and all. Fern's from a ranching family up by Yellowhouse Draw, and they've been sweethearts since they were teenagers. Great couple."

"Yellowhouse Draw? Where's that?" Maggie asked, not familiar with the name.

"And you profess to be a Texas Tech-educated woman! It's the old valley up north of town... has a museum about the area's Native Americans and animals? Fascinating exhibits... even an archeological dig."

"No idea what you're talking about. It's not on my list of things to see."

"Well, it should be. You really don't know where it is?" Colin asked surprised.

"I've never even heard of it. What's it close to that I would know?"

"Look there in the glove box. Should be a Lubbock map."

Maggie leaned over, pushing the old latch to open the ancient compartment, then gasped as papers and odd items fell out all over the floor even as she tried to grab them. "Arrughhh!" she cried as Colin winced.

"Sorry. I forgot it was full. Here, let me pull over and I'll take care of it." He slowed, finding an empty dirt road going off the main road and pulled in. They were still on the Cotton A land, surrounded by fields, so he wasn't worried about traffic. He climbed out to come around to the passenger side.

Maggie was attempting to straighten the items in her hands, when she jumped slightly as a wire fell out onto her lap from between some papers.

"What's this?" she said when he came around to the right side of the truck and opened the door. She held up two thin wires coiled together about eighteen inches long with small flat devices on each end. "Electrodes?" Maggie said, questioningly.

"No, just an old radio transmitter, that's all. Doesn't work," he said nonchalantly.

"Radio transmitter? Ooohh, like the cops use on TV? A bug? A wire?"

"Yeah, like the cops use on TV, but it's an old Bureau transmitter. Don't know why I still have it. Here, let me put this stuff back in. Here's the map," he said, taking the wire and papers from her and handing her the Lubbock map.

"You actually used that wire when you were with the FBI? What else have you got in there? A gun?"

"No, that's under the seat."

Maggie's eyes widened.

"I have a license for it, don't worry," he hastily added, silently kicking himself for mentioning it. No one knew about it... at least not until now.

"Once a G-man, always a G-man, huh?" she said teasingly, but she was surprised that he had a gun. She didn't think she'd ever known anyone who carried one, at least not in Dallas. Maybe guns were more prevalent in West Texas.

Ignoring her, he replaced all the items and closed the glove box, a little flustered as he came around to the driver's side again. "Yellowhouse Draw is in the northwest quadrant of the map. We should go to the museum sometime. I think you'd like it."

Smiling broadly at his discomfort, she said, "I'll make a deal with you, Professor Murphy. I'll go with you to Yellowhouse Draw if you'll tell me the details of how you used that little wire when you were a G-Man."

"I don't make deals, Mrs. Grant, and I don't talk about those days," he said in a flat, serious tone. "And I'd rather no one knew about the gun." He turned the truck abruptly around.

"Not a problem," Maggie said solemnly, starring straight ahead, feeling as though she'd been chastised.

He pulled the truck back onto the main road toward town, and they rode in silence for a short while. Finally Colin said lightly, "Look on the map. You can turn the dash light on if you need it." Tensions eased, Maggie unfolded it and looked in the northwest quadrant, but all she could find was Lubbock Lake.

"Lubbock Lake! That's it," he said.

"Well, I *know* where Lubbock Lake is. *Everybody* knows where Lubbock Lake is... but Yellowhouse Draw? Still never heard of it," she said refolding the map.

"Same place, I guess, just called two different things. But you'd really like the museum, I think. And we were talking about the Arbuckles, weren't we?"

"We were. Good people. So down to earth... and into the earth," she said as she raised her hands, examining the scratches and stains again. "It was a good day, Colin. Thanks."

They rode in silence for a while, each deep in thought. Maggie's distraction tactic was working and she thought of her boys and their families. She hoped they'd be described as a good family. She thought they were. She missed them, envying Russ and Fern their close-knit, as well as close-in-proximity family. But she knew she was in a good place. She was comfortable here.

Chapter 45 ~

Colin was lost in thought too, but definitely not comfortable. Damn, he thought, I should've put the wine between us. What was I thinking? I've been so careful with her, just like Sean said, that I've gotten too comfortable with her only as a friend. I shouldn't be sitting so close. How can she still smell so good after an afternoon in a cotton patch?

And I shouldn't have mentioned the gun. Stupid thing to do, Murphy.

Now what, Margaret Grant? Why'd you come into my life? I was content... But there's something about you that intrigues me. And when you smile, man. What would happen if I take it up a notch... kissed you the way you should be kissed? The way a real G-Man kisses?

When he pulled into Maggie's driveway, Colin thanked her for coming with him, and as they climbed out of the truck, she thanked him for letting her be a part of the wonderful event. The gratitude was getting a little nauseous, but it covered up other emotions and feelings. Why were they nervous all of a sudden?

"Would you like to come in?" she said tentatively, then quickly added, "For some wine?"

"I don't think so, Maggie." They'd reached the door and he stopped, thumbs hooked in his jeans front pockets. She turned to him, and looked up, disappointed, yet relieved at his answer.

"Well," she said, "Thanks again, Murphy—" Before she knew what was happening, he was taking her in his arms and crushing her mouth with a passion that left her breathless.

When she thought she would pass out, he let her go and turned abruptly, straightened his hat, and walked briskly back to the truck. She leaned back against the closed door to catch her breath. "Oh, my," was all she could say as she watched him drive away.

"Well, it's about time," Sharon said when Maggie related the kiss.

"What do you mean, about time?! We're friends and he... he... goodness... just thinking about it makes my heart race," Maggie said as they met for brunch after church the next day. Doug was at the music building.

"And, so, that's good, isn't it?" Sharon asked.

"I don't know. I... we were enjoying each other as friends. He's a fascinating man..."

"And damn good-looking."

"You know that doesn't enter into it... or shouldn't, at least. I'm just a plain Jane. What's he doing kissing me like that?" Maggie said in exasperation.

"Will you quit selling yourself short? You're intelligent, fun to be with, interesting, and any man with a lick of sense would be lucky to be kissing you like that. I thought this was the man you were ga-ga over just a few months ago... falling into his emerald eyes you said, or something maudlin like that?"

"That was before... when the physical was there."

"And it's not there now? Not even after that hot kiss?"

"It is," Maggie said tentatively, "I've just sort of put it on the back burner while I get to know him as a person, that's all."

"And he's wanting to move it to the front burner, is that what you're telling me?"

"I hope not, Phelps. I'm just not ready. Not yet."

Colin called later in that week, suggesting they meet at J&B Coffeehouse that evening.

"Oh, sorry," Maggie said. "Promised Sharon I'd go to a recital tonight. One of Doug's prize students is performing. Want to come?"

"Uh, no thanks. I think I'll just work on the cabinet tonight. Still a long way to gettin' done. Maybe we can get together over the weekend?"

"Sure, Murphy. Call or I'll call you. We'll see what we can work out."

When he'd said goodbye, she thought his tone was a little too casual. Why in the world did he kiss me like that on Saturday? They hadn't talked since then, and she was more than a little apprehensive about their next meeting. Surely the kiss meant he wanted to be more than friends? Dare she hope, or should she run away, scared out of her mind? Am I ready for more than friends? I don't think so... but that kiss...

As it turned out, neither called the other that weekend, and it was another week before they met for coffee. By then, whatever ardor there was had definitely cooled, and they were back to being comfortable friends. Just maybe, Maggie thought, the kiss was only breathless on her side, and he wasn't that impressed? She was out of practice, after all.

Good grief, Margaret Riley Grant, she chided herself, get over your insecurity and get on with just enjoying his friendship. And quit looking into his damn green eyes.

Colin, on the other hand, had been chiding himself severely for kissing her like that. He'd liked it, all right, but wondered how in the world that kiss could qualify as gentle as his twin had directed. He'd been afraid to call Maggie, thinking she might turn him down, but when he got up the courage, she did just that. Better back off, Buddy, he told himself. Now is not the time to ruin a good friendship with passion, no matter how much you'd like to kiss her again and again. Besides, Dad's cabinet needs to get finished before December. He would pour his passion into the wood instead of into Margaret Grant.

Chapter 46 ~

"**I** don't understand kids today," Sharon said in exasperation as she and Maggie shopped for more "treasures" at their favorite thrift store the next weekend. "Well, maybe I do, but it's frustrating."

"What's frustrating?" Maggie asked as she looked over the latest shipment of furniture. She'd brought a full-size mattress and box springs from Dallas for her master bedroom, but wanted an interesting headboard, and hadn't found one yet.

"I've been put in charge of Civil Engineering's once-every-four-years student survey. Lucky me!" she said rolling her eyes. "But we aren't getting much response from kids at all. I know they're busy, but the results of the survey could actually help them, so it's frustrating not to get more participation."

"How are you marketing it?" Maggie asked.

"I put fliers up on all the bulletin boards and asked professors to mention it in classes."

"How can they participate? Online? Hard copy?"

"Hard copy. Why?"

"How easy is it to put online? And what type of a deadline did you give them? Any incentives?"

"Fairly easy, I'd say. No deadline. We're stopping when we get enough, which may be never. And the incentive is that it will help with the next long-range planning for the department, which ultimately helps the kids."

"How many is enough?"

"What?"

"How many completed surveys do you want before you stop?" Maggie asked as she spotted a headboard possibility. "Come look at this one... it's heavy, and I like the lines. It might work. Did you bring the measuring tape?"

"A good engineer is never without a measure of some kind," Sharon said as she pulled a miniature tape out of her purse and laid it against the headboard, leaning close to see the tiny print. "Five hundred."

"It's five hundred inches wide?!"

"No, silly. Five hundred surveys is enough out of our two-thousand students. The headboard's the perfect size for your mattress."

"Good! I'll take it, and I've got some ideas for your survey. Let me talk with my staff on Monday and we'll work up a plan. What's your budget for it?"

"Budget? I don't have a budget for it... but I've got about $1,000 of discretionary funds I could use. Will that be enough?"

"More than enough. Help me get this thing up to the front. It'll need a good sanding and a coat of paint, but should be perfect if you measured right, Phelps," Maggie said teasingly.

Sharon gave her friend her own version of the evil eye but laughed as they dragged the new acquisition to the counter. She was glad she'd brought up her frustration to "Maggie the marketing genius"... at least she hoped she was a genius.

On Tuesday, Sharon arrived at Maggie's office to hear an overview of the marketing ideas, instantly agreeing to everything the Communications team had planned. "Looking forward to it," she said. "I'll have the survey put online in a couple of days and we can get started."

They began early the following Monday morning by putting red eighteen-inch square posters with a large black question mark in the middle of every wall in the Civil Engineering Building, making students and faculty alike wonder what they were for. On Wednesday, second squares were put up next to the first ones... these said, "Whadya." Nothing more, just that. On Friday, a third square appeared overnight that read, "think" with another large black question mark. Maggie had explained they were dealing with a perceptive audience. "So, let's intrigue them a little. Give them something to think about...to talk about... to puzzle about... and gradually, give them the answer."

Over the following weekend, the square posters were replaced with huge red and black posters saying, "Whadya think? Let us know through the Student Survey, hard copy or online. All participants will be entered into a random drawing for two cash prizes of $400 each."

"That gives this smart group of kids a more instant incentive, and drives them to the website or to the office to fill out the form. Next, in the second week, we'll hit them with more."

For the next strategies, the Communications team procured permission from the university Facilities Office. As students walked to the engineering building, they had to pass a series of six posters on stakes driven into the ground, about the size of residential For Sale signs, placed one after the other in rows. Reminiscent of old Burma Shave signs placed along highways, the signs had rhymes printed on them in sequence, once again, leading students to information about the student survey. Another rhyme was printed on the back for students leaving the building. A different set of rhymes was placed at each of the four entrances to the building.

An additional clever rhyme was sent once every other day to students' e-mail addresses as reminders. Normal communication routes of blogs, tweets and texts were utilized.

Students were hit with the message in classrooms, too. Ricky and Susan created a 3-foot by 4-foot old-fashioned sandwich board sign to match the big posters and paid a few students to take turns for two days walking the halls of the engineering building wearing it. They carried hard copies of the surveys. During each shift, the hired student donned a red body suit and a tall red and black Cat in the Hat felt chapeau, looking perfectly ridiculous, but garnering the needed attention. Poking their heads into classrooms before professors began their lessons, they presented a free Texas Tech pencil to anyone quickly filling out the survey—engineering students loved pencils.

The next day, in the dean's office where the stacks of hard-copy surveys were found, dozens of sugar cookies decorated in red with black question marks were offered for completion of a survey on the spot. Word spreads quickly about free food, and the office staff had to print more surveys to fill the demand before they ran out of the treats.

At daybreak, two days before the end of the survey campaign, Maggie's staff gathered at the Civil Engineering Building with colored chalk in hand. They wrote short sayings and messages on the sidewalks and steps leading to all the doors, with and without stick-figure pictures. Steven drew a full-sized hopscotch board, that read, "One, two, here's what you do. Three, four, fill out the form. Five six, you might get picked... to win $400!"

Another sidewalk graffiti said, "Dear Son, Please fill out the survey. I'm not made of money, you know. Love, Dad." And another, by Susan; "Dude, you got $400 just laying around somewhere? Fill out the survey!" And Maggie's favorite, from Ricky, "40,000 pennies for your thoughts!"

It didn't hurt that the *Daily Toreador* picked up the story and had a front page photo of the Steven's hopscotch graffiti the last day of the survey.

After the two weeks of marketing, Sharon happily reported

participation by 82 percent of her engineering students, making it the largest response in the history of the department. Other areas of campus heard about the success, and much to the Communications' staffers' delight, asked for assistance on several different campaigns.

Maggie detailed all this in her weekly e-mail summaries to Boyle, which she knew he never read, and that undoubtedly President Parker never saw.

Chapter 47 ~

In early October, Bennett Boyle stood in the third-floor outer office, fuming, waiting, checking his watch. None of the Communications staff seemed to be around and it was 9 a.m. on a Monday morning.

Maggie walked in, briefcase in hand, and stopped short at the sight of him. Uh-oh, she thought quickly. Whatever could've happened that she hadn't heard about? She had sources all over campus now, and normally heard immediately about even the smallest of problems. Must be something big for him to climb the stairs instead of sending Jonathan or a secretary. Maybe he's come back for the plant? Unlocking her inner office and inviting him in, she glanced back to make certain Phil was still there. He was.

She stood behind her desk as he followed her in.

"Where's your secretary?" he said curtly.

"She's out today. I gave her a comp day for working on Saturday. Why? Do you need her?" Maggie asked.

"You're late. It's after nine and I've been here for ten fucking minutes."

Maggie narrowed her eyes at his use of profanity. "Did we have an appointment, Mr. Boyle?" she asked, searching her brain for something she'd missed.

"Work hours begin at eight, not nine."

"I've been at the Engineering Building since 7:15 this morning, Mr. Boyle, working. I'm not late... and I know what the work hours are. How can I help you or did you climb those stairs just to chide me for being late?"

"Engineering? Why?"

"The Rube Goldberg Competition. They're announcing the winners right after lunch. My staff and I were... How can I help you, Mr. Boyle?"

He reached into his pocket and pulled out a mirror. It was one of the promotional items Elaine had handed out over the weekend at the Lubbock Convention Center's Women's Expo. A 2-by-3-inch makeup mirror in a convenient thick plastic casing, Texas Tech University stamped on the outside. It had been a big hit, as promotional items went, and Maggie was pleased when Elaine reported so many had been picked up.

"What the hell is this?" he said caustically, holding out the mirror.

Puzzled, Maggie thought it was fairly obvious what it was but obliged him by saying, questioningly, "A pocket mirror in a plastic casing?"

"I know what the fuck it is, God damn it. But where the hell did it come from?"

She took a deep breath. "Our department supplied them for the Women's Expo on Saturday. Please don't use that language with me, Mr. Boyle. I— "

"They're pink!"

"Yes, sir, they are," she answered defensively, looking at the hot pink plastic cover, still not understanding the cause of his displeasure.

"We don't do pink."

"Oh, well. National Breast Health Awareness Month... October. They're pink in honor of the national cause."

"The university's colors are red and black, not pink."

"Yes, sir, but lots of things all across the country are pink this month... and the thought behind the mirrors is that every time a woman reaches for it in her purse, she'll see the Double T printed on pink *instead* of the usual red or black school colors, and automatically think of October and the need to give herself a breast exam. It's a marketing tool with a health message. It promotes..." He cut her off.

"I don't care what it promotes, it's PINK!"

"Yes, and within university trademark guidelines. I checked with…"

"How many do you have?"

Maggie looked at him hard, saying testily, "Well, I think we ordered a couple thousand, but we gave away about five hundred on Saturday. We have several opportunities this month to hand them out."

"Get rid of them," he said, glaring at her.

"Get rid of them? But they're a great marketing tool."

"You keep forgetting I'm your direct supervisor and you answer to me. I said get rid of them. Throw them out. Don't give any more away. WE DON'T DO PINK!"

Bennett Boyle pitched the mirror on her desk and stomped out in a huff, narrowly missing Steven who had just stepped into Elaine's office to see what all the shouting was about. Steven looked at Boyle's back moving briskly down the hall, then at Maggie who still stood rigid at her desk. "What the hell was that all about?"

Maggie sat heavily, picking up the mirror and studying it. Quietly she said, "Seems we don't do pink."

Chapter 48 ~

"And you didn't throw them out, did you?" Sharon said as they walked toward the auditorium in the Civil Engineering Building for the awards ceremony.

"Of course not. I just put them away for later. That's a couple hundred dollars out of my paltry budget. I'm not about to waste them. Honestly, the man knows *nothing* about marketing. Even professional football teams are 'doing pink' this month. He's an absolute fool."

"Certifiable... Did his hair move while he screamed at you?" Sharon asked with a healthy dose of mischief in her voice.

Maggie laughed, the tension relieved. "No, but when he threw the mirror at me, his tie fluttered a little."

"Good heavens," Sharon said in mock surprise.

The auditorium was crowded with students, faculty and a couple of reporters and photographers, including Charlie. "Hey, boss," he said as she passed him to take a seat closer to the front with Sharon.

"Hey, Charlie. What type of shots you planning?" Maggie asked.

"Mostly close-ups of the winners faces as they hear their awards. Department's given me a list and where they're seated up on stage. It should be fairly easy to shoot. I'll mix 'em in with the ones we took this morning of the kids with their entries. Ricky's planning an extensive photo spread on the website, and Susan's done the main story. Steven's here to get a quote or two from the winners after it's over. And you know about the video we shot earlier this morning... we'll stream three of the winning entries on the web, too. Steven thinks folks will get a real kick out of watching them work. We should have it all up by late afternoon."

"Good work. Am I okay to sit here?" Maggie had a strict policy, as did most communication professionals—their staff was not to be in any photos unless they, themselves were receiving a prestigious award—and even then she preferred to show an example of the work instead.

"That's fine. I'll work around you."

"Do you think it's interesting enough to link to this week's *Insight?*"

Moving closer to the front, he said, "Yep, and Ricky's already saving a space for it. Got some really good entries this year."

Maggie knew Rube Goldberg had been a Pulitzer Prize-winning cartoonist and author who drew complicated and often absurdly nonsensical devices designed to complete simple tasks—such as a self-operating napkin, or a pencil sharpener involving motivation for a woodpecker that started with flying a kite. Silly, nonsensical things. She remembered her father's fondness for the inventive artist.

Today's competition for engineering student teams was similar in that they had to accomplish a simple task in a complicated manner. This year, their Rube Goldberg machines needed to move a two-inch cube horizontally onto a two-and-a-half-inch square. Students had to devise at least eight steps and could use at least two moving parts. Electrical components must be battery operated, and no flames or liquids could be used.

Proving Sharon's oft repeated contention that engineering is a creative science, this year's student machine components included boots, springs, pulleys, weights, feathers, steel ball bearings, plastic tubes, cups, ping pong balls and lots of string, just to name a few of the imaginative items. Many were mounted on backboards, but several were free standing.

Sharon said, "Don't they remind you of the Mousetrap Game from when we were kids? Remember, you built an elaborate device to let the mouse get the cheese, but trapped him? Or something like that."

"I do remember. My dad dragged it out on rainy days until I was a teenager," Maggie said. "He loved it, probably because it reminded him of Rube Goldberg. Doesn't one of the entries include a few pieces from an old Mousetrap game? I thought I saw one this morning."

"It does, but the team used the pieces in a different way, so they'll probably get extra points for creativity *and* nostalgia. It's just fun to watch them all, even when they don't work exactly like the kids plan."

"True. There were some pretty hilarious moments this morning when we filmed them. But that's part of the process, isn't it? Trial and error? I mean, the assignment's not just for fun, is it?"

Sharon replied in mock seriousness, "Engineers never do anything just for fun, my friend. But let me think. It teaches synthesis, analysis, team-work, the iterative, or repetitive process and evaluation procedures—all extremely important in engineering. After graduation, these kids will be building bridges, highways, hospitals, dams and the like. In all our classes we try to emphasize application of engineering knowledge to the solution of practical construction problems. Our students will one day not only have to design, but also write about the process so non-engineers can understand what they're doing."

"Like the science projects Michael and Ben did throughout school?"

"Exactly like those. So some of the kids here, probably the ones who used to win the blue ribbons at those science fairs, usually do pretty well at this. And most of the faculty love it, too." Looking around at the now-crowded auditorium, she said, "Looks like most of them are here. Once the awards are given, we'll go back down to the lab where you were this morning and the teams will demonstrate their machines during an open house. You should come."

"I saw most of them this morning. I'll see how long the award ceremony takes."

Maggie watched as team leaders were seated on stage, Jamie among them. He was the main reason she was here. Colin had a class and couldn't attend, and asked if she would be there for Jamie? She was happy to oblige.

Phil Nash, civil engineering instructor and researcher, began the proceedings, but stopped when President Parker came in and sat down off to the side. Nash nodded to him and introduced him briefly to polite applause before continuing his remarks about the competition and awarding the prizes. For both Maggie and Sharon, it was their first "presidential sighting."

Top prize went to an all-girl team, much to Sharon's delight. Not only was their entry the most attractive with brightly painted mechanical pieces in coordinated colors, but their design was the most complicated and inventive using a half-dozen moving parts and sixteen steps stretched out on a four-by-four-foot bright red felt board. At one point, a ball bearing made its way through a raised Double T maze, definitely garnering extra points for loyalty to the university. Jamie's team came in third, but out of the thirty-six teams entered, third place was a remarkably good showing and could be proudly included on his résumé.

Maggie congratulated him briefly, reminding him to call Murphy with the good news, but headed back to the office instead of going downstairs for the demonstrations. She had her own Rube Goldberg to deal with, but his name was Bennett Boyle. Funny, she thought, he really did make the simplest things extremely complicated.

Chapter 49 ~

Maggie was in the office early the next morning, quickly burying herself in work, hoping to get a huge portion of it done before the mid-morning Board of Regents meeting. She heard Elaine come in and greeted her without looking up. But Elaine walked into the inner office and asked cheerfully, "Coffee, boss?"

Coffee? Maggie thought. Elaine knew Maggie didn't drink coffee, and Elaine knew Maggie knew Elaine knew... so why the question? Looking up from her work, she found her answer.

Elaine was dressed head to toe in pink... pink shoes, pink tights, pink wool skirt with matching sweater, pink chiffon scarf, pink earrings. Even her fingernail polish was a shade of the now infamous color. To top it all off, literally, she'd donned a hot pink straight-haired wig which surprisingly fashionable next to her smooth cocoa face and large brown eyes.

"Elaine!" Maggie said laughing. "You look great! Thanks."

Keeping a straight face, Elaine said, "Thanks for what?"

"For the outfit."

"The outfit? Don't know what you mean. This was just next in line in my closet, that's all. I'm guessing you don't want coffee." With that she retreated to her own desk.

To Maggie's delight, each of her staff members was similarly dressed... although none as elaborately as Elaine. Of course all Ricky had to do was put on his Hawaiian shirt with flamingos—which probably *was* next in line in his closet.

She chuckled as each one made a point of coming into her office on a pretend errand just to show their loyalty. And each acted as innocent as Elaine.

When Maggie was ready mid-morning to head downstairs for the monthly Board meeting, Elaine insisted her boss borrow her chiffon scarf saying the hallways were a little chilly and she didn't want Maggie to catch cold.

Maggie obligingly tied the pink scarf around her neck, tucking it in the front of her jacket so that just a hint of the color showed above her dark brown suit. But it did show, and she hoped Bennett Boyle would notice, the idiot.

As she walked to the meeting, she was astounded to discover that at least half of the administration building's staff appeared to be in on the conspiracy, each wearing something pink. In the boardroom she sat next to Jake from the *A-J*, and waved to Miss Katherine, lovely in a bright pink blouse, and Winston, who winked at her and pointed to his pink bow tie. Even Russell Arbuckle sported a pink shirt visible behind the Board of Regent's table. Maggie couldn't imagine how he'd heard about it.

When Bennett Boyle arrived, it was impossible for him to ignore the sea of matching shirts, blouses, sweaters and ties. As all eyes smugly turned toward him, try as he might, he couldn't stop from joining in as his face turned a bright shade of angry pink.

During the administrative reporting section of the meeting, President Parker mentioned the Rube Goldberg Competition he'd attended the previous day, urging Regents to visit the university website to view the winning entries.

Maggie smiled, knowing her team had done another outstanding job on the report. But then the president said, "Mr. Boyle, Chief of Staff, is in charge of the university's website, and has done a good job of getting interesting activities such as this one up in a timely manner. He deserves acknowledgement of this good work."

Boyle was flustered, as the majority of the audience knew about his computer illiteracy. As he nodded at the president in thanks, once again his face turned a slight shade of pink. This time Maggie's did, too.

When the meeting adjourned, Winston stopped Maggie in the hallway. "My dear, you should have been the one being recognized, not Boyle."

"No, Steven, Charlie, Susan and Ricky should have been recognized. They did all the work," Maggie said resignedly. "But, thanks for wearing pink, Windy. It means a lot."

"And about that, don't worry. I told Bennett earlier to lighten up. And that it was his own damn fault anyway for being so 'assillogical.' "

Maggie smiled. Did that particular balderdash mean an illogical ass? If so, she thought that jabberwocky "approaptly" used.

Chapter 50 ~

That next weekend, Maggie made a quick trip to Dallas to see her granddaughters, delighting in how fast they were growing, the older one into a little lady, the younger one into a tomboy. As she left on Sunday, explaining to the tearful girls why they couldn't come to the airport and go with her, she assured them she'd see them in a few short weeks for Thanksgiving.

At Dallas's Love Field Airport, she turned in her rental car, and made the short trek to the gate, boarding pass in hand. As she walked up, she was surprised to see President Parker standing in line waiting for the same plane. They were flying Southwest Airlines and boarding was done by number on the boarding pass, then you chose any seat on the plane. Maggie had a low number, so would be one of the first on. Parker was several numbers behind her. As stealthily as she could, she moved behind a display, waiting until the big boss entered the plane before boarding herself.

Gracefully occupying the empty seat next to him, she said sweetly, "Why, Dr. Parker, what a nice surprise. I'm Margaret Grant, your director of Communications and Marketing. Nice to meet you." She stuck out her hand.

Parker looked startled to be recognized and unhappy to be trapped next to the window by an employee. It would've been awkward for him to move to another seat, but Maggie wasn't certain he wouldn't do just that. She'd already decided if he did, she'd follow him.

He shook her hand quickly but said nothing, turning his head to stare out the window.

"How nice we will have an hour together," she said seriously.

"Hmmph," was his only reply.

Maggie waited until they were about ten minutes into the flight and the drink orders had been taken before she turned to her "boss's boss." During takeoff she'd pleaded with God to put the right words in her mouth and decided to be blunt with Parker, seeing as no other communications techniques had worked thus far.

"Dr. Parker, I understand from Bennett Boyle that you don't like me?" She could see he was slightly startled but she pressed the issue nevertheless. "I don't think you know me well enough... yet... to not like me. May I ask why you don't?"

His eyes widened a bit, but he continued to stare out the window with as much of his back turned toward her as possible.

"You know," she said firmly, "even an axe murderer normally gets her day in court."

At that, the corner of his mouth turned up a little, but only a little— smiling was not a normal activity for him, especially since his arrival at Texas Tech. Slowly he turned to her and just looked, sizing her up.

Quickly taking advantage of what she knew would be a short opportunity, she looked him directly in the eyes and said, "I've never heard of an organization where the communications director didn't report directly to the president and have some type of access to him or her. What is it you so dislike about me, or my department, that I can't even get an appointment with you?"

He spoke slowly, meeting her stare with equal determination. "Dislike you? I don't even know you."

"Exactly my point. Allow me to remedy that. Hello. My name is Margaret Grant. I'm a Tech graduate with a master's in communications from Southern Methodist University. I worked with SMU for more than 15 years, the last ten as their director of Communications and Marketing. President Ramsey can attest to the quality of my work. I have extensive experience in media relations, marketing and communication plans, and can organize a formal dinner for 600 at the drop of a hat. I write speeches, press releases and scripts for promotional videos. I also know how important internal communication is to a university, and your office seems to be doing very little of that. My staff sent over a long list of ways for you to introduce yourself to the university staff and the community, but I don't see you following any of the suggestions, and I think that's a major mistake on your part. As the first African-American president of the university, you have more than an uphill battle with some of this community's less-than-forward thinkers, and our marketing campaign was designed to help you with that. Why can't I get an appointment with you to discuss these things?" She took a breath and waited.

His eyes had widened at her spiel and then narrowed questioningly. "Can't get an appointment with me? I wasn't aware you'd ever tried. Why don't you let me know what's going on?" he said testily.

"I've been trying since you first arrived. Bennett, um, Mr. Boyle keeps telling me you don't want to see me. And…"

"I've been going through Boyle because he's your direct senior report. He tells me you're not particularly interested in new ideas, and that he'll take care of anything I need. He also said you resent working for someone younger than you."

Wow, Maggie thought. Boyle is playing dirty. Okay, here goes political suicide. But her frustration with Boyle was at a breaking point. She'd been careful to not complain to anyone except a few close friends about his micromanaging and his complete ignorance of communications. She had tried to remain as professional as possible. But now, she couldn't hold back any longer. This might be her only chance to right the wrongs, so to speak. She swallowed hard and said, "I don't have a problem working for someone younger than me. I do, however, have a problem working for someone who tries to do my job for me and can't."

"Hmmph," he said again. "I've never seen a list of suggestions from your office. In fact, I'd never see anything from Communications if I didn't look at the website occasionally. I assume your department does the website at Boyle's direction?"

"We do the website, sir, but not at Mr. Boyle's direction. Bennett Boyle knows nothing about the website, probably never looks at it. In fact knows absolutely nothing about communications. It's a wonder I've been able to keep my talented staff the way he constantly interferes with us."

She took a breath, but continued before he could interrupt. "It appears he works overtime to block all our access to you, throwing impediments up for every move we try to make in communicating… to reporters, to faculty, to staff. I can't imagine how it can be easy for you without a professional communicator on the administrative team. And he shouldn't be doing my job, Dr. Parker, and neither should you. I'm perfectly capable of doing it myself. Why *are* you doing it?"

"Doing what?"

"Writing your own press releases… at least three that I know of when you first arrived. They made no sense and didn't enhance your presidency one iota. I don't understand why you would bypass the professional communicators to put out news that wasn't really news."

"I have no idea what you are talking about, Mrs. Grant. I don't write press releases. In the past, at my other universities I always relied on a quality communications team to do that."

"That's what I thought, sir," Maggie said, remembering Sharon's theory that Bennett Boyle was trying to set her up. Her call to Parker's last university confirmed he was a team player who didn't micromanage. She looked him squarely in the eyes to deliver the final question. "But then I still don't understand why you haven't contacted my office for assistance?"

He looked at her for a long moment. "It seems, Mrs. Grant, that I have been repeatedly pointed in the wrong direction. Mr. Boyle assured me he was sending my directives to you, but I never received any follow-up. Perhaps you never received them?"

"No, sir. Never."

"Well then," President Parker said. "I can't seem to get anyone on my administrative team to understand how I want to disseminate my plans, my concepts of how to move the university forward."

"Then tell me so I can help. I'm happy to work up some marketing plans. That's what I was hired for."

"Hmmph," he grunted again skeptically. He had been sorely disappointed in the lack of communication skills of his entire administrative staff, including his chief of staff. He'd mentioned the website at the Regents meeting because as the only bright spot he could find, he thought it might motivate Boyle to do better in other communication endeavors. He'd seriously wondered if he needed to replace several higher ups in order to reach his goals.

"Of course, Dr. Parker. That's what I do. What we do. And we're pretty damn good at it—when given a chance to do it."

This time there was no reply.

"How about we start now?" Maggie said. "I've got no place to go for another 40 minutes. What about you? Any pressing appointments?"

At that, he did smile, or rather his lip curled upward a little more than normal. Maggie took that as an assent, saying, "OK, here's what I need to know about your vision..."

They spent the remainder of the flight in deep conversation, with Maggie asking questions and taking copious notes. When the flight attendant announced the imminent landing, they were both surprised at how quickly the time had gone by.

Dr. Parker looked at his watch, then at Maggie. "Come to my office at 7a.m. tomorrow, Mrs. Grant, and we'll continue our discussion. I've another meeting at eight."

"Thank you, sir. I'll work up some preliminary marketing ideas tonight. And thank you for giving me my day in court."

"Hmmph," he said. "In the morning, be sure you leave your axe at home."

Sharon was waiting for Maggie at the baggage claim area and nodded to President Parker as he walked by. Moments later Maggie appeared and Sharon noticed a smug look on her face as well as a swing in her step.

"And just what makes you so happy on this dreary day?" she asked, giving her friend a welcome home hug as they headed out into the rain.

Maggie grinned. "I believe the war may soon be over."

Chapter 51 ~

The following Saturday, after Tech lost the football game to Texas A&M in an early afternoon thriller, Maggie and Colin walked from Jones Stadium to the Administration Building. Although the temperature hovered around the mid-forties, the sun had been warm on their faces for most of the game, and Maggie's nose was a little red. Her black Tech cap had helped shield her eyes. Walking in the shade of the numerous campus trees, she was glad she'd worn her heavy red wool jacket, black cashmere scarf and fur-lined leather gloves. Colin, presumably past the age of male pigheadedness about appropriately warm clothing, wore a sensible brown suede fur-lined bomber jacket and his old Notre Dame cap Maggie had finally returned.

When questioned earlier about his school spirit by a completely red-and-black-dressed Sharon, he pointed to the red scarf he'd tied around his neck and tucked inside his jacket saying, "My Tech spirit shows enough in this muffler. I wear the ND cap because it's comfortable. And I yell just as loud as you do, Miss Red Raider. Do *you* have a Red Raider bobble-head on your dash?"

Sharon's eyes widened. "You have a Tech bobble-head in your truck?"

Colin didn't know why he'd mentioned it and wished he hadn't, but now that he had, he stood straight and defended it, "Yes. A gift from the Saddle Tramp president. So?"

"So, I take it back," she said laughing. Besides, she admitted silently to herself, he did yell as loudly as she did, even heckling the referees at the right times.

"Good," was all he said.

Playing musical chairs with Sean and Doug and Sharon throughout the game, Maggie and Colin sat together during the first and third quarters, meeting at the southwest gate when the fourth quarter was over. Red Raiders 17, Aggies 21. Colin had promised to show Maggie the Saddle Tramp tower, but she'd agreed to go that day only if they lost. She didn't want to interrupt the victory bells, nor was she sure she wanted to be so close when they were ringing. If victory was on their side, the tour could wait until another time. Unfortunately, victory was illusive.

As they walked, she asked, "Do you really have a bobble-head doll in your truck?"

Embarrassed, he admitted he did. Jamie Chavez had given it to him last week, insisting it was perfect for his mentor's dashboard. He'd seemed so genuinely excited about it and so few things these days made Jamie smile, that Colin couldn't bear to refuse. So there it sat and there it would stay, bobbing its silly head up and down, up and down.

"I think that's sweet," Maggie said.

"Hmmph," was his only answer.

As they walked onto the north-south esplanade, in front of the long, narrow Civil Engineering Building, they had a view of the Administration Building, majestically anchoring the two-pronged key, Memorial Circle in the middle.

Maggie never tired of looking at the architecture. "It's really a beautiful campus, isn't it?" she asked, looking at how the red and gold leaves on the hundreds of campus trees enhanced the setting. Thousands of yellow chrysanthemums lined the walkways and gardens all across campus.

"That it is. The Admin Building looks like the façade of the University at Alcala de Henares, east of Madrid."

She looked up at him, questioningly. "You've been to Spain?"

"Cool, today. Isn't it?" he said. She didn't press. There were so many things she didn't know about this man—especially about those twenty years of doin' stuff for the government—but if he wanted to tell her more, she knew he would when he was ready.

The east door of the Administration Building was unlocked, and they headed up the old stone steps to the top floor.

On the third floor landing across from the entrance to the main hallway, seven narrow black steps led to a small plain white door, inconspicuous among the more stately wide oak doors throughout the building. Colin walked up and unlocked it. Stale, cool air rushed out, making Maggie pull her jacket tighter around her. Evidently, the towers had no heating or air conditioning.

The open door revealed a small landing and then a continuation of the steep stairs to the left, only much more narrow... seven steps to the first turn, then seven or eight to each of the five landings thereafter. The steps were covered in tattered red carpet with black rubber edges.

As they climbed up the first set of tower stairs, they passed an east-facing double window on the right, providing light and a splendid view over the treetops of the east esplanade down to Broadway Street. On the left, halfway up, the stairwell's open space had been filled in with a platform of sorts, about four feet square, tiled in black with a red Double T and edged with a foot-tall picket fence, painted red and black. A red door bordered the platform to the left—probably leading to a storage area under the staircase that continued up to the tower, Maggie guessed. The platform and storage area looked like later additions to the stairwell.

The walls were painted black for the first three or so feet up from the floor, then bordered with a wide red stripe before white paint extended up to the black and red ceiling high above. A huge Saddle Tramp cloth banner hung on the wall over the second set of stairs. A ten-foot Double T was expertly painted on the wall over the third flight. Then on the right, at the next landing, was another small door, this one painted black, leading into the attic area to the west.

In all, 53 steps led to the tower from the main building's third floor landing, making one and three quarter complete revolutions. On the final level, a wooden platform had been built about five feet high, painted red on the outside and white on the underside. A heavy brass railing outlined the top of the platform for safety.

Two long wooden black benches sat in the narrow spaces between the platform and the dozen floor-to-ceiling ornate casement windows that provided spectacular views of the campus in all directions. Between the windows, numerous Saddle Tramp plaques were hung, engraved with names of the organization's officers and those honored throughout the years.

When she walked around the platform, Maggie could see a second Double T centered in the five-foot-square tiled top. On the far side of the platform, a narrow black metal ladder began on the floor, rungs extending up across the edge of the platform to a red metal trap door in the middle of the ceiling high up above, directly over the Double T.

Two thick chains hung from the ceiling next to the metal door—she supposed these were attached to the bells. Two worn pairs of leather gloves lay near the ends of the chains. By climbing one-fourth of the way up the ladder and standing on the Double T platform, but never on the Double T—Colin explained it was sacred—the chains could be pulled to ring out victory on the bells above. Today they were silent.

One spotlight hung from the ceiling and she sensed it was rather dark up here at night, especially in the stairwell. The switch was down the stairs a ways. She hadn't noticed any other lights or switches. Maybe the lights from outside on the tower helped. Or were there lights on the towers? She'd have to look next time she was outside after dark.

Impressed with the view, although it was a little diffused through the dirty windows—she hesitated when Colin asked if she wanted to sit down after their long climb.

"I'm afraid I might stick," she said, looking down at the offered bench in amused disgust

"What?" he asked, examining it. The bench was, in fact, grimy with not only dirt and dust, but old food stuff, spilled drink residue and other unidentifiable splotches. "Oh, yeah, it's a little dirty. You know, guys don't always clean up after themselves."

"Raised two sons, remember?" she said looking around the interior. "But really, Colin, they bring dates up here? Isn't this a..." she stopped, just shaking her head and wrinkling her nose, hesitating to accurately describe the dilapidated "club house," not wanting to embarrass him.

He looked around, too, now more focused, and was astonished at what he saw, wrinkling his own nose. How could he have missed it? Scraps of discarded paper and food wrappers were strewn here and there, faded streamers hung from the corners, the shabby carpet was worn, dirty and unraveling in several places, the plaster walls were peeling, and the paint— completely gone in several places in the wake of old masking tape—was years beyond need of a fresh coat. Every inch of the place seemed to be neglected, and it was clear a broom or vacuum or mop hadn't been used in quite some time.

"It's a pig sty!" he said in genuine surprise. "Gosh, I'm sorry. I've never even noticed it. I'm not up here often. Guess I'd better talk to the guys about it. It's embarrassing... um, want to see the bells?" Maybe a diversion was in order.

"Of course," she said with a smile and looked up instinctively.

Colin climbed the thin metal ladder, which bowed under his weight but was securely bolted to the floor, platform edge and ceiling. When he pushed up the bright red trap door, even colder air rushed in to the small tower space. Maggie gazed up at the bottom of the smaller of the two bells, which Colin told her weighed in at "a mere" three hundred pounds, impressive clapper dangling, almost expectantly, as if waiting to fulfill its purpose.

Above it hung the larger bell, all nine hundred pounds, he said, of thick metal. A clear cloudless sky showed around the edges of the bells through the graceful, ornately carved open archways. She could only imagine how loudly the bells sounded to those Tramps lucky enough to be chosen as victory ringers. Hope they wear earplugs, she thought as Colin closed the trap door and came back down the ladder.

Maggie looked out across the administration building's red roof to the west, and studied the other tower. Its matching open archways revealed not just two, but a series of bells, the carillon bells that could produce melodic tunes, including of course, the Red Raider fight song. She was pretty certain those bells were played electronically rather than manually.

Shivering a little in the unheated tower, she suggested they find a warm place for dinner, and Colin agreed. He stepped back to allow her to go down the stairs first, and in doing so, accidently kicked one of the benches, moving it a little away from the wall. They heard something drop and both bent down to see what it was, bumping heads on the way.

"Yeowch!" Colin said, rubbing his head and laughing. "You've got a hard head, Margaret Grant!"

"And I'm not even Irish, unlike you who, ow, ow, ow, also have a hard head," she laughed, rubbing her own. "What fell?"

"I don't know. All I saw was stars!"

"Ha... ha... it wasn't that hard!"

He reached down under the bench and pulled out a small dusty black frame, glass cracked long ago. Brushing it off gingerly with his palm, he read it aloud:

"Like the soul of man, you can't put a finger on it, can't draw a picture of it. School Spirit just appears, when you need it, then disappears until it is needed again."
—*Arch Lamb, founder of the Saddle Tramps*

"I'll get a cleaning crew up here tomorrow," Colin said, shaking his head.

Chapter 52 ~

Fern Arbuckle had been true to her word and given Maggie details of the Bible study group at the Cotton A farmhouse scheduled to meet every Tuesday night. Earlier in the fall, Maggie had gone for the first meeting as a trial... to see if it was something she wanted to continue. She didn't think she could devote one night each week, but it would be nice to be able to attend on occasion.

Arriving just before seven, she was shocked to see the long line of cars parked around the house. And Colin's truck was there, too. Neither had spoken about the Bible Study, and each was surprised to see the other.

"I should have thought to ask you," Colin said as she sat down next to him in the crowded room. "I've been coming for several years. Glad you're here."

"Me, too," Maggie said, looking at the large crowd seated in rows of chairs in the Arbuckle's oversized living area. Tom and his wife Julie were there and she recognized several other church members, including the Bodeckers. She wondered how a crowd this large could study together... or was it a lecture? She didn't think that was what she needed.

Fern quieted the crowd a few minutes later, welcoming everyone and explaining the study procedures for the benefit of the newcomers. Tonight they would talk about several topics they wanted to discuss this fall, make a list and choose at least five topics. Each topic would have a volunteer leader who would prepare the next two weeks' lessons—using the Catechism of the Catholic Church as a reference. Then each week the large crowd, broken at random into five smaller groups, would rotate every other week to the various leaders, in essence, covering all five topics for two weeks each. Three topics would be presented here, and two more at Tom and Julie's house.

Maggie guessed from the discussion this process had been going on for several years, a theory Colin confirmed later. He'd been a member for more than eight years, he'd said, and had twice volunteered to lead a discussion group. Many participants enjoyed being the leaders, especially if the topic was one they wanted to explore further, while most preferred to move from topic to topic.

In all, ten weeks would be devoted to the fall Bible study, with a covered dish party the eleventh week, prior to Thanksgiving. If leaders had questions about their topics, Father Sean, although not a participant, and not present, was a willing reference source.

"What we find," Fern said later to Maggie, "is that the topics are fascinating and what lay people would really like to study. We don't have all the answers, but we learn a great deal by trying to find them. Sometimes, we repeat a topic the next year if there's still interest."

Maggie was impressed by the simplicity of the arrangement and by the interesting possibilities of the sessions. She straightaway decided this was something she wanted to be a part of as often as she could. She was disappointed, however, when she wasn't put in the same group as Colin.

As it turned out, though, being in different groups gave them an opportunity to discuss the sessions on a more personal level. Whether they met for coffee or dinner, they would touch on what they'd learned that week and compare their group discussion to the others, most of the time increasing their knowledge of the scriptures, and definitely their knowledge of each other.

One subject of particular interest to them both was confession. Not growing up Catholic, Maggie, along with the majority of Protestants she thought, had a definite misconception of this particular sacrament. She'd been surprised at how transformative the simple confession was for her, and after discussions with Colin, she knew he felt a relief after his visits, too.

Sexuality was the topic being led by Tom's wife Julie, but neither Colin nor Maggie had attended that one yet. For Colin it was his second to last topic, and for Maggie, the last. When she thought about it, perhaps it might be the most interesting discussion of all for the two of them. She'd definitely pose Sharon's query to better understand Saint Paul's admonitions. She wondered how well Colin and Saint Paul were acquainted.

Tuesday nights after the Bible Study was the perfect time for Maggie to "trespass" the cotton fields since she was already on the property. Being in different groups, Maggie and Colin came in separate cars—her second session was at Tom and Julie's—and she often would be one of the last to leave, turning off the main drive onto an isolated dirt road to take her far out into the cotton where no lights or highway sounds intruded on her thoughts. Maggie's refuge used to be activities—now it was the solitude of the cotton fields.

Josh's blanket, as she called it since its return, was often thrown on the Volvo's hood. Maggie climbed up to lean against the windshield, comfortably gazing up into the deep night sky. The first time she'd spread it out, she remembered the pleasant visit with Josh's parents in late July. Josh's mother, Carolyn, had wanted to thank the two ladies personally for their help, so they met at McAllister's where Josh still worked, and sat at one of his tables so his father could leave a big tip. It was a pleasant evening with both Maggie and Sharon insisting they had only done what anyone else who witnessed the accident would have done.

When Maggie went to the cotton fields during the early morning hours, mainly on weekends, she'd walk the furrows, gazing out over row upon row of red dirt and plants. Even when the cotton had been defoliated, crisp and brown and ready for harvest, something about the simple gift of the earth's bounty called to her. She couldn't wait until spring to watch the entire growing cycle up close. Tom had promised to let her ride in their newest tractor, one that pulled a 16-row planter. He beamed with pride as he talked about the planting process while showing her the massive equipment.

Even though oil and cattle at the Cotton A were his main jobs now, he helped out with planting and harvesting each year. "My granddaddy came to West Texas and plowed with a mule, one row at a time," he said proudly, then stopped when he noticed her nodding. "Guess you've heard that part of the story before."

"Yes, but go on, please, Tom. It's fascinating to me."

"Okay, then. Granddaddy stuck it out during the depression and was smart enough and fortunate enough to buy up land others gave up on, starting the acquisition of all our acres. In just three generations, we're using satellite guidance systems to run the tractors and irrigation wheels. I think my dad and his dad worked harder physically, but today's farmers work harder at the business end of it all. I need to know computers, statistics, trends, and GPS systems."

Maggie stood next to the six-foot high wheels of the huge John Deere tractor as Tom talked about the computers and guidance system on board that allowed them to plow perfectly concentric circles, most of it done with the tractor driving itself. Circles, rather than rows, allowed for more crop per acre. Tom explained most of his time in the air-conditioned cab was spent looking backwards to make certain all the parts of the planter were doing what they should—plow, plant, cover and fertilize. If all went well, then about six days later the precious seedlings would pop their pretty little heads out and reach up for the sun.

"Some of the fields are planted with wheat earlier in the spring. Once it ripens, we terminate it to give the sandy loam more stability so the West Texas wind doesn't blow all the dirt to Fort Worth. Other fields are planted with a grass-type plant between the rows that we allow to grow. It acts as a wind barrier for seedlings until they're about eight inches tall."

"Fascinating," was Maggie's constant and sincere reply.

Maggie chose different routes, different paths, different fields to get away from it all. The Cotton A comprised more than 12,000 acres stretching across Lubbock and Hockley counties. The western acres, more rugged than the plowed fields, were used for the cattle and oil businesses overseen by Tom. Maggie didn't think the middle of a cattle herd would be quite as peaceful, so she limited her forays to the cotton fields in the eastern acres.

Every so often, she would stumble upon a playa, once almost driving straight into one. Thousands of these shallow depressions pocketed the South Plains, providing seasonal water for wildlife, either native or migratory.

Playas, translated as "beaches" or "shores" in Spanish, are normally full of water and plant life. Within Lubbock city limits, lush green parks are built around the numerous small lakes. Ephemeral or permanent, playas are the holding tanks for rain runoff, keeping the water until it evaporates into the dry, semi-arid atmosphere. Maggie marveled at how even a little rainfall could quickly flood the streets of Lubbock—at her corner it often reached halfway to the house after an intense downpour—but then almost within a matter of minutes receded and disappeared without the assistance of storm drains. Nature had conveniently provided the flat plains with a natural drainage system—playas. The nearest one to her was in Flint Park, and after a heavy rainfall, often half the park's green area was under water for a short while.

As the Llano Estacado makes a gradual decline in elevation—an almost consistent ten feet per mile—water drains into the playas northwest to southeast, away from the Rocky Mountains which were originally formed eons ago. Where crops are planted, playas serve as runoff basins not only for rain, but also for furrow irrigation.

The irrigation runoff—tailwater—drains into playas and is then in turn pumped back into the fields. Energy costs of pumping from playas is much less than pumping from the underground Ogallala aquifer. And using the playas extends the life of the vast underground basin so vital to life on the South Plains.

When Maggie related her close encounter with the playa, Russ proudly told her it was Fern's doing that the Cotton A playas were alive and well today. Seems when she married into the family, she possessed a fondness for the desert jewels and was appalled Russ' dad had plowed over some of them.

She mounted an intense campaign and quickly convinced the elder Arbuckle to preserve them instead of destroy them. Then, over the next several decades, she supported local and state wildlife preservationists, environmental specialists and the Texas Water Commission as they campaigned the entire region to allow the playas to remain as God intended, natural runoff basins to support the abundant wildlife of the area. Assistance originally came from Texas Tech University's Department of Range and Wildlife Management, which spent a great deal of time convincing local farmers of the benefits of proper playa management.

Controversies surrounding playas increased in the mid-1970s when the Army Corps of Engineers, the United States Fish and Wildlife Service, the High Plains Underground Water Conservation District Number One, and many other agencies and groups bickered and argued over jurisdiction, regulatory control and the value of keeping the shallow basins. Some farmers loathed, cursed and tried to kill the hundreds of thousands of ducks, geese, red-winged blackbirds and sandhill cranes that migrated across the area, often destroying or crippling acres of crops. Russ said proudly that Fern was in the middle of it all. Her position was that God created the birds too, and after all, they were here first. She insisted a little respect went a long way. Today, several area farmers leased their "playa land" to duck hunters and made a tidy profit for their efforts, an interesting compromise.

When Maggie expressed an interest in learning more, Russ loaned her a book by area native Jim Steiert, *Playas, Jewels of the Plains*. The arresting photos by Wyman Meinzer reminded Maggie of the windmill photographs in Winston's museum office. She borrowed the book and spent many nights propped up in bed fascinated.

Late one night, she was so captivated by something she had just read that she called Sharon, who swore she hadn't been asleep but sounded drowsy all the same.

"You'll never guess what this books says, Phelps," Maggie said excitedly.

"No, I won't, so tell me quick, Maggie, my interest is fading fast." She yawned loudly to accentuate her statement.

"Llano Estacado has salt lakes on it! Salt lakes! Some of the playas are called salinas... salt... not many, but some! Why even Coronado knew about the salinas. I thought Utah had the only salt water between the oceans... Phelps? Are you there? This is fascinating!"

"Fascinating, Maggie. I'd love to hear all about it, but I need to... to wash my hair or something. We can talk about salt tomorrow..." she said sleepily and hung up.

Maggie continued devouring the book, oblivious to her friend's sarcasm.

185

Chapter 53 ~

Halloween fell on a weekday, so the Saturday morning before Maggie bought about ten pounds of candy for the event. She also rented two videos, inviting Colin to watch them with her Saturday evening. He'd seen the sweets when he came in, already in a bowl by the front door.

As Maggie cued up the DVDs, Colin commented, "That's a lot of candy, Maggie. You planning on inviting the whole city over?"

"It's my first Halloween in the house. I have no idea if any of the neighborhood kids trick-or-treat, so I just want to be prepared. If there's any left, I can donate it to the church daycare. Are you coming over on Halloween to carve a pumpkin with me?"

"Carve a pumpkin? I haven't carved a pumpkin since the '70s. They still do that?" he asked.

"Of course they still do that... I still do that... at least I used to do that for the boys and then for the grandkids. But yes, I'm still doing that. Will you come help? I'll give you some of the candy," she said playfully.

Colin went to the overflowing bowl and dug through it. "Let's see what kind you bought. Might not be worth it," he teased. "Okay, here's Snickers. I'll do it for five of these. Got five?"

"Yes, I've got more than five," she said laughing.

"Good. It's a date. I'll take one now on account," he said, putting it in his shirt pocket as they moved to the living room to watch the videos.

"On account of what?" Maggie asked.

"On account of I can."

Although that remark cost him a well-deserved punch in the arm, they settled in to watch "Cowboy G-Men," Vol. I and Vol. II. She'd seen the old black and white television series episodes advertised and couldn't resist renting them. She was still a little gun shy about talking with Colin on the subject of the FBI, so this was sort of a test to see if he had forgiven her.

He loved the videos and gave no indication he even remembered jumping down her throat about it after the hand-harvest. Plot lines and dialogue were so bad they both laughed the entire night, but Maggie fell in love with Stoney Crockett and Pat Gallagher, "partners dedicated to serving justice in the old west." Funny how the big rocks the bad guys used for ambushes looked identical in all episodes, whether they were supposed to be in Texas, Arizona or the Northwest Territory.

Colin declared it a great series, as the G-Men always "got their man." Unfortunately, he thought, it doesn't always happen like that in real life.

On Halloween, Elaine was decked out in her pink wig again, but this time it was coordinated with a heavily fringed roaring '20s flapper costume. Steven had on a red clown nose and huge polka dot bow tie with his usual designer clothes and Susan was in all black with witches' hat and broom. Charlie said he didn't like Halloween because it messed up any photos he had to take, so no costumes for him.

In his usual Hawaiian shirt, Ricky announced he'd dressed as Don Ho, his grandmother's favorite singer from Hawaii. Neither Susan nor Elaine had a clue as to who Don Ho was, so Ricky found a photo on the internet. Agreeing there was a slight resemblance, they still thought his "costume" a cop-out. He thought it was genius, as had the new young accountant lady from the second floor he was dating. Elaine had set them up and all seemed happy about it.

Maggie had worn her darkest suit and had an orange scarf draped around her neck. It was the most she would do but still felt festive. Mid-morning she was headed for another scheduled meeting with President Parker to talk about part of his mission—what he wanted to accomplish by the end of the school year. She hoped Bennett Boyle wouldn't be there. He almost always found something to object to whenever she presented an idea, still! At least Parker was talking to her now. She thought they'd made progress in that area, even though she still reported to Boyle, but she was sending copies of her weekly summaries directly to the president as well as to her boss.

Once again, she was working with Boyle in the way she knew worked, keeping her temper in check, especially after the now infamous "Pink Incident." As she walked downstairs, she chuckled as she remembered so many colleagues supporting her that day. Served the man right, she thought as she pushed open the door to the lengthy outside arcade.

She liked using the long way to get to the first-floor offices—liked going outside for a brief breath of fresh air and seeing the students scurrying to classes. It made her feel more a part of the university. Today was warm for late October, and the sun was shining. Early morning showers had forced her to drive to work, but they'd moved northeast and the skies were clear and crisp.

As she walked across under the south-side open-air arcade, she glanced at the Double T bench, occupied by three students this particular day. One young girl, dressed in a black and white spotted cow costume, was reading, feet up on the bench, obviously comfortable, book resting comically on her stiff plastic udders. Another girl was sitting with her eyes closed, face to the sun, soaking up the warmth. Maggie honestly couldn't tell if her Goth-like outfit was a costume or normal attire for her. The third student lounged with his head bent over a book, Dracula teeth protruding from his mouth, purple and black cape draped behind him. As she smiled at the scene, Maggie whispered to herself, "I love college campuses."

She walked along, quickly reaching the open archway that led to Memorial Circle. As one, the three students turned their heads toward her.

The seemingly choreographed movement caught Maggie's eye. It was as if she'd called out to them, which she hadn't. Strange. She glanced to her left to see if they were looking at someone beyond her and then heard what they obviously had heard. A siren.

It had been there, in her head, but sirens were common out on University Avenue. This one was getting louder. She stopped to listen and then walked toward the north side of the archway as the sound intensified and turned into campus. The phone rang on her belt.

Elaine said, "Fire. Civil Engineering building. Steven's on his way down with Susan and I'm calling Charlie."

"Call the president's office and tell them where I'm going," Maggie said quickly, turning to hurry toward the north/south esplanade as the fire engine made its way there.

When she reached the north side of the circle, she still saw no smoke, but heard a second siren and saw an ambulance turning from University Avenue. Someone's hurt, she thought, and quickened her pace.

People were streaming out of every exit of the long, narrow two-story building and she could hear the alarm sounding. Recognizing the fire chief from the library blaze, she approached and asked what he knew.

"Report is it's in a closet here on the first floor, but we're checking it out now."

"And the ambulance?" Maggie asked.

"Don't know yet. Could be merely precautionary. Give me a few more minutes."

Knowing Sharon's office was on the first floor, she thought she'd call her in a minute to find out what she knew. She didn't see her, assuming she'd evacuated out the east entrance. Maggie was on the west side.

Steven and Susan arrived, sans Halloween props, and she gave instructions on what she wanted them to do. Campus police were there, too, and began setting up a perimeter. Charlie appeared and was snapping photos. She pulled off her orange scarf and stuffed it in her pocket. Wouldn't look professional on camera if television reporters showed up.

Steven suggested a place for media, if the fire was big enough to warrant reporters, and at Maggie's instruction, he set out to make it happen. Susan headed around the building to ask some questions of those who had evacuated to the east side. Elaine called to say she'd spoken to the president's office and he was on his way to the scene. But Elaine couldn't find Boyle... she'd thought she'd better let him know too, since they did report to him, but he wasn't in his office. She'd left him a message.

"Good idea," Maggie told her. The fire chief came back out and headed for her.

"A small fire in a cleaning closet. It's out, for the most part. But one of the professors saw smoke and opened the door—caused a backdraft that burned her arm pretty good."

"*Her* arm?" Maggie said in alarm. There were only two female engineering professors. "Do you know her name?"

"Phelps, I think." Maggie moved immediately toward the building. "She's coming out now," the chief yelled after her.

Paramedics emerged carrying a gurney with Sharon lying on it, upper right arm wrapped in bandages, IV attached. Maggie moved quickly to her side, noticing her hair was singed and the side of her neck and ear were a deep red. "Are you all right?"

Walking alongside the gurney to the ambulance, Maggie tried to remain calm as Sharon turned her head to the familiar voice. "Sharon, talk to me," Maggie said.

In obvious pain, tears rimmed her tightly closed eyes. She opened them when she heard her name. Maggie could see the pain and fear.

"Stupid me opened the door. I knew I shouldn't but did it anyway. I've called Doug. He's meeting me at University Medical Center. They said it's not too terribly bad... sure hurts like hell, though."

"I'm coming with you," Maggie said as they prepared to put her into the ambulance.

"No, you stay and do your job. Doug will be there. Come when you're finished. Bring me balloons! You know I love balloons! I'll see you later... Yeowch! Careful there, guys. I break!"

"I love you!" Maggie said right before they closed the ambulance doors.

Steven came up at that moment, saying the media was here but so was Boyle, and he was trying to talk to them. Maggie stomped her foot in frustration, and said out loud, "Over my dead body." Following Steven, she headed toward the two reporters.

"Thank you, Mr. Boyle," Maggie said firmly as she stepped in front of him. "We've got it now." Turning to the reporters, she said, "Here's what we know so far..." and she filled them in on the facts.

Bennett Boyle had taken a few steps back in surprise and was once again incensed. Who does she think she is? He moved forward to intervene but stopped as he heard his name. Turning, he saw it was President Parker off to his left, motioning him to join him.

"Let's let them handle it, shall we, Mr. Boyle? I don't think they need us here right now. I'll walk with you back to the Administration Building." At that, he took Boyle's arm, turning him away from the scene and heading away from the chaos.

Just as she was wrapping up the full afternoon of calls from reporters and curious staffers, Maggie was summoned to the president's office. Please, she thought, don't ask me to stay late to make up the meeting we missed. She needed to go see Sharon, who was dismissed from the hospital about twenty minutes ago. And she needed to stop and get balloons on the way.

She hurried to the president's suite and was ushered in immediately. He asked her to have a seat. As she did, he said, "Chief Callahan tells me it was a relatively small fire with damage confined to the closet area. Boyle is getting estimates of the damages and I'm sure insurance will cover most of it."

"Yes, sir. I've talked with Chief Callahan myself. We've sent out a news release and e-mailed staff and students. Also, there's a story on the website."

"Yes, I saw them all. You and your staff did a good job today. You kept it contained, just released the facts, no speculation, and I think you covered all the bases. Well done," President Parker said.

Maggie hadn't had a compliment from administration in so long she was momentarily speechless. Recovering, she said, "Um, thank you, sir. That means a lot. I'll pass it along to the staff."

"I also know Chief Callahan thinks the fire was deliberately set."

"No, not again!" Maggie said, concerned. "Do they think it's the same person who started the library fire? Did they get any surveillance tape?"

"They don't know much at this point. And I'm told surveillance cameras are one of the many things in next year's budget. We won't release that piece of news—"

"Until the police department is ready," Maggie said absently, not even aware she had interrupted the president. She was deep in thought about it all. Parker smiled, deciding to tell her his latest decision.

"Mrs. Grant?" she looked at him. "I'm thinking it makes no sense for the Communications office to report to the chief of staff. I'll make the arrangements, so as of now, your office will report directly to me and you'll be part of the administrative team. Does my decision meet with your approval?" Parker said smugly.

She didn't think it possible to be stunned into silence twice within one minute, but it had happened. Her lower jaw involuntarily fell open. Sitting and staring at him, she came back into focus when he cleared his throat. Quickly she said, "Absolutely, sir. It's... it's perfect. Thank you, Dr. Parker. Thank you so much." A grin spread across her face she couldn't contain.

"Okay, then. Go see Dr. Phelps and give her my best. Wait and tell your staff tomorrow, because I haven't broken the news to Bennett Boyle yet. We'll talk again in the morning."

Maggie rose, still grinning. "You won't be sorry, Dr. Parker. I promise you that."

"See that I'm not. Now go! It's late and I'd like to go home."

Chapter 54 ~

When Maggie arrived at the Nest, she opened the Volvo's back door to reach in for the balloons. She had bought two each of red, orange, yellow, green, blue and purple—twice a rainbow, the clerk called it—and it had been no small feat to get all twelve of them stuffed into her car for the short ride from Market Street grocery store.

She'd brought a whole roasted chicken and several side dishes for dinner, already cooked and warm, knowing Doug would be too worried about Sharon to want to leave her side, even to cook.

She grabbed the ribbons and tugged at the balloons, pulling them out of the car one or two at a time, scraping and rubbing them against the car window, losing only one green one in the process. It floated up about 20 feet before hitting an overhanging tree branch and popping, making her jump as her phone rang at the exact same moment. Juggling balloons and grocery bags, she managed to answer the cell phone, holding it against her ear with her shoulder.

"Margaret Grant," she answered as she walked toward the Nest's front porch.

"I'm standing at your front door with a frog, a pirate and Tinkerbell. Are you here?"

"Colin! Oh, no, I completely forgot! Halloween. I'm so sorry! Um, the door's not locked, go ahead and give them some candy, if you don't mind. I am so sorry!"

When she briefed him on where she was and why, he said he'd come right over, but she said no, she was planning on delivering the balloons and food and then leaving so Sharon could rest. She'd be home within 30 minutes. Would he mind waiting?

He'd wait, he said. "Give Sharon a kiss for me."

Sharon was delighted with the balloons but too groggy from pain pills to talk much. Doug was grateful for the food and asked Maggie to stay. She declined, and after kissing Sharon on the forehead for Colin, left shortly after she arrived. Details about the fire and celebration of victory over Boyle could wait until tomorrow.

The delicious aroma coming from the kitchen hit her as soon as she walked in the door. She was pleased to find Colin making dinner. Miss Priss was pacing in the kitchen, tail switching as if scolding Murphy for his intrusion. Seeing her mistress, she daintily strutted to her corner and promptly closed her eyes, prepared for sleep, obviously trusting Maggie to take care of the situation now that she was finally home.

"Mushroom omelets, m'lady," he said, bowing to her, complete in bright red apron, spatula in hand. "Hope you like lots of cheese?"

"Love it," she smiled, leaning up to give him a generous kiss.

"Hmmm," he said, smiling himself. "If a simple egg dish gets me that kind of response, wonder what a thick juicy grilled steak might get me?" He gave her a mock leer. The doorbell rang.

"Silly man," she said as she went to answer. Returning to the kitchen a few minutes later, she said, "More trick-or-treaters. Those were adorable. A fairy princess and a cowboy. Then a tiny Yoda came up. So cute! Asked for Snickers only! But what happened to all the candy? The bowl's half empty."

"I've answered the door at least two dozen times already. Tell me, did this Yoda have on purple sneakers? And his dad out by the street had red hair?"

"Yes on both counts as a matter of fact. How'd you know?"

"Been here twice already. Second time said he only took Snickers. I gave 'em extra just for his excellent taste in candy."

The next day at noon, although Sharon was happy to see Maggie, she insisted she come back later for dinner so they could talk. She'd taken another pain pill a few minutes earlier and was growing more sleepy by the minute, so tonight would be better to provide details of the incident. Besides, there was plenty of food left from last night. Maggie promised to be back around six.

A she drove back to the office, Maggie thought about last night and Colin. They'd enjoyed their meal, although they were interrupted several more times by cute costumed kids of all shapes and sizes. The purple-shoed Yoda hadn't pressed his luck, but there were several trick-or-treaters who looked a little too old to be pilfering candy. Colin had given them a hard stare and a smaller portion. Finally, with a few remaining pieces of candy still in the bowl, the neighborhood was quiet.

Wine in hand, they'd settled on the couch as Maggie shared what she knew of the fire, which at this point wasn't much. Then she told him of the president's decision and how it would make life much easier for her entire staff. Colin toasted to her success, and she basked in the glow of their accomplishment, knowing it had been a total team effort.

She wondered if Colin felt as comfortable around her again as she did around him. She decided he must if he would forage in her kitchen and fix a meal. This was nice, she thought. And nicer still that it felt so natural. But what now? He'd left just before ten and held her tightly after a nice, warm, but not lingering kiss. She thought if she'd asked, though, he'd have been more than happy to stay the night.

But that would never do, she thought. I'm definitely not ready to do something so against what I think is right for me, even if he does make my insides do somersaults. She'd just have to worry about that another day. This one was already too busy.

And, she suddenly remembered, yesterday was so busy Colin had conveniently forgotten to remind her about pumpkin carving. Maybe she ought to demand return of the five Snickers.

Chapter 55 ~

Amanda gratefully accepted the invitation from her mother-in-law's friend, Sharon, for their annual Thanksgiving buffet, in part to be spared the task of cooking her first full holiday dinner, but mainly because she was dying to meet the man Maggie had "been seeing." Maggie had refused to call it "dating," saying she was too old for such nonsense—he was just a male friend she was "seeing."

"Ha," thought Amanda.

And a trip to Lubbock would be good for Ben, who needed to see his mother was indeed settled and perhaps even happy.

Michael and his wife were flying in from the Northwest and would be housed in Sharon and Doug's guest cottage, while Amanda and her brood would stay with Maggie. Although on visits to Dallas her mother-in-law had described how different her new house was from the old, until Amanda stepped inside she had no idea of the enormity of that difference.

The small foyer opened up to a large living area with a vaulted, beamed ceiling that had previously been attic space. Huge paintings in vivid colors graced the walls, most, it seems, done by Maggie's hand. Amanda recognized the heirloom desk, but most of the other furniture was new—or rather old. It was obvious Maggie had stayed away from the traditional chintz-fabric style of her Dallas home and instead furnished this house in a tasteful array of quality pieces from several different eras. Surprisingly warm and inviting, the eclectic style was at the same time stunning and tasteful in its arrangement. Amanda loved it and immediately began having quiet thoughts about how to achieve the same effect in her own home.

Ben's reaction upon entering had been a bit different. "Good grief, Mom. You live here? This is nothing like the old house in Dallas." Maggie raised her eyebrows. He continued, "This is not you!"

Taking her youngest son gently by the arm as he continued to stare at her home, she quietly said, "Yes, Benjamin, it *is* me. Just not the *me* you've ever known. This is the *me* before I had a family, and now it is the *me* I'm comfortable with again."

Ben looked down at her and then over her head at Amanda, who was definitely giving him a look that said, "Remember what we talked about?" He sighed and gave his mom a hug. "Okay," he said reluctantly. "I guess I can adjust to the new house, as long as you're still the same mother I know and love."

"No problem there," Maggie said, returning the affection. "Now, let's get you guys settled. We're due at Sharon's in less than an hour to help and I need to get changed."

"What about Michael and Karen?" Ben asked as his mother ushered him down the hallway to one of the guest rooms while Amanda took the girls into the one across the hall with twin beds.

"They arrived last night and are already at Sharon's. They're eager to see you. Oh, my pies!" Maggie cried as she hurried back to the kitchen to retrieve them from the oven.

When she returned a minute later to the guest room, she found Ben standing exactly where she had left him, stiff, luggage still in his hand, staring at a huge painting over the bed. Oh, she thought smiling, I'd forgotten about that, as she surveyed the portrait of her granddaughters. They were sitting in the grass, sun shining on their ribbon-tied hair, laughing and blowing bubbles. Absorbed in their play and in each other, they were oblivious to any audience. She'd snapped a picture of them in that pose last summer and used it as her guide. Although impressionistic in nature, there was no doubt as to their identities, especially to their stunned father.

Amanda walked in and stood between them, looking puzzled at her husband and mother-in-law standing silent as sentries, and followed their gaze. She gasped and reached for Ben, who dropped the luggage and put his arm around her, not taking his eyes off his little girls on the wall.

"Oh, Maggie," Amanda finally said softly. She reached over to pull her into the embrace.

"Do you like it?" Maggie whispered, asking them both.

They both answered with silent tears.

"Good," Maggie said, wiping away a tear herself. "It's your Christmas present."

Since it had been smoking on the back patio grill since before the sun came up, the twenty-pound turkey gave off a delectable aroma that infiltrated the house and had mouths watering and stomachs rumbling. There was an equally large ham in the oven inside and Doug was dividing his time between his duties at the grill, the kitchen and the oversized den where he was setting up two big-screen televisions. Seems loyalties, and therefore opinions, were divided almost evenly between which of the two important football games should be watched later that afternoon, and Doug, being the ultimate host, had decided the only fair course of action was to watch them both. Hence, two giant screens.

Not having a particularly good season, again, the Dallas Cowboys were hosting the Green Bay Packers, and Notre Dame was set against dreaded college rival University of Southern California in a special holiday matchup. As he moved in more chairs, Doug told Sharon he thought it would make for an interesting afternoon of competition. Nothing better than turkey and pigskin, or rather turkey, baked ham and pigskin.

Until kickoff, the house was a beehive of activity, with guests arriving loaded with festive dishes of every kind from spinach artichoke dip to green bean casserole to candied yams with orange juice and brown-sugar-coated pecans. The buffet tables in the dining room were crowded with cornbread dressing, asparagus tips, chili-pepper gravy and cherry-Coke Jell-O salad. Doug had managed to mix a couple of Italian dishes in with the traditional Thanksgiving fare, and as familiar as the guests were with his culinary genius, no one objected to the foreign delights among the strictly American cuisine.

One entire table was dedicated to desserts, as if anyone would have room for them, and it was overflowing with mouthwatering cakes, cobblers and pies of every imaginable sort, including Maggie's two specialties—pear and blueberry, both crisscrossed with homemade pastry, plucked from the oven just in the nick of time. Even with the twenty-five to thirty guests expected today, there was so much bounty leftovers would be packaged up for everyone to carry home.

Maggie was a little concerned about Sharon, as the fire and her resulting injury had occurred only a few weeks earlier. Amanda, a registered nurse, had readily agreed to check Sharon's burned arm to assure Maggie it was healing properly, and Sharon consented only to avoid an argument with her stubborn friend.

"Yep," Amanda said after a thorough check under the bandages and a redressing, "They did a great job. It seems to be healing nicely, Aunt Sharon."

Maggie was relieved, even as Sharon scolded her again for fussing. She was grateful, though, for Maggie's help and concern, as she still tired more quickly than normal. But the annual Thanksgiving potluck dinner had to go on, especially since Maggie's boys were here.

Childless herself, Sharon thought of Michael and Ben as her adopted sons, while Carol and Robert's two daughters held the same level of affection. She loved them all as if they were blood relatives. In fact, she loved them more than her only brother's three children, who lived in Kansas and never visited, which was just fine by her. She often stated that her brother may be her only brother, but he definitely was not her favorite brother. Maggie and Carol were the sisters she never had.

Aunt Sharon, as they called her, doted on her friends' children, sons- and daughters-in-law and Maggie's precious granddaughters. Once again she silently thanked Maggie and Carol for sharing them with her.

Amanda was helping set out the dishes, keeping one eye on her girls and one eye open to be the first to spot Maggie's new beau. She fairly bristled in anticipation as she stole frequent glances at the front door and at Maggie. Finally noting a distinct change in her mother-in-law's expression, she turned to the door just as a tall dark-haired man entered the house, followed by another tall dark-haired man. She had known this Colin Murphy had a twin, but these men were dead ringers for each other! And both were decidedly drop-dead gorgeous. Well, in an older man, sophisticated Mark Harmon sort of way.

The one who entered first looked around, greeted Sharon, Doug and several other guests, and handed over a bottle of wine while the second twin looked around until he spotted Maggie, and then had eyes only for her, making his way through the crowd toward her. Bending down, he caught her elbow to pull her closer and planted a soft kiss on her cheek. Maggie blushed slightly, returned the light peck, her eyes twinkling, and began looking around for her boys while at the same time steering Colin into the dining room so he could add his avocado-deviled eggs to the banquet. Amanda wiped away a tear and went in search of her Ben.

Introductions were made to Maggie's family, with Colin being respectful of their scrutiny and of any possible resentment her sons might have toward him. Their father had been gone for less than two years, and he wanted to tread lightly. Just as he shook the last hand of the last grandchild, Sean walked up quietly beside him and introductions were repeated.

"It's amazing, really," Michael said as he looked from one Murphy brother to the other. "Did you guys ever switch places in school?"

They laughed and looked at each other with knowing grins. "Every chance we got, and at home, too," Sean said, unzipping his Notre Dame jacket and revealing his white priest's collar. "Mom's the only one who could ever tell us apart, but sometimes even she has to look twice just to be sure."

"Right," Colin said. "Even today poor Dad can't tell one from the other unless Sean wears his priest's collar. At Saint Thomas parish school, we gave the nuns fits, and more than one declared it a miracle that 'Shameless Sean' made it into the priesthood. But you boys look quite a bit alike, too."

"Yeah, it's easy to see we're brothers, but I'm taller than my big brother," Ben said stretching up on his toes so he towered over Michael.

"But I'm more handsome, and so much older and wiser," Michael said.

"Eighteen months is not that much older," Ben said. "And if I recall, I had more girls than you in college."

"That's because I found Karen in my freshman year and didn't need any more girls," Michael said squeezing his smiling wife. "You didn't find

Amanda until you were a senior."

Maggie stood slightly back and kept silent, immensely enjoying the banter of her "men."

Chapter 56 ~

After the last plate was put away, the satisfied guests migrated either to the kitchen to pick at leftovers, to the patio out back to enjoy another glass of Doug's carefully chosen wines, or to the den to cheer on their favorite teams. Although Maggie loved football, she chatted in the kitchen populated mostly by women, nibbling on pumpkin pie, purposefully staying away from the guys.

Since Father Sean, Michael and Ben were all Notre Dame graduates, and Colin was a ravenous Fightin' Irish fan even though he heralded from Harvard—which he admitted shouldn't even attempt to field a team—the four of them formed an easy alliance against the two guests who favored USC. All guests agreed, however, that the Cowboys were the right team to cheer for.

Over the course of the next three hours of gridiron glory and gore, a bond was formed between the Murphys and the Grants, each pair silently analyzing and accepting the other side's current place in Maggie's life. When both the Irish and the Cowboys were victorious, although it was by a hair for each team, the day was deemed a complete success by all except the stunned USC fans.

Turkey and ham sandwiches were put together for the few remaining guests, who settled down in front of the fireplace in the den, with televisions pushed back against the wall and at last silent.

Most of the guests had departed at the end of the games, some after just one more piece of pie. Father Sean had left after two pieces of pie, loaded down with leftovers to take to Monsignor Fitzpatrick, who had dined that day with the bishop, no doubt also happy with the outcome of the games. That left the hosts, Maggie and her family, and Colin, all reluctant to end the happy day.

"Ah," said Doug sighing pleasantly. "Another great Thanksgiving with good friends—old," looking at Sharon, Maggie and her boys, and raising his wine glass to Colin "and new."

"It has been a good day," Sharon said. "And thanks to you all who came early to help and then helped all day long, even with the dishes. Now, isn't it time for our traditional story telling?"

"Oh, Aunt Sharon," Ben groaned, "Don't get Mom started."

"Yes, yes," Michael said. "Colin hasn't heard the costume story, has he?

Tell it Mom. The girls love it... at least I think they love it, don't you girls?" He looked at his nieces, fast asleep in an armchair in the corner, books fallen in their laps, heads together.

"Oh, well. Plenty of other Thanksgivings for them to hear it, but go ahead, Mom," Michael said. Sharon, Amanda and Maggie smiled. Ben looked stricken, and Doug and Colin looked puzzled.

"What costume story? I don't remember a costume story, do I?" Doug asked while refilling wine glasses and turning to Sharon for help.

"You'll remember," she said, smiling.

Colin looked from one to the other, then back to Maggie who was seated comfortably close to him on the couch. "Love to hear it," he said.

Maggie took another sip of wine, drew in a deep breath and then let it slowly out saying, "Okay, here goes... again. When Benjamin was about three, he came home from Preschool and announced that the next day they were having a 'tanksgivin' fearst' with 'Pilgims an' Injuns,' and they had all made hats to wear at school. He needed a costume to go with his hat."

"Mom, please," moaned Ben. "I didn't talk like that!"

"Yes, you did," Michael said. "Now shut up. Go on, Mom."

Maggie continued, "We said fine, are you a Pilgrim or an Indian? 'Pilgrim' was the reply, so Michael and I, and remember Michael was only five at the time, well, Michael and I found a black turtleneck sweater of mine, black pants and shoes, and put a pair of Jim's white tube socks over the bottom of the pants up to Ben's knees. We made aluminum foil buckles for his shoes and his belt. We used white construction paper for a big square collar and cone-shaped cuffs. He looked precious."

"Mom, please," Ben interrupted again, embarrassed.

"You did! Just adorable!" Maggie said, remembering her precious sons as children.

"Just adorable," Michael said sarcastically.

Maggie told her eldest to hush and continued, "So I got my camera out to take a picture of him. I said I wished he'd brought his Pilgrim hat home so we could include it in the photo and asked him what it looked like. He said, 'Oh, it's great, Mommy! It's a big brown band goin' round my head with a red feather sticking up real high.'

"We started all over again."

Chapter 57 ~

Friday and Saturday, Maggie enjoyed her family and showed them around Lubbock with trips to the Buddy Holly Museum, the Tech campus and her office, the Wind Museum, the Ranching Heritage Museum. She then steered them toward the popular cornfield maze out northwest of town where the girls ran through the corn, giggled while riding the small barrel train and posed for pictures standing next to giant circular hay bales painted to look like jack-o'-lanterns.

When the girls declared they had to come live with Grandma because this was the most fun they'd ever had in their whole long lives, Ben told them Dallas had just as many fun things to do and reminded them of the zoo they loved to visit. "Can we go to the zoo when we get home?" they asked brightly, today's fun already forgotten.

Colin stayed away to give them time alone but was surprised to find he wished he'd joined them. They'd asked, after all, but he didn't want to interfere with family. He'd sincerely liked Maggie's sons and gained an admiration for her late husband on how well he'd taught them to be men. And the munchkin granddaughters were really cute.

Sunday morning he did meet them at Mass as Father Sean preached on giving thanks, and Colin generously picked up the tab for a final dinner at Orlando's before they departed for the airport.

Asking if he could see her that night, he was surprised to feel genuinely rebuffed when Maggie politely declined, saying she had some work she had to get done before heading in to the office the next morning. He understood, he said, gave her a light kiss and left. But he didn't like leaving. He hadn't had her to himself since the previous weekend, and they hadn't had a chance to talk about the final Bible study lessons on sexuality. He really wanted to see what she thought about that, even though he thought he could guess. She didn't seem at all disapproving of Sharon and Doug's relationship. Maybe it was safe to move in that direction. He went to his studio to brood. And brood he did.

"This is insane," he told himself. "I'm not a family man. I'm a loner, a player. I like being on my own and being by myself. I like being with lots of women. But why am I always calling Maggie? Stop being such a chump, Murphy." He picked up his tools and walked around the cabinet he was working on, looking for a place to use up his energy. He walked around again, thinking, looking, thinking and finally threw the tools down saying, "Damn you, Margaret Grant. I don't want to want you." But Colin did, more than he'd wanted anything in a long time.

Maggie was brooding, too. She went to her studio, picked up her paintbrush and then put it down. Back in the house, she opened her laptop, stared at the screen and then closed it. Finally, as the sun went down and the air chilled, she lit a fire, made a cup of soup and sat in front of the blaze in flannel pajamas.

Both sons had called earlier to let her know they'd arrived home safely, and both, without any prompting from her, had broached the subject of

Colin. Michael told her Colin seemed like a decent guy even if he was a Harvard man. And Ben, after admitting Lubbock wasn't at all the barren wasteland he'd pictured, casually mentioned Amanda would welcome Colin in their home if Maggie wanted to invite him for Christmas. Wow, Maggie thought. Ben wouldn't have even broached the subject it if he hadn't agreed wholeheartedly.

So, in their own ways each had given permission for her to be with him—to be more than friends, in fact. Well, damn. Double damn. She really didn't expect this and wasn't really prepared.

And why not, she asked herself in front of the fire. Did she want them to voice objections? To tell her it was too soon? That nobody could take their father's place? Of course she would have argued with them and defended her right to a relationship, reiterating no one could or would ever take Jim's place in any of their hearts.

That, she realized, is exactly what she'd expected her sons to say. Then it would have been easy to tell Colin she simply couldn't move the relationship any further because her family wasn't ready.

Truth was, she wasn't ready. Wasn't ready to feel like she did, looking for him in crowds, getting light-headed when he walked into the room. Missing him when she was with her family, and thinking about him late at night, all by herself in her lonely bed.

Miss Priss jumped up onto the hearth, sharing the warmth and emitting a loud purr of contentment. She flicked her ears toward Maggie, who asked the cat, "He's a good man, isn't he? He's smart, creative, funny, interesting, isn't he? There's nothing wrong with having a casual relationship with another human being and enjoying his company, is there? We can be good friends, can't we?" Miss Priss blinked knowingly. "Good friends, and nothing more... and... and damn those green eyes."

The cat meowed in protest.

"Not yours. His."

Over the course of the next week, Maggie ignored Colin, and Colin ignored Maggie. "If he calls," Maggie said to Elaine, "I'm not in. OK?"

"Sure thing, Boss," Elaine replied, wondering what the man had done to her. But no calls came.

"If a call comes for me from a Margaret Grant," Colin told his student assistant, "I don't want to take it. Understood?"

"Understood, Professor Murphy." But no calls came.

By Friday, Maggie was exhausted from working hard and from working harder to ignore her feelings. She made a dinner date with Sharon at Café J, her treat. Over the seafood crepes, she poured it out to Sharon, who looked at her friend quizzically. "So, what, my dear, seems to be the problem? He's a great guy, and he's obviously crazy about you. And you're crazy about him. So?"

"So, I don't want to be crazy about him. I don't want to complicate my life. I don't want to... you know, want him all the time."

Sharon looked at her and said gently, "Jim's been gone almost two years."

"I know that!" Maggie said sharply. Then ashamed, she quietly said, "I know, Phelps. And I loved him and we were happy."

"So you're thinking how can you love another man? How can you betray Jim like that? Right?"

"No. Yes. Oh, I don't know! It feels different with Colin and not at all like the love I felt for Jim. How can it be a betrayal, but how can it not be?"

"It's not a betrayal. What you feel for Colin—isn't it like what you first felt for Jim? All giddy and silly and unfocused when you first dated? You know, that first flush of lust and craziness?"

Surprised, Maggie looked at her friend and said, "What? No, Jim and I just sort of drifted into it. We were friends, remember, and he graduated from law school and it was just the right time to settle down. So we got engaged, got married. You know, we were just right for each other."

Sharon put her head down and poked at her salad.

"What?! You didn't think we were right for each other? I thought you liked Jim? You were my maid of honor, remember?"

"Yes, and I knew you loved him in a way, and I know you were happy with him, but I never did think it was true love."

"True love? What the hell is true love? We were happy. We were faithful. We enjoyed each other and we raised two spectacular boys. What more is there?" she asked angrily.

"Now, listen, Maggie. I've been your friend since college, and I know you. You're a creative passionate girl, woman, and you channeled that into a successful traditional marriage with traditional Jim."

Maggie opened her mouth to protest, but Sharon waved her off. "And there's nothing wrong with traditional. You *were* happy, for God's sake. How many people actually have a chance to be happy like that? Damn few, if you ask me. Damn few."

"So?" Maggie said, still a little irritated even though she agreed with everything Sharon had said so far.

"So, fate has given you the opportunity to perhaps experience more than just happy. And I think you should take the opportunity to see if it's there."

"More than happy? What does that mean?"

"It means to have found your soul mate. To have found such a bond with another human being that it transcends all understanding. That you know you are totally, completely in sync with that person."

"Like you and me and Carol?" Maggie asked tentatively.

"Yes, exactly. What we have is special and rare. Except when you find a soul mate who is the opposite sex, it's even more... more than happy... more than special."

"More?"

"More, Maggie. Exquisitely more. With Doug, it's... I don't know how to put it into words... it's... it's magic all the time. Quiet magic knowing he's sitting beside me in church. Happy magic when he's cooking for me... and explosive, unrestrained divine magic every time we make love. More, Maggie, more. I don't think you had more with Jim, did you?"

"I... I don't know. We were happy."

"I know you were happy, dearest. I'm not saying you weren't. But... let me ask you this... twenty years ago, if you'd had to choose between remaining with Jim or remaining friends with Carol and me, would you have chosen Jim?"

"Don't be silly, Phelps, I couldn't choose. The boys."

"Forget you have children. I'm talking about if it was just Jim, and, oh, let's say Pinocchio's Blue Fairy came and told you to no longer be friends with us or no longer live with Jim. Would you do that? Could you choose Jim over us? Honestly?"

Maggie looked at her friend hard and didn't answer. Would she have allowed her love for Jim to keep her away from her best friends? Was her bond with him stronger than her bond with Sharon and Carol?

"If the Blue Fairy had asked me to choose," Sharon said quietly, "I would choose Doug."

Maggie looked at her sharply, suddenly wounded. "You would?"

"In a heartbeat, Maggie. Of course it would never happen, ever. We're talking hypothetical here. But, even hypothetically, if you couldn't say you would've chosen Jim in a heartbeat, then there's no way in the world he was your soul mate."

Maggie was stunned. Soul mate? Sharon and Doug had something more special than she'd had with Jim? More than the friendship she had with her and Carol? Of course there was the sex, but magic sitting next to each other? In the kitchen?

What about Carol? Did she feel that way about Robert? Now that she really thought about it, Carol had stayed away from Texas for him, and she loved Texas more than both Maggie and Sharon combined, which was saying a lot. And they do seem to have the same sense of constant excitement that exists between Sharon and Doug. She had always secretly envied that spark, hadn't she? That inexplicable something in couples you catch glimpses of here and there. It was rare, wasn't it?

Now that she considered it, her parents had had it, too. That spark.

Does it exist between her sons and their wives? She hoped so. She'd have to look closer.

But with Jim? She *had* loved Jim and they *were* happy, dammit. They were! But no, she reluctantly had to admit, there wasn't the more. If there'd been no children, and she *had* to choose, she knew how she'd have chosen... in a heartbeat.

Suddenly sad, and no longer hungry, she picked at her food. Sharon knew she had struck a sensitive cord, brought up long-buried feelings, but maybe that was what her friend needed right now. Brutal honesty in order to move forward.

She took Maggie's hand, saying gently, "Maybe, just maybe, you have a chance to find a soul mate this time and have a different type of love."

Sharon only hoped this man was good enough for Maggie... if not, if he hurt her, well, he'd have to answer to her and to Carol, and they were a powerful force in defense of their dearest friend.

Chapter 58 ~

By six o'clock it was almost dark, and Maggie, still working and extremely tired, wished she hadn't walked to work that morning, but there had been a good reason—the annual Carol of Lights was tonight and traffic would be as bad as on game days, at least at this end of campus. She would stay for the hour-long procession and ceremony and then head home on foot. Luckily, it was a fairly warm day in December, but she'd brought her heavy coat just in case. She'd learned no matter what the weather was in Lubbock, it was always cooler at night.

The Carol of Lights was a festive tradition at Texas Tech that began long before she was a student. Thirteen buildings facing Memorial Circle and the two esplanades, plus those in the science quadrangle, were outlined in more than 25,000 red, white and orange lights, creating a breathtaking holiday display of the Spanish-mission style arches and façades.

Students, faculty and Lubbock citizens flocked to Memorial Circle to watch the lighting ceremony as the Saddle Tramps marched in procession from Broadway Street at the east end of the esplanade, up around the circle and to the front of the Chemistry Building. This building's double staircase—two majestic marble flights of stairs rising away from each other and doubling back to the large first floor balcony—made the perfect setting for the celebration stage, with a two-story greenery wreath as a backdrop.

Each year around 6:30 p.m., all the lights in and around these buildings were turned off to highlight the dramatic procession. Decked out in white electric lights, Texas Tech's black stallion mascot, ridden by the Masked

Rider, slowly led the Saddle Tramps as they paraded up both sides of the esplanade from Broadway, past the Will Rogers statue, around Memorial Circle and into the adjoining science quad. Each Tramp carried a glowing red torch, held high, standing out against the darkened buildings. Luminarios—paper bags filled with sand and lighted candles—lined the circle where the giant Christmas tree stood, waiting to show its brilliant display of thousands of matching lights.

Maggie was told it normally takes about 20 minutes for the procession. Christmas carols are played throughout the march from the carillon in the west tower of the Administration Building. Once the procession ends, the president of the Student Residence Halls Association welcomes everyone and introduces the University Choir and a soloist, who delight the crowd with their talents. Finally, the Texas Tech Trombone Band plays a fanfare, and at the climax, the holiday lights are dramatically turned on with one switch. The spectacle is always worth the wait.

Doug was directing the Band tonight, and Sharon was nearby, assisting where she could. Maggie had not planned to meet up with them.

She donned her coat and left the building before the lights were turned out. She was right, she thought as she stepped outside, it was getting chilly, but not as cold as when they were seniors. That year temperatures had been so low the brass band didn't perform for fear of lips being frozen to the instruments. It hadn't mattered, because the crowds were sparse—not even one-percent of the normal crowd braved the sub-freezing temperatures. Turned out they were the smart ones. All three girls came down with colds immediately afterward, and coughed and sniffed through their finals and the holidays.

Tonight, however, the temperature was in the high 40s, so although the coat was needed, it was a fairly pleasant evening.

Colin hadn't called her—in fact it had been ten days since she'd seen or heard from him, the day her family left. Maybe the problem had solved itself. He'd lost interest, and she wouldn't have to worry about the "more"—about whether it might be there or not. It hurt—to love and not be loved in return—to a much greater extent than she imagined it would. Another lesson learned, right Lord?

But wait. What lesson was this? she asked God one night. That she shouldn't expect further happiness in her life? Shouldn't expect the "more"? She gave up trying to analyze—feelings were so hard to categorize into facts—and instead concentrated on work and completing her Christmas shopping to take her mind off of the possibilities of "more."

Problem was, it wasn't working.

Joining the growing throngs finding places to stand for the Carol of Lights ceremony—only the Saddle Tramps and dignitaries had chairs—she crossed the circle, ending up on the northwest side to get a good view of her building when the lights were switched on. She'd always thought the detail of lights on the ornate twin towers made up the most spectacular part of the display.

At the first site of the red torches, Maggie smiled remembering processions from decades ago. It was still a magical sight to her. When the parading Saddle Tramps came around Memorial Circle, she strained to see Jamie. As president, he would either be the first or the last. There he was! Marching proudly, first behind the Masked Rider on the south side of the circle. She watched him reach the science quad, and all but his torch disappeared behind the crowd. She knew once reaching the area below the stage, torches were extinguished in large barrels of water and marchers sat down with dignitaries. Standing up on tiptoe to see when his torch was put out, her view was suddenly blocked by a dark brown suede jacket. She looked up and, even in the dark, could see green eyes smiling down at her.

"Hello, Margaret Riley Grant," Colin said rather loudly to be heard over the carillon, pulling his hand out of his pocket and offering it to her for a shake.

She was surprised to see him, but recovering, smiled, took his hand firmly in hers, and returned the greeting, "Professor Cailean Patrick Murphy." She tried to pull away, but he held her hand tight.

"I've missed you," he said.

"Have you?" she asked, still lovingly looking in his eyes, happier to see him than she wanted to be.

"Every day for the last week and a half... and every night for longer." He let the moment stretch out and her insides turned over, the warmth of his touch radiating up her arm and scoring a direct hit on her heart before moving decidedly lower.

"Did your family get home all right?" he asked.

"What? Oh, yes. They did. Thank you."

He let go of her hand and moved to stand to her right, arm casually behind her waist, eyes looking over the crowd toward the stage. "Did you see Jamie?"

She gulped, then took a deep breath. Okay, she thought, we'll see where this goes. "I did. Right up front, on the other side. He looked good. Shouldn't you be up there with the Tramps or something?"

"Why, do you want me to leave?" He asked, looking down at her.

"NO!" she said too quickly and too loudly. Then she took another deep breath and said with more calm, "No. You can stay. I only thought this might be an activity where the Saddle Tramp sponsor was busy, that's all."

"Nope, I was with them this afternoon for moral support but they're big boys and have this down pat, just like most of their events. Speaking of which, Margaret Grant, the Saddle Tramps annual Red Rose Formal is

Saturday after next. Dinner and dancing. I wondered if you'd like to join me?"

She smiled, delighted, and then frowned, "Saturday after next?"

"Yep. You already have plans?" he said surprised and a little hurt. He knew he should have asked her sooner, should have called her right after Thanksgiving, but then he was too busy brooding.

He'd brooded for a week over wanting her, over the surprise feelings of wanting to be with her when her family was there—of wanting to be a part of them all. To shake that wanting, or so he'd hoped, he'd called Dixie for dinner last weekend, but much to the lady's chagrin, he hadn't talked much and dropped her off at her door before 9:30. It hadn't felt right, and he was more miserable than ever.

Yesterday, after another sleepless night of thinking about Maggie and how, or if, she was supposed to fit in his life, he'd finally decided he needed to stop being so gentle and see what happened. He knew women loved to be romanced, and he certainly knew how to pour on the charm, more successfully than most. Formal attire, flowers and a cozy hotel room afterward. It had always worked before. The Red Rose Formal might be the perfect time, if he could wait that long.

"I do have plans, as a matter of fact," Maggie said. "Ben's youngest is playing Mary in the Christmas pageant and I promised to be there. It's Saturday after next. I'm sorry, Colin. Really." And she was. Despite her better judgment, she wanted to continue the relationship... see where this new love she felt led. She was thrilled he seemed to want the same.

"Okay," he said casually, looking back toward the stage, but disappointment was evident on the face she couldn't see in the dark. "Maybe the following weekend." They lowered their voices as the procession and carillon had ended. The emcee was thanking the crowd for their attendance. The choir should be next, Colin thought.

"Definitely the following weekend. What about this weekend, though?" she said boldly. If he could ask she could, too. And she did want to see what developed.

"Sorry, I'm out of town Friday until late Sunday. Sean and I are flying to Chicago... Dad's 75th birthday. I shipped the cabinet yesterday." He hadn't been back home in a couple of years, and this date wasn't one he was willing to break, even for the possibility of moving to the next level with Maggie.

"Oh, that's right. I'd forgotten. I'm glad you finished it," she said, wondering if he'd been working on it for the last week and a half and that's why he hadn't called. "Then we'll just wait until two weeks from Saturday," Maggie said. "I'm heading to Dallas for Christmas week, but don't have to leave until Monday."

He turned to smile at her and confirm their date, and something caught his eye. He looked back up at the source, and in the darkened campus found a light coming from just above the trees... an orange glow.

Maggie turned to look too, and seeing the distinctive light, knew immediately what it meant.

Colin grabbed her elbow, steering her toward the Administration Building, even as she turned and headed that way. As they pushed through the crowed, Maggie pulled her phone from her belt, pushing the speed button she'd programmed after Halloween, and said, "Fire... East tower of the Admin Building. Hurry!"

The thousands who'd come to watch the Carol of Lights were focusing their attention to the west, to the stage where the choir sang. Only a few had seen the fire and that was only after Colin and Maggie had pushed their way through them, hurriedly heading in that direction.

"Boom!" One of the windows shattered from the heat, and most of the crowd turned around at the noise. By the time Colin and Maggie reached the building, all the windows had blown out, leaping flames dramatically visible against the darkened building and the clear, cold night sky.

Maggie pulled out her keys to unlock the east door, directly below the fire, desperately trying to remember the fire system in the old building. Ceilings had been dropped to add HVAC, and at the same time a sprinkler system. But up in the tower? There must not be a detector up there because no alarm was sounding or flashing.

Because the campus lights were out, they had to feel their way up the dark stairs to the tower's door on the third floor. Colin knew the construction of the tower was mainly brick and concrete, but if the fire was lower in the tower stairs or in the attic storage area, it could quickly spread to the main building and do major damage. He hoped the filthy old carpeting had already been removed in the "clubhouse," but he hadn't received a recent update on the cleaning project. He, too, tried to think if there was a fire extinguisher near the tower.

As they reached the third floor landing, they heard distant sirens. He moved up the narrow stairs, reached for the door handle, key ready, then pulled away quickly. It was hot... not scalding, yet, so he wasn't burned. He placed his palms gingerly on the thin narrow door. Definitely felt more than warm to the touch. If he opened it, he could create a backdraft, but larger than the one that burned Sharon. The sudden rush of oxygen to the fire would surely flash onto the entire landing. Or would it with the upstairs windows already blown out? He couldn't be sure. They'd have to wait for the firefighters. He wouldn't risk hurting Maggie.

Only then did Maggie think of the cleanup. She knew the Saddle Tramps were working to get finished by the new year but didn't know how far along they were. Maybe, just maybe, this fire was accidental—the result of something the Tramps did or didn't do—paint thinner, oily rags? Please don't let it be another arson fire, she prayed.

Two campus police officers came bounding up the stairs, extinguishers in hand, and insisted Maggie and Colin go back outside, which they were glad to do after warning of the possible danger at the door. They reached the east outside entrance as fire engines and more campus police drove up, so Maggie and Colin moved away from the activity. Maggie called her staff and Colin called Jamie.

"Hold the Tramps there, next to the stage," he told Jamie. "I'm coming through the crowd. Who's in charge of the renovations? Josh? Okay, the fire captain will probably need to speak to him. Thanks." He disappeared into the crowds as Maggie looked for the best place to set up the media area.

The ladder truck raised equipment high up against the clay tiled roof, and firefighters began pouring water into the tower through the shattered windows. Another crew disappeared into the building with a second hose.

Turning their attention to the fire activity, the Carol of Lights audience was no longer interested in the ceremony, and it was ended. Campus police moved the barricades previously blocking traffic, now using them to hold people back from the Administration Building.

Within 45 minutes, the fire was out, the smoke had dissipated and most of the crowd had departed along with the reporters who wanted to make the 10 o'clock news. Maggie had worked the media line with frequent updates of what she knew, which wasn't much. She promised to put out an updated statement as soon as she was able to obtain more from Chief Callahan, who'd once again called her Sweetheart, but this time with a twinkle in his eye. Once again she'd told him off, but with a grin. They were fast becoming friends.

Ricky and Susan were upstairs working on a general release for the website—firemen had given the all-clear signal for the main building and the lights were back on. President Parker had come by but didn't want to appear on camera, so she handled it all. Bennett Boyle made a brief appearance after the reporters had left but said nothing to her. She heard him tell Chief Callahan he didn't want to go up to see the damage.

"Send me photos," he'd told the campus police chief before turning briskly away. "And not through the computer."

Once her media duties were complete, Maggie talked to the arson chief. His preliminary inspection of the fire was complete. Power had been restored to all the buildings shortly after the fire trucks arrived, and floodlights were now being set up in the tower. Water dripped down the stairwell, still trickling out the door to the soggy grass. Maggie stood to the side of the door, attempting to stay out of the mud.

"The tower door was hot when we got here," Maggie said to the chief.

"Did the fire burn the entire stairwell, too?"

"No," he said. "Only the landing at the top. When firefighters entered the tower stairwell, they found a large space heater just inside the narrow door on the first tower landing, turned up to high. Interestingly, it was connected to a lantern battery with a trigger. That's what made the door warm."

The blaze upstairs had burned hot enough to destroy the wooden platform and shatter all the windows, he said, but the heater at the bottom of the tower stairs had nothing in front of it to catch on fire... it was only hot enough to heat the door, not set it on fire. It was almost as if the arsonist didn't want anyone to open the door until the fire upstairs was fully developed... or until it was out. Did the arsonist understand now about backdrafts? Had this heater been a warning to wait? An arsonist who didn't want someone to get hurt... this time?

Josh was the Saddle Tramp in charge of the cleanup. He told the fire captain he and a crew of Tramps had ripped the old carpet up last week and piled it up under the platform. They were going to haul it away this weekend.

"What about the plaques and memorabilia?" Colin had asked.

It was Jamie who spoke. "I took them down a couple weeks ago, right after you told us to clean the place. They're at our house in boxes in the garage."

"At least they're safe," Colin said. "That's something." He sent the young men home, saying they'd talk the next day.

Chief Callahan talked at length with the fire department officials. He relayed to Colin and Maggie that the attic storage was undamaged, the tower level the only area blistered and black. He thought the metal trap door to the bells would have to be replaced as would the now twisted metal ladder and the platform as well as all the windowpanes. A charred pile of debris lay on the floor where the platform and old carpeting had been.

From the description, Colin knew that new plaster, paint and a rebuilt platform would add significantly to their clean-up budget... but perhaps the university would now pay for it all with fire insurance funds. In any event, all of this would have to wait until engineers had thoroughly studied the tower to make certain it was still structurally sound.

It was late into the night when Maggie allowed Colin to walk her home. He promised to call her before the weekend, then headed out to his truck on the other side of campus. Once home, Maggie called Sharon's cell phone and Doug answered.

Yes, they were home now, too, he said. Sharon had been a little shaken, but he'd put her to work helping him get musicians and their instruments back to the music building and all accounted for, so they were not around to watch the fire being put out. She'd gone to bed, and Doug was sure she'd be fine. Maggie promised to call her in the morning.

Colin called the next day as promised but couldn't see her before he left for Chicago that weekend because of classes and Saddle Tramp business. She was disappointed beyond words. Seeing him at the Carol of Lights rekindled her feelings for him, and she knew that trying to keep busy would not keep him out of her thoughts.

When he called after his return from Chicago late Sunday night, Maggie was already in bed, reading, and they promised to try to meet for lunch the next day so she could hear about the birthday celebration. But she would see him before then, much to their mutual surprise.

Chapter 59 ~

Elaine answered the 9:30 a.m. call from Boyle's office. Her boss was wanted down there immediately. That was never good, Maggie thought. He'd really been leaving her alone since she didn't report to him anymore, and the autonomy she'd had in recent weeks was refreshing. She actually felt like they were moving forward with President Parker's goals. Whatever could Boyle want now?

When she stepped into Boyle's office, she was surprised to see Colin and Jamie sitting across from the massive desk. She looked at them questioningly, but their shrugs signaled they didn't know anything either.

"I need a news release posted. That's why you're here," Boyle said without welcome.

"What about?" Maggie asked, sitting in the chair next to Colin and opening her notepad.

"About the tower," he said with exasperation.

"We posted one the night of the fire," Maggie said. Surely he'd seen it? No, probably not.

"It's not about that," Boyle said testily.

"You've been up to see the damage?" Colin asked.

"I have not, nor will I... ever. Chief Callahan sent me photos."

"You know how the fire started, then?" Colin asked.

"No, I do not... nor do I care," he said with an exasperated sigh. "What I do care about is that your organization has damaged this historic building, and I am removing the Saddle Tramps from the tower, permanently. Please turn in your keys."

Colin was the first of the stunned trio to speak. "You're not serious?"

"Perfectly serious. Keys, please."

"But kicking the Saddle Tramps out of the tower? You can't, Boyle.

210

The tower belongs to the Saddle Tramps. It's belonged to them for more than half a century!" He was standing now, as was Maggie.

"I don't care how long it's belonged to them. It's a worthless organization. Nothing but a bunch of hypocrites. You will no longer be allowed access. Period. Put your keys on my desk."

Jamie still sat in stunned silence, a look of such loathing coming over his face that Maggie was afraid he might jump across the desk and strike the Chief of Staff. She quickly interceded.

"Mr. Boyle, Lubbock's Chief Graham thinks it was an arsonist, not the Saddle Tramps who did the damage. Surely, sir, even you wouldn't take away their rights to their tradition. And what about ringing the victory bells? How will they get up there to do that?"

"They won't. As of now, the bells in the east tower are silenced." He looked at Colin. "Maybe when they don't ring, your stupid organization will remember the fire and the significant costs the university now has to bear to restore it. Also because of the fire, we've been instructed by the Lubbock Fire department to extend the fire alarm and sprinklers to both towers, at another small fortune. I need those keys."

Colin reached in his pocket as he said, "Does President Parker—"

Boyle stood and looked directly at Colin. "The facilities are under the purview of the Chief of Staff's office. Are there other keys, Professor Murphy?"

Colin met his stare squarely, barely controlling his anger. "Josh, the sergeant-at-arms has one. I'll have it sent over this afternoon," Colin said, giving his key to Boyle. Turning to Jamie, he put out his hand, "Jamie, I'll need yours, son."

Jamie stood, keeping his malevolent gaze on Boyle, and threw his tower key on the desk. Turning briskly, he knocked his chair over, then pushed past Colin and stormed out of the office.

Colin followed him but only after he told Boyle he would fight this decision all the way to the Board of Regents if necessary. Maggie was now alone with Boyle and as furious as she had ever been. He sat back down and said to her, "Get a small release sent out saying the change in tradition is a result of the fire. Dismissed."

She left quickly, not bothering to right Jamie's chair and silently vowed to do everything she could to help the Saddle Tramps win back their "clubhouse."

On the way up to her office, she phoned Colin, offering her assistance. He accepted but then begged off from lunch to find and calm Jamie and inform the other Tramps. Maggie called a staff meeting to ask for input.

It was the next week before Maggie and Colin talked again, a few days after she returned from the Christmas pageant where the Virgin Mary had dropped the baby Jesus on his head. Luckily, it hadn't bothered either the baby doll or his four-year-old mother.

"We plan to call in a few extremely influential Saddle Tramp alums to speak to the board in January," Colin said when he called Maggie to confirm their date for the next Saturday.

"That might work. I'll make sure it gets on the agenda then. Also, what do you think about a student protest, or picket line at the Admin Building... just as the board arrives, or just outside their window. I can get the media out for that, and probably get an op ed piece in the *A-J* if the boys want to write one. What did President Parker say?" Maggie asked.

"Said he would meet with us after the holidays. Thinks the students should be concentrating on finals this week instead of traditions. I tend to agree with him on that point, but I'm not sure he understands the significance of throwing the most respected campus organization out of a space they've had since the 1940s. Maybe we can persuade him to change Boyle's directive, and then we won't have to go before the board."

"Here's hoping. Now, tell me, Professor Murphy, where are we going Saturday?"

"Um, a surprise, but wear something you'd wear to a fancy dance or to meet the Queen of England or something," Colin said. "And no more questions. Understood, Grant?"

Smiling because she liked surprises, she said, "Yes, sir."

"Good. I'll pick you up at 7:30. Be hungry."

Chapter 60 ~

Maggie couldn't imagine where he was taking her... or she could, actually, envisioning both the fancy steakhouse on Slide Road, and the Lubbock Country Club's formal dining room. She thought they had dancing on the weekends at the club, didn't they? She loved dancing. Is he a member? She didn't think so, but he probably knows someone who is, or Monsignor Fitzpatrick does.

Now, what to wear? There wasn't time to shop in Dallas, and Lubbock's limited shopping scene didn't offer a wide variety of formal wear. Maybe she'd pull out that red evening gown she wore two years ago for the Bishop's Annual Charity Christmas Ball in Dallas. It might work. She'd talk with Sharon.

Indeed it did work nicely, and Maggie was decked out in sleek deep red, complete with matching stole to keep her bare shoulders from freezing. With her hair piled up, she donned her favorite ruby earrings, but agreed with Sharon a necklace would spoil the effect of the low, strapless gown. Besides who owned ruby necklaces anyway?

Much less than buxom, Maggie liked the way the empire waist on the dress pressed upward to give her a rather impressive cleavage, even if it wasn't natural for her. She could cover it with the wrap if it wasn't appropriate for the surprise destination, but after all, she'd worn this for the bishop's gala. And he wasn't scandalized in the least.

When Colin arrived, flowers in hand, he whistled and kissed her in gratitude. He was dressed in a dark suit and stylish black turtleneck sweater, and looked every bit the part of the dashing, handsome hero. Her heart melted and she knew the night would be special. Hope he's washed the truck, she thought. When he walked her outside, she stopped dead in her tracks at the sight of a streamlined silver limousine parked at her curb.

"Your carriage, m'lady," he grinned as the chauffeur opened the door for them and bowed. Yes, this definitely was going to be a special night.

She was so taken with the luxury of the limo, the wine he offered and the soft classical music playing in their private "carriage," she hadn't noticed their direction. After about 15 minutes, she peeked outside. A sliver of moon was rising, and she could tell they were out of the city, but where?

Another few minutes and she had her answer. They pulled into the circular driveway of the area's newest resort, the LakeView Grand, a multimillion dollar project on the shores of Buffalo Lake, southeast of Lubbock. She'd read about it—the grand opening was last month—but hadn't visited or tried their cuisine. She was excited and pleased at his choice of elegance.

As she climbed out of the limo, she held tight to a Christmas gift wrapped in shiny gold paper tied with a big red bow. She'd brought it knowing this was the only time they would have to exchange presents because she was leaving for Dallas early Monday. They hadn't discussed gifts, though, and as Maggie realized, maybe they should have. With a quick look around the limo, she'd seen no present for her. Oh, well, she thought, tonight will be present enough.

Dazzling was the first word that came to mind as they entered the hotel lobby. Large crystal chandeliers graced the high ceilings, and sophisticated decor and furnishings filled the large foyer. Not a Southwest motif in sight! Watch out, Dallas, she thought—West Texas is catching on to elegance.

Dinner proved worthy of equal praise, and they ate slowly, enjoying each other's company, drinking copious amounts of wine and dancing to the string orchestra, made up mainly of Tech music students earning extra cash. The crowded dance floor allowed him to hold her tight and nibble her ear from time to time, and shivers of excitement pulsed through her at every touch. She never remembered feeling this feminine or cherished.

Finally exhausted and giddy with excitement and love for this man, she picked up his Christmas gift when they returned to their table. Amazon had delivered a newly released and rather expensive book on early 1900s furniture maker Gustav Stickley, and she hoped Colin would enjoy it. Also included was a DVD of a different genre.

Handing the package to him, she said, "I've brought you a Christmas present."

He looked at his watch and smiled, saying, "I'll open it after dessert." He stood up, and took her hand. "I've arranged for us to have a little more privacy. Do you mind?"

Mind? she thought happily. The man is romancing me with class and style, and he wonders if I mind. "Not at all," she said, gathering her evening bag, wrap and his gift. She walked with him to the elevator. The wine made her head spin slightly, and she grabbed his arm, giggling a little as she wondered where they were headed. At this point, she decided she didn't care where, as long as she was with him. Was this how Cinderella felt before midnight?

On the top floor, the elevator doors opened and Colin led her down the hall, pulling a hotel key from his pocket. He opened the door at the end of the hall, bowing for her to enter. She hesitated. A suite? He's taken a suite? Then she saw a white-draped table sitting with lighted candles, a bouquet of flowers matching those he'd given her at home and two places set with dessert and wine.

Maggie fairly floated in, turning left as she noticed the floor-to-ceiling windows. Just beyond, a wide balcony extended out over the lake, and the moon, now high in the star-filled cloudless sky, glimmered in reflection across the black water.

She turned as he came in and threw her arms around him, kissing him hard. He responded in kind but stopped to close the door. She walked unsteadily toward the table. "Colin, this is marvelous! What a wonderful surprise, even without the Queen of England!"

He laughed and moved up behind her, turning her and kissing her again, moving his hands down and across the small of her back, pressing her to him.

She took his kiss and returned it but pulled away a moment later, saying, "What's for dessert? I'm famished!"

He laughed again and seated her at the table. "After that huge lobster? We're having a cheesecake thing... I have no idea of the name, but the chef assures me it's his best. More wine?"

"Yes," Maggie said as she took a hungry bite of cheesecake, closing her eyes to the delicious flavor bursting in her mouth. Swallowing after savoring, she said, "All that dancing made me hungry again! You're pretty light on your feet, Professor Murphy. We must do this more often... dance I mean. It was fun! Wonder if the Cotton Club is still around. Can you boot scoot?" She took a second bite, washing it down with the smooth white wine in perfect complement.

Colin sat and watched her delight, nodding yes, he could boot scoot. "We did. Remember? At the hand-harvest?"

"Oh, yeah. Too much of this grape juice 'mudfuddles' my brain. It's so good!" she said with a mouthful of cheesecake.

"Mudfuddles?" Colin asked.

"Jabberwickety, or sump'en like that," was all she said. When she couldn't eat another bite, she stood up carefully and wobbled out onto the balcony. He followed, wrapping his coat around her bare shoulders. "Been a perfect night, Murphy. Thank you."

"You're welcome, Maggie. I've missed you. It's been too long since we've been alone. I wanted it to be special." He turned her towards him and held her tightly. She sighed, looking into the emeralds and believing she was a princess and he her handsome Prince Charming. A girl never got too old for that dream, did she?

He kissed her gently, and she moved her hands up around his neck, pulling him closer. He whispered in her ear, "I've wanted you so much, Maggie. I can't explain it, but I have this need for you." Now kissing her hard, she returned the intensity, pressing against him, wanting him, needing him, too. The coat fell to the ground, but neither one noticed.

He does love me, she thought as he thoroughly kissed her neck and shoulders. She whispered, "I never thought..." but her words ended as he covered her mouth with his again, reaching, exploring, testing her willingness. She lost herself in him, pulling him even closer, trying to meld their bodies.

"Oh, Maggie," he said, as she sighed under the kisses. "I didn't want to want you. I..." His hand moved down below the small of her back and she jolted slightly. He stopped and said, "You're cold. Let's go inside." She turned and went in to the table, found her wine glass and drained it.

Whoa, Maggie, she thought to herself. You're getting way ahead of yourself. You'd better call it a night and head home. Way too many smashed grapes. And not used to this romancing stuff.

Colin had gone to the bar and opened a drawer, picking something up. He went to her and took her hand. "Maggie, come sit with me."

She obliged, thinking she really needed to ask him to take her home. Maybe a few more minutes for Cinderella—it wasn't quite midnight. They sat together on the wide plush sofa in the living area. He cleared his throat, and turned to her. "Maggie, I've been a player all my life. I've had my share of women over the years."

"I'll bet you have, Murphy," she said giddily.

"I have, but I've never wanted a woman the way I want you."

Maggie was suddenly very sober. He wants me, she thought. What's he saying? He wants me. Her heart was in her throat as she looked at him with love, struggling to understand his words.

"I hope you want me too, and I thought, well, I thought it was time we moved this relationship a little further." He held up a small velvet box.

Oh, help, she thought. He's proposing? He is! He does love me... he does want to marry me. She reached over, putting her arms tight around his neck, kissing him with love and abandon. He responded in kind, and somehow within the blink of an eyelash she was lying on the couch, Colin half on top of her, kissing her over and over, telling her how much he wanted her. She was returning the kisses, wrapped in the passion of the moment, in her happiness and the promise of tomorrow. He kissed the deep hollow of her neck and she wound her hands into his long black hair. "Maggie, I want you, I want you."

She laughed and said, "You've got me, my darling..." He kissed her again, and again, moving down and kissing the top of her cleavage. Her head was swimming with wine and desire. He shifted slightly, reaching up to move the dress down so he could suckle her breast.

Maggie was slightly shocked, and whispered with a laugh, "No, Colin, don't do that." He didn't hear, and pulled the gown down to expose one breast, moving to take it into his mouth.

"No!" she said louder, trying to push him off, trying to sit up. "NO! Stop!"

He did stop, and looked at her in surprise. "Why?" he said, bewildered, moving to let her sit up. She straightened her dress and looked at him in equal surprise.

"Why? Because that kind of passion will have to wait for the wedding night, my darling."

"Wed... wedding night!" He stammered, standing up and moving away as if he'd been burned. "What... what wedding night?"

Her mouth fell open and she looked at him, unbelieving. Narrowing her eyes, she quietly said, "Didn't you just ask me to marry you?" He shook his head slightly, his eyes wide, his mind furiously replaying the last few minutes.

"Then what's this?" she said reaching to the floor for the fallen velvet box.

"It's... it's diamond earrings. What did you... you thought I was proposing? That it's a ring? Good God, Maggie, I wasn't proposing, I was asking you to be my lady... my... I want you. I want to take you to my bed." He moved toward her, hand out, but it was her turn to stand up and move away.

He looked at her, frowned and said firmly, "That's what I was asking— to bed you, Maggie. I'm not the marrying kind. You know that." She turned away from him and clutched her stomach. He ran his hand through his hair and looked helplessly at her back. "Oh, Lord."

Maggie was dumbfounded. He knew she wouldn't, couldn't be intimate without marriage. Or did he? They'd never talked about it. She just assumed he would know that about her. Her faith was everything to her. Didn't he know her at all? How could he not know?He wanted her to be his "lady"? Like the "lady" at *La Diosa*? He thought if he gave her diamonds she would give herself to him? Just like that?

She was humiliated and more hurt than she thought possible. And furious he thought so little of her as to want only to add her to his stable of "ladies." Damn those fucking green eyes, she thought angrily. With her back still to him, she walked to the table and put the velvet box, unopened, on top of the shiny gold paper, gathering her things before she walked out the door.

"Maggie, please don't go. I..." She closed the door quietly behind her.

Chapter 61 ~

Colin woke up the next morning with a monster headache. He found himself lying across the top of the luxurious resort king-sized bed, still completely dressed, and very much alone except for a gigantic hangover. After Maggie had left, he'd downed the remainder of the wine, miserable in his bewilderment of how he'd misjudged her so badly. Marriage? She had to be kidding. Her best friends, Sharon and Doug... they weren't married. And she was obviously all right with that.

Yes, he wanted her, but he wasn't the marrying kind. She knew that, didn't she? The look in her eyes when he'd said that... she was so hurt... she'd turned her back on him.

But he was so sure she was ready for the next step... ready for intimacy, for sex. She kissed him with such passion. It had been a long time since he'd been kissed like that. She had to have been ready... he certainly was.

They'd moved slower in their relationship than he'd ever moved with any woman in his entire life. Six months he'd been seeing her, and only her, except for one disastrous hollow dinner with Dixie. Six months, and nothing more than a few passionate kisses.

He was a man, after all. Six months was forever. How could he have misread her so badly? He must really be getting old.

Colin showered and changed, head feeling like cotton. The day before, he'd brought a change of clothes to the resort, along with the earrings, the flowers and explicit instructions for the suite setup.

Now what, he thought as he gathered his few belongings. He picked up the velvet box, opened it, and stared at the teardrop-shaped diamond earrings. He'd given diamonds before and the women had always been more than grateful. He touched them tenderly, thinking how lovely they would have looked against her pale skin. She'd been so beautiful last night, and they'd had such a perfect evening. Dinner, dancing, wine. The perfect prelude to what he thought would be an amazing night of intimacy.

He closed the box and slipped it into his pocket. Next he picked up the present she'd brought. He unwrapped it and shook his head—she'd taken care to give him two gifts he would really appreciate—she'd obviously put a lot of thought into them. The DVD was the 1939 classic *Dick Tracy's G-Men*. He opened the cover of the expensive Stickley book and found the inscription. "To Professor Murphy. With love, Maggie." Love. Had she said she loved him? She must love him if she was thinking wedding bells. She hadn't even looked at the diamonds.

Back in Lubbock, Colin was too preoccupied to participate in the final morning Mass. He stood up and sat down and kneeled along with the congregation, but didn't go up to Communion, or recite any of the Liturgy. And as far as he was concerned, Sean had preached about the man in the moon. He was too confused and miserable to concentrate.

Seated afterward in his brother's church office, Colin started by handing Sean the small velvet box. Sean's face lit up.

"You're proposing? That's great! I get to officiate, don't I? Mom will be so happy!"

Colin was horrified again, "No, Sean, no. I didn't propose. Open it."

Puzzled, Sean opened the box, looking at his brother in surprise. "Didn't? Uh-oh. She's seen these? Does she like diamonds? Doesn't seem the diamond type to me."

It was Colin's turn to be puzzled. "I've no idea. All women like diamonds, don't they?"

"No, big brother. Not all women like diamonds. How'd this go over with her? Obviously not well if I'm holding them now and you're looking utterly awful. What happened?"

"I tried to give them to her last night. Did the whole romance thing... you know limo, dinner, dancing, dessert up in a suite."

Sean closed the box abruptly, put it on his desk, and leaned back looking accusingly at his brother. "You took Margaret Grant to a suite?"

"Yes, I took her to a suite," Colin answered defensively. "I've been seeing her exclusively for half a year. Being gentle, like you said, for six months. It was the next step. And she shoved it back in my face. Walked out. I just wanted to take the next step with her."

"And sleep with her?" Sean asked.

"For God's sake Sean, we're consenting adults. Of course I wanted to sleep with her."

Father Sean shook his head and looked sadly at his brother. "The next step with a woman like Maggie Grant is marriage, you idiot."

218

Chapter 62 ~

Two days before New Year's, Maggie was heading back to the South Plains, determined to get back to work and to get over Professor Cailean Patrick Murphy. She still marveled at how she could have misjudged him so completely and love him when he was such a cad. Marriage indeed. Hmmph. He's not the marrying type, he'd said. She chided herself for being so stupidly naive.

Dressed in warm boots, gloves and heavy jacket, she had a blanket thrown over her legs as she drove. The heater on her beloved Volvo had stopped working on the pre-Christmas drive to Dallas a week ago, and she had stopped just east of Weatherford to retrieve extra clothes from her suitcase in order not to freeze 90 minutes before reaching Ben and Amanda's house. She also took the time to wash her face, hoping they wouldn't notice she'd been crying for the past five hours. Hot coffee, which she hated, helped warm her as well as keep her awake.

The morning after the disastrous date with Colin, she'd packed quickly after a sleepless night and left a day early for Dallas, wanting to put as much distance as she could between herself and the professor. She'd called Sharon after she was on the road and asked her to feed Miss Priss a day earlier than planned, giving her a hasty goodbye and Merry Christmas. She'd promised to be back January 30. They'd exchange gifts then.

"Mom, I've been tellin' you over and over to get rid of this old heap, and now look! You're frozen!" Ben had chided as he helped her bring her suitcase and bags of brightly wrapped presents into the house.

"Don't be silly, Ben. I'm fine. I'll get some hot tea. Bring in the rest of those, will you, and put them under the tree?"

With a shake of his head, he returned to the car for a second load. He recognized the huge flat, rectangular package on the bottom, knowing it had to be the portrait of his daughters he had seen at Thanksgiving. It was the reason Maggie had driven—the painting was much too big to fit on the plane, and she didn't want to take a chance damaging it during shipping.

"I'll take your Volvo in to my mechanic tomorrow," Ben offered, "although it might not get fixed... it's Christmastime, you know!" Maggie had already disappeared into the house.

Those few days away from Lubbock, from her heartache, were good for Maggie and she'd cherished the time with her family. Michael and Karen had flown in, and Ben and Amanda's home was large enough to hold them all. The traditional turkey dinner, cooked by Amanda with only a little help from Maggie, was delicious, and Ben puffed with pride at his wife's culinary success as he and Michael cleaned up the dishes afterwards.

Within an hour of her arrival in Dallas, she'd told them she was no longer seeing Colin, and would appreciate it if they wouldn't ask questions. They started to ask anyway, but "the look" silenced them all. During the entire visit, they respected her privacy, although all four of them sensed something was terribly wrong and hurt for her. The boys secretly plotted to fly to Lubbock after the New Year and beat the crap out of the man who'd hurt their mother.

The distractions of the holidays worked their magic, though, and Maggie fell quickly asleep each night, exhausted by the day's activities and grateful for family.

By far the best present she'd received was the news she was to be a grandmother for the third time—Michael and Karen were expecting their first child next summer.

Ben's mechanic said he could have the heater fixed in time, but the part he needed was nowhere to be found in or around Dallas. Luckily, it wasn't *that* cold when she headed back, but nearing Ranger, about 65 miles east of Abilene, the halfway point, it *got* that cold as she met an unexpected blizzard head on. As snow began falling, she stopped for hot chocolate and warmed her hands under the gas station restroom's hand dryer. By the time she drove past Abilene, the blizzard was in full-force. Thankfully, it was a dry snow and wasn't sticking, so the roads weren't icing up.

As she made the turn northwest outside of Sweetwater to Highway 84, the snowstorm limited visibility to about 50 feet and was beginning to accumulate on the sides of the road. She actually was a little concerned about making the remaining 115 miles, so, pulling over in Roscoe to warm her hands once more, she asked for a weather report at the gas station.

"Should blow o'er in no time a-tall," the greasy-haired station attendant had drawled, cigarette hanging out of the corner of his mouth as he rang up the cost of another hot chocolate. "Radar shows it's mostly to the south, though, so ya' shouldn't have trouble gettin' on up the road ta Lubbock, darlin'."

Somewhat reassured, she continued "gettin' on up" the road. Although snow usually delighted her as much as thunderstorms, Maggie remembered Josh's accident last March and was concerned with the possibility of deer, coyotes, or wild feral pigs suddenly jumping out in front of her. Any beauty that might surround her went unnoticed. Instead, she worried about running off the road and being stuck in a ditch in the blinding snowstorm. It was not her idea of a good time, especially in a car with no heat.

She also didn't notice they'd been right last spring—the hundreds of white wind turbines in the area weren't blighting the landscape—they'd been rendered invisible by the snowstorm.

About 40 minutes later, the greasy-haired guy was proven right. As she entered Snyder the snow was petering out, and by Post, the small town just below the Caprock, the sun was shining across a late afternoon's clear blue sky, although it was still well below freezing.

Now only thirty minutes from home, Maggie stopped at the small town's only McDonald's for another round of hot chocolate, her third, and one more hand warming, but only because she needed to use the facilities. What was it about cold weather that made you have to pee more often and more urgently, she wondered? She didn't think it was old age, but she couldn't be certain. These days she wasn't certain about much, except that she did feel old, cold and sad.

She called Sharon to report in and was easily persuaded to come straight to the Nest instead of her house because Doug was whipping up dinner and a fire was already blazing in the den.

"Why won't you call him? He's in agony, Maggie," Sharon said. "He's called here every day, and you said he'd left several messages for you, as well. What in the world happened?"

They were seated in front of the fire after having devoured dinner. Doug escaped to the music room, ostensibly to practice, and when they finished the dishes, the two friends took a plate of leftover Christmas cookies and eggnog to the den. Maggie hadn't told her the humiliating details, and Sharon knew better than to press too hard, understanding she'd tell her if she wanted or needed to tell her.

"Colin wants what I can't give him and I want what he can't give me... so it's best that we just move on and forget each other."

"But he loves you and I know you love him."

"Does he? Seems to me if he loved me, really loved me, he'd know me better. Know how I feel about things."

"Well, I know he misses you and wants to see you."

"That may be, Sharon, but for me that's not enough. I have to have the whole package, the whole commitment and... and..."

"And I know," Sharon said gently, "the whole marriage thing. I know you do, darlin'... I just don't think he can do that no matter how much he might love you."

Maggie balled her fists in frustration. "Don't you think I know that, Phelps? I know he can't do that. He's spent his whole life in temporary situations. Nothing permanent. Twenty years moving all over who knows where, doing who knows what for the FBI. And the man's never even owned a house, for God's sake... sorry, Lord," she said looking up. "Did I say house? He's never even bought a couch!"

Frustrated, she reached for another cookie. Chomping and dropping crumbs, she continued, "The only thing constant in his life is his love for his twin brother and his passion for Notre Dame football. How pathetic is that?!"

"Pathetic?" Sharon asked doubtfully. "I don't know. And I thought he owned the condo the lives in?"

"But it came furnished, and he just did it to help the boys. It's not a real home, but an investment property, he says. And, well, maybe not pathetic, but different, then, totally different from the way I live. I don't understand someone like that. Not to want to put down roots... not to build something solid."

"He makes pretty solid furniture. That's permanent, isn't it?"

"No, because he gives away or sells everything he makes, never using any of it in a real home. What kind of home is an investment property? Just like the women he's had—no investment other than bribing them with diamonds once in a while."

Sharon raised her eyebrows at that, but Maggie continued. "I like permanence... and I can't..." she admitted, lowering her voice to almost a whisper, "I can't be with a man unless he has made a promise before God to be with only me."

"Are you saying you think he's been with other women lately?" Sharon asked, surprised.

"No, no. I don't think that at all. In fact I'd bet my house he hasn't. I think... I know... oh, I don't know what I know anymore," she said in exasperation.

After a few more minutes of silence from them both, Maggie said, "Damn, Phelps. You know I've never been with anyone but Jim, and we waited until our wedding night, after we'd made public vows before God. It was amazing, and awkward, and embarrassing. I... I..."

She was lost in memories and smiled wryly, tears threatening to spill. Finally she said quietly, "It's just... it's... what Jim put inside my ring... did I ever show this to you? No, I've never shown it to anyone," she said pulling it off. "It was ours alone."

She read it silently, then handed it to her friend and turned away as the tears came forth.

Sharon read aloud, "*God and I~Always*. Oh, Mags," she said as her own tears began to fall, reaching to embrace Maggie.

"Always," Maggie whispered. "I want 'always' again Sharon. I won't settle for less than 'always' again."

Maggie stayed the night snugly tucked under quilts on the couch in front of the fireplace. They'd finally said goodnight after a good girlfriend cry, Maggie's heart in tatters, but determination steeling her against further involvement with Professor Colin Patrick Murphy.

Sharon's heart ached for her friend, and as she huddled against Doug's warm body upstairs in bed, she prayed for a way to help, deciding the best she could do now was to be there for her. Just like she had been since college. And tomorrow she would call Carol.

Slipping out before Sharon and Doug were up, Maggie had left a note of thanks, saying she needed to be alone so wouldn't be joining them to ring in the new year that night as planned. Maybe she would see them the next day.

She thought it might do her good to go out to the cotton field, but it was so cold that morning she didn't think she could concentrate, and she was a little tired of being cold.

Instead, throughout the morning, afternoon and most of the evening, she steadfastly worked on a new painting, diverting her mind again in hopes of allowing her heart to heal just a little. She would keep every minute of every day occupied and ignore most of the pain.

She could, couldn't she? Look how much practice she'd already had, first when her parents had died and then Jim. Both times she'd been devastated, but now she knew from experience that grief had to run its course—had to have its due. There wasn't a day went by she didn't still grieve for them, but time lessened the intensity, and acceptance slowly had taken its place. It had to, or she wouldn't have been able to love again.

So she would grieve again. Grieve for the "more" that might have been with Colin. But she wouldn't allow it to consume her. She would just grieve a little at a time each day, and it would fade away. Eventually. Maybe. God never gave you more than you could handle. She'd always believed that. Just now she wished He didn't think her so damn strong.

Too sad and too tired to stay awake after a light dinner, she went to bed early, tears soaking her pillow as she cried herself to sleep. She missed toasting in the New Year for the first time since she was a small child.

~ Part III ~ Puzzles To Be Solved ~

Chapter 63 ~

When Maggie opened her eyes early in the morning on January 1, the first thing she noticed about the New Year was that it was extraordinarily quiet. She got up and tiptoed to the window—somehow it felt like she should—and was delighted to find while she'd slept her world had been transformed into a magical white wonderland. A soft thick blanket of sparkling fresh snow had changed the landscape into an unrecognizable terrain that muffled the normal sounds of morning. The winter storm she'd passed through in Central West Texas two days ago had made an uncharacteristic wide turn back to the northwest, depositing just over a foot of the white wet stuff across most of the plains above the Caprock. It had been cold enough the past two weeks that the snow was likely to stick around for a while.

Donning boots and jacket over her flannel pajamas, she stepped out into the crisp freezing air to refill the bird feeder and look for the morning paper. Miss Priss ran out the door as soon as it opened but halted abruptly at the edge of the snow. Maggie laughed as the cat tested her footing, and then, sinking into the cold, white stuff, quickly jumped back onto the covered porch.

Maggie drew in a deep breath, letting the invigorating air fill her lungs, renewing and refreshing her from the inside out. She liked to think God had made this special setting just for her, as a reminder that even if her heart was broken, the world could be beautiful. Might be a tad egotistical, but she thanked Him, nonetheless. He could make everything right for her. She knew He could, and she hugged herself, content for the moment.

After providing breakfast for the neighborhood birds, she began to shiver, so she and Miss Priss returned to the warmth of the house—she to brew her morning tea and Miss Priss to find her litter box. As the tea brewed, Maggie said to the cat, "Guess I can read the newspaper online later." She hoped the paperboy had put double plastic on this morning's edition, still buried out there somewhere.

She was standing by her front picture window a few minutes later enjoying the serenity and softness of the new year when she was startled enough by the sudden ringing of the phone to spill her tea. As she brushed herself with a kitchen towel, she heard Sharon on the other end saying excitedly, "Remember our sophomore year when it snowed like this and we went to the open area by the Dairy Barn to make snow angels? Meet you there in 15?"

Maggie laughed, "Make it 30 and you're on, but bundle up, I've been out and it'll freeze your spiked hair off!"

Maggie walked to campus, not wanting to chance driving the side streets if ice had formed under the snow. Curbs and sidewalks had disappeared. She was thankful for her wide-soled snow boots that not only kept her warm but also allowed her to walk mainly on top of the snow rather than falling deep into each step. And once she was moving steadily, the cold didn't seem quite as bad.

She made good time, crossing 19th Street easily—there was no traffic yet. Spotting Sharon's SUV in the deserted Hulen-Gates Residence Hall parking lot, just a few feet off the street, she said, "Uh-oh." It looked like Sharon's car had hit the hidden curb, spun out and was wedged up against a snow bank. Great, we're going to have to dig her out, she thought as she heard her name from between the buildings ahead. Eerie how far sound traveled in the hush of the snow.

"Maggie! Come see! I've already started a snowman. This is perfect packin' snow!"

Maggie joined Sharon in the open area near the old Dairy Barn, just west of the library, and smiled with delight at the immense open field of glistening virgin snow... well, almost all untouched because Sharon had indeed "started" a snowman that was already almost as tall as her fuzzy red earmuffs. "I couldn't wait! Isn't this glorious? I feel like a kid again!" she beamed.

Maggie laughed, agreeing, and they spent a happy hour perfecting Mr. Snowman, building a family for him, including a dog that looked more like an armadillo, and making snow angels everywhere they could. Their noses were red, their cheeks were glowing and their clothes covered in snow, but they were oblivious to everything except their fun. It was as if God had picked them up and set them down in a world all their own. Sheltered by the empty buildings and surrounded by frozen white crystals, the only sounds were the crunching of snow and the muffled ripple of their laughter. They were 30 years younger and giggling at the slightest joke or statement, or just at the joy of being alive and together.

Maggie stood with hands on hips facing her latest snow angel and declared it positively, absolutely the best one yet. She then took a snowball hit directly in the back of the head, portions of it sneaking down her neck between scarf and jacket. Sharon whooped in joy at her excellent aim.

Knowing a second missile could be on its way, Maggie ducked and scooped up a handful of the wet stuff, forming her own weapon, wheeling around to fire it at her friend. Halfway through her delivery, she stopped, frozen in place by the sight of a tall figure coming around the far corner of the building.

Anticipating the retaliatory shot, Sharon had ducked and turned away also discovering the intruder walking determinedly toward them. She stood and watched Colin's steady approach and her eyes narrowed.

Chapter 64 ~

Nodding as he passed a frowning Sharon, Colin kept his pace steady and his eyes on Maggie. Uh-oh, he thought, she looks angry.

Maggie *was,* in fact, angry. Angry he was here, shattering their fantasy world. Angry her heart was doing those damn flip-flops again. Angry he'd treated her so cheaply. Angry she was happy to see him, but furious he had the gall to intrude into her life when she wanted him out of it. Permanently. She considered running, but the snow wouldn't make for a fast getaway. Considered smashing his face with the snowball in her hand, but knew she would have to stand her ground and deal with him, even as her heart cracked a little more.

She looked at Sharon, who started to step to her friend's defense. Maggie signaled she could take care of it. Sharon simply shrugged and waved goodbye, heading for her car.

"Sharon, wait!" Maggie called out, starting to move. "Your car. I'll help you dig it out."

"Already done," Colin said as he continued walking toward her, waving Sharon away.

"Okay, then, bye!" Sharon retreated quickly. Under her breath, she said, "Good luck, Professor." She then thought to herself if he blew this last chance and hurt her further, she'd have to punch him out no matter what Maggie said.

Sharon didn't know exactly what had transpired between these two erstwhile friends, but she knew Colin had hurt Maggie to the core. It was easy to see Maggie was in love with him... or at least had been in love with him until she left for Christmas holiday. And she thought the stubborn man-about-town Colin Murphy was in love with Maggie in return, but probably simply not aware of it. Guess they'd have to work it out themselves. She headed to the warmth of her own home and her own lover.

"Bye! Thanks!" Maggie said. Then turning to Collin she demanded, "What do you want? How'd you find me?"

"Tracked you."

"Tracked me?"

"Yep, went to your house and when you didn't answer, found the tracks from the back door and tracked you here. Got a little confused just before 19th Street... some kids pulling sleds heading for the park, I suspect, but picked your trail back up, then recognized Sharon's car. I dug it out and kept following the footsteps. And here you are." He kept his green-eyed gaze steady on her face.

Maggie forced herself to turn away. "Don't you have a bowl game or something to watch? I thought your beloved Notre Dame was playing today?"

"They are, but I wanted to talk to you."

"So talk," she said, still not meeting his eyes, but dropping her snowball and absently kicking it away.

"Let's walk while we talk," he said and reached for her elbow.

She pulled away. "I'm perfectly capable of walking by myself, thank you."

"I know you are, Maggie. Will you walk with me to see the horse statue?"

"The horse statue? I see it every day outside my office window," she replied with noticeable irritability.

Colin shook his head, "Not Soapsuds and Will Rogers, but the horse."

"The Masked Rider by the stadium? I've seen it, too, and I'm getting cold."

"No, the *other* horse," he said, with growing exasperation. "I'll show you if you'll come with me. Please, I want to talk to you," he said quietly.

Whatever could there be to talk about, she thought. She suddenly had a huge deja vu and was transported back more than 30 years, remembering a similar scene with a boy she dated here at Tech—the Saddle Tramp—how ironic. He'd wanted to talk to her, too, and she had walked with him across campus to... to where? Oh, the circle. Turned out he'd met someone else and was dumping Maggie, and felt obliged to tell her why in person. Something about honor or decency, or something. All she remembered was how much it hurt.

Is that what Colin wanted to do? To tell her why he was dumping her? But she knew why, didn't she. She wouldn't sleep with him, wouldn't be his "lady," so he was dumping her. But this time would be different because she was already hurt, and her heart had already dumped him back. She just hadn't told him. Fine, she thought. I can deal with this.

She nodded silently, and he motioned for her to go north out of the courtyard area, around the old silo next to the Dairy Barn. She complied and he walked next to her, careful to leave at least a foot of open space between them.

After a few steps, he glanced to the left, behind the English and Philosophy Building and said, "Bet the *Headwaters* fountain is frozen." It was a huge carved pair of hands, holding a jumbled alphabet, with water rippling over it all. Maggie glanced in its direction and nodded, but they were too far away to be sure.

He continued tentatively as they walked, "Did you know it was carved in Carrara, Italy? From African black granite and Kashmir gold granite? It's by Larry Kirkland. I met him when it was installed a few years ago."

Maggie didn't comment, wondering why he was giving her a description of the sculpture. Was he nervous? Confident, comfortable

Professor Colin Murphy nervous? She couldn't imagine. But she didn't ask, just listened and walked and hurt.

Despite her lack of response, he continued. "The hands full of letters are supposed to symbolize the potential for communication, and the water is the unquenchable thirst for knowledge. I like the heavy feel of it. The stability. It reminds me of the bulls."

The bulls, Maggie knew, were the enormous bronze figures in front of the Animal and Food Sciences Building at the west end of campus. Each year at graduation, Ag students fashioned giant mortarboards and placed them on the bulls' heads. The huge beasts were favorites of Maggie's because of their playfulness and satirical laziness—both bulls were nonchalantly resting, legs seemingly tucked up beneath their massive bodies. She imagined they looked different today all covered in snow.

When she didn't say anything, Colin continued, "The bulls draw attention to the relationship between convex and concave forms that create shadows in the sand around them."

Maggie looked at him sharply, "What'd you do, memorize the University Art Collection brochure?"

He blushed and Maggie thought perhaps he'd done just that. Immediately embarrassed for her childish ridicule of him, she quickly asked, "Who's the artist?"

"Peter Woytuk," Colin said, suddenly reluctant to continue talking. He had, in fact, read the brochure again an hour or so ago, trying to compose just the right words so she would know exactly how he felt, thinking perhaps art, one of her passions, might help him make her understand. He was embarrassed he *was* reciting some of it and was making an awkward mess of things.

They walked on in silence, and he used the time to send up fervent prayers to every saint he could think of—except Saint Jude, the patron saint of lost causes—he didn't want to jinx this.

Still heading north across campus west of Stangel/Murdock residence complex, they were getting close to Carpenter/Wells Complex, the once-progressive residence halls built shortly before Maggie was a student. Maybe they were heading to the clock tower, Maggie thought, a fairly recent addition that was an obvious attempt to bring some of the Spanish-style architecture to that end of the campus. Did it have a horse carved on it? She didn't remember.

Just before the clock tower, Colin stopped, turning toward her. "We're almost there, but I need you to close your eyes."

"What? Why?"

"Just trust me on this Maggie, please?" he asked quietly.

"Okay, but if you lead me into a ditch or wall, you'll pay for it, Professor Murphy." Her anger had cooled with the long walk, and now she just wondered where he was taking her, and why, and how much longer she'd have to endure the pain of being close to him. She closed her eyes and felt his hand gently but firmly take hold of her elbow. She wanted to pull away but didn't.

"This way," Colin said, and she allowed him to lead her, hands out front a little in case there was indeed a wall she needed to avoid.

He turned her to the right and walked her about 150 paces, stopped and let go of her arm. "You can open your eyes now."

It took her a minute to see anything as the bright sun reflecting off the snow blinded her and she quickly closed her eyes again. This is why people wear snow goggles, she thought, rubbing her eyes and then squinting them open, one at a time. Once her vision returned, she spotted a sculpture, one she'd never seen, and put her hands to her heart in astonishment. About twenty feet in front of her was a magnificent life-size horse, standing with solid assurance in a circle of snow-covered prairie grass, his powerful curved neck suggesting an easy, confident tension. "Oh," was all she could say as she let her breath out slowly. How long had it been here? How had she missed it in all the time she'd been at Tech? How did Colin know she would be captivated by its beauty?

Finally, after taking a few tentative steps closer, she whispered, "Driftwood? No, it can't be. It wouldn't last." But it looked just like driftwood and other scraps of natural wood shaped by nature. Twisting and writhing in form, the pieces were the lines, giving the suggestion of the animal, as if a powerful dry brush painting had suddenly become a frozen three-dimensional life form.

Crisp clean wind moved undeterred through dozens of openings between the sections of wood swimming in and out of each other. Somehow the artist had picked up the right pieces of this jigsaw puzzle and fitted them perfectly to form a glorious work of open-air art.

Colin's tension left him as he studied her reactions. "Yes, it's driftwood... or was. The artist, Deborah Butterfield, takes pieces of wood and fits them together for a bronze mold. So, it's really bronze formed from wood. This is *Wind River.*"

"It's magnificent," she said, still staring at it, overwhelmed by the beauty of it, walking up and around and touching it everywhere as if petting the huge wild beast, knocking the snow off.

Colin followed and then bent down to sweep the snow off one of the surrounding granite walls on the periphery of the sculpture. Straddling the wall, he took off his gloves and watched her. He decided he'd better send up one final plea for assistance... but this time to the Man himself. There were some times, he reasoned, you just had to go straight to the top.

After a few minutes he said, "Sculptures of hers are all over the country. There's one in Washington, D.C., at the National Portrait Gallery.

And four that I know of in Portland, Oregon, where your son Michael lives. Three of them at the airport, in fact."

She continued walking around and touching the horse, brushing snow off of it, hearing Colin, but not really focusing as she said absently, "You've been to Portland?"

Chuckling to himself, he knew she hadn't even heard herself ask the question that required no answer. "Here, let's sit down a while," he said reaching again for her arm as she passed him. He pulled her gently to the granite seat. Keeping her eyes on the horse, she allowed him to guide her and sat down, oblivious not only to the cold chair, but to his warmth next to her.

"Maggie," he said softly. She turned and looked at him. Something in his eyes compelled her to look more closely, to be drawn in. Then remembering her pain and the last time she saw him, she put her head down. He reached up and gently lifted her chin, studying. "You're so lovely when you smile. Please smile for me, Maggie." She looked up at him and love overflowed, intensifying the hurt and making her smile with rue. Just get it over with, she thought. It hurts so much.

"I brought you here for a specific reason," he continued, turning his gaze to the horse. She followed his eyes and resumed her consumption of the art. "This sculpture represents... well, represents a transformation. At first the wood was trees and shrubs and had life, had purpose. Then wind and the weather changed it into driftwood, and it sat on a beach some-where, soaking up the sun, being washed by waves or floating in the water, not ever being tied down. Then God sent someone to pick it up and transform it yet again, into something permanent, something solid, something beautiful in a new way."

He paused, and Maggie wondered why he was telling her this. Somehow, he'd taken her gloves off, too, putting her hands in his, but she didn't pull away, didn't feel the cold, only the warmth of his touch. Listening intently, she turned toward him again as he looked at her.

"That's what you have done for me, Maggie. You have transformed me."

Her heart stopped and she couldn't breathe. What was he saying?

"The sight of you stirs me, Margaret Riley Grant. Seeing you smile, making you smile, I feel comfortable, and God knows I like comfortable. But at the same time, you stir in me a longing I never knew was there.

"It's not just a longing to have you in my bed..." Now she did try to pull her hands away, but he held firm. "...but it's a longing to have you by my side. I want you to be there when I wake up, when I go to sleep, when I work... when I laugh... and when I pray. Maggie, I have this unrelenting longing for the whole you. Don't get me wrong, I still want you in my bed in the worst way, but I want all of you. I want all of you, Maggie, always."

She whispered questioningly, "Always?"

He nodded and continued. "You have made me want to be permanent, to be steady and transformed. I love you with all that I am, and I am humbled by the hope you might still return that love. I'm so sorry for trying to make you into what you can't be... shouldn't be... something just temporary. I don't want you to be temporary, Maggie. I want you to be permanent in my life. I want you to marry me."

She was crying, and her hands were over her mouth to stifle the sobs, and his were on her face, wiping away her tears. "Don't cry, Love, your tears will freeze," he said gently.

Finally she said, "Oh, Colin. Are you sure? Are you sure you can do 'always'?"

"Sure enough to want to give you this." He opened his fisted hand, revealing an antique emerald ring, the same clear green of his eyes. "Will you wear it for me, Maggie?"

She looked at the large stone and then at her left hand, the hand with Jim's ring on it.

He looked at Jim's ring, too, and quickly said, "You don't have to take that one off. I don't mean to replace the love of the man you were married to for thirty years. I couldn't, and wouldn't ever do that. I mean to *add* to it... so you can wear this with it or on the other hand if you want to."

"Oh, Colin," she said as she pulled Jim's ring off and moved it to her right hand. Holding her empty hand up to him, she said with a smile, "I love additions."

He laughed as he slipped the emerald on and leaned down to kiss her, gently.

She accepted his kiss. She then pulled back, looking him squarely in the eyes, smiling, and still crying. "Are you sure, Colin?"

"Absolutely sure."

Maggie grabbed him by the collar of his jacket, pulled him to her for a much longer, much more passionate kiss—one that held a promise of things to come.

Chapter 65 ~
The End of January

"**Oh**, he's here!" Maggie called out excitedly when the doorbell rang. "Are you ready? How do I look?"

"Well, let me see, girlfriend," Sharon said coming in from the adjoining upstairs room, motioning her to twirl around. Maggie complied, her deep emerald gown swishing around her ankles in elegant swirls of satin.

"Gorgeous!" grinned Sharon as Maggie beamed.

"It is gorgeous, isn't it," Maggie said, admiring the way her engagement ring sparkled next to the satin.

"Yes, IT is, but I meant you, Maggie. You're gorgeous, especially with your hair piled up like that," Sharon said.

"You just say that because you love me, but I'm still the plain Margaret Riley you met in college... just older. But I do like what you did with my hair. Hope Colin does. Normally he likes it down."

"Up or down, the poor man won't know what hit him. Maybe you should wear that dress for the wedding? It's fantastic!"

"No, no," Maggie laughed, swirling around one more time just because it was fun to feel so girly. She had to admit the elegant gown was about the most beautiful one she'd ever owned, and certainly the most expensive. Not to mention the most daring, with tight-fitted high-neck bodice, billowing skirt, full length sleeves, and the added surprise of absolutely no back.

"The wedding is simple, and this, well, this is a party dress!" She turned to Sharon. "But let me look at you! Twirl, yourself, Phelps!" Maggie let out a low whistle as Sharon obliged. She was donned in a floor-length jeweled tight-fitting red gown with low neckline. The elbow-length sleeves completely covered her upper arm burn from the Halloween fire. "You look wonderful! Has Doug seen you in it yet?"

"Absolutely not! When we got back from Dallas, I hid it. Neiman's dresses are always so worth the wait, don't you think? Thank goodness Winston made this party for the wind museum a formal affair. It's so fun to shop for glamour!"

"Definitely, my friend," Maggie agreed, admiring them both as they posed together in front of the mirror. They turned their heads towards the door as male voices drifted up the stairs. Reaching for her matching wrap and evening bag, Maggie said, "I love that you brought me over here to dress... we can regally descend the staircase. I've always wanted to do that, by the way. Like Eliza Doolittle in *My Fair Lady*. Wow, you in scandalous scarlet and me in elegant emerald. Why, those guys ain't got a chance!"

"Amen. Let me get my things and we can go down. Doug's probably already given Colin a beer, and most likely had two himself, so we'd better go now if we want them to be conscious enough to appreciate us."

Returning from the next room with her evening bag and coat, she put her arm through Maggie's. "Let's knock 'em dead!"

At the top of the curved staircase, Sharon cleared her throat loudly enough for Doug and Colin to turn around and look up. Staring open-jawed at the women coming toward them, they then grinned broadly. "Colin," Doug said, I don't know where Sharon and Maggie are, but let's take these beautiful creatures and go party. I'm taking the red sparkles."

"Fine with me. I'll take the green. Matches my eyes."

As the ladies descended, Maggie's heart started doing the now-frequent flip-flops as she looked at her new love. Resplendent in black tuxedo, he was truly as drop-dead gorgeous as her daughter-in-law Amanda had said. What's that line from the movie *Funny Girl*? "The groom was prettier than the bride?" I think I'm one lucky old woman. Thanks, again, Lord.

Just over two hours later, she would again be saying prayers, but much more fervent ones.

The Wind Museum, at the northwest corner of the Texas Tech University campus, had been transformed into a winter wonderland for the late January gala, celebrating the completion of the first phase of the massive expansion made possible by the Arbuckle's generous donation. Although the museum was not quite as resplendent as Mother Nature had done three weeks earlier, it was hard to believe you weren't in a snowy fairyland. Miniature white lights crisscrossed the immense ceiling behind hundreds of yards of filmy, gently draped white material. Sparkling silver and white floral arrangements topped the dozens of dinner tables, and thousands of small glass mirrors attached to white satin ribbons hung floor to ceiling in front of the fabric extending down the walls, reflecting the candlelight and sparkles back on to the partygoers.

The two couples were amazed as they walked inside, looking up and around, dazzled by the splendor.

"Wow. They sure know how to throw a party," Doug said, still gaping.

"Or at least how to decorate one," Sharon said. "Mags, let's find the ladies room first, the wind wasn't kind to your hair. I need to fix it. Doug, sweetie, we'll meet you at our table. I'd love a white wine."

"Me too?" Maggie asked Colin when he looked at her with raised eyebrows, "then I need to briefly check on the media."

As director of communications for the university, Maggie was officially on duty tonight. At least two local television stations were covering the gala for their 10 o'clock newscasts, as well as her reporter friend Jake from the *A-J* along with his staff photographer. Charlie, the university's official photographer was there, and would handle any requests from the others, but Maggie had told him she would check in with him when she arrived to see if assistance was needed.

First, though, she'd better see about her hair. She led Sharon down the hallway to the left. She knew the largest restrooms were in the other direction, but here, close to the main offices, she remembered an older, smaller one that might be less crowded.

As they entered the short corridor, they encountered Winston P. Whitaker III, dressed in a dark blue tuxedo, velvet bow tie and an enormous blue brocade cummerbund that surprisingly looked appropriate for him. He was coming out of the office area, closing and locking the door behind him.

"Oh, my dears!" he said as he planted light kisses on their cheeks. "How wonderful you look!"

"Thank you, Winston," Sharon said. "The museum looks amazing. You've done a marvelous job with the decor, especially for an engineer!"

"Why thank you, Dr. Phelps, but much of the credit goes to our lovely Margaret Grant here, you know what I mean?"

"Uh, no, I don't know what you mean," Sharon said as she studied Maggie's now blushing face.

"Why, it was she who suggested the theme for tonight and even did some sketches for the decorators."

It was a small favor for Windy, and Maggie hadn't thought to mention it. She didn't believe favors of kindness needed to be discussed. She much preferred to keep it between the recipient and herself.

"This is so much more, though, Windy," she said. "You've brought the fabric all the way to the floor. It's really spectacular. Um, we were heading down to the ladies room?"

"Yes, yes, of course. Keeping it for the hired staff, tonight, but you ladies go right ahead. I need to attend to my other guests. Can't make Miss Katherine do all the work!" He stepped quickly away.

Before dinner, hors d'oeuvres and wine were served to the guests as they chatted happily at their assigned tables, listened to the Tech Student Chamber Orchestra, or wandered the museum floor, examining the new exhibits. Purposefully, a large area at the front of the renovated museum, about one-quarter of the floor space, had been left empty for just such an occasion as this. It would also make a perfect classroom, Sharon had said, even though plans for the next phase of the renovations included an extensive educational wing.

With most of the displays toward the back of the building and the west, but close enough to make guests at any table feel a part of it, Maggie thought it also would be a perfect site for business meetings, or receptions, or even weddings. Windy had told her that was exactly what he had in mind. A little added revenue, he had said, although it probably meant putting on additional staff to handle it. But the publicity would be great. And Windy dearly loved publicity.

Across the entire front of the museum, the old small windows had been replaced with a half-dozen sets of elegant French doors that opened to a huge flagstone patio, extending the party outside and doubling the capacity for events. But not tonight, as the late-January evening was much too cold.

As in the previous exhibit, windmills of all shapes and sizes were displayed throughout the area, some of them spinning ten- to fifteen-foot

236

blades on motors that purred contentedly. Winston had successfully exhibited the full-size modern wind turbine blades and a motor similar to the working turbine outside—two of the blades were buried about one-third into the floor with the third massive blade reaching high up into the three-story addition. Winston's pride and joy, it was the hit of the evening, as patrons marveled at its size. Somehow, out on the plains, and even out front, the white metal blades didn't look quite this big!

Windy had outdone himself, Maggie thought as she read an exhibit plaque about the Aermotor windmills, manufactured since 1888. Sharon had begged off a few minutes before, saying she'd read and seen all she needed to read and see about windmills for the evening, and where could she find more of those delightful shrimp thingys? Doug and Colin had eagerly offered to help her in her quest. Traitors, Maggie thought. She, herself, was fascinated by the exhibit, and wanted to look a few minutes longer, promising to join them at their table shortly. How could there possibly be this many styles and sizes of windmills?

She was interrupted by a familiar voice, and turned to see a shyly smiling Jamie Chavez himself, the Saddle Tramp president, handsome in short-waisted red waiter's coat with crisp white tuxedo shirt, pressed black pants and bolo tie. He offered one of the glasses of wine he expertly balanced on a silver tray.

"Jamie!" Maggie exclaimed as she took one of the proffered glasses. "How nice to see you. Thank you. I didn't know you were working here tonight. How are classes going?"

"Going well, Mrs. Grant. Thanks. I, um, I haven't had a chance to say, I mean, congratulations and all. I think it's great, you and Murphy. Really great."

"Thank you, Jamie," she said, thinking how his words didn't match the sadness in his expressive eyes. The grief over his mother's death was still so evident. Maybe she needed to talk with him again? She would if he asked, but she wouldn't push him. "I think it's pretty great, too, Jamie. Murphy's back over that way someplace," she said, looking out over the crowd.

She didn't see Colin, but instead noticed Winston in the near corner, behind the enormous Southern Cross windmill wheel set close to the floor, talking animatedly with Bennett Boyle. Both their backs were to her and the crowd, but it was obvious they weren't exactly exchanging pleasantries. She wondered what the problem was, thinking this definitely was not the time or place for an argument.

"Jamie," she said, "See Dr. Whitaker over there? Why don't you go offer him a glass?" Maggie thought an interruption might calm them down before others, especially one of the news photographers, noticed the heated exchange. She watched as Jamie obligingly headed in their direction.

As he approached the men, Jamie heard Dr. Whitaker say, "I won't do it that way, B.J."

Rubbing his forehead, Bennett replied angrily, "You have to. I told you last week he was asking questions. Do it, or else."

"Or else what? It's your..." He stopped in surprise as Jamie approached clearing his throat.

"Wine, gentlemen?" Jamie asked in a flat voice.

"What? No, thank you, son," Winston said.

Jamie held his ground and looked at Boyle. "And you, Mr. Boyle?" he said forcefully.

"No. Now get lost," Boyle said dismissing him with a wave of his hand.

"Sure thing, Prick," Jamie said under his breath as he turned to leave.

"What did you just say?" Boyle demanded as he caught Jamie's free arm and pulled him back around, nearly upsetting the wine glasses.

Jamie looked up at him with disgust and pulled away. "Nothing."

"Nothing, sir," Bennett said staring hard at him.

"Nothing, sir," Jamie replied with contempt. He turned again, put his silver tray down on a nearby table, and moved quickly to the kitchen door, angrily pushing his way through and almost knocking down a fellow caterer.

"What was that all about?" Winston said.

"I have no idea," Bennett said. "Stupid kids. Listen, I've been seen by the damn president and talked to that idiot board chairman, so I'm leaving."

"Leaving? The party's just getting started, Bennett. Stay a while longer. Have some more wine."

"Just do as I said," Bennett scowled as he pushed him aside, weaving his way hurriedly through the crowd toward the front door.

Winston shook his head, smiled slightly and then noticed Maggie several yards away, who gave him a questioning look. Winston shrugged, and picked up two fresh wine glasses from the discarded tray before he made his way in the opposite direction.

He made a beeline to Mrs. Fauntly, a smartly dressed and extremely wealthy widow who hadn't donated any of her millions to the museum in at least six months.

"Mrs. Fauntly," he gushed as he handed her a glass, "Don't you look simply 'stunfabulous' this evening!"

Chapter 66 ~

Dinner was delicious. The museum had obviously spared no expense in choosing the menu of prime rib and smoked salmon, with delicate asparagus spears lightly covered in a French white wine sauce Doug vowed to find the recipe for, even if it wasn't Italian.

Jamie seemed to have gotten over his "mad," and half-smiled at Maggie and Sharon as he continued helping serve the dinner plates and pouring more wine and coffee.

"I'm sure he's still angry with Bennett for throwing the Tramps out of the tower," Colin had said when Maggie told him of the incident. "He seems so depressed this year. I worry about him, but I'm sure he'll be fine tonight. I'll talk to him later."

Maggie relaxed because all the media had left as dinner was served, having gotten their allotted footage, quotes and photos. Their tendency was to not hang around if they could help it. And Winston was paying to have it all taped for posterity anyway, so they could borrow footage if needed.

Winston stopped by Maggie's table, and the two women introduced him to their dates. When he moved on, Doug said, "Well, I'll be damned. You're right. He does look a little like the White Rabbit."

"Shh!" Sharon said quickly, looking to make certain Winston hadn't heard. He hadn't, but she playfully slapped at Doug's arm anyway.

"I kinda agree, I think," Colin said. "That is if I remember what the White Rabbit looks like. From *Alice in Wonderland*, right?"

Doug said, "Yep. Looks like Whitaker, except with long white ears. He even has a pocket watch and chain! Why does he dress like that?"

"He does it to create an older persona," Maggie explained. "We talked about it, and he explained he does it for the opportunity to be more friendly with wealthy women."

"What?" Doug said. "That doesn't make sense."

"Sure it does, Honey," Sharon replied. "If their husbands think they're giving money to some old guy who likes windmills, they're fine with that. They've met him and find nothing at all to be jealous about. Would you be jealous if I spent a lot of time with him?"

"No. He's just a funny old guy. Sort of comical."

Sharon smiled. "That's precisely why he does it. The men don't see him as a threat, and the women adore him. He's so charming!"

"Exactly," said Maggie. "Witty, charming and a gracious host."

Miss Katherine was making the rounds at the same time, resplendent in a navy satin gown that stylishly showed off her delicate bare shoulders.

"Who's a gracious host?" she asked.

"Why, you!" Maggie replied, rising to give her a hug. "You've done a great job, Katherine. Everything is perfect!"

"Why, thank you, Maggie. I tell you, I'm having the time of my life! I'm so glad to be working here with Dr. Whitaker. He's such a charming old gentleman!"

As the sated patrons were finishing up the crème brûlée with fresh raspberries, Winston took his place on the first landing of the new steel and glass staircase. It provided central access to a five-foot-wide glass walkway spanning the museum's main floor from east to west. Although it was about 15 feet up in the air, the bridge served to visually separate the open area from the exhibits. Made entirely of metal and clear glass—even the floor section—Colin said it reminded him of the fairly new Calatrava glass bridge in Venice.

"You've been to Venice?" Maggie asked innocently. Colin smiled but didn't reply.

Affording an entirely different perspective on the exhibits, especially those in the pit that had been moved toward the back, and being only a few feet wide, the walkway allowed the majority of the first floor to remain open to the new ceiling, also made of glass. During the day, the natural light was a perfect setting for the windmills. Tonight, a few bright West Texas stars could just barely be seen twinkling between the floating decorations.

From the first landing, about eight feet up, Winston had an unobstructed view of the entire museum floor and stood there for a moment admiring the scene, enjoying the packed house and the splendor of the evening. Only one chair was empty... Bennett Boyle's. Stupid fool, Winston thought. His loss.

He switched on the microphone placed there for the evening and cleared his throat before loudly saying, "Good evening, my dear friends!" Silence followed, as all heads turned toward him, anticipating. This was what he had worked for all his life, he thought happily, this recognition, this splendor, this spotlight. And he was prepared.

"My dear friends," he began. "It is with extreme joy that I welcome you to this gala 'festavelebration' upon the completion of the first of five phases for the expansion of my Wind Museum, destined to become the premier institution for all things 'Windy.'"

The audience laughed at his obvious self-serving play on words, but they loved him and expected nothing less.

He continued, "My heart tonight is 'overglowing' with gratitude to so many people. Let me introduce a few special ones tonight. First, our new president, Dr. Raymond Parker and his lovely wife, Ruth." Dr. and Mrs. Parker stood to the applause and bowed graciously to Winston, who then, in turn, introduced the board chair, other board members and, of course, Russ and Fern Arbuckle, the philanthropists who had made the evening possible. They received a standing ovation.

After all introductions, Winston continued, "I know you have been enjoying the new space and the new exhibit, but I want to give you a brief outline of what else we have deliciously planned, and not just for the next meal, but for the Wind Museum expansion. Our next phase—"

A scream pierced the air, and Winston and guests turned toward the sound. Mrs. Fauntly was standing, screaming loudly and looking wide-eyed

240

at the northeast wall. A figure in familiar catering clothes had emerged from the office hallway, back and hair fully engulfed in flames. In obvious agony, he stumbled, moaned and fell against the wall, becoming entangled in the mirrored ribbons and two of the white fabric columns that hung from the ceiling. Glass mirrors crashed to the floor and the fabric caught fire. The large-framed Mrs. Fauntly fainted, falling heavily to the ground a few feet away from the burning man.

More screams erupted and then an immediate pushing back of chairs as most guests began moving away from the danger and the now billowing smoke rushing in from the hallway. Colin had jumped up before Maggie could even comprehend what she was seeing. He reached the fallen man just as a campus police officer rushed in, extinguisher in hand. The officer quickly doused the flames on the man and started checking his vital signs.

Colin reached to pull the burning cloths down, but the flames had been too quick and were already halfway up the wall, spreading to other fabric as smoke started to curl on the glass ceiling. He knew the extinguisher wouldn't reach that high. "Where's the sprinkler system?" he shouted to the guard.

"I pulled the alarm, but nothing happened," the officer shouted back. He called on his radio for an ambulance. He had already called the fire department from outside. Several guests stepped forward at the officer's direction and were picking up the burned man just as others helped a revived Mrs. Fauntly towards the front doors. The officer pulled Colin away from the wall saying, "It's too late! We've got to get all those other doors open!"

Colin looked up once more at the spreading flames, then glanced at the hallway where the waiter had come from. He could see a wall of orange through the thickening smoke, and thought the entire back office area must be burning. He turned, looking for Maggie, but still headed toward the doors.

Jamie appeared suddenly at his side, saying the kitchen was cleared out the back and asking what he could do? "Open the last two doors. We've got these!" Colin said, turning back to look again for Maggie. Their table was empty.

When Maggie realized Colin was heading for the burning man, she got up to help him but a quick glance at Sharon stopped her. Phelps sat as if in a trance, staring at the flames beginning to shoot up the wall. Sharon's left arm was clamped protectively over her right shoulder, exactly where she had been burned three months earlier.

Maggie reached for her, but Doug had immediately sensed his lover's terror, and was already pulling her to her feet, saying, "I've got her, Maggie. I've got her. Come on, Baby. Let's get your coat on and go home. Party's over. Come on, Baby." He gently but firmly made her stand, put her coat on and then looked at Maggie. "Let's go!"

Maggie nodded, and looked again for Colin who was heading for the French doors. Was that her closest exit? Sweeping the room, something caught her eye and she looked up at the glass stairway landing behind her. Winston stood stock still, eyes wide and hands gripping the railing tightly, staring at the growing fire.

"Maggie! Come on!" Doug shouted, already two tables away, holding Sharon protectively against the crush of the panicked crowd. They were quickly absorbed by the throng, but Maggie again looked instead for Colin. All the doors were open now, and cold air rushed in as the hundreds of guests rushed out into the night. Maggie's table was in the southeast corner of the open space, the fire to her left, the doors behind her. She was alone in her area—all others had instinctively fled away from the fire. She scrambled over upturned chairs, discarded coats and dropped glassware, heading for Winston, screaming his name as she ran.

As she reached the bottom of the glass stairs, he seemed to finally hear her and looked down as she raced up toward him. Recovering, he said, "Yes, yes. I'm coming. I'm coming!"

Without use of the railing, he sprinted down to her, grabbing her arm and turning her around to lead her out as she reached the fifth step. Maggie had to shake the notion that he was old and feeble, as he always seemed, remembering he was actually much younger and still in fairly good condition despite his girth. He was helping her out instead of the other way around.

As they hit the bottom of the stairs, they heard a loud pop overhead, and then a gushing sound, and a few moments later, just as they were about to reach the doors, they were showered with water. The sprinkler system had kicked in at last and was doing a good job of putting out the fire in the exhibit hall.

"Thank God," Winston said as they exited the doors leading to the patio.

Colin grabbed Maggie from behind, turned her around and crushed her against him tightly. "Thank God," he said over and over, oblivious to her wet hair and soggy satin gown.

"I'm fine, Colin. Really. Did everyone get out?"

He took off his coat and wrapped it around her as she began to shiver and then held her protectively again. "Yes, I think so, but we haven't been able to get to the office area. It's still burning. Fire department's just arrived. They'll check, but I can't imagine anyone surviving in there."

"Sharon and Doug?" she asked.

"Saw them. They're fine. I sent them home. Sharon didn't need to watch this again," he said quietly.

"Fern and Russ?"

"Out and safe. Fern is organizing those who need medical attention and Russ is moving people to their cars."

Winston had slumped heavily on the porch's stone wall as soon as they exited, and Maggie thought he was once more transformed into an old man. A Good Samaritan placed an overcoat around his wet shoulders.

"Why did this happen?" Winston said to no one in particular, shaking his head and trying unsuccessfully to pull the warm coat around him. "Why here? Why now? Oh, my windmills."

Many of the guests had left, but just as many stood in the parking lot or sat in their cars watching the old east part of the building burn, flames now coming through the one-story roof despite the best efforts of the Lubbock firemen. Winston stood up and shuffled over to Colin and Maggie. "Is anyone else hurt badly? That poor man..." His voice was hoarse.

Colin said, "Some bruises and a few cuts. Someone broke out a window with a chair, I think, before we opened all the doors... and a sprained ankle or two from pushing their way out. Good thing there were so many doors. I think everyone else is fairly okay, except the waiter. Must've been in the men's room back there. They're taking him across to the Medical Center. He's still alive thanks to the officer, but he's got some pretty serious burns. Patrol cop said he'd seen the flames through the outside office window, so he came in with the extinguisher from his patrol car."

"And the lady who fainted?" Maggie asked.

"Oh, she's fine. Refused to go to the Medical Center—tough old bird. Said she wanted to stay and watch the excitement. By the way, Dr. Whitaker, she also said she would personally donate enough to rebuild what was lost tonight. Said it several times, in fact."

"Really? Mrs. Fauntly?" Winston asked, somewhat recovering. "Guess I need to go make sure she's all right, you know what I mean?" Maggie smiled and then pulled away from Colin, putting her arms through the sleeves of his coat, buttoning it and rolling up the sleeves. It would have to do, she thought, as she pulled pins from her soggy hair. Smoothing it back straight and pinning it tightly in her old-style chignon, she said to Colin, "Time for me to go to work. Reporters will be coming back soon. I'll find you later. Can you figure out a way to get home since Doug took the car? I might be a while."

She'd had the forethought to grab her evening bag as she raced to save Winston, so she pulled her phone out and began dialing her staff as she walked away.

"I'm going with you, and yes, I'll find a ride for us both," he said as he followed her toward the fire trucks and chaos. No way he was letting her out of his sight again tonight.

Chapter 67 ~

Colin marveled at the way she worked, moving from one official to the other, pulling information, asking questions, directing the press area to be set up. Maggie prepared a short statement for a grateful President Parker. There were some times, like now, audiences wanted to see the person in charge actually *be* in charge, so she had him memorize a couple of lines to give on camera and then she stepped in to take any questions.

Winston had asked her twice if he shouldn't be the one talking to reporters, but Maggie convinced him she could take care of it. She knew his persona didn't work as well on television as it did in person. No telling what audiences would make of his occasional jabberwocky which he still couldn't resist.

She had returned Colin's coat when Elaine showed up with a warmer one much closer to her size. Bless her, she'd also brought warm leather gloves and flat shoes that fit perfectly with Reginald's thick wool socks. Maggie hadn't asked for anything but the jacket, but Elaine knew her boss would be on her feet for a few hours and any woman with any fashion sense would be wearing very high heels under a Neiman Marcus evening gown. She'd been aware of the shopping trip to Dallas a few weeks earlier.

Steven and Susan arrived to assist, and one or the other was in constant contact with Ricky who'd gone to the office to put out a campus-wide bulletin and post the news on the website, mainly to give assurances to parents of only one serious injury and it wasn't a student. That alone would save several thousand phone calls.

Charlie had been working the gala and was continuing to capture the event with his Nikon, transmitting the photos to Ricky through his laptop.

Every 15 minutes, Maggie returned to the press area to give an update and then went back to gather more facts and confer with her staff. Through Ricky, she took a call from CNN, who would be there early tomorrow for video, and did a radio interview with the local Tech public radio station. She had to tactfully ask the board chairman to step further away from the building—he'd been making jokes with other regents to cut some of the tension, but laughter at a disaster scene didn't look good on camera.

Out of the corner of her eye, she noticed Bennett Boyle had returned, in more casual clothes and a heavy overcoat. He was talking with Winston, a little more calmly this time. Thankfully, he didn't try to interfere with her or her staff and she dismissed him from her mind as she went to find Chief Callahan for an update. Callahan finished talking with an officer when she walked up.

"We've just gotta stop meetin' like this, Sweetheart," the chief said with a wry smile.

"Yes, we do, and don't call me Sweetheart," she said matter-of-factly.

Then she asked in serious frustration, "Was it an accident, do you think? Or is it the same as the others?"

"No idea, yet, Sweetheart. My man who called it in said he tried the fire pull, but it didn't kick in for about five minutes. And the fire captain said the sprinkler apparently didn't go off at all in the office area. He also said his inspector had been out here earlier this week and everythin' passed with flyin' colors. So, that's somethin' we'll be lookin' into. We've got our best men workin' on it. Since this is the fourth campus fire, we'll put a priority on it."

"Thanks, Chief. Do we have an ID on the injured waiter yet?"

Callahan pulled out a notepad. "Yep. Henry Cassidy, age 42. Plumber. Been with Tech catering as a second job for about 20 years, they said. One of their best."

"Latest condition report?"

"Critical, but stable. His upper back and neck were pretty bad. Said he was taking a leak in the men's room when he smelled smoke. Went down the hallway to investigate and saw smoke coming up under the office door. Opened it and tried to see where the flames were and the ceiling fell in on him. Poor guy. It must've been burning for a while."

"Can we release his name and condition?" Maggie asked, writing down what he had said.

"Yes, the Medical Center already has. His wife is with him. Seems she's a nurse and was on duty tonight, and she gave permission for the release."

"Thanks, again, Chief," Maggie said as she left to give the latest to the reporters.

"No problem, Sweetheart!" he called after her.

"Thanks again for the ride, Jamie," Colin said as he helped Maggie out of the car in front of Sharon and Doug's house. It was close to midnight.

"Happy to, Murphy. Glad you're okay. What a mess. We've been hired to go back and clean it up first thing in the morning. It'll be good overtime, but I sure hate that it happened."

"We do, too, son. Goodnight," Colin said.

Doug was waiting at the front door and welcomed them with steaming cups of hot buttered rum. Maggie's ruined gown was dry by now, but she still shivered and welcomed the drink and the fire in the den. Doug had given Sharon a sedative earlier and stayed with her until she fell into a deep sleep. She'd want to see Maggie first thing in the morning, but Maggie knew she'd need to be at the office to take calls most of the day, even if it was a Saturday, so she politely declined the offer to stay overnight.

After warming up slightly and personally checking on a sleeping Sharon, Maggie let Colin drive her home, where he insisted on staying—in one of the guest beds. He didn't want to be across town just now. In fact, he didn't want to even be in another bed, but he knew better than to push the issue.

At 7a.m., which came much too fast for both of them, he made a breakfast of scrambled eggs while Maggie showered. After breakfast, she kissed him goodbye and headed for the office. He promised to clean up the kitchen before he left. Definitely a man worth keeping, Maggie thought.

Chapter 68 ~

That evening, Maggie and Colin dined again with their friends, and although Doug's cuisine was no less delicious than the fancy meal the night before, none of them really tasted it. Maggie had relayed the sad news that Henry Cassidy, the waiter, had died earlier in the afternoon, leaving a grieving wife and two teenage daughters. He had underlying health problems and his heart couldn't cope with the trauma.

The communications team had put in a hard day updating staff, students, parents, community and interested news stations from around the country. Maggie had to dissuade Winston again from going on camera, so instead Dr. Whitaker busied himself, along with the ever-faithful Miss Katherine, with overseeing the cleanup and getting a new workplace set up. Mrs. Fauntly had sent over an office trailer from one of her company's construction sites early that morning, complete with phone, fax and computer lines and equipment, telling Winston to spare no expense in getting things back to normal.

Had it been a tragic accident, they asked themselves. Or was it the arsonist again? Colin had suggested they pool their collective creative minds and work through the four fires, trying to find commonalities. He knew the campus police were already doing that, in fact had been doing that for several months with the first three, but fresh eyes never hurt. And, he reasoned, it gave them all something productive to concentrate on instead of the close call they'd had, especially Sharon.

When dinner was finished, Colin asked Sharon if she was okay to talk about it.

"Yes, of course. I apologize for my behavior last night. It just... I don't know what happened."

"It's fine, really, Sharon," Colin said quickly. "I only wanted to make sure you were up for this, that's all."

"Right, Phelps. No need to apologize," Maggie added as Doug moved protectively closer to her.

"I'm fine, now, really," Sharon said firmly. "So quit fussing, and let's figure out who the bastard is and stop this insanity."

Doug was a man of details. Having talked with Colin earlier in the day, he'd borrowed two large dry erase boards from the music department and set them up on easels in the den. He'd asked Colin when he called if this is how they did it back in his Bureau days.

"Yep," was his reply. "You wouldn't believe how seeing things written down can help the thinking process."

Colin started the discussion. "We need to put down everything we can remember about each fire, then look for similarities. Don't neglect anything, even the smallest thing you can think of or remember might help. First, we'll list the dates."

In the top corner on the far left, he wrote *Library/Mid September.* Then came *Engineering/End of October, Tower/Early December* and, finally, *Wind Museum/ End of January.*

Under each heading, one at a time, they discussed what they knew about the fires. They knew how the first and second had been set but were still waiting for completed information on the tower accelerant. And, of course, they knew nothing yet about the one last night, except that again it appeared to be arson because the sprinklers were disabled and delayed, and it had completely destroyed the office area. But this time it had killed an innocent man.

Doug, the music professor said, "First thing I notice is the meter is off, isn't even." To their quizzical looks he added, "The meter—the rhythm. The time between isn't consistent. Nothing in November, not the same number of weeks in between any of the fires. Longer between the September and October fires than between the October and December fires, and then much longer between the December fire and the one last night."

"Good... and bad," Colin said. "Good that the arsonist—if it is just one person doing all this—doesn't seem to be on a schedule. But it also means we can't predict when the next one might occur. But good catch, Doug."

Sharon said, "Also, the times of day are different, aren't they?"

"You're right, they are," Colin said, writing times under each heading. Early evening, morning, and the last two at night, with about an hour's difference.

"Maggie," Colin asked. "Do you remember seeing anyone at all four fires? Anyone who stands out? Start with the library. Who did you see?"

"Well, there was the student librarian, but he was so terrified he puked all over me. I can't imagine him setting it, and I don't remember him at any of the other fires. There were lots of students, all going down the stairwell. Any of them could have also been at the next two fires, but no one particularly stood out. Then I talked with the Campus Police. That's all.

"Oh, wait, Jamie was outside in the rain. Said he'd come up from the basement, I think. He took charge of the librarian for me. That's it. They said Bennett Boyle was there talking to reporters, but I hadn't seen him beforehand and he was gone by the time I was allowed out."

Colin listed student librarian, Boyle and Jamie under *Library*.

"Okay, how about the next one? At Engineering? Sharon?"

"Students, of course, and colleagues, but Boyle was in the building, too. Maggie, did you see him there?" Sharon asked.

"I did, but I thought he'd come from his office. I didn't really pay attention to him until he tried to take over. Luckily, Dr. Parker stopped him. I don't know if Boyle was there before the fire."

"He was. I saw him about ten minutes earlier in the main office and wondered what had brought him to our hallowed halls," Sharon said sarcastically. "I don't think I've ever seen him there before... ever."

Colin listed Boyle under *Engineering*. "Maggie, you certain you didn't see the librarian at the second fire?"

"I'm sure I would have remembered him. No, I didn't see him... but I did see Jamie, I think. Didn't you, Sharon?"

"I don't know for sure. But he's an engineering major. I see him all the time and he's in one of my classes this semester. I don't think that's significant."

"I'll still list him, although I agree with you," Colin said.

"Right. Jamie's just one of the few students I actually know by name, that's all," Maggie said.

Under *Tower*, they couldn't list anyone, because they saw no one near the fire. And Boyle didn't come until about an hour later, after most of the crowd had left, saying he was caught in traffic.

Doug said, "But he was there afterward, so I think you should put his name down."

"I agree," said Colin, writing Bennett's name on the board.

"Well," Maggie said tentatively, "maybe you should put my name down. I was there for all four of them."

Colin looked at her and said, "Did you set the fires, Maggie?"

"Of course I didn't!" she said indignantly. "But maybe..."

"Maybe what?" Colin said. "This is brainstorming, Maggie. Out with it."

"Maybe someone is setting them because of me."

"Because of you?" Doug said skeptically.

"No, Doug," Colin said, thinking about it seriously. "She may be on to something. Who has to be on camera and talk about each fire? Who has to answer phones the next day and put out news releases. And she was actually in the library and the museum when the fires started. Maybe...?"

"But I don't do those things by myself. I have a staff. Colin, you don't seriously think one of my staff has been setting the fires, do you?"

He raised his eyebrows as if it might be a possibility. "I don't know, Maggie. Would be a good way to get some overtime hours, all right."

"They're all salaried. They get comp time, but no extra money."

Sharon speculated, "Maybe one of them thrives on the excitement. Who was at the fires from your staff?"

"I had to call them for each one, except your fire, Sharon. Charlie was at all of them, of course. But he was there to record for the website."

"You saw Charlie at all the fires?" Doug asked.

"Yes... No, not at the library. But I was inside with the fire chief and police. There were some of his photos on the website, but I don't remember seeing him there."

"Okay," Colin said, "but we know he was there shortly afterwards. Let's pull up the website archives and see what we've got, if we can tell how soon after the alarm he was there."

Doug opened his laptop and began surfing for the photos. "Maybe we can also see some of the same people in the crowds. They do say those who start fires like to watch the chaos they create. I'll print them and we can tape them up."

"Good idea. What about Engineering? Maggie, was Charlie in your office or at the Engineering Building?" Colin asked.

"My staff was in the office—Elaine, Ricky, Susan and Steven. I'm sure they were. Charlie? He was at the scene, taking photos like he should and feeding them to Ricky. I... no, wait, he'd been somewhere else on campus when I first heard the fire engine, not in the office, because I remember Elaine saying she'd call him... but then he's always out of the office. He's a busy guy." With a pained expression, Maggie looked at Colin. "It can't be Charlie."

"Right now, Love, we're just writing down everything, remember? Not making accusations. He was also at the Carol of Lights and the Museum, wasn't he?"

"Yes, he was," Maggie said quietly.

A review of Charlie's photos showed fire engines arriving at each fire, meaning Charlie had been on the scene almost immediately, if not before. But Maggie refused to believe he was a suspect. Nevertheless, Colin listed him under each heading. And they found no one in the crowds who showed up in all four places.

"Okay, who else?" Colin asked the group. He prodded them to think of the next fire in the tower. But still, no one came to mind.

Sharon said, "Well, Jamie was there again, but he was leading the procession."

"Right," Colin said. "And I was with him for about three hours before that getting things ready for the ceremony. But, I'll list him anyway." He put his name under Charlie's and Boyle's.

"He was also at the museum," Maggie said quietly. "So was Charlie and so was Boyle. All three were there, Charlie taking photos, Jamie waiting on tables, and Boyle... well, Boyle left early, before dinner in fact. He and Winston had argued about something. Then he said something to Jamie that made him furious."

Sharon said, "Probably about throwing the Saddle Tramps out of the tower. I still can't believe Boyle did that. What's the status on reversing Boyle's decision, Colin?"

"President Parker has postponed our talking with the Board of Regents until March or April. Said he's still trying to get more information about the fire. Doesn't want to make too much of it until we find out who did it, so we're on hold."

"What about how the fires were set?" Doug asked. "What do we know?"

"Not much," Colin said. "I've talked with Chief Callahan, and he said the first one, in the library, was fairly easy to set. Perp pulled old magazines with ancient paper and set them on fire, closing and then disabling the stacks. Put some metal rods in the tracks to block the movement. Seemed to know air could reach the fire, but the firemen couldn't, at least not until they pulled the stacks apart."

"What did they burn?" Doug asked. "Which books?"

"Good question. I've no idea. Maggie?"

"It was in the 'T' section. I remember seeing the letters when I was trying to get the stacks apart. I thought the chief told me it was *Scientific America* publications, from the 1860s, I think, and something else...?"

"That's right, it was," Sharon said. "Now I remember. We had to put out requests all over the country to get some replacements. We have them all on computer, but wanted some originals. Some old *Iron Age* magazines burned, too, beginning in 1911. All destroyed."

Colin said, "All old paper and extremely flammable."

"And about science, engineering," Doug said. "Maybe we need to look for a disgruntled science or engineering student."

"Why do you think it's a student?" Sharon asked, defensive of her kids.

"Just a hunch. Plus, there are more of them around than anyone else, that's all."

"You could be right," Colin said, and wrote it down. "But it also could be a professor or any staff member. And maybe he... or she... was more interested in the location of the fire. Close to the stairwell for a quick exit? We just need to look at everything. Now, what else?"

"Well," Maggie ventured, "What burned at the other fires? Books and magazines in September, paper towels soaked in some type of accelerant in October, old carpeting and the wooden platform in December, and last night? An entire office building." Colin was writing furiously. "But what do they have in common?" Maggie asked.

Standing back and looking at the boards when he finished, Colin said,

"They increase in intensity... each one burned hotter and bigger than the last."

"You're right!" Doug said. "Our arsonist—if it's only one—is getting bolder each time."

"That's a scary thought," Maggie said quietly.

"What about the fuses or what he uses to ignite the fires?" Sharon asked. "Is he getting better at them each time, too? Is he setting bigger fires because he understands them better after each one?"

"That's a good question," Doug said. "Or were we just lucky enough to find the first two before they could get bigger?"

"I don't think so," Colin said, "because he had to have known there were others on the library floor. Didn't you tell me, Maggie, that the elevator bell rang loudly, so he must have known someone was there? And didn't you also say you used the copier?"

"Yes, I did. For about 15 minutes. It's really noisy and I used it right before I heard the southwest exit door close. He had to have known I was there. So, he either thought one person, me, would be able to get out, or, he didn't want too many casualties." An involuntary shiver ran up her spine.

"No, unless someone knew it was you up there," Sharon said with a sudden insight. "What was the name of that girl from HR you forced out?"

"Allison?" Maggie cried, shaking her head. "She's so stupid I'm not sure she knows how to strike a match, much less deliberately plan four fires. And I haven't seen her since last spring. No, I can't imagine it being Allison. And besides Boyle, I don't really have any other enemies, do I?" she said, trying to think of anyone else she might have crossed.

Colin wrote Allison's name on the board.

About an hour later, they photographed the now full boards and Colin e-mailed the photos to Chief Callahan. The chief had told Colin he welcomed any help from the ex-agent, but the group wasn't certain their random thoughts were anything but random thoughts. They had many more questions than they had answers.

Chapter 69 ~

In their Monday morning staff meeting, the Communications team debriefed about their work with the latest fire. Maggie praised Elaine for her quick thinking with the flat shoes, gloves and the warm socks, saying that once again, they had all done their jobs well.

But silently Maggie was ashamed she was paying particular attention to everything Charlie said. She was still certain in her heart he was not guilty.

However, his name had remained on the board.

As the meeting was wrapping up, Charlie spoke. "My wife knows Henry Cassidy's widow from the high school PTA. She volunteers there, my wife, I mean—it's her alma mater. Anyway, she said they have two girls who are a few years away from college. She wondered if Tech could, or would, set up a scholarship fund for them... to help. He was an employee, after all."

Steven said, "My wife knows her, too, from the hospital. Says she's one of their best nurses. I think it's a great idea."

"Good," Maggie said. "I'll bring it up to President Parker this morning. Or perhaps the Wind Museum could initiate it. Surely, something can be done. Thanks for the suggestion, Charlie."

He wouldn't be so kind to the family if Cassidy had died because of him, would he, she thought. Or maybe that's *why* he was being kind—out of guilt?

On Wednesday, Chief Callahan asked Colin to join them in their own brainstorming session. An extra investigator, even a retired FBI investigator, couldn't hurt. Colin was happy to oblige, but they seemed to be going in circles, too. The only new piece of information Colin learned is they'd been correct on the increasing intensity of the fires and the increasing sophistication of the ignitions.

The first was a simple paper trail fire, with torn-out pages of old books and magazines as the fuel. By the time the police had arrived and pulled the stacks apart, it had almost burned itself out. Books, as a general rule, don't burn that well unless torn apart and sprayed with an accelerant of some type. The fire department's arson dog had found no vapors from an accelerant. It was the torn and crumpled, decades-old dry paper that caused the massive amount of smoke.

Colin thought the arsonist must have set it all up while Maggie was at the copy machine for those 15 minutes. That would have covered any noise. To test the theory, he and the chief went early the next morning to experiment before the library opened. Standing where Maggie said she sat, Colin listened as the chief moved the stacks, but the only thing audible was a light ping preceding the movement and Maggie might not have heard it. Then he used the copier, while Callahan crumpled paper near the area of the fire. Colin heard nothing but the copier. Their conclusion was the arsonist had put it together while she was at the copy machine, then left using the stairs. Maggie's stuffy nose that day had obviously prevented her from detecting the smoke until she saw it.

In the Halloween fire in the engineering building, cleaning supplies from the burned closet were used as an accelerant on paper towels and old rags. Again, it was a relatively small confined fire and should easily have gone out by itself after damaging the inside of the closet. Unfortunately, Sharon had opened the door to investigate creating a backdraft that burned her and allowed the flames to spread briefly into the hallway. Luckily, Professor Nash, Sharon's colleague, had used an extinguisher to knock it down and close the door before the sprinklers were activated and flooded the hall.

In the tower fire, the stair's worn carpeting and the old wooden benches were piled up and soaked with gasoline. A simple trigger device had ignited the fire, though they didn't yet know how it had been turned on. It was a bigger pile of fuel than the last two. And the heater at the bottom of the stairwell warming the door was interesting—the arsonist must not have wanted anyone to be accidently hurt this time... although according to the arson investigator, with the windows blown out, a backdraft would not have occurred.

Was their arsonist still an amateur, not quite understanding how fires worked? And an arsonist who didn't want anyone burned? Was more than one person doing this? How were the fires connected? Four fires since September, yet no fires anywhere at the university in the five previous years. Still, more questions than answers, Colin thought.

Accelerant was used at the Wind Museum fire. Lubbock's arson chief said the fire was started with papers as fuel up against the northeast corner walls. But which accelerants and how much was another unknown at this point.

More than likely, one reason the fire had spread so rapidly was because holes had been made in the north and east inside walls so the flames quickly expanded to the attic area and to old insulation between sheetrock and brick. They'd found not only evidence of the holes, but the charred remains of a timing device that had served as the trigger. It could have been set as early as an hour before the fire started, giving the arsonist plenty of time to leave the scene, or as close as two minutes. Guests were concentrating on having a good time instead of noticing anyone entering or leaving the office area. An outside office door could have been used instead of the one to the hallway—the one Cassidy had opened. However, the doorknob on the outside door was locked.

Yes, it appeared the arsonist was learning. That bit of analysis scared the hell out of them all.

Chapter 70 ~

Working late in his studio several days later, Colin was surprised when Jamie walked in. Colin thought it was a good time for a break and put his tools down.

"Hey, Murphy," Jamie said, somewhat hesitantly. Colin thought he looked a little nervous.

"Hey," he replied, picking up his thermos of coffee to pour a cup. "What brings you to this side of campus?"

"I... um, I needed to check on the schedule for the Habitat for Humanity project for next week. Wondered if you'd look at it and see if there's anything we might need to change."

Colin narrowed his eyes and studied the boy. "I can... but I've never had to look at them before. What's this really about, Jamie?" He took a sip of the still hot liquid.

The young man shifted from one foot to the other, hesitating.

"Sit down, son. You're making me nervous. What is it?" Colin hoped it was about the boy's obvious continued depression so he could offer some help. He had been increasingly worried about Jamie.

Jamie sat on the offered stool. "I... I just wanted to ask you something personal, that's all."

"Personal? Go ahead, ask," Colin said, immediately thinking about Maggie. *Maybe he wants to ask me about marriage? With only his mother raising him, maybe he wants a man's perspective on marriage.*

"I was wondering what you thought about becoming a priest?"

"A priest?" Colin sputtered. "Um, my future wife probably wouldn't be too keen on the idea. And I think I'm a little too old for the priesthood."

"No, I meant me. The priesthood for me."

Colin was stunned and hoped his face didn't show it as Jamie appeared quite serious.

"Well, son, that's an interesting question," he said, recovering. "I've always admired the men who give their lives to the church, especially my brother. It's a difficult decision and one that shouldn't be taken lightly. But shouldn't you be talking to Father Sean about this? He's much more knowledgeable on the subject than I am."

"I know, but I wanted to know what you thought first. Do you think I'd make a good priest, I mean. Am I good enough like your brother to be a priest?" His face was contorted in pain.

Colin pulled another stool next to the young man and sat down. He took another sip before he answered. "I don't think it's a matter of being good enough, Jamie."

"What if you've made some mistakes? Some big mistakes. Can they be forgiven enough for you... I mean for me... to join the priesthood?"

"Jamie, everybody makes mistakes. Even big ones. And yes, I believe we can be forgiven for mistakes we make, even big ones. We just have to ask. Heaven knows my brother was no saint when he was ordained. All humans make mistakes, and often big ones. No, I don't think it's a matter of being good enough, because if that were a prerequisite, I doubt there'd be any priests at all. I think Father Sean would tell you it has to do with hearing a definite call from God to serve. You really need to talk with him about it."

Jamie looked unhappy with that answer and stood up to leave. Colin rose, too, and walked with him to the workshop door, thinking he needed to give him something more.

"Why don't you go talk with him tomorrow? I know he'll make himself available for you."

"Thanks, Murphy, I will."

"And Jamie," Colin said as the Saddle Tramp walked away. "I think you'd make a hell of a priest."

Chapter 71 ~

The early morning sunshine promised a clear, unusually warm late February day, so Maggie walked to work Friday morning. She knew a cold front was due in later tonight but for now, she enjoyed the warmth. "I'm getting married three weeks from tomorrow," she whispered to herself as she made her way across campus. What a miracle. How blessed she was to find love twice in one lifetime. She was almost giddy with happiness, the spring in her step reflecting her joy.

Late in the afternoon, she was deep in a project for the athletic department, and realizing it was going to take her longer than she'd anticipated, phoned Colin to tell him she would be working late—she wanted the weekend free for wedding planning.

He was doing the same, he said—working late, that is, not wedding planning; he knew enough to leave all of that to the bride and her friends—and offered to pick her up about eight for a late dinner.

"Best proposal I've had all day," she said brightly. "See you then. I'll look for you out front by the circle and come right down."

Around 7:00 p.m., she was surprised to get a call from Bennett Boyle's office on her desk phone. When she answered, Boyle said in his usual flat tone, "You're still in the building. Can you come down here? I need to ask you about parts of Parker's Washington speech. I told him it would be ready first thing Monday morning."

President Parker was scheduled to be in D.C. on Tuesday at a congressional hearing on higher educational needs, and Maggie had spent considerable time last week researching and composing his testimony. What in the world did Boyle want to change now, she thought. Before she had a chance to answer, he spoke a word that she thought was foreign to him.

"Please? It shouldn't take long."

Recovering after a moment, she said, "Of course, if you can give me about 15, 20 minutes to wrap up what I'm doing here. Is that all right? I can be down then."

"Twenty minutes is fine," he said and then uttered another foreign word, "Thanks."

Maggie was astounded. Since the department had been moved under the president late last semester, she rarely even saw Boyle, except in administrative staff meetings, and he didn't talk much during those meetings except to contradict her now and then. For him to ask for her help and to utter the two magic words? Unbelievable. Well, maybe not. She *had* been praying for him, at least once in a while. Who knows? God works in mysterious ways, doesn't He?

She finished up the section she was editing, and nineteen minutes later headed to Boyle's office with a final copy of the speech in hand, deciding to take the third floor hallway to the east stairs and head down that way. Normally she took the path of down first, then over to the east wing through the outside arcade and fresh air. She wasn't sure of the weather, though. Had the cold front arrived? And sometimes the outside door was locked at night.

As she rounded the corner to the east stairs landing, she noticed the small door to the bell tower was slightly open at the top of the narrow stairs. She winced at the absence of the red and black inside, her first glimpse since the fire. The walls were now institutional beige and there was no carpeting on the bare, concrete steps. What a shame that the Tramps were thrown out, she thought. Boyle was such a prick, even if he has learned to use the magic words. Colin was working on reversing the order and thought the Saddle Tramps might be given permission to reclaim their "clubhouse" by summer.

She refocused. Who in the world would be up there at this hour? And why? She knew of no athletic games tonight. Besides, they weren't ringing victory bells anyway. She walked across the landing toward the open door, thinking maybe someone had accidently left it open.

She stopped as she heard a man's voice call out, "No!" then a deep scream that ended as something or someone fell. It sounded like Bennett Boyle's voice, and she took two steps up inside the door, calling up the stairwell, "Hello? Who's there?"

She heard movement, then silence. It wouldn't be Boyle, she reasoned, he's downstairs in his office. "Hello?" she said even louder. She leaned against the outside wall, straining to see upward, but remembered the sightline was limited, not only by the platforms spanning the stairwell spaces, but also by the lack of lighting. She reached for her phone on her belt, only to discover she'd left it on her desk.

She took a few more tentative steps up the bare cement, calling out again. She thought she heard a low moan and quickened her pace, climbing higher and higher... third set, fourth set, fifth set... all the while calling out. "Hello? Is someone there? Are you all right?" She kept her hands tight on the old wooden railing to make certain of her footing in the dim light. Now she could see the one hanging spotlight at the top. It was not lit. She flipped the switch at the bottom of the last set of stairs but the light didn't come on.

The only light was a reflective glow coming in the windows, but it was enough for her to make out a dark figure lying on the floor up ahead—he was on his back on the top level, feet hanging over the edge of the last step. His hands were clasped to his chest and he wasn't moving.

"Mr. Boyle?" Recognizing him as she moved closer, Maggie cried out, "Boyle!" She knelt down beside him, thinking perhaps he'd had a heart attack, but up here? She repeated, "Boyle! What's happened? Did you fall?" His eyelids opened slightly and he turned his head to look at her.

"Anna?" he said weakly. He put his hand to Maggie's cheek, but his hand was wet and sticky. Maggie recoiled, confused by the mercury smell and Boyle's touch. His hand fell back across his chest where a dark wetness was spreading rapidly across his starched white shirt. Blood! There was blood all over his shirt! Maggie started to get up to go for help, but he grabbed her arm, and pulled her back down, grimacing in pain.

"Did I hurt you, Anna? Oh, my love," he continued to whisper, still holding her arm, but barely able to talk. "I'm so sorry, please forgive me. We didn't mean to... Oh, Mars, I'm so sorry." His eyes closed and he let go of her arm. Then he said in a shallow voice, "Anna? I love you. I've always loved you." Grasping his chest with both hands in obvious extreme pain, Bennett Boyle looked directly in Maggie's eyes once more and whispered forcefully, "Oh, God, Mars... God forgive me." His eyes closed and his head fell to one side.

"Bennett!" she shouted.

She heard a noise behind her, but before she could turn, her world went dark.

Chapter 72 ~

Maggie's first thought as she regained consciousness was that she was cold—her blanket must have fallen off. But she wasn't at home in bed, she was somewhere else, somewhere strange. And she was dressed. She opened her eyes and looked around. What was she doing on the floor in this cold dimly lit room? She tried to sit up, but the back of her head throbbed and she felt as though she were in a fog.

She slowly pushed herself up to a sitting position, palms against the cold floor, head bent down as she tried to focus. Strange, she thought, noticing the papers scattered around her, a page or two halfway down the stairs... stairs... she remembered she was taking something down the stairs to... Oh, God! Boyle! She frantically looked up and then grabbed her head in pain. She almost fainted but steadied herself on the platform post. She took deep breaths and opened her eyes again, looking around behind her in the dark room. There he was, sitting up against the far wall... he'd moved!

"Bennett!" she shouted, slowly crawling over to him, oblivious to the continued searing pain in her head. His eyes were closed and the stain on his shirt was immense. She put her fingers on his neck, but his body was so cold she knew she wouldn't find a pulse. He was dead.

She sat back heavily against the wall opposite him, crossed herself and then reached up instinctively to touch the egg-sized bump on the back of her head. She felt not only the wound, but also the dried blood that had matted her hair and run down the back of her neck. Who had done this? God, who had done this?

She wondered how long she'd been out—it must've been hours judging by the caked blood, the much colder temperature and the lack of any traffic noise from outside.

Colin! He was coming for me at eight! Maggie pushed herself up, almost retching from the pain, black spots dancing before her eyes. She leaned against the wall for a minute or two and became a little steadier and more focused. She stepped around the body and felt her way to the stairs, leaning heavily on the railing, supporting herself with the wall and the old wooden banister as her head screamed in agony.

After what seemed like an endless descent, she reached the door at the darkened bottom of the stairwell, discovering it not only closed, but locked. And it was a keyed lock. Someone had locked her in the tower!

She banged on the door, calling for help, again and again, but no one came. "Please, God," she prayed, slumping against the wall in exhaustion. "Help me." Then she turned and forced herself to go back up the stairs, pulling her shivering weary body up by the railing, slowly enough to keep the pain from making her faint. It took an eternity.

Stepping once again around the body, willing herself not to look at Boyle's face, she went from window to window, trying to pull one open. Recently painted shut, they wouldn't budge, and the new glass was now reinforced with wire, so breaking one was not an option. Besides, the Saddle Tramp benches had been burned in the fire last December, so she had nothing to use to even try to hit them with. She sat down on the floor on the far side of the platform, away from Boyle, to think.

Facts, Maggie. What are the facts? Fact one: the door downstairs is locked from the outside and no one is around to unlock it. Fact two: in the morning, maybe someone would be around and would hear her and unlock it, but who knew how early or even if someone might come on a Saturday?

And to sit all night alone in the dark with a dead man was not her idea of how to spend the night. Besides, she was cold! She wished she'd worn pants today instead of her wool skirt and jacket. At least it was wool, she thought, hugging herself.

She thought of Colin again. He must be frantic trying to find her. She had to get out.

She leaned her head back to rest it on the wall behind her, mindful of her painful lump, and noticed the platform above. The platform had been rebuilt... she thought it was strange Boyle had it rebuilt if they weren't going to be ringing the bells. Now that Boyle was dead, maybe... Focus on now, Maggie. How are you going to get out of here?

In addition to the rebuilt platform, a new ladder was bolted to the floor, resting against the platform and continuing up to the trapdoor below the bells. She could climb to the platform, pull one of the chains hanging down and ring a bell! Someone would come to see who was ringing it in the middle of the night! Hadn't Jimmy Stewart climbed up a bell tower in that Hitchcock movie? But he climbed a rope... I've got a ladder... Focus, Maggie, focus.

Once again she struggled to pull herself up, reaching for the rungs of the metal ladder to steady herself. Surely she could climb four little ladder steps? Then she could crawl over to pull the chain.

Gathering her strength, she used the cold ladder rungs and the platform's railing to drag herself to the top and began crawling across the hard frigid tiles. Oh, she thought, they've relaid the tiles in a Double T... mustn't step on it... focus, Maggie. Get to the chains.

They weren't there! The killer had either cut the chains or drawn them up on the roof with the bells. No, maybe Boyle had them taken off. If they weren't going to ring the bells anymore, why would they need chains? The leather gloves were gone, too, probably burned in the fire. She could've used their warmth. She sat down, placing her cold hands under her arms, and leaned against the new railing. Not brass this time, but a metal mesh. Looking up, she estimated it was another eight or nine rungs up to the trap door. Hard to tell in the dark. Could she climb up, and push it open?

She didn't think she had the strength.

Fact three... or was it fact four? Her brain was getting fuzzy. Whatever number, fact was she didn't know how much blood she'd lost—her blouse was stuck to her back, presumably with dried blood. How serious was her injury? She knew she shouldn't wait much longer to get medical attention.

Fact: If she wanted to get out tonight, she'd have to climb up through the trap door into the open tower next to the bells.

Maggie said another prayer as she reached again for the ladder and pulled herself to stand. One step at a time, Grant... just one step at a time. Her slick leather-soled shoes slipped on the rungs. Her arms ached, her head screamed at every small movement. Hooking not only her hands but her elbows around the ladder, she slowly, painfully dragged her unwilling body up and up toward the trap door.

After what seemed to Maggie like another eternity, she put her right palm under the trap door to push. She was sweating now from the exertion, numb to the pain in her head, fingers stiff from the cold metal ladder, and she had grown more debilitated with each step.

She pushed upward and slipped again, this time losing her footing. As she swung over the edge of the ladder, she frantically grabbed at the rungs to stop from falling to the unforgiving tile surface below. Gathering her last reserves, she righted herself. Her slippery shoes were kicked off so she could firmly plant her bare feet. Next she heaved open the trap door and hauled herself up to sit beside the lower bell.

Breathing heavily, she took in gulps of the frigid night air. The predicted cold front had definitely arrived. It seared her lungs, but also somewhat revived her as she looked for the chains. Spotting them coiled up on the opposite side of the bell's ledge, she said weakly, "No way."

There isn't room to crawl around the bell up here, she wearily thought. She'd have to go back down the ladder a few steps and drag herself up the other side to reach the chains—at this point an impossible task in her weakened condition.

Despairing, she lay back with her feet hanging out over the open trap door, caught her breath and weighed her new options, if indeed she had any.

She was bitterly cold again so she wrapped her arms around herself and tried to curl up into a ball for warmth. As she raised her legs, bending her knees to pull them up, she accidently kicked the bell, bruising her heel. "Damn," she winced, but inspiration was born. She put her legs back down and painfully pushed herself up to a sitting position.

She stared at the bell. "Worth a shot," she whispered. Slowly she lay back down, head spinning. Placing her hands under her thighs, she drew her legs up to her chest and put the bottoms of her bare feet on the side of the frigid 300-pound bell. She pushed. It moved slightly, but the huge clapper barely stirred.

With considerable effort, Maggie scooted back a little and pushed again with her freezing feet. The bell moved more and she pushed over and over until it gave a slight ping, encouraging her. Moving back even further, groaning from the pain and energy expended, she was now up against the bottom of an open arch. The stone was cold and rough on the back of her already pounding head. She pulled her knees up to her chest again and pushed in steady movement toward the bell. It moved with her feet, again and again, and then went further, swinging back to catch her feet again. She pushed again, moving it even more. Once more. It rang! She pushed again, and it rang again, and again and again. After the sixth successful shove, Maggie fell to her side exhausted while the bell continued ringing loudly with the momentum. "God," she prayed, "Please let someone hear. I'm so cold..."

Once again, her world went dark.

Chapter 73 ~

This time Maggie's first thought when she regained consciousness was that she was cozily tucked under her warm quilt at home and she smiled, eyes still shut. But something was wrong... this wasn't her bedroom... the smell wasn't right. She smelled flowers and... and antiseptic.

She slowly opened her eyes to a roomful of bouquets and worried faces. And Colin. She reached her hand toward him and he was immediately by her side, brow furrowed, green eyes ringed from exhaustion, stroking her cheek.

"Maggie, Love, how do you feel? You're in University Medical Center. Doctor says you have a concussion, but once you woke up, you'd be just fine... and now you're awake!" he said, eyes wide with obvious relief.

"Hi, honey," Sharon was now holding her other hand and smiling at her.

"What happened?" Maggie whispered, her mind still in a fog.

"We found you in the bell tower, unconscious," Colin said. "Boyle..."

Maggie shut her eyes again as she remembered Bennett Boyle, covered in blood.

"Oh, God, Colin. He's dead! They killed him and hit me and locked us in the tower. Oh, God, Colin."

"I know, Love. We found him. Don't cry, Love. Who, Maggie? Who did this?"

"I don't know... I don't know. I didn't see anyone... only Boyle... and then I had to ring the bell. I was so cold... You heard the bell?"

"Yes, we did, Love. Good thinking or we might not have found you for a while."

Sharon let go of her hand and moved to allow a nurse to take her vitals. Maggie looked up questioningly through tears at the familiar face. The nurse smiled and said, "Yes, I'm Steven's better half. He told me to take good care of you, and that's just what we're doing. Be still for me, now."

Maggie was thinking she was too tired to be anything but still when her son's head popped up behind the nurse, cell phone to his ear.

"Benjamin!" she cried.

"Hi, Mom, I brought the nurse!" he said, looking at his mother with love, concern and relief. Then holding the phone up a second, he said, "Calling Michael. He insisted I call him the minute you woke up." Then into the phone he said, "She's awake. Nurse is checking her now, but she's talking and... what? No, she looks good considering she's got a bandaged head..."

Maggie reached up to find a wide bandage wrapped around her head. Underneath, it hurt big time.

"She also looks very unlike our fashionable mother in this incredibly ugly hospital gown that's just not her color. Yeah. I will. I gotta go call Amanda. Later, Bro." Then to Maggie, "Michael sends his love. He wanted to come, but Portland's airport is snowed in. I told him he could pray just as well from there and to stay by the phone. Karen sends her love, too. One of these huge flower bunches is from them. I don't remember which one. I gotta call Amanda. She and the girls are beside themselves with worry."

Nurse Jackson turned to Ben with her version of "the look," thinking that was entirely too much talking and she didn't like cell phones in her patients' rooms. Patients needed rest. Ben got the message and said, "I'll just call her out in the hallway, Mom. Be right back!"

The nurse smiled and continued taking vitals. "Looks pretty good, considering, Mrs. Grant. You've got 15 stitches in your head, but you're doing fine. The doctor will be along on rounds in another hour, but I think you'll be staying with us at least another night."

"Another night?" Maggie said hoarsely. "What day is it? What time is it?"

"It's early Sunday afternoon, Love," Colin said. "You've been sleeping for quite some time. Doctor said it was normal, though, from the blow to your head and the cold. Don't worry. Do you feel up to talking to Chief Callahan? He wanted to see you as soon as possible."

"I don't know much, but I can talk to him. Is that all right, Nurse Jackson?"

Nurse Jackson said yes, but told Colin not to let Maggie get too tired. "I'll order a dinner tray to be brought up," she said before leaving. Maggie immediately realized how hungry she was and hoped it wasn't just broth and Jell-O.

The door opened again and Carol came in, rushing to Maggie's side, saying, "Ben said you were awake. I went to get coffee. Oh, Maggie, you had us all so scared!"

"Carol! What are you doing here!?"

"When Sharon called, I wanted to come right then, but I waited a day for further reports. When the doctors said you'd be fine but needed lots of rest, I just packed everything up and came two weeks earlier than planned for the wedding! I'm now your new roommate and am at your service to get everything done at home in time for you to walk beautifully down the aisle with this handsome man of yours!"

"Oh, Carol," was all Maggie could say through more tears—but tears of gratitude.

Chapter 74 ~

Chief Callahan arrived shortly after the doctor's rounds and the broth, Jell-O and weak tea were brought in. Maggie gulped it all down hungrily as she tried to recreate the night. And she asked a lot of questions as well. Once again, she was both interviewee and interviewer.

She learned Colin had arrived as scheduled Friday night and was puzzled to see her office light out. Thinking she must have seen him driving up and was on her way down, he waited. When she didn't appear within ten minutes, he called her cell. No answer. He got out, but found the building locked tight.

Maybe she'd forgotten their date and walked home, he thought, so he drove her normal route, but her house was dark, her Volvo parked in the driveway, and there was no sign of her on the streets. He called Sharon, who hadn't seen or heard from her all day.

He went back to campus, checked the library, the SUB and all places in between. Knowing this just wasn't like her, he finally called campus security. An officer met him back at the Administration Building, and they went inside, but found her office the same as all others in the building—dark, quiet and locked. He called her cell again and again. Nothing.

Completely baffled, he called Sean, who checked the church and the small chapel, which also turned up empty.

By now, Sharon was worried as well, and she and Doug donned heavy coats and joined Colin at the Double T bench in the courtyard with the campus police officer. Sean arrived soon after.

Sharon asked if they had gone *into* Maggie's office? They hadn't, so the officer and Colin headed that way to look for a possible appointment book entry. Sharon and Sean went to wait at Maggie's house and call the local hospitals while Doug went back to the Nest in case she called its landline.

In Maggie's office, Colin and the officer found nothing on her calendar but were alarmed to see her briefcase sitting next to her desk, keys and wallet inside. Her cell phone, sitting on top of the desk, had been turned off.

They quickly walked the halls of the building again, all three floors, and found nothing and no one. All offices were locked and all lights were off. The officer called in for assistance, but still nothing after another hour or so of searching and waiting. It was as if she'd just vanished.

Colin confirmed the only car in the parking lot was not Maggie's.

By midnight, Colin was frantic and called Chief Callahan at home— he'd given Colin his private number after the January fire. Then Colin called Elaine, who hadn't seen Maggie since her own departure at five. Elaine remembered Maggie had been wearing a dark wool suit that day. Colin promised to call Elaine again as soon as they found her boss.

An obviously concerned Callahan joined them in the courtyard about twenty minutes later, directing two of his men to retrace Maggie's usual route through campus and to look in all the bushes and dark doorways. He called the Lubbock Police for assistance in searching around her home and nearby park. Then he checked on the one parked car, finding it belonged to the chief of staff. Boyle didn't answer his cell either, and a second check of his dark office turned up nothing unusual. Had Maggie actually been the target all along? Was Bennett Boyle the arsonist?

They were baffled. Both Maggie and Bennett Boyle missing? Callahan sent an officer to Boyle's condo to check on him, but Colin could not, would not believe they were somewhere together—at least not willingly. Maggie still avoided the man like the plague.

Because it was too cold to stay outside much longer, Chief Callahan moved them inside to the president's suite on the first floor to continue coordination of the search. President Parker was notified and asked to be kept updated.

"We don't have surveillance cameras on this building," Callahan said. "It's in next year's budget. But we can pull the footage from the few we do have on surrounding buildings to see if she, or Boyle, might have crossed their line of sight. Normally, though, most of the cameras are focused on entrances, not on the grounds. We can get them in the morn..." He stopped and turned his head slightly. "Listen," he whispered.

A bell rang, and then rang again and again.

"The tower! Someone's in the tower!" Colin shouted as he rushed out the heavy oak doors heading for the east stairs, closely followed by two young officers and Chief Callahan. By the time they reached the third floor landing, Colin was frantic trying to imagine why in the world Maggie might be in the bell tower. The door was locked. He pounded on it and called her name, cursing Boyle for taking his key. He stepped aside anxiously as one of the officers pulled out a master key and slowly opened the door, peering inside the darkness with his flashlight.

"Go!" Callahan said to his officers. "Professor, they go first." Colin stayed back, but not by choice. He and the chief followed behind the officers who had their weapons drawn and were proceeding cautiously but quickly up the stairs, flashlights leading the way. The bell had stopped ringing. Colin thought he was much too far behind, and he wished desperately for his gun.

"There's a body up here!" one of the officers shouted down, and Colin blanched, falling against the wall. "No, God, no. Maggie..." he prayed aloud.

Then he heard, "Get an ambulance. One of 'em's alive!" Chief Callahan called it in as Colin raced up the remaining stairs, two at a time. The young officers had found Boyle. Then seeing a woman's shoe next to him, and feeling the cold night air coming in, shined their flashlights up toward the ceiling. Maggie's bare feet hung out over the opening of the trap door, and one of the officers scrambled up to her. Upon finding a pulse and no injuries except the bump on her head, he slung her over his shoulder, fireman-rescue style, and carried her down to the platform.

Colin was up there in a flash, helping the officers get her down, then cradling her in his arms as he sat on the frigid sacred Double T. She was so cold! He took off his jacket and wrapped it around her. An officer climbed back up and shut the trap door. Then all three men rubbed her hands and feet, trying to get her circulation moving. When the paramedics arrived, they took over, assessed her head wound and started an IV.

Colin had been standing at the edge of the platform watching the medical team work when Chief Callahan asked him to take a look at the body. He reluctantly took his eyes off her and obliged, just then realizing the dead man was Boyle. He hadn't noticed or cared as he stepped over him to get to his Maggie.

He shifted his mind to investigative mode and quickly assessed the scene, noting the placement of the body, the strewn papers, the amount of blood. Boyle had been stabbed in the chest, but no weapon had been found as yet.

After he gave his professional opinions, Colin left it to Callahan's CSI team, and rode with Maggie in the ambulance to UMC. He was joined at the hospital by Doug, Sharon and Sean—who was immensely relieved he wouldn't need to perform Last Rites for his future sister-in-law. She was alive, and although unconscious, the doctors thought it was exposure that was her immediate, but not life-threatening problem.

Sharon then called Ben and Michael and Carol. Ben arrived on the first flight from Dallas, calling in hourly reports to Michael who couldn't get out of Portland. Carol had arrived early Sunday, moving into Maggie's guest bedroom and taking care of Miss Priss and everything else that needed to be taken care of.

Chapter 75 ~

Maggie told Chief Callahan she was sorry she couldn't remember much, except finding Bennett Boyle and seeing all the blood.

"Did he say anything before he died? Did he say who did this?" the chief asked.

No, Maggie only remembered him saying he was sorry, thinking she was some other woman. She couldn't remember the name. And she didn't know if he'd still been alive when she was knocked out—she didn't think so. She knew for certain he was dead, though, when she came to a few hours later. She explained about the door being locked and trying to figure out how to get out. The bell had been the only thing she could think of.

Chief Callahan assured her it was the smartest option, marveling to himself they hadn't found two bodies instead of only one. "Looks like the killer thought they were alone. When he heard you call up the stairs, he must've hidden in one of the storage areas or under the platform until you passed by, then came up behind you. Good thing you didn't see him, or he might have killed you, too."

Maggie was taken aback at that and tightened her grip on Colin's hand, but the thought had crossed Colin's mind much earlier—in fact, back at the crime scene he'd known the assailant must have thought Boyle was dead when Maggie found him... because if he thought Boyle talked to Maggie, she would've been dead, too. He would be forever grateful the killer had thought wrong.

The chief continued, "We found a two-by-four with blood and hair on it in the storage area. We've tested it, but no fingerprints. And you're sure Boyle didn't say anything else?"

"Nothing I can remember, Chief. I'm sorry."

"He'd never married and didn't have a significant other anyone knows of... his mother's name was Gayle. Does Gayle sound familiar?"

Maggie shook her head, then winced in pain at the movement.

"Okay, don't worry about it now. If you remember the name of the woman, let me know. What about your office? We found it dark and locked and your phone was turned off."

"I left it open and my phone was turned on," Maggie said, puzzled.

Colin interjected, "The killer must have gone to both offices and locked them. But he would have needed keys, wouldn't he? Maggie's were in her briefcase."

"We'll check to see if he took Boyle's. Don't worry. We'll find him. Has to be someone who hated Boyle."

When Maggie and Colin looked at him with raised eyebrows, the Chief said, "Yeah, I know... long list. But listen, Sweetheart," he said as he prepared to leave, "We've really got to stop meeting like this."

She managed a thin smile, dutifully whispering her line, "Don't call me sweetheart." Her eyelids were heavy. She was asleep before Callahan reached the elevator.

Maggie woke to a semi-dark room, this time her throbbing headache telling her immediately where she was and why. She saw Colin sleeping in the chair next to her and reached for his hand. He startled at her touch and pulled away, trying to remember where *he* was. "Colin," she said softly. He smiled and took her hand, moving to sit beside her on the bed, "No, it's Sean, Maggie. Colin's just down the hall getting some more coffee."

"Oh, Sean, thanks for being here for him." Just then the right Murphy brother came through the door with two cups of coffee and said in mock seriousness, "I told you, little brother, I saw her first."

Sean said, "Yes, but I get to hold her hand when you're not around. It's a brother's prerogative." He took the offered coffee, changing places with Colin as a nurse walked in to give the grateful patient some much-needed pain medicine.

As the nurse left, Father Sean said, "Maggie, please convince this stubborn Irish pig-headed brother of mine to go home and get some sleep. He's been here since Friday night and I'm embarrassed by his appearance! People will think I'm the slob!"

"Colin, you haven't left? Go home! I'm fine," Maggie said, now noticing the two-day old beard on his normally clean-shaven face and the dark circles under his tired eyes.

"I've slept some in the chair," he protested.

"Really, Professor Murphy. The doctor said I was fine now. And I've just taken more pain medicine so I'll probably be off to dreamland again in a minute or two. Go get some sleep. You can come back in the morning to take me home. I'm out of danger and just need to rest. Please. I'll rest better if I know you're getting some, too."

"Yeah, Murphy, go home," Sharon said as she and Carol walked in. "We're taking the night shift. You took the last two! Besides, you don't smell so good. Go to the Nest. Doug and Ben are putting beer on ice, lasagna in the oven, and you can use our shower. Father Sean, take your smelly brother outta here and over to my house. It's our turn to fuss over Maggie. We loved her first."

Colin knew he was outnumbered and truly was dead on his feet. He kissed Maggie gently on the forehead and promised to be back before she woke in the morning.

When they'd gone, Maggie sighed, "Doug's lasagna. Oh, that sounds good. I'm starving. Is the hospital kitchen still open, do you think?"

"No, it's after 9 o'clock, but we brought you some dinner," Carol said, eyes twinkling. She held up a shopping bag.

"Doug's lasagna?" Maggie asked hopefully.

"Nope, we did you one better," Sharon said boldly. "But don't tell Doug I said that. Café J's seafood crepes... three of them and crème brûlée for dessert."

Carol added, "We asked the nurse and she said it was fine. You need sustenance."

"Oh, wow. You two are my bestest BFFs!" Maggie exclaimed giddily as she sat up and began unwrapping her dinner.

Carol turned to Sharon, whispering, "Bestest BFFs?"

Sharon shook her head and whispered back, "She's just woozy from the pain medication. Makes her slip into preteen language, or something." She turned to the patient and said, "Honestly, Maggie, BFFs?"

Chapter 76 ~

True to his word, Colin was at the hospital before Maggie woke up and to her eyes looked a little more refreshed. He'd showered and shaved and slept as ordered, and was anxious to talk again with the doctor. Ben was there to say his farewell. He had to get back home to Dallas, but would return for the wedding as scheduled. Sharon was home preparing for a class and Carol was at Maggie's house, but would come help move her home if the doctor allowed it.

When they were alone, Maggie asked Colin again, "Who did this?"

He moved to sit by her and reached over to gently brush her hair across her forehead. "No idea yet, but Callahan is working on it. Your job is to not worry about it but to get well. We've an important date coming up, Love."

"What?" Maggie said, obviously concentrating on her attacker instead of Colin. She looked up at him. "Oh, yeah. A wedding." She smiled and lost herself once again in pools of green.

Mid-morning when the doctor made his rounds, Colin asked, "You're sure, then, that she'll be fine?"

With practiced indulgence, the doctor nodded, "Yes. Just needs bed rest and lots of fluids. I've given her some pain pills, but she should gradually wean herself off of them in another day or two. She can probably go back to work when she feels up to it, but not today or tomorrow."

To Maggie he said, "And no driving until you're off the medication. I'll want to see you in a week. But call me before then if something doesn't feel right. Now I'll send someone in to get you checked out of here."

Once home, Colin fussed until Carol finally tried to shoo him out,

"You're in the way. Don't you have classes to teach or something?"

"I do, but I wanted to make sure Maggie was comfortable." He looked at Miss Priss, curled up on the end of Maggie's bed and wished he could take her place.

When Maggie had come home, carried in by an insistent Colin, the cat that normally spent her days outside took a sudden interest in what was happening inside. As Maggie was tucked neatly under the covers in the master bedroom, she was astounded when Miss Priss jumped up on the bed, tail high in the air. Maggie tentatively put out her hand and the formerly untouchable cat moved under it, generously accepting Maggie's light petting. Then she prissed down to Maggie's feet and settled in, blinking up at Colin and Carol as if saying, "I've got her now. You can go."

Chapter 77 ~
Three weeks later

When the music started at noon, a nervous Maggie turned to her best friends and said, "Am I really doing this?"

Their smiles were reassuring. Sharon and Carol were picture perfect in their closely matching dark green suits, similar in style to Maggie's tailored ivory linen suit. She insisted she was way too old for a traditional wedding dress and matching bridesmaid's gowns. The two each carried a single yellow rose of Texas. Maggie carried a small nosegay of deep yellow and white roses with dangling ivory satin ribbons. Her salt and pepper hair was piled up at the back of her head, completely covering the bald spot and fast-healing wound, small yellow sweetheart roses sprinkled elegantly throughout the curls. Pearl earrings fell to just the right length in accompaniment to her mother's pearl necklace. Maggie didn't care if Saint Paul did disapprove.

Wanting only a small, intimate wedding, she and Colin had chosen to be married in the original St. Elizabeth's tiny chapel on the northeast corner of the church grounds. Outside, the Texas Historical Commission plaque described the chapel: "Built in 1936. Eclectic design shows Byzantine and Spanish Colonial influences with elaborate stonework featuring stylistic elements and religious symbolism."

Dark beams crisscrossed the rich wood interior of the small simple chapel, and bright sunlight streamed in through the plain glass windows. A few candles helped to light the scene along with the ornate Byzantine chandeliers. Two simple bouquets of long-stemmed yellow and white roses were the only extra altar decorations.

When the music started, her two girlfriends walked arm in arm out of the small waiting room of the old church—both designated as honor attendants, but Sharon went down the aisle first, insisting because their heights were so different. With the two granddaughters as picture-perfect flower girls, their procession was shortest to tallest. Fine, Maggie had said, not worrying about the details.

Ben and Michael then stepped up, each offering their mother an arm, escorting her to a waiting Colin, who flushed when he saw her. She smiled broadly at him, knowing she had been right back in January, the groom *was* prettier than the bride—but then so was the priest!

Father Sean was the Mass celebrant, and Colin had asked their older brother Patrick, who could have been a triplet, to stand for him along with Tom Arbuckle. These tall, smiling men were handsome in their dark suits and yellow rose boutonnieres—Father Sean outfitted in his finest priestly vestments.

At the end of the Mass, Father Sean gave them the same Irish blessing his parents had received decades earlier on their wedding day:

> Deep peace of the running wave to you.
> Deep peace of the flowing air to you.
> Deep peace of the quiet earth to you.
> Deep peace of the shining stars to you.
> Deep peace of the Son of Peace to you.

Sharon and Doug hosted the wedding luncheon at the Nest, although the bridal couple insisted on having the simple affair catered. They wouldn't even allow Doug to tend his own bar, saying it was enough he and a few friends were providing beautiful stringed-instrument music for the ceremony. The Tech Catering crew was taking care of everything, and Jamie easily switched from wedding guest to bartender, earning some extra cash that day.

Other guests included Maggie's family and a few friends. Most of Colin's family had flown in from the Chicago area, leaving behind two feet of snow. They were still marveling at the warm spring weather and the flat empty land of West Texas. Doug had opened the patio doors so guests could spill out to enjoy the sunshine around the pool. When the groom's father remarked again about the amazingly warm weather, Doug told him this was Texas and if he waited a minute or two, it was likely to change. Late spring snowstorms were not at all uncommon.

Carol's husband Robert had flown in from the East Coast. Russ, Fern, and Tom's wife Julie were there, as were Winston, Jonathan and his wife. Monsignor Fitzpatrick was in attendance, along with Maggie's staff members, including Charlie who served as the official photographer. At the couple's request, he was taking only informal shots—no posed photos were allowed.

All the out-of-town guests were either flying or driving home that afternoon, and Colin was taking Maggie to Santa Fe that night, a five- to six-hour drive, so they didn't linger at the luncheon.

Colin convinced Jamie to housesit at Maggie's to not only watch the place, but set up a surprise for his new bride, and to feed the cat. Colin continued to be worried about Jamie and made a mental note to talk with Sean about the young man when they returned later this week. Surely there was something they could do to bring him out of his seemingly unending depression?

By 2:30, Maggie had hugged and kissed everyone goodbye. She climbed into the old pickup—the heater was still out on her car and they were heading into snowy mountains. With the old bench seat, she was happy to be able to snuggle next to her new husband the entire way.

Chapter 78 ~

As they headed north out of the city, Maggie nestled next to Colin, the Texas Tech Red Raider bobble-head doll right in front of her, continuously bouncing as if nodding at her. She reached up to steady the head, but it was made for movement.

"Can I at least turn it around?" she asked.

"Sure. He'd probably like to see where he's going anyway."

She gave a small chuckle, still thinking the gift from Jamie was sweet... but sweeter was her new husband's ready acceptance of it.

New husband, she thought, hardly believing she was now, once again, a wife. And delighted she was going to have Colin for always, or as always as God allowed. But she trusted Him and would savor every day as if there might not be a next. That was a lesson she had learned too well.

Their wedding Mass had been simple yet beautiful, and she'd kneeled next to her new love and prayed with him. And just like Sharon had said, it *was* magic. It had been so different than her first wedding, and it was hard not to compare the two. With Jim, they were both so young and naive, and the minuscule details of the wedding, from the right lace on her dress to the right flavor of cake frosting and complementing filling were among her priorities. Today, her priorities had been Colin and his being comfortable with his first, and she hoped only, wedding. She concentrated on him instead of on things, and it made so much difference. Maturity definitely had its good points.

Quickly eating up the miles, they talked comfortably about their guests, and how strange it was for Monsignor Fitzpatrick to sit in the pew as a guest instead of presiding. He'd said he rather enjoyed it, but nobody believed him. He liked the spotlight too much.

Doug's music had been amazing, floating with joyful elegance from the small church's choir loft. How the five musicians and their instruments had all fit inside the tiny space was a mystery—or a miracle.

And they talked about Colin's family. The thirteen of them who'd been able to attend arrived two days ago and had been adopted by Russ, Fern, Tom and Julie, who insisted they all stay out on the Cotton A. There was plenty of room at the two houses, and they got to see firsthand how a West Texas farm/ranch worked. Colin's parents, just slightly older than the Arbuckles, quickly became the older Arbuckle's new best friends, promising this wouldn't be their last visit to the South Plains, especially now Colin was finally settling down.

After a little more than an hour of heading north on Interstate 27, Maggie wondered at Colin's earlier decision not to take the Clovis Highway out of Lubbock, a more direct route to Santa Fe. Maybe he'd rather hit Interstate 40 in Amarillo and head west? It was a wider interstate but not the most direct route. She finally decided to ask.

"We're heading up to I-40 and over?"

"Nope," he said matter-of-factly.

"You missed the Clovis Highway about an hour back, then."

"Yep."

"Aren't we going to Santa Fe? To the La Fonda Hotel?"

He continued to look at the road ahead. "Not tonight."

"What?! Where *are* we going, Colin?"

His smile broadened, slowly, menacingly, Maggie thought, still not looking at her, but concentrating on the highway.

She stomped her foot, if that was possible while seated in a pickup. "Talk, Murphy. Now!"

He turned to her, grinning, "Margaret Grant Murphy. You didn't really think that after waiting all these long months to bed you, I was going to wait another whole six hours, did you?" His eyes turned back to the road.

She opened her mouth in retort but hadn't a clue what to say so shut it again and looked out at the long, flat landscape. Finally she asked again, "So where are we going?"

"You'll see. Only about 20 minutes away, Love."

At Canyon, home of West Texas A&M University, they turned east, definitely not the way to New Mexico. Ten miles outside of town they turned into Palo Duro State Park.

"We're going to camp on our wedding night?" Maggie asked tentatively, afraid of the answer. It wasn't exactly her idea of a romantic way to spend their first night together. The luxury suite at the La Fonda would be so much more comfortable than a sleeping bag on the rocky ground.

"You'll see," was all he said, looking at his watch. With that, he pulled in to the ranger station and disappeared inside for a few minutes. Returning, he went to the back of the pickup and started unloading their suitcases, telling Maggie, "Get out, Wife."

She got out of the truck, slammed its door, and stomped her foot, unhappy about this "surprise." She took a deep breath, looked to the heavens asking for patience, and then thought it really shouldn't matter where their first night was, as long as they were together. She thought she heard Colin chuckle. Calmer now, she walked around to him and asked what she could carry.

"This," he said, handing her a small duffle bag, "and pull this, please." It was a Coleman cooler on wheels. She hadn't noticed it before.

Colin picked up their suitcases and headed around the side of the ranger station. Maggie followed, amazed she was here... in a state park... on her wedding day. She chuckled to herself that being married to this professor who made furniture, this ex-G-man with a deep faith in God, certainly wasn't going to be dull. It hadn't been so far!

As she rounded the corner of the ranger station, Maggie was concentrating on pulling the cooler over the rough ground. She nearly ran into Colin, who'd stopped. She stopped, too, then looking up, quickly took a step back, nearly falling over the cooler. Her eyes widened. They stood on the edge of the north rim of the canyon, looking out over a breathtaking view of steep, eroded cliffs, colorfully red and brown in the mid-afternoon spring sunshine. Palo Duro Canyon was part of the Caprock to the High Plains. Called the Grand Canyon of Texas, it was a miniature at no more than 800 feet deep. Didn't she remember this state park was established somewhere back in the 1930s?

Evidence of settlement as far back as 12,000 years gave the canyon an ancient feel, smell and taste that often humbled visitors into accepting their own insignificance. Here tribes of Native Americans had sought shelter from winter storms, had found water during dry seasons and made use of the limited shade of the juniper and cottonwood trees, cedars and scrub brush that grew on the canyon floor. Until 1874, Kiowa, Cheyenne, Apache and Comanche tribes inhabited the area at various times, before the bloody Red River War resulted in displacing all Native Americans from the southern plains to the Oklahoma Territory.

Colin headed for the top of a trail that must take them down to the canyon floor. Maggie no longer cared about sleeping on the ground—the beauty was overwhelming—she just hoped she didn't have to manage the cooler for too long—she wasn't exactly wearing hiking boots.

She'd been here before, but then she was twenty and on an adventure with Sharon and Carol. They'd spent a cold night on the side of the canyon in sleeping bags and loved it. Yes, she decided, she would love it tonight, too.

The steep trail was roughed out of the cliff, sloping sharply with intermittent rock steps. Concentrating on keeping her footing and not losing the cooler contents, whatever they were, about 30 feet down the trail Maggie once again almost ran into her new husband. She looked up and followed his gaze. To her amazement, three small weathered stone cabins were solidly perched on the canyon rim, facing southwest.

"We're here," Colin said brightly. He held up a key and said, "Leave the gear. Let's go look." Maggie followed him to the third cabin, grateful she wouldn't have to sleep on the canyon floor and wondering if at least they'd have bunks that were off the ground.

Colin unlocked the door. He opened it slightly, stuck his head in and then turned back to her with a wide grin, "Yep, it's ready, Love. Go on in and see what you think."

He stepped back to let her into the doorway. The walls of the small cabin were the same rustic stone as the exterior, and the fireplace was original, much like hers at home, wood piled high but not lit on this warm afternoon. But nothing else inside the fifteen-by-fifteen foot interior was anywhere near rustic. Dominating the room by taking up most of the small cabin's floor space was a huge king-size four-poster mahogany bed, delivered that morning from Lubbock's finest furniture store. Maggie and Colin had seen it a few weeks earlier when shopping. Colin didn't think he would fit in her current full-size bed with thrift store headboard. They'd talked about the need to eventually buy a bigger bed, but with Maggie's tower incident, they hadn't found the time, or so she thought.

Six fluffy pillows, covered in crisp new cotton pillowcases rested across the oversized headboard, and matching sheets were tucked out over the largest quilt Maggie had ever seen. It was a colorful crazy quilt pattern, in blues and greens, with the tiniest touch of purple, and Maggie knew it would be heavy and warm, just the way she liked.

Fresh yellow and white rose petals were scattered across the linens and up over the pillows.

A handsome matching nightstand sat near the north window, with a bouquet of long-stemmed yellow roses gleaming in the sunshine. A small door to the right led to the bath, where she could see two hotel-quality plush white terry cloth bathrobes hanging expectantly.

Colin said quietly, "I thought our first time should be in our own bed. So, it's ours, and tomorrow they'll take it and put it in your—our house. Will that work for you?"

"Will that work for me? Oh, Colin, it's perfect! It's wonderful. It's... I thought you were going to make me sleep in a sleeping bag on the ground. This is wonderful. Just wonderful."

Grinning, he said, "And you would have slept on the ground on our wedding night?"

Maggie nodded, not taking her eyes off the new bed.

"Okay, then," Colin said, slightly amazed. "Make yourself at home, and I'll bring in the suitcases. Oh, my mom made the quilt. Hope you like it." He disappeared out the door, thoroughly satisfied with the surprise for his bride.

"She made it?" But he didn't hear. Maggie walked over to it, and ran her hand lovingly over the pattern, marveling at the quality craftsmanship and relishing the softness. Obviously stitched with love, she thought. And the perfect colors for their master bedroom.

How in the world had he arranged all this? What a wonderful surprise! Unable to resist, she took her shoes off and lay down, head resting on the supple pillows. Realization came that her hair was still pinned up with roses in it, so she sat back up to take it down. She set the roses on the pillow next to her among the petals, the pins went to the side table.

As she ran her fingers through her hair to untangle it, she thought of Sharon and Carol fussing over her this morning, expertly covering her bare spot, arguing about how many roses should actually adorn her tresses. Did they know about this surprise? Probably, and so probably did everyone else, she thought. Some friends, she thought... keeping secrets from her. Smiling, she lay back, clasping her hands behind her head thinking this was a pretty wonderful surprise to keep secret. She had such good friends.

Colin came in and saw her relaxing on their bed, smiling at him in a way that had him quickly dumping everything in the corner, closing the door and joining her.

"Think you might need to take your boots off your mother's quilt first, Murphy," she said as he reached for her.

"Oh, yeah," he replied sheepishly as he sat up and pulled them off. "Mom never allows boots on beds."

"Smart woman," Maggie said, as he reached for her again. She put her arms around his neck, leaning in to kiss him. He let his hands explore her back, reaching down to cup her firm but ample buttocks and pull her closer to him. He'd waited a long time to get his hands on her backside, and he wasn't letting go anytime soon.

Chapter 79 ~

Even through their layers of clothing, Maggie could feel he was more than ready to "bed her"... and she was more than ready, too.

But she pulled back as he started to help her out of her blazer. "Wait. I have a silk negligee I bought just for tonight."

"It's not tonight, yet... it's now," he said, continuing to kiss her neck and helping her out of the jacket. "You can put it on later." He stopped and looked at her intently. "Let me undress you."

Damn those green eyes, Maggie thought. She'd let him do anything he wanted when he looked at her like that, now that they were married, of course. So she let him, while helping him out of his clothes at the same time. Despite the warm afternoon, goose bumps raised on her arms when only her black silk lingerie remained, and they quickly moved under the covers, slipping deep beneath the cool, crisp cotton sheets and the warm weight of the quilt. Colin held her there a moment, kissing her softly, feeling the smoothness of the silk against the smoothness of her skin, liking how it felt, passion held in check.

He whispered to her, "Thank you, Maggie."

"For what, Murphy? We haven't done very much yet. I'm just getting started."

He laughed at that, and then said softly, "Thank you for being a permanent kind of woman, for changing me, for making me comfortable with more than temporary, for giving me this." He held up his left hand with its new silver wedding band.

Deeply touched, tears threatening, she lightened the moment by saying, "Wait about an hour, Murphy, and then you'll really have something to thank me for."

"A whole hour? Goodness, woman, I'm an old man! Go ahead, then, make me thankful!" Much to his delight, she did.

Maggie rolled on top of him, put her hands on his bare, broad shoulders, and pushed herself up with her arms, quilt sliding off her back. Her hair fell on the sides of her face, soft and slightly curled. He pushed it back behind her ears, then put his hands on either side of her waist and watched her eyes as she studied him in the soft afternoon light. They had undressed too quickly for her to see all of him, but she'd take advantage of what she could see now and study his upper half. The lower half would just have to wait.

He had dark skin, and a little bit of black hair on his chest. He also had a large scar on his right shoulder, and another on the left side of his chest, something she'd ask about later. She looked at his strong chin, his full dark lips and moved her gaze up to his eyes.

Slowly she smiled, inviting with a confidence that was new to her, and he moved his hands up across her pale smooth back, under her bra, deftly unhooking it. Ah, she thought, laughing a little, he's done this before. His return smile showed just a touch of cockiness, as if to say, I've had lots of practice, woman.

She let the expensive black silk and lace fall off her shoulders, allowing her breasts to be freed. Lifting one arm, then the other, she tossed it aside and unselfconsciously let him look at her. And she watched him look, hoping she would meet with his approval.

She remembered feeling inadequate when she was younger because her breasts were just shy of average size, smaller than most of her friends'. But as the years passed, she realized there was less to sag, and even at their current age, her "girls" sat up rather nicely without much help from Victoria's Secret weapons. There were advantages to being less than buxom, especially as you grew older.

Colin moved his large hands up and around her sides, his thumbs reached her nipples, and he teased them back and forth a little. Quick to respond, they stood out straight and erect. Her first reaction was to pull away, because they were sensitive, not having been handled in so long. But he held her gently, moving his whole hands around to enclose them as he pleasured her while at the same time reassuring her.

She put her head back and closed her eyes, trusting him and enjoying the warmth that spread to pulsing sensations lower down. After a few minutes, he gently pushed her on her side and then exchanged positions as he bent down to tenderly kiss her mouth, her neck, and then her left breast, taking it into his mouth and sucking softly while still caressing the other with his hand.

Fighting to check his passion, Colin could have taken her quickly but knew he needed to be tender with her. He'd been gentle for months, and only when he'd treated her roughly and thoughtlessly had she run, and he was certain he'd lost her forever. He didn't want to make her run now, not when she was finally, really his. He moved to the other breast, giving it the same thorough attention.

Maggie moaned softly under him, her legs moving, one of them coming up around his waist of its own accord. She lost herself in his touch, and nothing mattered except the feel of him, the love of him. Putting her hands in his thick hair, she pulled him up and kissed him thoroughly, allowing his tongue to explore her mouth, then returned the favor, hands moving more intensely over his rough back as he moved slowly against her.

They were on their sides now, lovingly exploring one another's bodies, kissing deeply and hungrily. Somehow, the last silk and lace fell away, and she wrapped her leg around him tightly. Taking this as a silent signal—he could feel the warmth and wetness between her now that she was uncovered—he reached a hand down over her firm derriere and under her raised leg to be certain.

She arched at his touch, and he quickly turned her on her back, straddling her once again as she murmured his name, eyes closed. Entering her, he pushed in slowly but forcefully, holding his taut body just inches above hers, watching her face as he did. When he reached his full length, she opened her eyes, looked at him and smiled.

This is different, something told him. This is different. He pulled out slowly and then thrust again, bringing her a little higher, her eyes now again closed. He willed himself to have control, to savor each different sensation. This was his Maggie, and he wanted to do this right for her the first time, every time. But especially the first time. He slowed down and bent to take a breast again, eliciting a different sound from her.

He'd never had to use control before and had always taken what was easily offered. Not to say he slept around all the time with whoever was there, but he'd availed himself of beautiful or interesting women from time to time since college. He didn't exactly feel like he was using them, but more like they used each other.

And yet he'd always felt slightly uncomfortable afterward, like maybe he needed to say he was sorry? Or maybe go to confession? Seldom acting on that impulse, he simply stopped seeing that particular partner, allowing each one only a temporary place in his life.

He also couldn't understand how Sean had given up sex for his love of the church, yet at the same time he deeply envied his twin brother's devotion, self-constraint and conviction.

Colin shifted, moving them to their sides again and pulled her closer.

"Murphy," she said, voice husky, "I'm... I'm..."

He kissed her words away, deeply, passionately, and she began moving again, slowly, slowly, feeling every part of him deep inside of her.

"Oh, Love," he said, as he felt her position herself under him again, pulling him on top, wanting more, needing more, begging for more. He obliged willingly, ready to give up his control and drive deep within her over and over, faster and faster, as she moaned louder, clutching his arms and moving in rhythm with him and against him. Quickly now reaching her peak and exploding over the edge in exquisite agony, she moved with abandon as he, too, erupted in spasms of unparalleled satisfaction.

Spent beyond words, he lay on top of her, his head turned away, conscious of the fact he was probably crushing her, but at the moment unable to do anything about it. Maggie was breathing as hard as Colin was, but moved her head to nibble his shoulder. He mumbled something about being too heavy, and she whispered, "Move, Murphy, and I'll throttle you." She liked the feel of him on her skin, the weight of him pressing down, covering, protecting her, and the intense pleasure of a little of him still left inside of her.

Quilt long ago abandoned, they lay still until their physical passion ebbed and she could feel little goose bumps forming on his back as she caressed him. Completely covered by him, she was warm and cozy and could have stayed underneath him through the night. Finally, when he shivered just a bit, Maggie whispered, "I think we'd better light a fire, Murphy, or you'll freeze before I'm through with you."

He laughed at that, and she whimpered in quiet protest as all of him slipped out and off of her. She quickly pulled the quilt up over herself as he just as quickly lit the logs. He grabbed two small towels from the bathroom and climbed back in beside her, cradling her in his arms after they each wiped the stickiness off. Kissing the top of her head, she lightly kissed his collarbone.

"What do you mean, before you're through with me? I'm spent, woman. I'm an old man, remember? I need rest!"

"You've had enough rest, and it hasn't been an hour yet," she said as she kissed his neck, then progressed up to his ear, turning him on his back, ready to love him again. Helpless to protest, he let her have her way with him.

Maggie boldly declared she was now going to touch every part of him, slowly, deliberately and without mercy—with her fingertips, her lips and/or her tongue, then she began to do just that. Within seconds, he joined in the mutual torture by doing the same to her. They laughed and sighed and touched and tasted. The blazing fire had warmed the room, so the quilt was once again tossed to the side, neither of them the least bit shy about their nakedness.

Now was her chance to study the rest of him, and she asked him to lie back on the pillows. He obliged her request, putting his arms behind his head, wondering what she was up to now. She sat up and looked.

Oh, my, was her first thought at seeing his "maleness," still a little flaccid after its last extended use. She never was comfortable saying the "P" word and somehow she always thought that particular part of the male anatomy was misnamed. "Manhood," "maleness," even "babymaker" seemed more appropriate. ell, maybe not "babymaker" at their age. After their recently completed first encounter, "woman pleaser" would do nicely.

She had seen only two men completely naked—Jim, who was tall but of a slighter build, and now Colin. With only two actual sightings in her sheltered life, it was hard not to compare. Oh, my, was all she thought, again, reaching to touch the massive organ. No wonder it had felt different.

She hesitated, looking to Colin for his permission. He was grinning, watching her in fascination, and nodded his assent. She moved her hand over the rough texture of the skin, surprised he hadn't been circumcised. Jim had been. She gently reached down underneath and felt the weight of his pouches heavy against his inner thighs. Moving back up, she took him in her hand, gently pulling back the foreskin revealing the crown that reminded her of a giant acorn. The acorn responded to her grasp by filling her fist. She smiled, and he smiled, dazzled by her. He sat up and pulled her to his lap.

"Just looking, Murphy," she said softly, arms now around his neck, head resting on his chest.

"Time to do more than look, Love," he said, moving to take her mouth again, his hand touching between her thighs. Exploration resuming, his manhood took on a life of its own, and they mapped each other's curves and bumps and surfaces as the afternoon waned and evening's soft light came through the windows.

This time, even though the foreplay was long and exquisitely drawn out, their mutual passion built so powerfully it reached a fever pitch neither had ever known, and Colin took her hard, using her roughly while she bit and scratched, begging him to take her harder. When they climaxed together, neither was sure who had ravished whom, and neither really cared. They fell into a deep exhausted sleep, clinging desperately to each other.

Chapter 80 ~

More than an hour later, he awoke first, marveling that she'd been able to make him ready and eager again, and at how aggressive she'd been. But so many things about sex with this woman—his wife—were a marvel to him. It really was different when the one you were with was the one you loved. This was lovemaking—sex at its finest, obviously the way God Almighty had intended it to be. He thought it must be his first.

He wondered now how he could have lived his whole life with just physical sex. Of course he'd cared for the women he bedded, well at least for most of them, and at least for a short time. But now, it seemed so shallow, so physical, so lacking. Maybe he *should* go to confession. This... this was different.

When she awoke, he asked her if he was too rough with her, and she looked at him frankly, saying, "No. I liked it... but didn't know I would. Never done it like that." Shrugging and giving him one of her transforming smiles, she got up to bathe. He sat up and stared after her, dumbfounded, but happy as a kid on Christmas morning.

While Colin was showering and utilizing the larger of the plush terry cloth robes he'd had placed in the cabin, Maggie donned her wedding negligee. Then she opened the cooler to discover a feast. The Coleman was packed with a picnic wedding supper, and now she was certain her friends been in on the surprise. She'd assumed she and Colin would be dining in a fancy restaurant in Santa Fe, but the note inside this well-kept secret said it was a gift from them all.

She pulled out seedless grapes, two varieties of cheese, fresh pears, olives, thick slices of chicken and French bread. Maggie spread the fare on the large platter provided and balanced it cautiously on the quilt. A cold bottle of champagne had been thoughtfully added, complete with two crystal flutes, carefully wrapped in linen napkins. Strawberry tarts rounded out the dinner essentials.

The newlyweds enjoyed every bite sitting cross-legged facing each other, platter between them, feeding themselves and each other. They consumed the last tart as the sun set completely.

Colin had actually reserved all three of the cabins, assuring their privacy and providing a place for the rustic bunks and thin mattresses from their cabin to be stored for the night. Maggie wasn't surprised at how quiet it was, even just off the road, because the back of the cabin was nestled against part of the cliff. Built in the 1930s by the Civilian Conservation Corps, the sturdy stone cabins were actually on a ledge jutting out thirty feet below the top rim of the canyon. Access was limited, making the seclusion and solitude well worth the short climb down.

Once dinner and the champagne were consumed, crumbs from the quilt were shaken outside for the nocturnal mice or morning birds. Maggie twirled a little unsteadily in her silk negligee, saying as she frowned, "See, Murphy, I was prepared to try looking beautiful for you to seduce you. Direct from Lord & Taylors in Dallas, and very expensive. All that money wasted. You should be ashamed."

He lay across the bed admiring her and laughing at her, loving that she was this comfortable with him, and he with her. "You don't need an expensive gown to seduce me, Love. You just need to smile." And so she did, and he was up in an instant, holding her and kissing her. He picked her up and took her once again to the bed where they made love into the night, silk and terry cloth puddled together on the floor.

Sometime close to dawn, Maggie awakened and listened to the quiet. Carefully she moved Colin's arm from around her waist and stepped silently to the bath to wash herself. She wrapped the other robe tightly around her. The fire was stirred and received another thick log. Maggie was trying not to disturb her husband. He turned over, snoring slightly as she walked to the door and stepped out into the silence of the night.

A rough-hewn log bench was just outside the door. Maggie sat and tucked her legs up under her for warmth, looking up into the clear dark sky. Thousands of stars twinkled across the vast heavens, and she said a silent prayer of praise for their beauty. Then in the deep quiet, she thanked God for her new love and for this night of loving him, hoping it was only the beginning of years of being together.

Then she thought of Jim. Silently grieving for him anew, she wondered if she was betraying him by loving again.

"No," she clearly heard him say, "I want you to be happy. It's okay, Margaret."

Funny, she hadn't heard him since that night in Dallas when he told her to take the new job, but she somehow knew it was him and was content.

Looking up, she whispered, "Thank you, Jim."

At that moment, a shooting star caught her eye and streaked across the night in a dazzling display of light, making her heart sing.

"God does good work, doesn't He?" Colin said as he surveyed the stars.

Slightly startled, Maggie turned to see him standing at the door, wrapped in his own robe, carrying the heavy quilt. She smiled contentedly as he sat down, covering them both in the warmth of the thick fabric.

"Indeed, He does," Maggie said softly. A moment or two later she asked, "Murphy, is it always like this for you?"

"Is what always like this for me? Oh," he said looking at her and understanding. He looked back out over the dark canyon. "Actually, it's never been like this for me, Love."

"Never?" she said surprised.

"Nope, never. I thought earlier it must be because all the other times were not with someone I loved."

Her heart swelled, but she was silent for a minute and then asked quietly, "You've never loved before, Murphy? Really?"

"Guess not, because I've never wanted permanence before, and before it was just sex."

"Um, well that was definitely sex I was doing, Murphy. What were you doing?"

He waited a few moments before answering. "Making love."

"Oh," she said softly, touched again, and once more she thought of Jim. She guessed she had always only made love, and never just had sex.

"It's natural for you to think of Jim," Colin said, still looking into the night sky.

She was silent for a moment, then said softly, "How'd you know?"

"Because you've only been with a man you were married to, right? So, there's only the two of us who've had the privilege... I, um, I only hope I compare favorably," he said with a little hesitancy.

She laughed, and thought he turned red, although she couldn't see his face in the dark. Uncomfortable, he said, "Okay, then, I guess that's not so great for me, huh?"

"Oh, Colin," she said as she crawled into his lap, putting her hands under his robe, over his bare chest and around behind his back. He carefully tucked the quilt up around them. She laughed again, "You overgrown little boy. Why is it you males are so damn competitive? Is everything a contest for you? You just have to win? What is it with guys?"

"Whoa, there, missy. I just wanted to make certain you were, you know, satisfied. That's all." Now he was definitely red in the face.

"Satisfied? Damn, Colin, how could any woman not be satisfied with you?"

282

He pushed her back to see if she was still laughing. She wasn't.

Seeing his doubt, she tried to explain, finding the words hard to come by. "It's just that, well, Jim and I were young and naive and we were convenient when time came to settle down, that's all. We loved each other, and had good sex—I mean good lovemaking—but, it was mixed with growing up and then children and responsibilities. We were good with each other. We did love each other and I think we made a happy home for our boys. That's important to me, and I'm grateful for it.

"But this... this tonight? Oh, Colin, this is something I never even dreamed was possible." Relief flooded him, and he held her tighter. She continued, "Never, ever have I felt so completely... what's the word I'm looking for?"

"Comfortable?" he offered.

"Comfortable? No, I mean yes, I am completely comfortable with you, but I was thinking more like open... no, that's not right. Maybe unrestrained... uninhibited... more willing to lose myself in what I'm feeling and doing with you. Tonight I didn't look at facts and analyze how to approach the situation. I just let myself go."

"I'll say," Colin said remembering her unbridled passion and feeling his "woman pleaser" coming to life once again.

"Yeah, well... It's like nothing I've ever experienced. It's a gift, Colin, a gift I didn't even know existed to wish for." She turned her head to lean back on his shoulder, gazing at the ever-lightening sky. "Thank you, Murphy. Thank you for this gift."

"I can assure you, Love, the pleasure is all mine," he said, smiling with gratitude as he stroked her hair. Another dazzling light raced across the sky. "Make a wish," he said quietly.

"There's nothing else in the world I want," she whispered and turned to show him once again just how unrestrained she could be.

Chapter 81 ~

Later that morning, they drove the four hours to Santa Fe, straight west on Interstate 40, turning north at Clines Corner into the now visible Sangre de Cristo Mountains. Setting a good pace but staying within the posted speed limit, they arrived in plenty of time to test the hotel's luxurious bed—not as comfortable as their own, they declared—and still make Sunday evening Mass at the downtown Cathedral Basilica of St. Francis of Assisi, just down the street from the hotel, off the Santa Fe Plaza.

Built during 1869 and 1886 in the French Romanesque Revival style, with huge stained glass windows and elaborate gold and marble altars and carvings, its ornate design accomplished the goal of hushed reverence among worshipers even today.

"Exquisite," Maggie whispered when they first walked in, and then again when they walked out after the service.

For the next three days, they discovered Santa Fe—it was a first visit for them both—and enjoyed its galleries, historical sites, and more delicious food than they could ever imagine. At noon one day, Maggie insisted they sit at the Woolworth's lunch counter on the square, ordering grilled cheese sandwiches, fries and strawberry sodas, because she had done so as a child with her parents at the Woolworth's in downtown Dallas. They laughed through the entire meal as Colin barely fit on the spinning stool, his knees bumping up under the counter. But the food was good and he was with his Maggie, so everything was right with the world.

The hotel had recommended dinner at Café Pascuáls, named for the folk saint of Mexican and New Mexican kitchens and cooks, one block southwest of the Plaza, but they would need reservations, which the hotel was happy to make for them. The small Pueblo-style adobe cafe seated only 50 patrons at a time, and a long line of hungry tourists was almost always out the door and often down the block, no matter the time of year.

The festive though small, dining room was lined with hand-painted Mexican tiles and murals by Leovigildo Martinez, a Mexican painter Maggie was not familiar with, but the artist's repeated stylistic depictions of the moon intrigued her.

The Southwest cuisine menu was extensive and it took them a while to decide. Finally, Maggie opted for Talas Wind Ranch Lamb Osso Buco with orange, lemon, parsley and garlic cremolata, served with Anson Mills polenta and steamed mustard greens. Colin decided on the Plato Supremo – chile relleno, Rosie's chicken móle and a taco barbacóa, complete with a skewer of grilled beef carne asáda. As an appetizer, they chose banana leaf-wrapped black bean, corn and jack cheese tamales.

"Mustard greens?" he asked Maggie after they'd ordered.

"Great stuff. Haven't had them in years. My great aunt Bertie—-on my mother's side—used to cook them. She was from Mississippi. You should try them."

"No, thanks. I've ordered plenty of food for myself."

A pleasant hour later, but stuffed beyond comfort, they tried walking dinner off with a late-night stroll around the plaza but ended up going straight to bed, quickly falling into deep sonorous sleep, waking long after the sun rose. Delicious as it had been, for the rest of the honeymoon they chose lighter fare.

One afternoon, Colin took them to a nearby ancient Indian burial site. On the return trip, they walked across the Plaza to the Palace of the

Governors, built in 1610, the nation's oldest continuously used public building. Maggie found a pair of turquoise earrings she loved made by one of the numerous colorfully dressed Native Americans whose wares were spread on wool blankets outside the palace. Colin bought them for her. They found other gifts, too, for friends and family.

One of the highlights for them both was a visit to the Loretto Chapel, another short walk from the Plaza. Modeled after King Louis IX's Sainte Chapelle in Paris, which each had visited, the small Gothic-Revival-style chapel was completed in the late 1800s.

Maggie picked up a brochure and studied it, while Colin studied the chapel's famous staircase.

"Listen to this, Murphy," Maggie said, reading from the brochure. *"The church was built for the Sisters of the Loretto, who established a school in Santa Fe in 1853. According to legend, St. Joseph the Carpenter had a role in the building of the chapel's Miraculous Staircase, constructed sometime between 1877 and 1881 with two 360-degree turns and no apparent means of support."*

"Definitely no visible means of support," Colin said as he looked at the staircase. Then he looked off into his remembrances. "Dated a woman once, very buxom, you see, who wore this black mystery dress."

"Mystery dress?" Maggie asked, taking the bait.

"Yes, it was a mystery how she kept the thing from falling to her ankles. Being cut so low 'tweren't any visible means of support."

"Really, Colin! We're in a chapel!" Maggie whispered with twinkling eyes.

"Oh yeah, so we are. What else does the brochure say about the good sisters of Loretto?"

"When the Loretto Chapel was completed in 1878, there was no way to access the choir loft twenty-two feet above. Carpenters were called in to address the problem, but they all concluded access to the loft would have to be via ladder, as a staircase would interfere with the interior space of the small Chapel.

"Legend says that to find a solution to the problem, the Sisters of the Chapel made a novena to St. Joseph, the patron saint of carpenters. On the ninth and final day of prayer, a man appeared at the Chapel with a donkey and a toolbox looking for work. Months later, the elegant circular staircase was completed. It rests solely on its base and against the choir loft. The risers of the 33 steps are all of the same height. Made of an apparently extinct wood species, it was constructed with only square wooden pegs without glue or nails."

"Amazing," he said. "Look at the craftsmanship."

"Wait, there's a little more. *The carpenter disappeared without pay or thanks. After searching for the man (an ad even ran in the local newspaper) and finding no trace of him, some concluded that he was St. Joseph himself, having come in answer to the sisters' prayers.*

"So, what do you think, Colin? Is it Saint Joseph's work?"

Unable to walk on the stairs or even move completely around it—its age rendering it off limits to everyone—Colin leaned over the rope barriers as far as he could to study the structure, fascinated. After careful inspection, he said, "I won't say it wasn't. It's remarkable artistry, to say the least. I'd be interested in hearing what Sean thinks. He's been here before, I think. Let's take the brochure home and ask him."

Their days in the beautiful old city flew by, and when Thursday came, they were reluctant to leave, having not only spent the time exploring the town, but also exploring each other. Colin was amazed to find that each time they made love, he learned something new about his bride, and it simply gave him more reasons to be fascinated by her. Maggie continued to be amazed at how blessed she was to have found this good man, and she enjoyed him and his athletic body to the fullest. This was definitely the "more" Sharon had talked about.

Chapter 82 ~

Thursday's weather forecast predicted a significant spring snowstorm moving across the Santa Fe area, heading for Amarillo, but they left confident they could completely miss it by traveling the Clovis Highway route. Near Santa Rosa, however, their luck changed. Just two miles before they were to turn southeast off I-40, they became part of a major traffic jam. Up ahead, an oil tanker had jackknifed when the driver fell asleep and then tried to overcompensate, flipping his rig and setting it on fire. Although he was able to escape, wreckage was strewn across the two eastbound lanes, with burning diesel fuel spilling to one of the westbound lanes as well, creating a thick pillar of black smoke.

Three hours later, the roadway was cleared and they were able to resume their homeward trek. By then, the snowstorm had almost caught up and was turning more toward Lubbock. It would be sheer luck for them to outrun the storm and make it home by dark.

Stopping only once briefly for gas, they crossed the Texas border by nightfall. Colin called Jamie's cell to let him know they'd be late but Jamie didn't pick up, so Colin left a message. Since Saturday afternoon, Jamie was using a guest room, tending the cat, seeing to the placement of the new bed from the cabin at Palo Duro, and had promised to leave early afternoon before the honeymooners arrived home. He had a major research paper due the next week, and the quiet of their house had been a good place to get it done. Colin had generously given him a hefty check in return for the light housesitting duties.

By the time they pulled into their driveway, huge wet snowflakes were falling and turning everything white. They got out, and Colin said, "Let me see the keys, Love."

"I never lock my door, remember? This is Lubbock, and now that I have a big strong ex-G-man living here to protect me, I still don't have to lock it... and besides, Jamie's truck is here. I thought he was leaving this afternoon?"

"He was. Maybe a friend picked him up. No lights on."

Miss Priss stepped out from under the porch bench and meowed a greeting, stretching up to the doorknob and batting at it with her paw.

"Miss Priss! What are you doing out here?" Maggie cooed to the cat. "Did Jamie forget to let you in? Why didn't you go through your private door in the back? You'll freeze with this blizzard coming in."

Maggie reached the front door, turned the knob and pushed the door open a little before Colin put his arm around her waist and said with a wide grin, "Just a minute, bride. I think I should do this right." He bent down and picked her up. Delighted, she wrapped her arms around his neck and gave him a quick kiss. As he carried her over the threshold, he teasingly said, "Good thing you lost those twenty pounds."

As he stepped inside and closed the door behind him with his foot, the hair on the back of his neck stood up, and in the semi-dark room he noticed Miss Priss had stopped, too, back slightly arched. Maggie started to protest about the weight joke, but his suddenly serious demeanor stopped her. He put her down abruptly and quickly moved in front of her, shielding her from some unknown danger in the darkened house.

"What is it?" she asked.

"Something's wrong. Stay back," he commanded in a low voice, reaching instinctively for the gun at his side that wasn't there.

She immediately sniffed for smoke, and smelling none, reached over and flicked the light switch on, saying, "Don't be silly." She turned toward the living room, gasped, then fell back against the wall, holding back a scream with both hands over her mouth as she crumpled to the floor.

Jamie's body hung from a rafter, his fingers tightly tucked downward in between the rope and his neck, as if at the last minute he'd changed his mind about dying. Maggie's thrift store lime green chair was lying on its side inches beneath his dangling feet.

Chapter 83 ~

Colin instinctively moved toward him, desperately wanting to take him down, even though he knew it was much too late. His Bureau training took over and he stopped, knowing not to contaminate the scene. He crossed himself, sent up a silent prayer, then put his arm up over his nose in an attempt to block out the sickly smell of death.

Forcing himself to look at the body and the room with an investigator's eye, he focused in on Jamie's laptop, sitting on the desk a few feet away, screen up, plugged in, but dark. Colin took his penknife from his pocket, opened the blade and touched the corner of the mouse pad lightly, bringing the screen to life. He scanned the message and then reread it, closed his knife and put it away. He quickly returned to Maggie who was quietly sobbing, head buried in her hands. He gathered her up in his arms once again and carried her back over the threshold.

As Maggie sat crying in the truck, heater turned up high with the snowstorm arriving in full force, Colin called 911, then Sean, and then Doug. Arriving first, Sharon and Doug were asked by Colin to take Maggie to the Nest so he could talk with the police.

"Come on, Baby," Sharon said gently to the now silent, staring Maggie. "Let's get you outta here." Receiving no answer, she nodded to Doug, who moved in and scooped an unresponsive Maggie into his arms and into his car. Sharon drove the three of them home. Doug placed her in front of a roaring fire and Sharon covered her with an Afghan and tried to get her to sip some brandy.

About an hour later, fearing Maggie was in shock as she continued to stare unspeaking into the fire, brandy untouched, Sharon decided she needed to be more forceful or she'd have to take her friend to the hospital.

"Maggie, you must take some of this. I know it's hard, but you've got to pull yourself together. Your husband will be coming through that door any minute and he doesn't need to worry about you at a time like this."

My husband, Maggie thought. Jim's coming? No, not Jim. She looked at Sharon, seeing her for the first time and said, "Colin. Colin's coming?"

"Yes, dearest. Now drink some of this and let's get you pulled together. You and Colin will be staying here for a while. I've opened the guest cottage for you two, and Doug's putting something together in the kitchen. There now," she said as Maggie finally took a sip of the strong warming liquid. "That's better. A couple more swallows. You've got to think of Colin. He'll need you to be strong, Maggie. Jamie was like a son to him. He'll need you."

When Colin came through the door looking stricken and lost, Maggie rose and gently put her arms around him, head on his chest. He held her tight and began to sob. Maggie cried too but knew Phelps had been right. She had to be the strong one now.

Slipping out as soon as Maggie rose, Sharon quietly closed the door behind her, finding her own surcease in Doug's waiting arms.

That night, Doug and Sharon asked no questions, knowing now wasn't the time. They did what they could, fed their friends—though no one had much of an appetite—hugged them and sent them to sleep out in the cottage. Maggie and Colin clung to each other until each, in his own time, fell into an exhausted but fitful sleep near dawn.

Early the next morning, Maggie asked Steven to put out the news release on the death of Jamie Chavez, senior Texas Tech University engineering student and the president of the Saddle Tramps organization. His death was ruled a suicide by the investigating officer who said a note had been found on the laptop, but the contents were not made public... yet. The investigation was ongoing and funeral arrangements were pending.

Also early in the morning, the remnants of the blizzard already melting, Colin drove to Canyon to find the local priest to accompany him in breaking the tragic news to Jamie's grandparents, who were grateful Colin had come to tell them personally. Along with the priest and the grieving grandparents, Colin then made arrangements for the funeral to be held the following Tuesday. Father Sean would be in touch with the priest, as he would like to be a part of the Funeral Mass.

Maggie had wanted to accompany Colin, thinking he shouldn't be alone, but he said he needed the time to sort some things out. He'd see her that evening back at the Nest.

Even though Sharon objected, Maggie borrowed a car shortly after Colin left and drove out to the solitude of the cotton fields. Four hours after leaving, she returned, clothes muddy from the knees down.

Chapter 84 ~

Over a light dinner that evening, Colin asked if Maggie felt up to talking about it, because he had something to share with all of them. She could if he could. She was determined to be brave for him, to help him through his grief, even as she worked through her own.

"When we found him," Colin began, "I tried to survey the scene—like I used to do. His laptop was open, but dark. I found the message police are calling his suicide note."

"Oh, Colin," Maggie said, reaching for his hand. "I didn't see you... I..."

"It's okay, Love. I memorized it and wrote it down before the police got there. I wanted to be able to look at it again... to study it. Here's a copy."

Looking at him as if she didn't want to see it, Maggie hesitatingly took it from him at his nod. Doug and Sharon read it with her.

can't live withoutmother withguilt — setfires — gave bastardevil Boyle his due — wanted2cut heart out — sorry — pleaseforgive J

"Apparently," he said with a face full of grief and pain, "Jamie was our guy all along."

"And killed Boyle?" Maggie said in stunned disbelief. "No, Colin. He couldn't!"

"Which means he was the one who attacked you in the tower. I can't believe it either, Maggie, but look at the note. He called Boyle a bastard, said he was evil, and couldn't live with the guilt."

Sharon said, "Boyle *was* a bastard. But to kill him?"

Doug shook his head and said, "He must have been more devastated by his mother's death than anyone knew. And then humiliated when Boyle threw the Saddle Tramps out during his senior year as their president. Grief can be a changing force in some people... completely throw them for a loop. Make them do things totally out of character."

"But to set fires and to kill Boyle? And three of the fires were before they were kicked out. How does that make sense?" Sharon asked the group.

"It doesn't," Colin said. "But as Doug said, grief does strange things. I once hiked the mountains for several weeks trying to get hold of my grief. I was about Jamie's age then."

Maggie considered what Colin had said, shrugged and then replied with resignation, "And I poured myself into any activity to would take my mind off the pain when my parents died. I coped by filling every minute of every day. Then I met Jim and threw myself into marriage and family. I guess it's different for everyone. Oh, poor Jamie."

She reached over and put her hand on Colin's again. This has been so hard on him, she thought. Much harder for him than anyone here. "Have you talked with Sean about the note, Colin? I know he and Jamie were fairly close, weren't they?"

"They were, and no, I haven't shown him the note yet. I need to let him know. Once this gets out—and you know it will because it solves the fires and Boyle's murder—then Sean might be able to... I don't know, maybe he can help me explain it to the other Tramps... and... He was Jamie's confessor, but I can't imagine he knew this."

Sharon said slowly, "You called him last night to give Last Rites, didn't you?"

"He couldn't actually give Last Rites," Colin said, voice cracking. "Last Rites involve confession to a priest just before death, not a note. Sacraments are for the living." He took a deep breath. "But he did pray for him. It's allowed. I'll talk to him tomorrow and see what he might have known."

"Known? If he's Jamie's confessor, he might have known it all, but he can't tell you, can he?" Maggie asked. "He's sworn to secrecy in the confessional."

Doug looked from Maggie to Colin. "But Jamie's dead. Is Father Sean still bound by it?"

"I don't know..." Colin said dejectedly. "I just know I need more of an explanation than we have now. On the road today, I tried to look for clues to his behavior since last summer, since his mom died, but I don't know what I missed. I just didn't see anything except depression. But setting fires and killing Boyle? I just didn't see it."

"No one saw it, Colin," Doug said, laying a hand on Colin's shoulder. "We listed him on our white boards in January, but we all agreed it was not plausible for him to set those fires... Wait, he couldn't have set the tower fire, could he? We all saw him in the procession at the time the fire was supposed to have started."

"Yes, we saw him" Colin said slowly. "But he could have set it. The day before the wedding Chief Callahan called to tell me they finally got back all the results of the tower fire investigation, and they're pretty sure it was set by remote control... not a timer, but a detonation device he could have set off as he walked past the building that night. The range was close enough as he rounded Memorial Circle."

"Good Lord," Doug said. "Why? So he could be sure it didn't start until after they marched in? So he had the glory of marching in as president and a damn good alibi? Wow."

Sharon shook her head in disbelief. "And the museum fire? How was it set?"

"With a simple clock timer. But he was there, remember, working the event. Could have set it after he had words with Boyle."

Sharon looked at him quizzically and then said, "But the theory was each fire was more sophisticated than the last. If the museum fire was set with a 'simple clock timer,' as you call it, how is that more sophisticated than a remote detonation device?"

"The accelerant was larger. He used not only cleaning supplies—acetone—as he did in the engineering fire," Colin said as he watched Sharon instinctively reaching for her arm. "But he added hydraulic fluid used in windmills to make the fire hotter and faster at the museum. And somehow he dismantled the sprinkler system in the office area and had the museum area system on delay. It was creative engineering."

Sharon groaned at his use of her oft-spoken words.

Maggie said, "But why? Why would he set the museum fire, or any of them?"

"Maybe," Doug ventured, "just maybe the fires made him feel in control of something? Sometimes the death of a loved one makes people feel impotent, helpless... and they need to do something, anything that allows them to regain some sense of control. He then used Boyle as his target, to deflect the grief." To Maggie's questioning look he shrugged, "Majored in music, minored in psychology."

Colin thought about it. "That's something I'll ask Sean tomorrow. He'll tell me."

Chapter 85 ~

The next afternoon, Sean looked at his twin in disbelief. "You can't actually expect me to reveal what Jamie told me in confession, Colin! You know good and well I'm bound by Inviolable Secrecy in the Sacrament of Reconciliation. I can't tell you anything, you know that."

"But he's dead, Sean," Colin said, angry. "I need to know if he really did this. If he was capable of doing these horrid things. I need to know."

"Well, you can't know anything from me. The Seal of Confession remains even after the death of the penitent. I can tell you nothing he said in the confessional, Colin. Nothing."

"Fine. How does that help anyone, then?" he said, frustration framing his words.

"It doesn't. You knew him, didn't you? Better than I did. What do you think? Do you think he was capable of doing this? Of murder?" Sean asked, as frustrated as his brother.

"No, I don't. He'd talked about exploring the priesthood. You don't talk about becoming a priest and then kill somebody, do you? I thought he'd discussed it with you? When was it, in February? I advised him to talk with you, not me. It was before Boyle was killed. Did he? Did he talk to you about becoming a priest? What did he say to you about that?"

Sean was silent.

"For God's sake, Sean, tell me something!" Colin cried.

"All right, but I can only talk about what was said *outside* of confession, so let me think a minute. He was conflicted and extremely depressed but you knew that. He still couldn't understand why God had taken his mother who had only done good in her life. He asked me if the priesthood was less painful than normal life." Father Sean laughed sardonically. "Less painful? I asked him if he noticed my hair had more gray than yours. Truth be told, being a priest is more stressful than not being a priest."

Colin narrowed his eyes. "Then in your professional, more-stressful-life-than-my life opinion, was he serious about the priesthood? Or just looking for an escape?"

Ignoring his brother's sarcasm, knowing it was coming from his pain,

Sean was thoughtful for a moment. "While it's true some think the priesthood is an escape, those of us who have been in a while try to explain the 'call' to young men like Jamie. I was called to do this work. I seriously believe God actually picked me out to do His bidding, and I knew for a long time He was asking me to follow this path. You know that... we've talked about it many times before. But I don't think Jamie had gotten the call—yet. Only a desire to find peace after his mother's death. But we can never really know what is in another man's heart, or mind. That's all I can tell you, Colin. I'm more sorry about his death than I can say. To take one's own life is not in God's plan."

"But we can pray for him, can't we? We can petition God to be merciful, can't we?" he pleaded in obvious anguish.

"God is always merciful, but yes, He will certainly hear our petitions. And Colin, by ways known to Him alone, God can provide the opportunity for salutary repentance. The Church prays for persons who have taken their own lives, just as they pray for all who die."

Both brothers were silent for a few minutes, each deep in thought. Finally, Sean asked, "You mentioned to the priest in Canyon I'd like to be part of the Funeral Mass, didn't you?"

"Yes. He's expecting your call," Colin said flatly. "It's Tuesday morning. You want to drive up with us?"

"No, thanks. Monsignor wants me to drive him. He was fond of the boy, too."

Colin stood to leave. Sean rose, too, and walked him to the church door, hand on his brother's shoulder. "Let me know if you want me to talk with the Saddle Tramps about it. I'll do what I can, you know I will. I'm sorry I can't be of more help to you, brother."

Colin shook his head and walked to his car without a goodbye. But Colin knew his sibling too well. He was his twin, after all. They'd started life together at conception and there was little one could get past the other. Sean didn't have to tell him what Jamie had said or not said in confession. Colin could read his brother well enough to know.

Chapter 86 ~

In the days that followed, Maggie and Colin slowly, quietly, got back to their work. They'd endured the wake and funeral service not only for their own sake but for the grieving grandparents who were amazed at the overflowing crowd of mourners in the tiny church in Canyon. Devastated by the loss of their only grandchild coming less than a year after they'd said goodbye to their daughter, Colin was worried about them. But they were steadfast in their faith and their parish priest assured Colin they would be taken care of with abundant love by their congregation and community.

At the gravesite, Father Sean had prayed, "Lord, God, you are attentive to the voice of our pleading. Let us find in your Son comfort in our sadness, certainty in our doubt and courage to live through this hour. Lord, our beloved son, grandson and friend, Jamie Chavez, is gone now from this earthly dwelling, and has left behind those who mourn his absence. Grant that we may hold his memory dear, never bitter for what we have lost nor in regret for the past, but always in hope of the eternal kingdom where you will bring us together again. We ask this through Christ our Lord. Amen."

And so Maggie and Colin began their married life under a cloud of intense heartache. The passionate lovemaking of their honeymoon had vanished. Each night since their return, they'd held each other tight, too immersed in raw emotion to even consider physical love.

The night of the funeral, they retired to the cottage early, wanting, needing to be alone. Tonight, when no more "death duties" loomed ahead... nothing except normal life... tonight was different.

Maggie had tried to be strong for her new husband. Jamie had been so close, and Colin's grief knew no comfort. She had to try, though. It hurt her to see him in such torment. As usual, she laid her head on his shoulder when they settled into the cottage's bed. He put his arm around her, and as usual, stared at the ceiling. There didn't seem to be words just yet. He didn't know if there ever would be.

Tentatively, Maggie turned her head and kissed him gently on the neck. He held her tighter. Shifting, she kissed his cheek as he turned to her. Searching his eyes to see if he needed more, she kissed him on the lips. He didn't kiss back, as if he hadn't felt her touch. She pulled back and looked at him again, searching for how to give him what he needed.

Suddenly he moved on top of her by roughly flipping her on her back and ravishing her mouth with his.

In the first moment she was stunned and almost resisted. Then passion and desire seized her and had her responding in kind. The transformation from one minute to the next was as if they'd turned on a light switch after being in the dark for so long.

Grabbing each other roughly, they tore at each other's night clothes. They were frantic to use and abuse each other, as if in forcing their will upon the other they would somehow release their deep shackles of grief.

Colin seized her breasts as if molesting her... she scratched his back and bit his shoulders as if daring him to be more callous. He assaulted her mouth, forcing it open to thrust his tongue roughly inside, bruising her lips and hurting her where he held her. She pulled him to her as if trying to push his soul through hers, leaving deep marks on his shoulders, back and buttocks.

When he did take her, it was brutally, without the slightest consideration of gentleness or love, but she yearned for more brutality, daring him, taunting him. This was pure raw sex at its basest level, and they dishonored and defiled each other in equal measure in a desperate attempt to block out the pain of Jamie's betrayal and to convince themselves they were still alive. Neither had known anything like this before, yet they couldn't, wouldn't, stop, captivated by the violence and necessity of it all.

Finally, the chains broke, the shackles came off and they found release. As Colin lay spent on top of her, Maggie could feel the tears dripping down his face, mixing with her own. Raising up, he said hoarsely, "Maggie, I'm sor..."

"No," she said quickly, but quietly. "It's what we needed."

He moved off of her and carefully gathering her in his arms he asked tenderly, "Are you hurt, Love?"

"No," she lied. "Sleep now, darling, and tomorrow we'll begin again."

He kissed her tenderly on the top of her head and within minutes was deep in a peaceful sleep—the first he'd had since their return. Maggie lay awake for a while longer, astonished at what had just occurred but grateful for it. Yes, she thought, it was exactly what they needed. Then she, too, slept peacefully.

Chapter 87 ~

Refusing to return to her house, Maggie told Colin to sell it as quickly as he could. She insisted, however, that all prospective buyers be told of the suicide. Colin agreed and hired a competent, honest young real estate agent who quickly found an eager buyer, despite the home's now-tainted history. Although she had been in the house less than a year, as Colin had predicted Maggie was going to reap a huge profit on the upgraded property, but he knew not to bring it up.

Sharon dug up the irises, allowing Maggie to transplant them once again in the garden next to the cottage. To everyone's surprise, they bloomed heavily in late April, even though transplanted rhizomes normally wait a year before producing flowers.

Miss Priss was utilizing the cat door Doug and Colin had put in for her at the cottage. Surprisingly, as if she knew they were moving, she'd walked right into the pet carrier Colin put down to transport her to the Nest. Since Maggie's tower incident, the feline rarely left her side, although she stayed off the bed Colin now shared with her mistress. She slept in a nearby corner.

It took several evenings and a full weekend for Colin, Doug and Tom Arbuckle to empty the house, putting some of the furniture once again in storage. Several pieces were donated back to the DAV Thrift Store. The rest of it was taken to an auction house for sale. Maggie simply couldn't bear to keep most of it, afraid every time she saw it she would picture Jamie. Her father's desk, her mother's table, the little she had brought from Dallas—those things were untainted in her eyes, but the rest had to go. Their new bed was kept because Maggie had never seen it in the house, so it held only good memories for her.

As for the lime green chair? She asked Colin to burn it, which he did along with the Texas Tech bobble-head doll.

Staying gratefully at the Nest's cottage, Maggie and Colin slowly made unenthusiastic attempts at looking for a place to call their own. Both knew without saying it couldn't be even remotely close to the Tech Terrace area—it had to be somewhere away from campus, away from reminders.

Colin had already decided to keep his condo near campus so now five junior or senior Tramps could live there. He dropped by once in a while to make certain they were keeping it clean. It was still a good investment property.

President Parker allowed the Saddle Tramps to move back into the east tower. They began repainting it in red and black and the victory bells would ring again.

Tom offered to sell the newlyweds a few open acres of their land for a new house, but Colin and Maggie didn't want to build something from scratch. So they took their time in deciding where to make their new home, enjoying the shelter of the cottage at the Nest and the closeness of their friends. Father Sean joined them for dinner as often as he could. He knew his brother needed him, too.

Closing out the semester, Colin and Maggie attended graduation to watch proudly as the senior Saddle Tramps, including Josh, walked across the stage. They bravely faced the pain of not seeing Jamie complete his college journey.

The Wind Museum foundation, at Winston's insistence, set up a generous trust fund for Henry Cassidy's family, while Tech offered full scholarships for both daughters. Jonathan Long was named the new Chief of Staff and was quickly making a positive impact on the faculty and staff.

President Parker was becoming more accepted at all area organizations after finally following some of the Communications Department's advice, and had a solid long-range vision of growth and prosperity for the university.

Chapter 88 ~

Two days after graduation, eight weeks after their wedding, Colin told Maggie he was picking her up after work to show her something.

"Show me what, Murphy?"

"Just something. We'll come back and pick up your car later. Can you be ready at five?" She'd finally traded in her old Volvo for a new one—she needed reliable transportation since she no longer walked to campus.

Maggie smiled. They'd gotten back to their lovemaking and were making a valiant attempt at being happy, the mourning creeping in only at the most unguarded moments now.

Early last January, they'd chosen not to participate in the Cotton A Bible Study this semester, knowing they'd be too distracted with the wedding—and with so many other events happening since the new year, it turned out to be a wise decision—but they were looking forward to resuming it in the fall. Maggie hadn't been back out to the cotton fields since the day after Jamie's death.

Promptly at five, she went down the stairs of the Admin Building to meet Colin out front. His truck was a little cleaner these days, and Maggie marveled at the small changes marriage could make in a person.

Colin drove down the east esplanade and turned north on University, driving in front of the football stadium and across the Marsha Sharp freeway. Maggie asked again what he wanted to show her. "You'll see," was all he would say.

They reached the Clovis highway and turned left, heading northwest, leaving the city limits in no time—Lubbock still had no traffic to speak of, especially this far from campus. Knowing how stubborn her Irish husband could be, Maggie resigned to wait to learn anything until they got wherever they were going.

Colin turned southwest just before Shallowater, the same exit Maggie had used for the Corn Maze her granddaughters had loved last Thanksgiving, but Colin drove past the site, heading into the sun.

Gazing out at cotton fields sprinkled with old homes, Maggie was surprised when Colin turned the truck down a long tree-lined drive. An old two-story farmhouse, much like Russ and Fern's, stood proudly at the end of the lane. Looking at his watch, he said, "We're right on time. What do you think?"

"What do I think about what?" She looked around and spotted the For Sale sign. She drew in a deep breath. "It's for sale? The house! You want to live way out here?"

"I don't know yet, but our enterprising realtor thinks it has possibilities. He made an appointment for us to see it, so let's go take a look, okay?"

An old farmhouse, ten miles from work? She looked around the grounds. The soft gray two-story structure sat on about three acres of neat grass- and flower-covered grounds, well away from any main roads, with not one oil pump jack or wind turbine marring the horizon... nothing but cotton fields all around the edges of the huge yard. One lone windmill turned slowly in the light breeze behind the tree-shaded house. Maggie climbed out of the truck, skeptical, but intrigued.

The realty agent who'd made a small fortune selling Maggie's house walked out the front door to greet them. On a whim, he'd called Colin when the property came on the market that morning, thinking it might be a long shot but worth a try. The owner had recently died and the out-of-town heirs wanted to sell the house that had been in the family for generations.

Maggie immediately liked the two-story clapboard farmhouse. It had a wide covered porch that stretched around both sides, probably continuing around the back. A late-blooming wisteria climbed a porch column and graced the entrance with huge purple blossoms hanging like massive grape clusters. Large windows occupied all the walls—the house having been built back when air conditioning consisted of opening windows for cross ventilation. A sturdy brick chimney poked up off either side of the newer dark gray metal roof.

As they stepped inside the empty house, they faced a graceful oak staircase with a beautifully carved banister, original to the house, Colin speculated. To the left, a large dining room; to the right, a good-sized living area, brick fireplace with carved oak mantle dominating the room.

Upstairs they found four bedrooms and two full baths. Knocking down a wall between the two east bedrooms would make a nice-sized master, especially if they could incorporate and enlarge one of the baths and add another closet. Their king-sized bed, now in storage, would fit with plenty of room to spare.

Back downstairs, they walked through the dining room to a homey kitchen, cozy despite its enormous size. It sported a cooking fireplace and a huge well-used free-standing butcher's block that would stay with the house. A utility area was next to the kitchen with a half-bath tucked under the stairs. A large cellar, or basement as Colin called it, had been built to equal the size of the first floor and could be reached from either inside or outside the house.

Maggie thought the old house had definite character and was only a little rough around the edges. Colin could work his magic here, she knew. And wouldn't it be fun to furnish? The possibilities were beginning to excite her.

She glanced out the back windows and spied an enormous old barn close to the windmill. "You know, Murphy, I never figured you for a farmer."

"And you figured right," he said as he stepped out the kitchen door to the back porch, facing the barn. Maggie followed, noticing a porch swing in need of repair, a large fallow vegetable garden to the right and an opening in the cotton fields beyond that led to a substantial playa about an acre away.

Colin quickly sized up the property. "Realtor says all the fields are leased to real farmers who are eager to keep working the land. And the barn looks about the right size for a studio... room enough for us both. We could make your wall of windows on one side. I think it's pretty comfortable, don't you?"

He turned around to look at Maggie. She was wearing the largest smile he'd seen since their honeymoon.

Chapter 89 ~

So Maggie and Colin bought a house, quickly settling on a fair price a few days after they'd seen it, and signing up the tenants to continue their labor on the accompanying 540 acres. Maggie was tickled at how nervous Colin seemed signing the papers of home ownership—a first for Colin. Planning and renovations would keep them occupied for a couple of years, at least. And Maggie was more than thrilled she was going to have her own cotton fields to roam right outside her back door.

She'd mentioned to Winston about their new land and set up an appointment with him one Friday afternoon in late May to get more information about their old windmill—it was still drawing water. Besides, she thought, it's time I got a Wind Museum construction update for the Tech website. He'd be delighted to see her, he said, so in the early afternoon she found Winston in the construction trailer.

"Oh, my dear! Come right in! Would you like some tea?" Winston said, ushering her into his temporary office—a permanent fixture since the museum fire. Maggie thought it'd been more than enough time to construct a new office area, but Winston enthusiastically explained it was more economical to build the new office in conjunction with the new educational wing, Phase II of the master plan. "'Incorperstruct' it all together in one design, you know what I mean?" Construction was already started. Incorporation and construction were in full swing, and the east and south sides of the museum were a beehive of activity and noise. "We hope to have it all completed by late fall in plenty of time for the next spring semester."

Maggie looked around, surprised at how the humble trailer had been transformed into a comfortable, upscale office. Winston had set himself up quite elegantly, but then he would, wouldn't he, she thought. She sat across a massive desk from her friend, looking at all the trappings of a successful museum curator. He's had to replace everything he lost in the fire, she thought, and it looks like he's been able to do it quite well.

Texas Tech University had provided reproductions of his beloved diplomas. Hanging on the walls were new photos of him posing with various dignitaries, including a new autographed picture of Winston posing with Diane Sawyer on the Good Morning America set. At least a dozen snapshots of windmills of all shapes and sizes, the kind you find in expensive coffee table books, also bedecked the walls.

Pricey curtains replete with a vintage windmill design graced the two windows, one high above the side of his desk, doing a good job of keeping out the warm afternoon sun. He saw her looking at them and said, "Another gift from dear Mrs. Fauntly. Do you think she made them herself?" Winston asked with a mischievous twinkle.

Maggie giggled, trying to imagine the elite Mrs. Fauntly laboring at a sewing machine. She shook her head.

Next to the file cabinet was a sturdy polished steel windmill reproduction, about four feet high and quite authentic in detail. An eight-inch-tall duplicate sat prominently on Winston's desk. Typical Windy, she thought with amusement.

"Now tell me about this marvelous new acquisition of yours, my dear," he asked, eyes sparkling as they normally did when he discussed his passion for "anything windy."

"I brought a picture, hoping you could tell me a little about it," Maggie said, taking photo enlargements out of her briefcase. "Then we can talk about the museum construction," she laughed. "I *am* supposed to be working."

"Goodness, my dear, we're between semesters and everybody takes a breather or two these few weeks. But of course, I can give you a tour of the construction in a minute. Let me take a good look at this beauty and see if it's 'historelically signiftiquated.'"

Maggie laughed, handing him the photos. "I hope it is," she said, knowing his jabberwocky meant historically significant, but didn't he throw in relic and antiquated, too? "Your mind is always a wonder, Windy," she said with admiration.

"Thank you, my dear," he replied, humbly amused. "Let's see, oh, yes, this is quite old, and quite rare... where did you say it was? I don't remember if I've ever climbed this one..."

"I'm sure a climb can be arranged, but we haven't moved out there yet. It's ten miles northwest of here. The old Hemphill place. Do you know what kind is it? And how old?

"Oh, my dear," he said after studying the photos for a moment. "Let's go to the museum floor. One of my precious pieces is a close cousin of yours. I can tell you all about their fascinating history."

He walked her to the door and said, "Come along my dear Mags, and I'll show you a real beauty!" His eyes were twinkling like diamonds.

Maggie spent the next two hours at the museum, happily receiving her second lesson on all things Windy. She hadn't returned since the fire, and was pleased to have him lead her up and across the glass bridge that gave a "spectaspecial" view of the windmill wheels. She learned all about her new acquisition and took notes for Colin.

Finally, Winston took her on a tour of the construction for the office and educational wing. Looking at blueprints and asking questions of the construction boss, she was duly impressed with the largesse of the project, thinking it a fitting tribute to the history of West Texas civilization, as well as to its future.

Close to five o'clock, Maggie bid Winston goodbye in the parking lot, thanking him once again for convincing the museum's foundation to set up the trust fund for Henry Cassidy's children.

"It was my pleasure, my dear," he said pulling his pocket watch out and looking at the time. "Oh, dear, I'm late!" Watching him hurrying away to his office trailer, Maggie chuckled, wondering if he knew how perfect his imitation was of the White Rabbit.

Chapter 90 ~

Sharon and Maggie were putting dishes in the dishwasher. Doug was outside cleaning up the grill and Colin was at his workshop on campus. It had been a long week, but with students gone before the summer sessions started, it was quieter in all of their offices. Maggie had related her visit with Winston that afternoon, and Sharon laughed with her about his comical persona. She just might join him on his climb up Maggie's windmill. She'd always wondered what it would be like. And hadn't Doug expressed an interest, too?

"When do you think you'll be ready to move in?" Sharon asked.

"Are you trying to get rid of me, of us?" Maggie teased.

"Don't be silly. We love having you 50 feet away, and Doug is enjoying Colin's company. Plus, as long as you're here, my mother won't visit and bring me any more stupid bird paraphernalia. But I know you're both eager to start your new life by yourselves. I know you won't be really comfortable until you're way out there in Shallowater."

"Way out there? It's less than ten miles! And we still need to get several more pieces of furniture before we can move in. Colin's almost finished with the master bath—that's what he's working on tonight—the last cabinet—and once that's done, we'll start on the kitchen. He insists we'll move in then, even if the rest of the house is still a mess and there's no place to sit except the bed!"

"Well, that's the most important piece anyway," Sharon retorted.

Maggie laughed as she put the last plate in the dishwasher. She took a damp rag over to the dining room table to wipe it clean.

Sharon had her own rag and was wiping down the counter tops. "Why don't we go shopping tomorrow? We can look for some furniture at that new antique shop on 34th. I hear it's great."

Shopping, Maggie thought. Maybe.

"Did you hear me? Mags? It's Anna's Antiques or something like that."

Maggie stopped suddenly, stiffening. "What did you say?"

"Shopping. Let's go shopping."

"No, what did you call me?" Maggie turned to look out the patio window, seemingly staring into space.

"Um, Mags... short for Maggie, short for Margaret? What is it?" She looked out the patio doors, too, trying to see what her friend was looking at.

"And the name of the shop?"

"Um, I think it's Anna's Antiques? Why?"

"That's it.... that's what he said!" Maggie threw the rag toward her friend and raced out the door, heading for the cottage.

Sharon looked after her, bewildered. "That's what WHO said? Maggie, WAIT!"

Chapter 91 ~

But she couldn't wait. Wheels were turning in her head too fast to comprehend, but there was something there... something significant... something Winston had said, too... something just out of reach. She only needed a few more facts.

She raced into the cottage and grabbed her phone. She called Colin's number, then stomped her foot and hung up when he didn't answer. She quickly dialed another number and reached Chief Callahan. It took him a minute to find what she wanted, and she nervously paced the cottage floor while she waited. When she got the answer she thought she might, she thanked him and hung up. Quickly she dialed Jonathan's home phone.

He answered on the third ring. "Jonathan. How did Bennett Boyle and

Dr. Whitaker know each other? Just through the museum?"

"Good evening to you, too, Maggie," he said. When she didn't reply, he answered her, "The museum? No, they go way back. In college, I think."

"But Winston graduated from Tech. Boyle was an Aggie, wasn't he?

"He was, but did his first two or three years here at Tech. I actually thought they'd been roommates, he and Dr. Whitaker, but maybe not. Boyle never talked about his college days."

"When, Jonathan? Do you know exactly *when* Boyle was at Tech?"

"Let me think. I saw his diplomas often enough on the walls while I was just standing there in his office, waiting for him to acknowledge me and..."

"When, Jonathan? When?"

"Sorry. He graduated from A&M, um, let's see… twenty-four years ago if my math is correct. So he would have been at Tech twenty-five to twenty-seven years ago. Somewhere around then..." He pulled the phone away from his ear and stared at it. She'd hung up.

Maggie grabbed her keys, jacket and briefcase, and raced outside. Damn, she thought, I forgot I've got Colin's truck. She went back inside for the right set of keys and her briefcase. Her new Volvo was making a strange noise so they'd dropped it off at the dealership service center that morning. Colin had been in his workshop all day saying he'd call when he needed to be picked up.

She jumped in the old Chevy, and headed for the library as the sun was setting behind her. She found a nearby parking spot on the lot just south of the building, and raced up the steps and into the almost deserted learning center. A quick computer search took her to Stack Level 2, northwest corner. What is it with these corners, she thought as she quickly marched the full length of the library to find the right shelf.

Maggie pulled one copy after another of the old *La Ventanna* yearbooks from the shelf, lugged them to the nearest study cubical and looked through the back indexes. Third time's the charm, she thought as she found what she wanted in yearbook number three. He was there, listed in the index under Boyle, B.J., p. 56, 192, 193.

B.J. Bennett James... B.J. Hadn't she heard Windy call him B.J. before? The picture on page 56 confirmed it was indeed a much younger Bennett James Boyle, junior business major, attending Tech. But a different Boyle than she'd known. This Bennett Boyle was smiling, confident, happy.

Then she looked up Whitaker, Winston P. and there was Windy, page 64, surprisingly white-headed even then, a junior majoring in engineering. Pages 192 and 193 had been listed after his name, too, so she turned to them.

Saddle Tramp pages! There was Boyle again, listed not only as a member, but as First Vice President B.J. Boyle.

Under his name was Sergeant-at-Arms Windy Whitaker.

Maggie fell back in the chair in astonishment. Bennett Boyle had thrown the Saddle Tramps out of the tower after the fire saying the Saddle Tramps were, what? He'd said they were a "worthless organization of hypocrites." And he wouldn't go into the tower to even look at the damage. But he went there the night he was murdered. Said the organization shouldn't be allowed access. But he was once a Saddle Tramp himself! They both were!

Had she known Windy was a Saddle Tramp? Had he ever mentioned it? She was sure he hadn't. But why not? Being a Tramp was something to be proud of.

What had happened? She couldn't imagine but knew she needed to find out.

Maggie scanned the rest of the photos on the two pages. They showed Saddle Tramps volunteering at the local retirement center, helping tutor elementary students in a poor neighborhood. There they were at the always important football activities. Next to the Carol of Lights photo was the Annual Christmas Ball picture, now the more politically correct Annual Red Rose Formal... And there in a shiny black tuxedo was Bennett, or B.J. as he was called back then... his arm around a lovely Hispanic girl with dark brown hair and beautiful soft brown eyes. Where had Maggie seen those eyes before? Let's see, the caption says... Anna Garza. Anna. Anna. That must be who Bennett thought I was the night he died. He'd said he loved her. Certainly looks as though she loves him.

How else did she know that name? She looked again at the smiling young girl who was looking up longingly at B.J. Boyle. The index listing for Anna Garza took Maggie to page 58. There she was, a junior majoring in biology. Those eyes... "Oh, God," Maggie said as a piece of the puzzle clicked into place... "Jamie." Is she Anna Chavez? Jamie's mother? Had she married someone named Chavez and changed her name from Garza to Chavez? It had to be her... Jamie was a carbon copy of this lovely young woman with the soft brown eyes.

Her mind reeled at the possibilities, trying desperately to remember what Colin had told her about Jamie... what his obituary had said. She could look up the obit, but first, she turned back to the Saddle Tramp pages.

Next to the happy pair was another couple posing for the camera at the Christmas Ball—Windy Whitaker and Mars White.

Mars?... Mars White... Anna and Mars... the two names Bennett Boyle whispered as he was dying. The two names she finally remembered. Anna and Mars... Mars... could it be? The index confirmed that Mars White was listed as White, Marsha, p. 64, 193. Maggie swallowed hard, her heart racing. Was this photographer Charlie's little sister? Page 64 showed a better photo of Marsha White, and there was definitely a resemblance to Charlie.

Ten more minutes searching on the computer helped her fill her mental fact sheet. Texas Tech University junior Marsha White had died in a fall from the Biology Building the spring following the photo with Winston. The *Lubbock Avalanche Journal* had printed, "Police have ruled her death a suicide."

Maggie opened the *La Ventanna* from the following year, and of the four, only Whitaker, Winston P. was listed. Anna Garza—or Chavez—and Bennett Boyle were not at Tech that year. And of course, neither was Marsha White. On page 185, Maggie found a photo of the new Saddle Tramp officers, including, much to her surprise, President Winston P. Whitaker, III.

And this poem, as a tribute to Lewis Carroll:

> "Beware the Jabberwock of service,
> Ye trung and toble naves.
> 'Tis truth and good we seek whilst here
> Thrunce balderdash to thine caves.

> "Whilst passing through these callayed halls
> Hold hither yon learnest lamps.
> And spread your frabjous ploys of giving
> Ye vaingallant Saddle Tramps!"

She reread it and then closed the book, thinking, searching, putting together what facts she had. Then she sat back stunned. "Oh my God. Forgive me, Lord, for being so blind."

Maggie dialed Colin's number as she headed out of the library, yearbook under her arm. As she hurried past the checkout counter, she heard the student on duty call out, "Wait, Ma'am, you can't take that!"

She didn't stop, but instead shouted over her shoulder, "Administration emergency! I'll bring it back!" Then as she raced to the truck she whispered into the ringing phone, "Pick up, Colin, please pick up..."

"This is Murphy's voice mail. I'm busy creating, so leave a message."

After the click she breathlessly cried, "Colin, we were wrong about Jamie... I have to find Windy. We were wrong!"

Chapter 92 ~

Maggie parked the truck in back of the museum next to Winston's car and noticed a light coming from the trailer. It was after closing and the museum was now dark. Construction crews had long since left, but Windy was still here, working.

She sat a few minutes longer, deciding what to do. Should she wait for Colin? Should she go get him first? Had he even gotten her message? No, I need to know, she thought. I need the facts. I can do this, she said to herself. She formulated a plan, took her briefcase, walked to the trailer and knocked on the door.

Winston opened it questioningly but seemed delighted to see her. "My goodness, my dear! Come right in! What a nice surprise. Twice in one day! More questions about your wonderful windmill? Would you like some tea? Sit down, sit down," he said escorting her to his desk at the far end of the trailer.

His jacket was off and draped carefully on the back of his leather chair. His bow tie was undone and his spectacles were folded on the desk next to his enormous pocket watch and chain. Maggie thought this was the first time she'd seen him out of his complete "costume." Did he look younger? She knew now for certain how much younger he really was.

He moved around to the other side of his huge desk, grinning at her. "Please, my dear, sit down. To what do I owe this unexpected visit?"

Maggie looked at him and wondered if she wasn't mistaken after all. For the most part, he still fit the White Rabbit profile, harmless and intent on his museum mission. She remained standing, not returning his smile. After placing her briefcase in the chair, she opened it and reached in. She took out the yearbook and held it out to him. Windy looked at her, questioning, and then at the book.

"I found a photo of you and Bennett Boyle in this old yearbook. He was B.J. back then and dated Anna, Jamie's mother... He was Jamie's father, wasn't he?"

Winston tensed, and sat down heavily with a sigh. "Yes, I believe so, my dear."

"And in the picture, you were with Marsha White. She's the girl who supposedly jumped off the biology building that spring. Charlie White's little sister."

"Ah, yes, good old *La Ventanna*. I meant to get to the library this semester to snatch their latest copy, but got too busy. My museum takes up so much of my time, you know what I mean? No matter how many I destroy, someone is diligent in finding a copy of that particular year and replacing it on the shelf."

"What happened, Windy?"

He looked up at her for a long moment, as if trying to decide what to say. He sighed heavily again and said, almost resignedly, "Alas, poor Mars. She had such illusions. I only dated her to keep up appearances, you know what I mean? She said she was in love with me. Imagine that. When I told her I was gay and was breaking it off with her, she went crazy. Silly girl thought we were going to get engaged, just like B.J. and Anna."

"They were engaged?"

"Not officially. But, of course, they'd slept together so thought they loved each other, you know what I mean?"

Maggie put the yearbook back in her briefcase and moved it to the floor. She sat in the previously offered chair across from him and waited.

"Anyway, Mars was obsessed with wanting to get married. She kept telling me I couldn't be gay, she would've been able to tell! And here's the kicker, if I *was* gay, she knew she could love me enough to turn me straight. Such nonsense. She wouldn't leave me alone, you know what I mean? Kept calling me, sending me notes. That night she followed me to the science building. Said she thought I was going to see another girl. Then when she saw B.J. and me copying the biology exam—"

"What!"

"Life science was not our forte, B.J.'s or mine. The only way we would pass the stupid course was to borrow the exam questions ahead of time. And we had to pass. They don't like it when Saddle Tramps fail courses, you know what I mean? Especially B.J. He was to be president the next year. Anyway, we went that night to get the exam, had most of it copied when she showed up. Stupid girl. Like I said, she must have followed me.

"She... ," he laughed, "she talked about the honor code of the 'vaingallant' Saddle Tramps and all that crap."

Maggie had a sudden sickening insight. "She didn't kill herself, did she, Winston?"

He looked at her hard, trying to decide how much she knew, what she'd figured out from the god-damned yearbook. Now he'd have to deal with her just like he dealt with all the rest. He frowned, remembering the night twenty-five years ago. "She was going to turn us in and wouldn't listen to reason. Started getting loud, hysterical... I was just trying to get her to calm down, keep her quiet, you know what I mean?" He shrugged and then continued calmly. "So I slapped her. She fell back and must've tripped on something... her head hit the corner of the lab table.

"B.J. panicked and wanted to call an ambulance, but I knew she was dead. It was just a horrible freak accident.

"I almost had to slap Bennett, too, but he finally came around and knew what we had to do. I typed up the suicide note and put it in her pocket. It was perfect. Everyone knew she'd freaked out when we broke up, so it was easy for everyone to believe the note.

"While B.J. cleaned up the blood in the lab, I took her to the roof. She was just a little wisp of a girl, you know what I mean? I threw her off so it looked like she jumped. Her head hit the stone steps so the original wound blended in nicely. Then I finished copying the exam, put it back and we left." He shrugged his shoulders as if that was all there was to it. Just a little cleaning up.

"They found her the next morning, and because of the note, no one even looked in the lab for anything."

Tapping his head, he continued, "That was smart thinking on my part, you know what I mean? And of course the 'imbecilistodgy' police readily bought the suicide angle. Forensics wasn't much in play back in those days. And definitely no security cameras or anything.

"But Anna didn't buy it. She kept saying there was no way Mars would have killed herself. Too religious and all. She wouldn't let it go. Day of the funeral, I told friends I was too distraught to attend. But I should have gone. B.J. was definitely stressed. I never should have left him alone.

"Anyway, he and Anna argued about Mars' death. He told her to drop it or he'd leave her. But it was Anna who left. Just up and disappeared, you know what I mean? B.J. was frantic to find her. He really loved her. The fool didn't even use the exam questions we took and failed the damn course.

"Didn't matter, though, because he immediately transferred to A&M. I think if Anna had stayed, he might have, too. After a couple of weeks, though, he stopped looking for her. I think he was afraid she somehow knew what we did, or was afraid she would eventually guess and he'd lose her all over again."

"And you?"

"And me what? Oh, the exam? Well of course I used it, but just enough to pass so as not to raise suspicion. Always thinking, always thinking, you know what I mean?" He was tapping his head again.

Maggie shook her head angrily and gave him a direct stare. "I meant, hasn't it bothered you all these years?"

"Oh, goodness, no, my dear. It was just an accident. Wasn't my fault. But it would have ruined everything... everything. Since then, B.J. and I have kept our little secret, and evidently so did Anna, if indeed she'd figured it out. I tried for years to find her, just to be sure she hadn't guessed the truth, to tie up that loose end, but to no avail. Did you know she changed her last name? Yes, of course you knew that, didn't you.

"Anyway, I understand she died last summer—of natural causes—but seems she left a different loose end."

"Jamie..." Maggie said, more pieces beginning to fit in the puzzle.

"Yes, Jamie. Bennett's bastard son. Apparently, just before she died, Anna told Jamie about Bennett—about him being his father, I mean. Sort of a deathbed confession. So the boy was naturally curious. Right after the museum fire, he came around asking questions about B.J. I lied and told him I didn't know Bennett well at all. I had hoped that was the end of it. But as you know, he saw me arguing with Bennett at the gala... said he'd seen me talking with him at several functions he had worked last fall, too...

thought perhaps we were friends. Hmmph... as if anyone could be friends with B.J. Boyle.

"Anyway, the young man kept coming back after class, asking more questions. He was in my wind energy class last semester, did you know? I couldn't understand why he kept asking about B.J. And there was something so familiar about him... about his mannerisms... and his eyes... Anna had the most lovely eyes," he said dreamily.

After a long moment, he shook his head and looked directly at Maggie. "Imagine my surprise when I realized he was Anna's son, their son... and was right here at Tech... and a Saddle Tramp of all things."

"Imagine," Maggie said carefully, thinking she should just get up and leave. Okay, Lord, tell me when...

Winston had a far away look in his eyes again. "Idaho. Jamie said they lived in Idaho. I never thought to look in Idaho. I mean who moves to Idaho on purpose?"

He shook his head again, then looked back at Maggie across the massive desk. "Anyway, I finally asked him if Bennett was his father and he said yes, he was curious about him now that he knew, and he was looking into the past.

"He begged me not to tell Bennett. Jamie intensely hated B.J. for leaving his mother and he didn't want to give him the satisfaction of knowing he had a son. Well, of course I wouldn't tell him. That wouldn't have been smart on my part. What if B.J. suddenly got all paternal or something and decided to tell his long-lost son the truth about why his mother had left? Why he wasn't there to be a daddy for him? What if he was tired of keeping our little secret? I couldn't take the chance, you know what I mean?"

"So why did you kill Bennett?" Maggie asked, hoping she'd guessed right again, but praying she was wrong. She didn't relish the thought of being alone with a murderer. Where was Colin? I shouldn't have come alone.

She shifted in her chair to calculate the distance to the door behind her. He'd have to come out from behind the desk, she thought. I might be able to push it up against him, pin him back there. No, the desk looks too heavy. I think I could make it to the door—but I need to know it all.

"Why, Winston? He didn't find out about Jamie, did he?"

"So you know it was me instead of Jamie? Smart girl. No, Bennett never knew about his son. But he was getting pushy. He'd come back to Tech years ago at my insistence. Shortly after he graduated from that dreaded Aggie school, I threatened to reveal it all if he didn't come back here. I thought I needed to keep an eye on him. I needed to keep him close, you know what I mean?

So he came and worked his way up quickly to chief financial officer. He really was quite brilliant with money, you know. I had the perfect set up. Bennett would pretty much do anything I wanted... And we created the Wind Museum Foundation, skimming just a little off the top from the university—"

"You embezzled university funds?" Maggie asked incredulously, forgetting for the moment the danger she might be in, desperately wanting to get all the facts.

"Not me, my dear. Bennett James Boyle, chief financial officer. Certainly not enough to matter to the university, you know what I mean, but enough so I was able to build my dream." He spread his arms wide indicating the museum.

"Funny thing is, we probably didn't even need it. When my parents died, I sold the old homestead for the museum's seed money. And turns out I'm not the only West Texan who fancies windmills. We've received more than enough donations to sustain us lavishly for several more decades, which of course you know. Made me a rather wealthy man in the meantime."

"So why kill him?"

"President Parker, for one thing," Winston said flatly.

"President Parker?" Maggie asked, unable to make the connection.

"Yes, of course. Seems Parker's a financial wizard, too, and had noticed some anomalies in the audits from a few years back. He kept telling Bennett he wanted to see the museum's foundation books. No president has ever asked to see my books," he said with indignation. "Bennett wanted me to straighten them out so he could show them to Parker. But ten years of books to clean up? I didn't want to go to all the trouble and couldn't have done it without Miss Katherine getting suspicious."

"That's what you and Boyle argued about at the museum gala? The books?" Maggie asked, vividly remembering the scene.

"Yes, my dear. Rather than clean them up, so to speak, I did him one better."

"The museum office fire," Maggie said, understanding. "You set it to get rid of the financial records." Then she looked up, startled. "Did you set all of the fires?"

"All? Oh no, my dear, but they were the perfect cover, don't you know. Surprisingly, our young friend Jamie actually set the first three fires. Imagine that!

"Set them to punish Bennett, he said. He was so angry at B.J. for leaving his mother that in some twisted way he thought he was punishing Bennett by setting fire to different parts of the campus. Said he was really sorry your friend got hurt in Engineering. He didn't mean for it to happen. You, of course, noted the next one in the tower? He made sure no one was around... heated the door to keep people out... even saved the Saddle

Tramp plaques and memorabilia. Wasn't that just like a good Tramp?" Windy added with sarcasm.

He continued, shaking his head and smiling, "Stupid boy, as though something as tame as a few fires could phase B.J. And then Bennett kicked the Saddle Tramps out of the tower! How ironic was that?!"

Maggie closed her eyes in anguish, praying Colin would hurry.

Winston continued, "But it was perfect for me, the fires, I mean, no matter who had set them. Ours was quite a 'spectaspecial' night, don't you think? National publicity. Even CNN came. And I got to meet Diane Sawyer! You just can't buy that kind of exposure, can you? No matter how good the marketing plan might be... and yours was good, my dear, but the fire got us so much more.

"And then the money just poured in after the fire, you know what I mean? Easily more than made up for the damage. I knew it would. People open their wallets wide when they feel pity for you. And it took care of the records at the same time. Two birds with one stone, don't you see?"

Maggie was horrified, looking at the man she thought she knew so well.

"But a man died, Windy!"

"Oh, yes, my dear. My fault, entirely. I'd locked the office, but halfway through dinner slipped back in to set the timer and neglected to lock it again. That was too bad, but really helped with the sympathy angle. And he was just a waiter, nothing more."

Maggie was sick to her stomach, but knew she had to keep him talking, had to get the whole story. Where was Colin! Didn't he get my message? Keep him talking...

"So then, *why* kill Boyle? I don't understand—if the records were gone and he didn't know about Jamie?"

"I couldn't be certain he wouldn't find out about his son. I'd finally recognized Jamie as Anna's son, didn't I? I couldn't take the chance that Boyle might do the same. Or that Jamie might decide to tell his dear old daddy who he was."

"So you murdered him," she said sadly, remembering Boyle's last moments. "But how did you get him to go up into the tower? He hated that place. And how did you get up there without a key? They keep it locked."

"That was simple. I used B.J.s." He looked over her head as if focusing on a remembrance.

"How did you get it?"

His eyes returned to Maggie and he frowned. "Easy. I walked into his office and told him after all these years I'd found some information on Anna, but I would only tell him about her up in the tower—"

"That's who he thought I was," Maggie interrupted. "He called me Anna just before he died."

Winston's eyes flew open wide. "He was alive? He spoke to you!"

"Yes. That's how I made the first connection. This afternoon you called me Mags. Mags... Mars... nicknames, not often used. Bennett called me Anna and asked Mars to forgive him. I didn't remember the names until tonight, though, and started to put it together."

"The bastard. If I'd known that, I would have had to let you die that night, too, my dear. I hate loose ends," he said flatly.

Maggie shivered, deciding it definitely hadn't been a good idea to come here alone after all. But still, she needed to know everything. She might as well get it all.

Chuckling to himself, Winston continued as if he hadn't been angry a moment before, "At first I was worried he didn't have the courage to come up to the tower, too many memories, you know what I mean? We used to take Mars and Anna up there... I wonder if that's where the boy was conceived?"

Maggie's stomach lurched, and she choked down bile while trying to comprehend what kind of monster thinks of things like that while confessing so calmly to the murder of another human being. She swallowed hard, glancing once more toward the door, calculating the number of steps.

Winston continued, and she turned back to him as he said, "But I took the key from him and he came up after me that night. Soon as he came up the tower stairs, I just turned to him and pushed the knife in. I was waiting on the top step, so it was easy to get him in the chest. So easy. He was so surprised, the stupid fool.

"Then I heard you call out, so I had to hide in the storage closet until you passed by. Almost didn't make it in time. I didn't realize anyone else was in the building. Bennett's was the only car," he said questioningly.

Realizing he expected her to explain, she said flatly, "I'd walked."

"Oh, well, then... Anyway, I am sorry I had to hit you, my dear, but it wouldn't do for anyone to find me there. He wasn't supposed to be found until at least Monday, and then you spoiled it. I had to have time to make my get away, you know what I mean? If I'd known he talked to you..."

Maggie closed her eyes and dropped her head. "God, Winston. I don't know who you are. How could you?" At that instant, the last piece fell into place. She was certain her hunch in the library was right. She looked up at him hard. "So then you staged Jamie's suicide, too, letting him take the blame for Boyle's death, didn't you?"

"Seemed a good way to tie things up neatly. What was it the newspaper said? 'Student, still grieving for mother, kills administrator who kicked Saddle Tramps out of tower. Hangs himself in guilt.' Just like Mars, the pieces fit, so everyone bought it." He smiled.

"See?" he said, tapping his head again. "Always thinking, always thinking. I knew he was housesitting for you—how was the honeymoon, by the way? It was a lovely wedding—so I went over before sunup that last morning—to avoid nosey neighbors, you know what I mean? He was asleep, but answered my knock. I told him I'd remembered some more about his parents, so he let me in. It was so easy. Just like his stupid father.

"I showed him the knife I used to kill Bennett and he was shocked. Truly, he hadn't even come close to figuring out about Mars, just too caught up in mourning his mother, and then in hating Bennett. Being the benevolent soul that I am, I filled in the gaps for him, just like I've done for you this evening. That's when he told me he'd set the other fires to punish his absent father."

Winston glanced at the small window next to his desk, high up on the wall, covered in heavy curtains. "It is a lovely evening, isn't it?"

His reality is slipping, Maggie thought, nodding slightly, much more frightened now. Still, she had to know. "But how did you manage to have him hang himself? He wasn't threatened by the knife, was he?" she asked, unable to imagine that Jamie couldn't somehow have gotten away from a man almost twenty-five years older.

"Oh, no, my dear, I used this," and he pulled a gun out from under the desk, pointing it straight at Maggie's chest.

Chapter 93 ~

Maggie started to stand, but he motioned her back down. She dared not move after that.

Winston continued, talking even faster than normal now. "I told him if he didn't hang himself, then the two of us would wait for the newlyweds to come home and I'd kill all three of you. Make it look like a murder/suicide instead of only a suicide."

Maggie held back a strangled sob. Jamie was protecting them. God, oh, God...

Winston interrupted her thoughts, "Damn shame I had to kill him, you know what I mean? Bright young kid. But I couldn't take the chance he might figure it out and talk. Hmmph... when he understood he was to die, too, do you know what he did?"

Maggie shook her head, too terrified to speak.

"He prayed for me... prayed for my sins. Isn't that a hoot? He's the one about to die, yet he prayed for *me*."

Maggie swallowed hard to keep back the tears. How could we have doubted him? I'm so sorry, Jamie. Why didn't we know better? Keep him talking, she thought. Please come, Murphy. Please, God. She swallowed again, her throat dry but she managed a hoarse whisper, "I'll pray for you, too, Windy. Just let me have the gun and this will all be over." Reaching her hand out slowly toward him, she did indeed pray for them both.

He stood up, keeping the gun on her. "You'll pray for me, too? Oh, how kind of you, my dear," he said with a mocking laugh, holding his other hand to his heart. "But no thanks. You see, I haven't done anything wrong. I've only tried to set things right. Keep them on the straight path. I had no choice, you know what I mean?

"What if Mars had turned us in? What if Bennett talked to his son about it... or if young Jamie figured it out by himself?" He shook his head, "Too many loose ends. It's all their fault. I just did what I had to do to protect my windmills, my museum, my legacy, you know what I mean? Get up," he commanded, waving the gun. "Get up!" he yelled. Then in a calmer voice, "We're going outside. Give me your attaché."

She reached over for her briefcase and rose slowly, keeping her eyes on the gun, praying fervently, for both herself and for her one-time friend as she moved toward the door of the trailer. He put his coat on, then took the leather briefcase from her before giving her a rough shove toward the door.

When they were both outside and under the floodlight, she stopped, hoping someone might see them, but what would they see, really? He'd put the gun in his pocket, now directing her toward the deserted construction area where it was darker. Maggie began to walk, slowly.

"And now you, my dear," he said from behind her. "What a shame you couldn't leave it alone. How did you figure it all out, by the way? Connect me to Bennett? What was the last tumbler that fell into place to unlock the truth?"

"The jabberwocky," Maggie said flatly, frantically trying to think of a way to escape.

"What?" Winston replied.

Maggie stopped before they rounded the dark corner and turned to face him. He took the gun out of his pocket, still pointing it toward her. "The jabberwocky," she repeated. "The nonsensical word in Jamie's suicide note. They thought it was just a typo, but it wasn't. 'Bastardevil' wasn't 'bastard' and 'evil.' It was 'bastar-devil.' Bastard plus devil. It was a jabberwocky. It was you. It's how you wrote the tribute on the Saddle Tramp yearbook page back when you were president... how you write your foundation speeches... how you talk... always with some balderdash and jabberwocky."

Winston seemed impressed. "Hmmm. So you've slain the Jabberwock, have you, Alice? Clever girl. Didn't really think anyone would catch that. Too bad you did. Now turn here, we're going over to my Axtel windmill where you'll climb up and accidently and conveniently fall off."

But she didn't turn, she continued facing him. "Why, Windy? Surely you can't think you can get away with another murder? What's the reason for my being up there at night? How will you explain this one?"

God, please, she prayed, tell me the right time. "Now," God said to her, but before she could speak again, she was struck hard on the side of the face by her briefcase and fell to the ground.

Winston stood over her and waved the gun at her, his eyes as cold and hard as his voice. "Shut the fuck up, bitch. Just give me a minute to think."

She dared not move and probably couldn't anyway with the side of her face in agony.

"You're right," he said at last, in a calmer voice. "Too many questions. I can't really let them find your body... but you can disappear. I'll just shoot you and... and then bury you—like I did the knife. Deep in the construction. That's what I'll do," he said, making up his mind. "No one will ever find you. No one will ever know."

"No, Windy. They'll know," she said slowly sitting up in the dirt and looking up at him. "They'll know."

"How will they know?" he said. "We're all alone out here and it's too far away for anyone to see or hear anything."

"Let me stand up and I'll show you."

He looked at her, puzzled, but backed up a step, motioning for her to stand, the gun still pointing at her menacingly. "Show me what?"

"Here, Windy, in my pocket. Let me reach in so I can show you." She moved her hand slowly toward her jacket pocket.

"No!" he said putting the briefcase down in the dirt, moving closer to her. "I'll do it."

She quickly moved her hand up in the air, and he reached into her pocket, looking puzzled as he felt something. Winston pulled the object out and looked at it for a long moment. Finally recognizing what it was, eyes widening, he dropped it, stepping back as if it had burned his hand.

"A transmitter? You're wired?" he said incredulously. "You bitch!" He moved forward, this time raising the gun to strike her.

Maggie cringed, covering her already painful cheek waiting for the blow, but instead was knocked flat to the ground by the full weight of Winston P. Whitaker.

Chapter 94 ~

Maggie fell hard on her right side, thought she heard something crack, and felt an immediate intense pain just below her shoulder. Am I shot? she thought. She hadn't heard the gun go off, had she?

Winston rolled off her in a flash, scrambling to quickly regain his feet. Once again, Maggie was astonished at his agility, telling herself she really shouldn't be surprised by now. His old and feeble act was just that—an act.

Maggie slowly and painfully rolled herself off her broken right arm and into a half-kneeling position. She'd fallen hard on a construction stake. And she was sure her ribs were bruised if not also broken. Protectively reaching for her arm just below her shoulder, she looked up at Winston, who no longer pointed the gun at her but at something nearby. Following Winston's malevolent gaze, she was astonished to see Colin sprawled a few feet away, staring up at Winston.

"Maggie, Love, are you alright?" he said with a steady voice, keeping his eyes on Winston.

She winced in agony, but said, "Just grand, Murphy. Just grand."

"Get up, both of you," Winston commanded harshly, breathing heavily. Colin put up a hand indicating his intention. He crawled over to Maggie.

"You lied," he whispered as he gently helped her up, positioning himself between her and the gun. Then he looked squarely at the other man and said in a strong voice, "Now what, Whitaker? She's wired, I heard and recorded everything, and Chief Callahan is on his way."

On cue, a siren was heard in the far distance to Maggie's everlasting relief. Winston cocked his head, hearing it, too.

Holding out one hand to Winston while supporting his wife with the other, Colin said, "It's over, Whitaker. Just like she said. Give me the gun."

Winston sighed. "No. Get in the trailer... both of you. NOW!"

The siren grew louder. Holding her up, Colin walked them to the trailer and up the steps. As soon as they were inside, the door slammed shut behind them. They heard the padlock clicking in place.

Colin quickly moved them away from the door, found the switch and killed the lights, telling Maggie to get down and stay down, an idea she was definitely in favor of. The glow of Colin's cell phone appeared in the dark, and he quickly said, "FBI agent needs immediate assistance..." and continued with the where and the why, giving Winston's description, telling them he was armed. When he hung up, he moved toward the back of the room.

"I thought you'd already called Callahan," Maggie said through gritted teeth as her head started to swim from the pain. It was definitely getting worse.

"No, Love, I was bluffing... just like you. Nice job, by the way."

"But the siren?" she asked.

"There's a hospital across the street, remember?"

Maggie smiled at that. How clever her G-man was. As her eyes adjusted to the darkness, she could see the outline of furniture. A small amount of light from the museum's outside security lights filtered in through Mrs. Fauntly's heavy curtains, enough to make out Colin's shadowy form moving around the trailer.

They were both startled by a heavy thud against the outside of the trailer door, and then the sound of rushing air. "Quick, Maggie, come here," Colin said with some urgency. She tried to get up, but wasn't steady on her feet, and said in a whisper, "Not sure I can..."

He found her in an instant, put his arm around her waist, and moved her quickly to the opposite end of the trailer. He sat her in a large leather chair. We must be at Windy's desk, she thought. "What is it, Colin?"

He'd let go and moved to the heavy curtains, ripping them down. More light poured in, and Maggie could clearly see him pushing the massive oak desk in front of her closer to the window. The window was shoulder high, and not terribly large.

What's that smell, Maggie thought? Then her brain pushed past the pain, adrenaline pumping as she abruptly stood, backing fearfully into the wall saying, "Smoke... he's burning the trailer... Colin, we've got to get out!"

"Working on it," he said calmly as he climbed up on the desk. The solid, top-of-the-line construction trailer was built for security and had only two reinforced windows that didn't open without a key, the other window close to the door and the fire. Air ventilation was from the top of the unit, and came in and out through two eight-inch square vents, which obviously wouldn't work as an escape route, especially now that one was bringing smoke in.

After a couple of tries, Colin gave up his attempt to knock the window out with his elbow. Smoke was beginning to come across the ceiling. He scanned the room for something heavy to use as a battering ram. Maggie realized what he needed and pointed to the corner, shouting "There!"

He jumped down from the desk and picked up the four-foot tall steel windmill, sending up his hundredth plea for help that night. He pulled at the blades, separating the wheel from the tower section after a few hard tugs. The tower design made a strong pointed end.

Maggie was doing her own praying, as she tied a piece of the torn curtain around her arm, wincing in pain. The sticky warm wetness on her jacket and the metallic smell of blood told her the bone had protruded through the skin, and she knew the bleeding had to be stopped. She didn't want to go into shock.

Colin was back on the desk, head down, shoulders against the ceiling so he could stand as high as possible for leverage. Knees slightly bent, feet apart, he held the windmill's tower halfway up and at the base, and swung it back and then forward to gain momentum, then back and forward again, ramming it into the window. He heard a crack. He rammed again, and again, and on the fourth try the window frame and reinforced glass fell out, letting in the cool night air. He threw the windmill out after it.

Quickly finding the other discarded curtain, he placed it across the bottom of the sill. He then helped Maggie up onto the desk as she winced in pain. By now, smoke was beginning to fill the room, and the little light they had from the outside floodlight was growing dim.

"I'm going to let you down, but it will still be a drop for you, Maggie. Try to land on your left side, away from the glass. Understand?"

Maggie nodded as he helped her out the window. Holding her under her arms, her stomach was flat against the outside of the trailer. Over his shoulder, she could suddenly see an orange glow.

Hearing her gasp of fear, Colin said steadily, "Okay, Love, I'm letting you go now. Ready?"

She looked up into his eyes, those amazing emerald eyes that had first attracted her to him, and she knew she would be fine... knew they both would be fine. She smiled and nodded and he smiled and gently let her go. She hit the ground hard and rolled left just as she'd been told, missing the glass. Then everything went black.

He was beside her in seconds, urgently calling her name to rouse her, helping her up, half dragging her a safe distance away from the burning trailer. He sat her down against the patio wall. She was awake and in pain, holding her broken arm. Thinking she might faint again, she willed herself to stay conscious.

Another siren was closing in now. Help *was* on the way this time, but Colin said, "Chief's coming, but I can't let Winston get away."

Thinking he meant to go to the truck for his gun, Maggie put her hand on his arm. "Your gun's not there..." she said weakly.

"I know, I checked the truck..."

A shot rang out and Colin instinctively shielded Maggie. But the bullet hadn't come their direction. "What!" he said, frantically looking around.

"Oh, God," Maggie whimpered, looking up.

Colin turned to her and then to where she looked. "Oh, damn," he said angrily, sitting back heavily against the wall next to her. He crossed himself, then put his arm protectively around his injured wife.

Winston P. Whitaker, III sat at the top of his Axtell Standard windmill, the one he'd brought from his family's farm. Sat on the sturdy old wooden platform directly under the giant turning wheel, white hair blowin' in the wind, eyes staring out over the flat West Texas horizon, gunshot hole through the side of his head.

Chapter 95 ~

Lubbock's fire department quickly dealt with the trailer fire, declaring

318

it a total loss. Colin dealt with the police. The paramedics dealt with Maggie, and the coroner dealt with Dr. Whitaker. Chief Callahan walked up to Maggie as the paramedics finished. He kissed her gently on the forehead.

Smiling up at him, she said weakly, "Thanks, Sweetheart."

He smiled back and then made a stern face, wagging his finger at her. "I don't know how you get yourself into these things, Maggie, but you should've let us handle it. We were getting there, you know."

"Getting there?" Maggie whispered.

Colin answered. "I've been working with Callahan and his task force. Winston has been the prime suspect for quite a while, but we couldn't figure out all the motives and we had no evidence."

"What? Why didn't you tell me?" Maggie croaked out, giving Colin a jaundiced look.

"Because one of the first rules of investigations is to keep the list of those who know what you know to a minimum. Honestly, Love, if you knew we suspected Winston, would you have believed us? Or would you have been able to keep it from him?"

Maggie looked down and said quietly, "No, probably not. He killed Boyle... and Jamie. He killed them both."

Colin nodded, "We thought so. The museum fire didn't fit the pattern of the others. It was too sophisticated, with the sprinkler system alterations. The fire burns the office, all their records and files, but not even one windmill? President Parker told us he'd been asking to see the museum's financial records shortly before they were all destroyed. And the engineering was too creative for it to have been done by a student, even a senior student like Jamie."

"Plus," Chief Callahan said, "your husband here convinced us young Jamie wouldn't have killed Boyle, so we looked at Dr. Whitaker for that, too."

Colin added, "And none of us thought Jamie killed *himself*. We just didn't have enough proof to arrest Whitaker."

"What made you think it wasn't suicide?" Maggie asked. "I thought you'd only found Jamie's fingerprints on the keyboard?"

"We did, on every key. About a week after the funeral I had a thought and went to Callahan. He checked it out. The letters used in the suicide note? Only *those* letters on the keyboard had microscopic pricks in their keys, like the one my penknife put in the mouse pad when I lit the screen. The killer used the tip of a knife to type the note, leaving only Jamie's prints. If I remember right, the note had, let's see, two c's and something like eleven t's and there were two corresponding pricks on the 'c' key and a matching number on the 't'. In any case, the pricks exactly matched the letters in the note."

Maggie's eyes widened questioningly.

"Well, we looked hard at everything because I knew Jamie didn't do it," Colin said firmly. He shook his head, thinking of Jamie and of Sean. Knowing his brother so well allowed him to know for certain Jamie hadn't killed Boyle, or at least hadn't confessed it. And he knew Sean didn't think Jamie capable of murder or suicide either, and Sean was a damn good judge of character.

"And the style of the writing on the suicide note," Chief Callahan said, "the misspelled words and missed spaces."

"Yeah. That's what led me here," Maggie said.

"Hmmph," the police chief said. "Well, I'd seen that style before, years ago when I first came on the force. I showed it to your husband, here, who agreed the two notes were too similar for it to be a coincidence. Jamie's note closely matches a suicide note of a Tech student."

Maggie nodded, "Marsha White."

"Yes," the chief said as both he and Colin looked at her in disbelief.

Maggie said wearily, "I finally remembered what Bennett Boyle whispered to me as he died. He called me Anna and asked Mars to forgive him. Mars for Marsha." She shook her head. "It's a long story," she said flatly, shifting to try to ease the pain.

Colin said, "When I finally heard the two messages tonight, I was—"

"Two? I only left one message," Maggie said.

"One was from me," Chief Callahan said. "I called him right after you called asking me to read Jamie's note to you. You neglected to tell me where you were going, so I called you back and the line was busy, so I tried to call your husband. Had to leave a message."

Colin continued, "Once I heard your message, I was afraid you'd found something we hadn't, and I ran here from my studio to try to stop you from talking to Whitaker and raising his suspicions. I thought it might ruin our investigation. Sorry I didn't call you, Callahan." Looking back at Maggie, he said, "I did call *you* back, Maggie, but you didn't pick up. Guess I was a little late."

Maggie sighed, reaching again for her arm. "I'd put my phone on mute so I wouldn't be interrupted. Actually, Murphy, your timing wasn't too bad. I got the whole story."

Chief Callahan said, "So, Sweetheart, can you fill in the blanks for us? Feel up to answering questions now, or do you want to wait?"

"Don't need to," she said, wearily. "Windy told us everything."

Colin, thinking the pain was making her mind fuzzy, gently said, "No, Love. That old wire transmitter wasn't connected to anything, remember? It's broken. No one heard a thing except you."

"You will. My briefcase? Out there in the dark someplace? I recorded it all."

Chief Callahan grinned at her and turned to go find the briefcase with

Maggie's tape recorder.

She called out after him, "Colin's gun is in there, too. And be careful with the yearbook. I need to return it to the library!"

Colin looked at her in amazement and not without a healthy dose of pride. "Clever girl. Sure you weren't ever a G-Man?"

Chapter 96 ~

Safely settled back at the Nest, cast on her reset arm, tape around her bruised but not broken ribs, Maggie was now sitting alone in the den with Charlie White, tears running down his cheeks.

"All these years," he said quietly, "I wondered how my baby sister could do that. She was so happy and fun-loving. To kill herself over some guy? Now you're telling me it wasn't true?"

"No, Charlie, it wasn't true," Maggie said, continuing to speak gently. "She died because she was trying to do the right thing. It was a horrible freak accident."

"Dr. Whitaker? She dated Dr. Whitaker? Isn't he much older?"

Maggie shook her head. "You... your family... never knew who she was dating?"

"No. I lived in D.C. when she was in college, and Mom and Dad were never ones to pry. And when Mars died, we were so devastated we didn't want details. Then her roommate, Anna? She'd disappeared right after the funeral so there wasn't anyone to ask. Funny, Marsha had told Mom that when she came home that summer she would have a surprise for us. Mom said she was so happy. I guess Mars thought she'd be engaged. And now to find out she didn't..." He sighed heavily, and wiped away his tears. "Thanks, Boss. It means everything to me. To my parents. I'll need to go see them."

"Of course, Charlie. Take all the time you need."

Jake Humphrey's well-written article in the *A-J* exonerated Jamie Chavez and named Winston Whitaker as a murderer and an arsonist. Chief Callahan saw no reason to mention it might have been Jamie who actually started the first three fires to punish his newly discovered father—they had no real evidence—so he allowed the White Rabbit to take the blame for everything. Bennett Boyle's long-secret relationship to Jamie was also left out.

Callahan did disclose that evidence pointed to the accidental death of Marsha White twenty-five years ago at the hands of Whitaker, rather than to suicide. The entire story was picked up by the wire services and quickly spread across the country.

Winston would have loved the publicity.

Mrs. Fauntly and the Arbuckles asked the Museum Foundation to immediately appoint Miss Katherine as the new director of the Wind Museum, and the construction of new offices and the educational wing resumed. The murder weapon remains buried.

Colin and Father Sean contacted all the Saddle Tramps to let them know that Jamie, their much-liked president, had committed neither suicide nor murder.

Together the brothers traveled to the little churchyard in Canyon to place flowers on Jamie's grave, ask forgiveness from him for their doubts, and to arrange for the local florist to have a weekly bouquet placed there.

Jamie's grandparents presented Maggie and Colin with an exquisitely hand-carved wooden crucifix whittled by the abuelo in gratitude for finding the truth. The Murphys proudly hung it in a place of honor in their new home.

Charlie White began taking assignments in the Biology Building.

Maggie threw away the Jabberwocky poem when her entire department moved back downstairs into the larger offices next to the presidential suite.

Colin bought a new Texas Tech University Red Raider Bobble-Head for his truck.

Chapter 97 ~

"Ya'll need to seriously think about coming over with us next summer. Maybe we could get Carol and Robert to join us for a while. It'd be great!" Sharon said, eyes sparkling as she took another sip of wine.

The four friends were comfortably seated on the back porch, enjoying the quiet of the country setting and the cool evening air. Maggie, Colin and Miss Priss had moved ten miles northwest of Lubbock to a cotton farm, where earlier that evening Monsignor Fitzpatrick and Father Sean had belatedly blessed the fields, as well as provided a special blessing for the couple's new home.

Slightly to the left at the back of the house was the massive old barn, being slowly renovated by Colin into a sun-filled studio for painting and furniture building. All around, they could see the distant rows of the cotton fields, strong dark green plants growing tall and sturdy in the well-tended fields. A sizable vegetable garden was thriving off to the right, bordered by Maggie's once-again-transplanted irises. The setting sun glimmered off the playa far beyond the garden. Their Aermotor windmill turned slowly and steadily in the light breeze.

Colin smiled as he surveyed it all, amazingly comfortable with his new wife, new life and new home—not just an investment property. "Italy next summer?" he said. "We might be able to work a trip into our schedules. What say you, Mrs. Murphy?"

"I say it's a great idea, Professor Murphy," Maggie said, smiling. "Think Miss Priss would watch the place for us?"

Colin looked at the fat tabby cat curled on the far edge of the porch, asleep with one eye open next to a barrel of blooming red bougainvillaes. "*For* us? She thinks she owns the place and we're just the visitors. She wouldn't even miss us with all the mice she's catching. I'm sure we can get away for a few weeks." He raised his wine glass.

"Here's to Doug and Sharon, for their loyal friendship, for letting us stay in their cottage for so long, for loaning their muscles to get us moved in—"

"Oh, Maggie," Sharon interrupted. "I just remembered, I absolutely love the new couch you moved in the other day. The colors are wonderfully rich and it's so comfortable. I forgot to ask where you found it?"

Both Colin and Doug looked at her in mock exasperation, rolling their eyes. Colin lowered his glass.

"I didn't find it," Maggie said. "Colin did. Isn't it perfect!"

"It is... but Colin, since when do you buy furniture, or even have an interest in buying stuff... besides the bed, I mean?" Sharon asked, truly surprised.

"Actually, I'm finding it's kinda not too bad to shop for stuff for a house—a home. Never done it before... never needed to... but it's not bad... not bad at all."

Maggie's heart swelled with love for this man who had transformed *for* her and *with* her. What a gift from God to have this life, she thought, especially after being blessed by God with another whole life before. It was as though she'd been given her second wind.

"Now if you don't mind, Dr. Phelps," Colin said in a teasingly harsh voice, "I'll continue my toast." He gave Sharon his newly learned version of "the look." Not quite as effective as Maggie's, but nonetheless impressive.

Cowering in feigned fright, Sharon said weakly, "Sorry, Professor! Go right ahead. Don't let me stop you!"

He gave a smug grin and raised his glass again, "Now where was I?

Oh, yes... and to their annual trip to Italy starting tomorrow morning. A whole month roaming beautiful countryside, seeing magnificent art, ogling gorgeous Italian women—"

"Say!" Sharon cried, looking at Doug who quickly put his hands up.

"I don't. I won't. I'm innocent!" Doug protested.

Laughing, Colin continued, eyes twinkling, glass raised once more, "And to enjoying family while there, to exploring the history, to finding new recipes, to eating gelato—"

He lowered his glass yet again and looked at Doug. "Seriously, man, the best gelato in the whole of Italy is at Rome's Piazza Navona, just to the northwest of Bernini's *Fountain of the Four Rivers*. Try the pistachio."

Surprise registered on Maggie's face.

"You've been to Rome?"

The End

~Acknowledgements~

Thanks go to **Roger K. Haldenby**, former vice president, operations, Plains Cotton Growers, Inc., for his time and knowledge about growing cotton on Llano Estacado.

To **Dahlen Hancock**, West Texas cotton farmer extraordinaire, for explanations of all things cotton—and for the lone cotton seed that flourished in my backyard garden in Dallas. Not quite enough to make a new pair of jeans.

To **Coy Harris** of the **American Windmill Center**, Lubbock, who in no way resembles the character in the book. His love of windmills and windpower is a joy to behold. You need to go see this fabulous museum that is NOT on the Tech campus, but in McKenzie Park in Lubbock.

To **Wayne Kohout**, longtime friend, resident of Lubbock, for his eager tidbits and edits of the city he loves, and all things playas.

To **Jim Steiert** and **Wyman Meinzer** for their stunning book *Playas, Jewels of the Plains*, borrowed from Wayne! Texas Tech University Press, 1995.

To **Lewis Carroll** for *Jabberwocky* from *Through the Looking Glass, and What Alice Found There*, England: McMillan, 1872.

To **Captain Randall E. Sanders** and **Sgt. Dennis Wilson** of the Dallas Fire Department, arson and bomb squads, respectively, for their assistance with several scenarios.

To **Phil Nash**, Professional Engineer, Texas Tech University professor, for his eager explanations of the Rube Goldberg competition. I hope he doesn't mind that I put him in the book.

To **Cameron Carter**, Saddle Tramp President, 2009-2010, for everything good and glorious about his beloved organization. And for allowing me to visit and photograph the inside of the sacred Saddle Tramp bell tower. Loved those red corduroy shirts…

To **Texas Tech University Library**, for assistance with research.

Continued…

Thanks to the **lady in the elevator of the Architecture Building** who suggested I find Nolan Barrick's book *Texas Tech University, The Unobserved Heritage*, Texas Tech University Press, 1985, about the architecture of early campus buildings. I did, and it helped.

To **Texas Tech University Facilities and Planning Department** for their willing help in showing blue prints and details of buildings.

To **Kristine Hughes**, Dallas; **Chris McKinney**, Phoenix; and **Russ Arendell** and **Fern Arendell**, Lubbock; for reading the rough draft and offering invaluable insight into how to make it better. And the real Russ and Fern are not nearly as old nor as wealthy as the Arbuckles in the book, but plenty rich in love, friendships and faith.

To dear friends **Sharon Kohout** and **Carol LaGasse** for allowing me to use them as the basis for the character's "bestest BFFs."

To fellow writers of the **Dallas Fort Worth Writer's Workshop** who helped me learn the value of "No word wasted."

And to **Joe Guerra**, husband of "too many years to count," for supporting the efforts of this book, not minding the missed dinners and the long hours I was married to the MacIntosh instead of him. His deep faith in God and in me has helped sustain and transform me.

GO RED RAIDERS!
&
LOVE THOSE FIGHTIN' IRISH

50782092R00184

Made in the USA
Lexington, KY
29 March 2016